BES   The Best From Orbit
      ed. Knight, D.F.

Best Stories from
ORBIT

Volumes 1–10

BEST STORIES
FROM
ORBIT

Volumes 1–10

Edited by Damon Knight

34,165

Published by
BERKLEY PUBLISHING COMPANY
Distributed by
G. P. PUTNAM'S SONS, NEW YORK

Excerpt from a speech delivered at the Baltimore Science Fiction Conference, February 21, 1970:

> And I thought then, wouldn't it be great if there were a magazine, the top of its field, paying the best rates, that would find some good writers and within very broad limits just let them write whatever they wanted to. That was in the fifties, and that's why *Orbit* is the way it is now. I buy a story in fear and trembling, in April, and in December that story seems to me a perfectly ordinary and conventional thing.

A question from the floor:

> Q: If you feel that way about spaceships and things like that, why did you call the book *Orbit*?
> A.: It was an accident. When I wrote the proposal for this series, I said we would call it something like *Orbit*, expecting a lot of discussion about that, but instead they just called it *Orbit*. It doesn't matter. A name means what you put into it.

From the introduction to *Nebula Award Stories Four,* edited by Poul Anderson:

> [Science fiction] still tells stories, wherein things happen. It remains more interested in the glamour and mystery of existence, the survival and triumph and tragedy of heroes and thinkers, than in the neuroses of some sniveling faggot.

Contents

A SORT OF INTRODUCTION
Damon Knight
    1

THE SECRET PLACE
Richard McKenna
    3

THE LOOLIES ARE HERE
Allison Rice
    18

THE DOCTOR
Ted Thomas
    24

BABY, YOU WERE GREAT
Kate Wilhelm
    31

THE HOLE ON THE CORNER
R. A. Lafferty
    45

I GAVE HER SACK AND SHERRY
Joanna Russ
    56

MOTHER TO THE WORLD
Richard Wilson
    71

DON'T WASH THE CARATS
Philip José Farmer
    104

THE PLANNERS
Kate Wilhelm
    109

THE CHANGELING
Gene Wolfe
    124

PASSENGERS   135
    Robert Silverberg

SHATTERED LIKE A GLASS GOBLIN   147
    Harlan Ellison

THE TIME MACHINE   156
    Langdon Jones

LOOK, YOU THINK YOU'VE GOT TROUBLES   176
    Carol Carr

THE BIG FLASH   187
    Norman Spinrad

JIM AND MARY G   206
    James Sallis

THE END   212
    Ursula K. Le Guin

CONTINUED ON NEXT ROCK   221
    R. A. Lafferty

THE ISLAND OF DOCTOR DEATH
  AND OTHER STORIES   242
    Gene Wolfe

HORSE OF AIR   259
    Gardner R. Dozois

ONE LIFE, FURNISHED IN EARLY POVERTY   273
    Harlan Ellison

RITE OF SPRING   288
    Avram Davidson

THE BYSTANDER   295
Thom Lee Wharton

THE ENCOUNTER   313
Kate Wilhelm

GLEEPSITE   334
Joanna Russ

BINARIES   339
James Sallis

AL   350
Carol Emshwiller

LIVE, FROM BERCHTESGADEN   363
George Alec Effinger

A SORT OF INTRODUCTION

(which, however, continues throughout the anthology, so perhaps we ought to call it a perduction.)

The other day I read a review of *Orbit*, a good and thoughtful review, by someone who said in effect that the science fiction fan would find new and exciting ideas here, and unusually good writing, but would miss the comfortable sense of familiarity he expects from a science fiction anthology. And I said to myself, how peculiar to think of science fiction as comfortable and familiar! Of course ninety percent of it is predictable, mediocre and safe. But good science fiction is not and never has been like that—it is not a pony cart but a roller coaster. For comfort and safety you must go to bad s.f., or a lending-library nurse novel—or what about a nice cup of tea and an aspirin?

At various times in its short history American science fiction has gone through episodes of great excitement and enthusiasm. These bursts of energy seemed to me like the sounds of an engine that catches and runs for a few seconds, than stalls again. If you will tolerate this metaphor a moment longer, I have been trying to tinker with the engine since about 1952. At first, because I could not do anything about it directly, I resorted to backseat methods: I wrote book reviews. They were collected in a volume called *In Search of Wonder* (Advent, 1956; second edition, revised and expanded, 1967). It is still in print, and I like to think it has had some indirect influence, but it was not enough.

Orbit is the continuation of *In Search of Wonder* by other means. I made it a series of books rather than a magazine because I thought no publisher in his senses would start a new science fiction magazine at a time when the existing magazines had been in deep trouble for over ten years.

Books have certain built-in advantages over magazines. They are not tied to a rigid schedule; their sales life is longer. In hardcover, paperback and book club editions, *Orbit* can reach several times as many readers as the

1

average s.f. magazine; it can afford to pay its authors better, and treat them with more courtesy.

I am proud of the awards *Orbit*'s fiction has won, and even more of the writers who have given it their best: Gene Wolfe, Kate Wilhelm, Joanna Russ, R. A. Lafferty, Gardner R. Dozois, Robert Thurston, George Alec Effinger, and many others. I want to express my deepest gratitude to them, and to Thomas A. Dardis, formerly editor-in-chief of Berkley Publishing Corporation, who began the publication of this series and saw it patiently through its early years.

In the following pages I propose to offer you twenty-eight of the short pieces *Orbit* has published in its first ten volumes, together with excerpts from my correspondence with the authors, the publishers and an occasional reader. Wherever possible, I have arranged these excerpts to throw light on the stories. Some stories, however, have no correspondence worth mentioning connected with them—I just bought and published them. Rather than invent something about these stories, I have simply put them in without comment where they belong in the sequence.

To Thomas A. Dardis, December 4, 1964:

> Dear Tom:
> Here are some comments on the proposed split of *Orbit* royalties. As I mentioned on the phone, most science fiction anthologists take 50% of all royalties, right down the line. Whether this is fair or not, I think, depends on how much work the anthologist puts in. For example, in the case of a magazine editor who only has to thumb over his own back files and write an introduction, I think it is robbery. On the other hand, an anthologist like Judith Merril, who reads every damn s.f. story published over a year's time to produce one SF collection, in my opinion earns her 50%. . . .
> Fifty percent to the authors certainly seems low if you compare it to the 100% of royalties received by the author of a novel, but I think this is misleading. *Orbit* will be comparable to an anthology or an issue of a magazine, and comparison must be made to the usual anthologist's share and the editor's salary.

To Eva McKenna, February 12, 1965:

> Dear Eva,
> Do you remember a story of Mac's about a young man who saw

2

through time, kind of, glimpsed dinosaurs and so on? I would tell you more about it if I could, but that's all I can remember except that it took place in some Western state. If you can locate the story, can I have another look at it? I'm doing a collection of unpublished s.f. stories for Berkley and would like to include something of Mac's. The rates will be pretty good, at least 4¢ a word as an advance against a share of one-half of all royalties.

McKenna, a good friend, had died the year before. Eva sent the story, I published it, and it won a Nebula.

THE SECRET PLACE

by *Richard McKenna*

(Nebula Award, Best Short Story, 1966)

This morning my son asked me what I did in the war. He's fifteen and I don't know why he never asked me before. I don't know why I never anticipated the question.

He was just leaving for camp, and I was able to put him off by saying I did government work. He'll be two weeks at camp. As long as the counselors keep pressure on him, he'll do well enough at group activities. The moment they relax it, he'll be off studying an ant colony or reading one of his books. He's on astronomy now. The moment he comes home, he'll ask me again just what I did in the war, and I'll have to tell him.

But I don't understand just what I did in the war. Sometimes I think my group fought a death fight with a local myth and only Colonel Lewis realized it. I don't know who won. All I know is that war demands of some men risks more obscure and ignoble than death in battle. I know it did of me.

It began in 1931, when a local boy was found dead in the desert near Barker, Oregon. He had with him a sack of gold ore and one thumb-sized crystal of uranium oxide. The crystal ended as a curiosity in a Salt Lake City assay office until, in 1942, it became of strangely great importance. Army agents traced its probable origin to a hundred-square-mile area near Barker.

3

Dr. Lewis was called to duty as a reserve colonel and ordered to find the vein. But the whole area was overlain by thousands of feet of Miocene lava flows and of course it was geological insanity to look there for a pegmatite vein. The area had no drainage pattern and had never been glaciated. Dr. Lewis protested that the crystal could have gotten there only by prior human agency.

It did him no good. He was told his not to reason why. People very high up would not be placated until much money and scientific effort had been spent in a search. The army sent him young geology graduates, including me, and demanded progress reports. For the sake of morale, in a kind of frustrated desperation, Dr. Lewis decided to make the project a model textbook exercise in mapping the number and thickness of the basalt beds over the search area all the way down to the pre-volcanic Miocene surface. That would at least be a useful addition to Columbia Plateau lithology. It would also be proof positive that no uranium ore existed there, so it was not really cheating.

That Oregon countryside was a dreary place. The search area was flat, featureless country with black lava outcropping everywhere through scanty gray soil in which sagebrush grew hardly knee high. It was hot and dry in summer and dismal with thin snow in winter. Winds howled across it at all seasons. Barker was about a hundred wooden houses on dusty streets, and some hay farms along a canal. All the young people were away at war or war jobs, and the old people seemed to resent us. There were twenty of us, apart from the contract drill crews who lived in their own trailer camps, and we were gown against town, in a way. We slept and ate at Colthorpe House, a block down the street from our headquarters. We had our own "gown" table there, and we might as well have been men from Mars.

I enjoyed it, just the same. Dr. Lewis treated us like students, with lectures and quizzes and assigned reading. He was a fine teacher and a brilliant scientist, and we loved him. He gave us all a turn at each phase of the work. I started on surface mapping and then worked with the drill crews, who were taking cores through the basalt and into the granite thousands of feet beneath. Then I worked on taking gravimetric and seismic readings. We had fine team spirit and we all knew we were getting priceless training in field geophysics. I decided privately that after the war I would take my doctorate in geophysics. Under Dr. Lewis, of course.

In early summer of 1944 the field phase ended. The contract drillers left. We packed tons of well logs and many boxes of gravimetric data sheets and seismic tapes for a move to Dr. Lewis's Midwestern university. There we would get more months of valuable training while we worked our data into a set of structure contour maps. We were all excited and talked a lot about

4

being with girls again and going to parties. Then the army said part of the staff had to continue the field search. For technical compliance, Dr. Lewis decided to leave one man, and he chose me.

It hit me hard. It was like being flunked out unfairly. I thought he was heartlessly brusque about it.

"Take a jeep run through the area with a Geiger once a day," he said. "Then sit in the office and answer the phone."

"What if the army calls when I'm away?" I asked sullenly.

"Hire a secretary," he said. "You've an allowance for that."

So off they went and left me, with the title of field chief and only myself to boss. I felt betrayed to the hostile town. I decided I hated Colonel Lewis and wished I could get revenge. A few days later old Dave Gentry told me how.

He was a lean, leathery old man with a white mustache and I sat next to him in my new place at the "town" table. Those were grim meals. I heard remarks about healthy young men skulking out of uniform and wasting tax money. One night I slammed my fork into my half-emptied plate and stood up.

"The army sent me here and the army keeps me here," I told the dozen old men and women at the table. "I'd like to go overseas and cut Japanese throats for you kind hearts and gentle people, I really would! Why don't you all write your congressman?"

I stamped outside and stood at one end of the veranda, boiling. Old Dave followed me out.

"Hold your horses, son," he said. "They hate the government, not you. But government's like the weather, and you're a man they can get aholt of."

"With their teeth," I said bitterly.

"They got reasons," Dave said. "Lost mines ain't supposed to be found the way you people are going at it. Besides that, the Crazy Kid mine belongs to us here in Barker."

He was past seventy and he looked after horses in the local feedyard. He wore a shabby, open vest over faded suspenders and gray flannel shirts and nobody would ever have looked for wisdom in that old man. But it was there.

"This is big, new, lonesome country and it's hard on people," he said. "Every town's got a story about a lost mine or a lost gold cache. Only kids go looking for it. It's enough for most folks just to know it's there. It helps 'em to stand the country."

"I see," I said. Something stirred in the back of my mind.

"Barker never got its lost mine until thirteen years ago," Dave said. "Folks just naturally can't stand to see you people find it this way, by main force and so soon after."

5

"We know there isn't any mine," I said. "We're just proving it isn't there."

"If you could prove that, it'd be worse yet," he said. "Only you can't. We all saw and handled that ore. It was quartz, just rotten with gold in wires and flakes. The boy went on foot from his house to get it. The lode's got to be right close by out there."

He waved toward our search area. The air above it was luminous with twilight and I felt a curious surge of interest. Colonel Lewis had always discouraged us from speculating on that story. If one of us brought it up, I was usually the one who led the hooting and we all suggested he go over the search area with a dowsing rod. It was an article of faith with us that the vein did not exist. But now I was all alone and my own field boss.

We each put up one foot on the veranda rail and rested our arms on our knees. Dave bit off a chew of tobacco and told me about Owen Price.

"He was always a crazy kid and I guess he read every book in town," Dave said. "He had a curious heart, that boy."

I'm no folklorist, but even I could see how myth elements were already creeping into the story. For one thing, Dave insisted the boy's shirt was torn off and he had lacerations on his back.

"Like a cougar clawed him," Dave said. "Only they ain't never been cougars in that desert. We backtracked that boy till his trail crossed itself so many times it was no use, but we never found one cougar track."

I could discount that stuff, of course, but still the story gripped me. Maybe it was Dave's slow, sure voice; perhaps the queer twilight; possibly my own wounded pride. I thought of how great lava upwellings sometimes tear loose and carry along huge masses of the country rock. Maybe such an erratic mass lay out there, perhaps only a few hundred feet across and so missed by our drill cores, but rotten with uranium. If I could find it, I would make a fool of Colonel Lewis. I would discredit the whole science of geology. I, Duard Campbell, the despised and rejected one, could do that. The front of my mind shouted that it was nonsense, but something far back in my mind began composing a devastating letter to Colonel Lewis and comfort flowed into me.

"There's some say the boy's youngest sister could tell where he found it, if she wanted," Dave said. "She used to go into that desert with him a lot. She took on pretty wild when it happened and then was struck dumb, but I hear she talks again now." He shook his head. "Poor little Helen. She promised to be a pretty girl."

"Where does she live?" I asked.

"With her mother in Salem," Dave said. "She went to business school and I hear she works for a lawyer there."

Mrs. Price was a flinty old woman who seemed to control her daughter absolutely. She agreed Helen would be my secretary as soon as I told her the salary. I got Helen's security clearance with one phone call; she had already been investigated as part of tracing that uranium crystal. Mrs. Price arranged for Helen to stay with a family she knew in Barker, to protect her reputation. It was in no danger. I meant to make love to her, if I had to, to charm her out of her secret, if she had one, but I would not harm her. I knew perfectly well that I was only playing a game called "The Revenge of Duard Campbell." I knew I would not find any uranium.

Helen was a plain little girl and she was made of frightened ice. She wore low-heeled shoes and cotton stockings and plain dresses with white cuffs and collars. Her one good feature was her flawless fair skin against which her peaked, black Welsh eyebrows and smoky blue eyes gave her an elfin look at times. She liked to sit neatly tucked into herself, feet together, elbows in, eyes cast down, voice hardly audible, as smoothly self-contained as an egg. The desk I gave her faced mine and she sat like that across from me and did the busy work I gave her and I could not get through to her at all.

I tried joking and I tried polite little gifts and attentions, and I tried being sad and needing sympathy. She listened and worked and stayed as far away as the moon. It was only after two weeks and by pure accident that I found the key to her.

I was trying the sympathy gambit. I said it was not so bad, being exiled from friends and family, but what I could not stand was the dreary sameness of that search area. Every spot was like every other spot and there was no single, recognizable *place* in the whole expanse. It sparked something in her and she roused up at me.

"It's full of just wonderful places," she said.

"Come out with me in the jeep and show me one," I challenged.

She was reluctant, but I hustled her along regardless. I guided the jeep between outcrops, jouncing and lurching. I had our map photographed on my mind and I knew where we were every minute, but only by map coordinates. The desert had our marks on it: well sites, seismic blast holes, wooden stakes, cans, bottles and papers blowing in that everlasting wind, and it was all dismally the same anyway.

"Tell me when we pass a 'place' and I'll stop," I said.

"It's all places," she said. "Right here's a place."

I stopped the jeep and looked at her in surprise. Her voice was strong and throaty. She opened her eyes wide and smiled; I had never seen her look like that.

"What's special, that makes it a place?" I asked.

She did not answer. She got out and walked a few steps. Her whole

7

posture was changed. She almost danced along. I followed and touched her shoulder.

"Tell me what's special," I said.

She faced around and stared right past me. She had a new grace and vitality and she was a very pretty girl.

"It's where all the dogs are," she said.

"Dogs?"

I looked around at the scrubby sagebrush and thin soil and ugly black rock and back at Helen. Something was wrong.

"Big, stupid dogs that go in herds and eat grass," she said. She kept turning and gazing. "Big cats chase the dogs and eat them. The dogs scream and scream. Can't you hear them?"

"That's crazy!" I said. "What's the matter with you?"

I might as well have slugged her. She crumpled instantly back into herself and I could hardly hear her answer.

"I'm sorry. My brother and I used to play out fairy tales here. All this was a kind of of fairyland to us." Tears formed in her eyes. "I haven't been here since . . . I forgot myself. I'm sorry."

I had to swear I needed to dictate "field notes" to force Helen into that desert again. She sat stiffly with pad and pencil in the jeep while I put on my act with the Geiger and rattled off jargon. Her lips were pale and compressed and I could see her fighting against the spell the desert had for her, and I could see her slowly losing.

She finally broke down into that strange mood and I took good care not to break it. It was weird but wonderful, and I got a lot of data. I made her go out for "field notes" every morning and each time it was easier to break her down. Back in the office she always froze again and I marveled at how two such different persons could inhabit the same body. I called her two phases "Office Helen" and "Desert Helen."

I often talked with old Dave on the veranda after dinner. One night he cautioned me.

"Folks here think Helen ain't been right in the head since her brother died," he said. "They're worrying about you and her."

"I feel like a big brother to her," I said. "I'd never hurt her, Dave. If we find the lode, I'll stake the best claim for her."

He shook his head. I wished I could explain to him how it was only a harmless game I was playing and no one would ever find gold out there. Yet, as a game, it fascinated me.

Desert Helen charmed me when, helplessly, she had to uncover her secret

8

life. She was a little girl in a woman's body. Her voice became strong and breathless with excitement and she touched me with the same wonder that turned her own face vivid and elfin. She ran laughing through the black rocks and scrubby sagebrush and momentarily she made them beautiful. She would pull me along by the hand and sometimes we ran as much as a mile away from the jeep. She treated me as if I were a blind or foolish child.

"No, no, Duard, that's a cliff!" she would say, pulling me back.

She would go first, so I could find the stepping stones across streams. I played up. She pointed out woods and streams and cliffs and castles. There were shaggy horses with claws, golden birds, camels, witches, elephants and many other creatures. I pretended to see them all, and it made her trust me. She talked and acted out the fairy tales she had once played with Owen. Sometimes he was enchanted and sometimes she, and the one had to dare the evil magic of a witch or giant to rescue the other. Sometimes I was Duard and other times I almost thought I was Owen.

Helen and I crept into sleeping castles, and we hid with pounding hearts while the giant grumbled in search of us and we fled, hand in hand, before his wrath.

Well, I had her now. I played Helen's game, but I never lost sight of my own. Every night I sketched in on my map whatever I had learned that day of the fairyland topography. Its geomorphology was remarkably consistent.

When we played, I often hinted about the giant's treasure. Helen never denied it existed, but she seemed troubled and evasive about it. She would put her finger to her lips and look at me with solemn, round eyes.

"You only take the things nobody cares about," she would say. "If you take the gold or jewels, it brings you terrible bad luck."

"I got a charm against bad luck and I'll let you have it too," I said once. "It's the biggest, strongest charm in the whole world."

"No. It all turns into trash. It turns into goat beans and dead snakes and things," she said crossly. "Owen told me. It's a rule, in fairyland."

Another time we talked about it as we sat in a gloomy ravine near a waterfall. We had to keep our voices low or we would wake up the giant. The waterfall was really the giant snoring and it was also the wind that blew forever across that desert.

"Doesn't Owen ever take anything?" I asked.

I had learned by then that I must always speak of Owen in the present tense.

"Sometimes he has to," she said. "Once right here the witch had me enchanted into an ugly toad. Owen put a flower on my head and that made me be Helen again."

"A really truly flower? That you could take home with you?"

"A red and yellow flower bigger than my two hands," she said. "I tried to take it home, but all the petals came off."

"Does Owen ever take anything home?"

"Rocks, sometimes," she said. "We keep them in a secret nest in the shed. We think they might be magic eggs."

I stood up. "Come and show me."

She shook her head vigorously and drew back. "I don't want to go home," she said. "Not ever."

She squirmed and pouted, but I pulled her to her feet.

"Please, Helen, for me," I said. "Just for one little minute."

I pulled her back to the jeep and we drove to the old Price place. I had never seen her look at it when we passed it and she did not look now. She was freezing fast back into Office Helen. But she led me around the sagging old house with its broken windows and into a tumbledown shed. She scratched away some straw in one corner, and there were the rocks. I did not realize how excited I was until disappointment hit me like a blow in the stomach.

They were worthless waterworn pebbles of quartz and rosy granite. The only thing special about them was that they could never have originated on that basalt desert.

After a few weeks we dropped the pretense of field notes and simply went into the desert to play. I had Helen's fairyland almost completely mapped. It seemed to be a recent fault block mountain with a river parallel to its base and a gently sloping plain across the river. The scarp face was wooded and cut by deep ravines and it had castles perched on its truncated spurs. I kept checking Helen on it and never found her inconsistent. Several times when she was in doubt I was able to tell her where she was, and that let me even more deeply into her secret life. One morning I discovered just how deeply.

She was sitting on a log in the forest and plaiting a little basket out of fern fronds. I stood beside her. She looked up at me and smiled.

"What shall we play today, Owen?" she asked.

I had not expected that, and I was proud of how quickly I rose to it. I capered and bounded away and then back to her and crouched at her feet.

"Little sister, little sister, I'm enchanted," I said. "Only you in all the world can uncharm me."

"I'll uncharm you," she said, in that little girl voice. "What are you, brother?"

"A big, black dog," I said. "A wicked giant named Lewis Rawbones keeps me chained up behind his castle while he takes all the other dogs out hunting."

10

She smoothed her gray skirt over her knees. Her mouth drooped.

"You're lonesome and you howl all day and you howl all night," she said. "Poor doggie."

I threw back my head and howled.

"He's a terrible, wicked giant and he's got all kinds of terrible magic," I said. "You mustn't be afraid, little sister. As soon as you uncharm me I'll be a handsome prince and I'll cut off his head."

"I'm not afraid." Her eyes sparkled. "I'm not afraid of fire or snakes or pins or needles or anything."

"I'll take you away to my kingdom and we'll live happily ever afterward. You'll be the most beautiful queen in the world and everybody will love you."

I wagged my tail and laid my head on her knees. She stroked my silky head and pulled my long black ears.

"Everybody will love me." She was very serious now. "Will magic water uncharm you, poor old doggie?"

"You have to touch my forehead with a piece of the giant's treasure," I said. "That's the only onliest way to uncharm me."

I felt her shrink away from me. She stood up, her face suddenly crumpled with grief and anger.

"You're not Owen, you're just a man! Owen's enchanted and I'm enchanted too and nobody will ever uncharm us!"

She ran away from me and she was already Office Helen by the time she reached the jeep.

After that day she refused flatly to go into the desert with me. It looked as if my game was played out. But I gambled that Desert Helen could still hear me, underneath somewhere, and I tried a new strategy. The office was an upstairs room over the old dance hall and, I suppose, in frontier days skirmishing had gone on there between men and women. I doubt anything went on as strange as my new game with Helen.

I always had paced and talked while Helen worked. Now I began mixing common-sense talk with fairyland talk and I kept coming back to the wicked giant, Lewis Rawbones. Office Helen tried not to pay attention, but now and then I caught Desert Helen peeping at me out of her eyes. I spoke of my blighted career as a geologist and how it would be restored to me if I found the lode. I mused on how I would live and work in exotic places and how I would need a wife to keep house for me and help with my paper work. It disturbed Office Helen. She made typing mistakes and dropped things. I kept it up for days, trying for just the right mixture of fact and fantasy, and it was hard on Office Helen.

11

One night old Dave warned me again.

"Helen's looking peaked, and there's talk around. Miz Fowler says Helen don't sleep and she cries at night and she won't tell Miz Fowler what's wrong. You don't happen to know what's bothering her, do you?"

"I only talk business stuff to her," I said. "Maybe she's homesick. I'll ask her if she wants a vacation." I did not like the way Dave looked at me. "I haven't hurt her. I don't mean her any harm, Dave," I said.

"People get killed for what they do, not for what they mean," he said. "Son, there's men in this here town would kill you quick as a coyote, if you hurt Helen Price."

I worked on Helen all the next day and in the afternoon I hit just the right note and I broke her defenses. I was not prepared for the way it worked out. I had just said, "All life is a kind of playing. If you think about it right, everything we do is a game." She poised her pencil and looked straight at me, as she had never done in that office, and I felt my heart speed up.

"You taught me how to play, Helen. I was so serious that I didn't know how to play."

"Owen taught me to play. He had magic. My sisters couldn't play anything but dolls and rich husbands and I hated them."

Her eyes opened wide and her lips trembled and she was almost Desert Helen right there in the office.

"There's magic and enchantment in regular life, if you look at it right," I said. "Don't you think so, Helen?"

"I know it!" she said. She turned pale and dropped her pencil. "Owen was enchanted into having a wife and three daughters and he was just a boy. But he was the only man we had and all of them but me hated him because we were so poor." She began to tremble and her voice went flat. "He couldn't stand it. He took the treasure and it killed him." Tears ran down her cheeks. "I tried to think he was only enchanted into play-dead and if I didn't speak or laugh for seven years, I'd uncharm him."

She dropped her head on her hands. I was alarmed. I came over and put my hand on her shoulder.

"I did speak." Her shoulders heaved with sobs. "They made me speak, and now Owen won't ever come back."

I bent and put my arm across her shoulders.

"Don't cry, Helen. He'll come back," I said. "There are other magics to bring him back."

I hardly knew what I was saying. I was afraid of what I had done, and I wanted to comfort her. She jumped up and threw off my arm.

"I can't stand it! I'm going home!"

She ran out into the hall and down the stairs and from the window I saw her run down the street, still crying. All of a sudden my game seemed cruel and stupid to me and right that moment I stopped it. I tore up my map of fairyland and my letters to Colonel Lewis and I wondered how in the world I could ever have done all that.

After dinner that night old Dave motioned me out to one end of the veranda. His face looked carved out of wood.

"I don't know what happened in your office today, and for your sake I better not find out. But you send Helen back to her mother on the morning stage, you hear me?"

"All right, if she wants to go," I said. "I can't just fire her."

"I'm speaking for the boys. You better put her on that morning stage, or we'll be around to talk to you."

"All right, I will, Dave."

I wanted to tell him how the game was stopped now and how I wanted a chance to make things up with Helen, but I thought I had better not. Dave's voice was flat and savage with contempt and, old as he was, he frightened me.

Helen did not come to work in the morning. At nine o'clock I went out myself for the mail. I brought a large mailing tube and some letters back to the office. The first letter I opened was from Dr. Lewis, and almost like magic it solved all my problems.

On the basis of his preliminary structure contour maps Dr. Lewis had gotten permission to close out the field phase. Copies of the maps were in the mailing tube, for my information. I was to hold an inventory and be ready to turn everything over to an army quartermaster team coming in a few days. There was still a great mass of data to be worked up in refining the maps. I was to join the group again and I would have a chance at the lab work after all.

I felt pretty good. I paced and whistled and snapped my fingers. I wished Helen would come, to help on the inventory. Then I opened the tube and looked idly at the maps. There were a lot of them, featureless bed after bed of basalt, like layers of a cake ten miles across. But when I came to the bottom map, of the prevolcanic Miocene landscape, the hair on my neck stood up.

I had made that map myself. It was Helen's fairyland. The topography was point by point the same.

I clenched my fists and stopped breathing. Then it hit me a second time, and the skin crawled up my back.

The game was real. I couldn't end it. All the time the game had been playing me. It was still playing me.

13

I ran out and down the street and overtook old Dave hurrying toward the feedyard. He had a holstered gun on each hip.

"Dave, I've got to find Helen," I said.

"Somebody seen her hiking into the desert just at daylight," he said. "I'm on my way for a horse." He did not slow his stride. "You better get out there in your stinkwagon. If you don't find her before we do, you better just keep on going, son."

I ran back and got the jeep and roared it out across the scrubby sagebrush. I hit rocks and I do not know why I did not break something. I knew where to go and feared what I would find there. I knew I loved Helen Price more than my own life and I knew I had driven her to her death.

I saw her far off, running and dodging. I headed the jeep to intercept her and I shouted, but she neither saw me nor heard me. I stopped and jumped out and ran after her and the world darkened. Helen was all I could see, and I could not catch up with her.

"Wait for me, little sister!" I screamed after her. "I love you, Helen! Wait for me!"

She stopped and crouched and I almost ran over her. I knelt and put my arms around her and then it was on us.

They say in an earthquake, when the direction of up and down tilts and wobbles, people feel a fear that drives them mad if they can not forget it afterward. This was worse. Up and down and here and there and now and then all rushed together. The wind roared through the rock beneath us and the air thickened crushingly above our heads. I know we clung to each other, and we were there for each other while nothing else was and that is all I know, until we were in the jeep and I was guiding it back toward town as headlong as I had come.

Then the world had shape again under a bright sun. I saw a knot of horsemen on the horizon. They were heading for where Owen had been found. That boy had run a long way, alone and hurt and burdened.

I got Helen up to the office. She sat at her desk with her head down on her hands and she quivered violently. I kept my arm around her.

"It was only a storm inside our two heads, Helen," I said, over and over. "Something black blew away out of us. The game is finished and we're free and I love you."

Over and over I said that, for my sake as well as hers. I meant and believed it. I said she was my wife and we would marry and go a thousand miles away from that desert to raise our children. She quieted to a trembling, but she would not speak. Then I heard hoofbeats and the creak of leather in the street below and then I heard slow footsteps on the stairs.

14

Old Dave stood in the doorway. His two guns looked as natural on him as hands and feet. He looked at Helen, bowed over the desk, and then at me, standing beside her.

"Come on down, son. The boys want to talk to you," he said.

I followed him into the hall and stopped.

"She isn't hurt," I said. "The lode is really out there, Dave, but nobody is ever going to find it."

"Tell that to the boys."

"We're closing out the project in a few more days," I said. "I'm going to marry Helen and take her away with me."

"Come down or we'll drag you down!" he said harshly. "We'll send Helen back to her mother."

I was afraid. I did not know what to do.

"No, you won't send me back to my mother!"

It was Helen beside me in the hall. She was Desert Helen, but grown up and wonderful. She was pale, pretty, aware and sure of herself.

"I'm going with Duard," she said. "Nobody in the world is ever going to send me around like a package again."

Dave rubbed his jaw and squinted his eyes at her.

"I love her, Dave," I said. "I'll take care of her all my life."

I put my left arm around her and she nestled against me. The tautness went out of old Dave and he smiled. He kept his eyes on Helen.

"Little Helen Price," he said, wonderingly. "Who ever would've thought it?" He reached out and shook us both gently. "Bless you youngsters," he said, and blinked his eyes. "I'll tell the boys it's all right."

He turned and went slowly down the stairs. Helen and I looked at each other, and I think she saw a new face too.

That was sixteen years ago. I am a professor myself now, graying a bit at the temples. I am as positivistic a scientist as you will find anywhere in the Mississippi drainage basin. When I tell a seminar student "That assertion is operationally meaningless," I can make it sound downright obscene. The students blush and hate me, but it is for their own good. Science is the only safe game, and it's safe only if it is kept pure. I work hard at that, I have yet to meet the student I can not handle.

My son is another matter. We named him Owen Lewis, and he has Helen's eyes and hair and complexion. He learned to read on the modern sane and sterile children's books. We haven't a fairy tale in the house—but I have a science library. And Owen makes fairy tales out of science. He is taking the measure of space and time now, with Jeans and Eddington. He

15

cannot possibly understand a tenth of what he reads, in the way I understand it. But he understands all of it in some other way privately his own.

Not long ago he said to me, "You know, Dad, it isn't only space that's expanding. Time's expanding too, and that's what makes us keep getting farther away from when we used to be."

And I have to tell him just what I did in the war. I know I found manhood and a wife. The how and why of it I think and hope I am incapable of fully understanding. But Owen has, through Helen, that strangely curious heart. I'm afraid. I'm afraid he will understand.

To Joseph P. Elder, Scott Meredith Literary Agency, March 7, 1965:

> Dear Joe,
> I've been thinking off & on about "It's a Wise Child," by John Wyndham, one of the stories I returned on Feb. 24, and it seems to me that it could be salvaged. There are two things wrong with the story in its present form: it is about 2,000 words too long for its one-punch plot, and the surprise ending is telegraphed a mile. . . .
> If Wyndham would like to rewrite the story along these lines at about 3,000 or 3,500 words, I would be very glad to see it again, and would pay $200 for a successful rewrite.

The story subsequently appeared, just as the author wrote it, in *Playboy*.

To Robert P. Mills, March 15, 1965:

> Dear Bob,
> I think "The Loolies Are Here" is one of the freshest and funniest things I've seen in many a year, & it would be a dirty shame if it never got published because it has no story. It builds and builds, beautifully, for four & a half pages, and then we get to the end, and it just goes flooo. . . .
> I found an item here and there in the text that I could not puzzle out, & I will list these for whatever they may be worth. . . . P. 1, last par., your hands full of runny? Noses? P. 2, par. 2, what are

16

hydrators? My wife, who comes from Kentucky, explained doodledy squat to me, but she never heard of hydrators either. . . . P. 5, I am trying hard, but can't quite visualize a dog escaping in a slather of canned tomatoes.

All this probably makes me sound pretty square, but in my own defense I will state that Katie just now came in to see if I was all right: I had run across "something terrible with a bite out of it" for the fifth time and was laughing like a fool.

To Mills from Jane Rice (one of the two authors of "The Loolies Are Here"), June 27, 1965:

Dear Bob:

I fain would lie down. How about you? If D.K. doesn't like THIS ending the Hell with it.

THE LOOLIES ARE HERE

by Allison Rice

They are. I've seen one. He (it?) was standing in the washbasin in our bathroom, during an electrical storm, in the middle of the night. He was about a foot high in his bare feet and he had a whiskery face and he smiled at me . . . slowly. I don't care to dwell on it. They have more teeth than we do—or *something*, and this one was wearing a little pockety-looking garment somewhat on the order of a shoemaker's apron. He must have been able to see in the dark because he was reading a threatening note I had written milord and scotch-taped *firmly* to the mirror.

In case you're thinking what I think you're thinking, the answer is—No, I don't. Nor am I subconsciously fulfilling a psychological need. I am the mother of four small boys and I need a loolie like milord needs a coat hanger caught in the lawnmower.

Anyhow, to the inevitable queries—Why are they called loolies? Where do they come from, et cetera?—I can only reply through a mouthful of clothespins, I haven't time to bat this over the head with a rolled-up research

17

paper. I guess they're called loolies for the same reason that brownies are called brownies. It is their name. Maybe they come from the same place. Et cetera. Wherever that is. However and where*as* a brownie is a good-natured goblin who performs helpful services at night (that's what I need, begod, a reliable brownie, with an eyeshade and some counterfeiting equipment) a loolie will leave you lop-legged. And probably already he has. I'm not sure a loolie is a goblin either.

No matter. Think back. Do you own a listless, slump-shouldered voltage-starved appliance that brightens, clicks its dials, and does a sexy Flamenco the minute the repair truck turns into the driveway? Does your gravel sprout grass, your lawn nourish moles, and your iced tea get cloudy? Do your paper bags jump out of the cupboard at you when you've got your eggbeater full of runny so that you get splaat all over? Are your children behaving like subversives in the employ of a foreign power? Are your groceries being delivered with the cans on top of the grapes on top of the potato chips? Does someone whom you haven't seen since your pink tulle and corsage days —such as an old Sigma Chi beau—drop in from Paris en route to the Orient when you've just returned from a catfish fry at Thick Lake and are going with your tongue hanging out looking like doodledy squat? Do drawers stick? Gutters runneth over? Sheets split down the middle? What always makes three too many of those floorboard screeks you hear in the dark? Where are your car keys? (Wanna bet?)

That's enough for a sample. Try them for size. If they fit, Welcome to the Club. The password is May Day and don't say you weren't warned. Another thing, pay attention to what your wee ones jabber at you when you find the sink stopped up, the ceiling leaking milk, and the baby licking the flyswatter. Let me be a lesson to you. I didn't listen and now I wear a size Gulp dress and my house is shrinking. Your motto should be WATCH OUT, lest thy hoe handle uprise and whack thee in thy teeth.

If you're the It-Can't-Happen-Here type, get down on the kitchen floor where everything else usually is and hunt for eeny-weeny footprints. Act at once. The neck you save may be your own, honey. I learned the hard way, with a stray roller skate as my Cinderella slipper (a typical loolie ploy) and an ironing board for a partner. Recognizing this prone situation as a seldom-come-by pooprtunity,* I rested a spell. Which is how I saw the footprints.

When I was a new bride I would've thought MICE but I have realized that mice ain't much, comparatively speaking, and that eeeeek don't solve nuthin'. Therefore I merely shifted onto one elbow and ruminated hmmmmm. If I dipped snuff I'd've dipped some.

*This is *not* a typographical error.

18

The prints were too large for mice. And they all had fairly human-looking toes, which is how human toes generally look. Was a lost doll walking around the neighborhood trying to beam in on Ma-Ma? Considering whatall dolls do nowadays this idea wasn't far-fetched. Could it be a baby robot, for that matter? Or, a ditto Martian, a very likely possibility. Perhaps it was loolies. Maybe it was—

. . . loolies . . .

! and ? Suppose loolies weren't scapegoats invented by our imaginative progeny? Suppose loolies were the truth? It was idiotic to suppose that loolies had painted our car wheels, when I had collared the syndicate white-handed, but suppose loolies were the *Master*minds. Lor' luv a duck . . .

A succession of past events blipped across my inner eye, like the fruit on a slot machine. The Great Sugar Fight and Toothpaste Squirt. The company's-coming, big, old-fashioned Thanksgiving dinner which *dis*interested the company mightily when milord, probing the golden-brown-turkey-dripping-with-delicious-goodness, came up with a soggy wool mitten. The day our offspring sneaked their scraggly, half-grown, spook-footed, purple Easter chickens into the car trunk and we didn't discover the witless, scrawky, whap-flap THINGS until we arrived at our destination, a downtown hotel in Louisville. The day they built the snowman, indoors. The day I was sure I had erected an impregnable barricade to defend a freshly varnished floor when here they came, huffing and puffing, to show me how thistledown worked.

And what about like weevils in the flour. Cobwebs overnight. Holes in socks. All those long lost, tenor, *s'wahoo ol' buddy* buddies milord finds at Homecomings, and places. And all those ol' midnight invitations for beckon and eggsh at our housh while I weigh my chances of beating the rap on a murder charge.

Y'know something? An all-woman jury would be a cinch. They wouldn't bother to leave the box. They would simply continue to knit one, purl two as they murmured in unison, "Justifiable homicide." Their modish foreman (not a grease spot on her, not one bead of sweat) would stand and say, "Your Honor . . . we find the defendant . . . NOT THE LEAST BITTY BIT GUILTY." Pandemonium. Judge pounds gavel, to no avail. Jury pounds prosecuting attorney. Snake dance forms . . . flambeaux . . . floats . . . bunting . . . banners . . . loudspeakers . . . *Allison Rice for President!* A prominent (size 42, D cup) society matron climbs up on the Helen Hayes Theatre marquee and does the split. Huzzah! Huzzah! Wall Street and ticker tape . . . Pennsylvania Avenue . . . the Inaugural Ball . . . and there, beside me, in the spotlight, my fambly. Milord has just met a long-lost, *tattooed* buddy.

Our children have been eating dirt. The smallest is holding a one-eyed alley cat with a bad case of mange. They are showing a prominent society matron a bottle of spit they've saved up. They espy Lady Bird (a Mrs. Lady Bird Jackson, who is famous for her salt-rising bread) and wave and yell for her to come watch how they can piddle-puddle through a knothole. I confront them with the footprints. Loolies? My voice booms over the microphones. There is a skitter of amusement. A widening sputter of mirth. A surge, a roar of jelly-belly laughter. I am horrified to discover I am the sole lady present who is not wearing a topless evening gown. The scene mercifully fades. . . .

Let's see. Where—

Ah, *there* you are. What are you doing way over there? Never mind, let us hurry on, past milord's theory that the loolie prints could've been made by any of the following: turtles, hamsters, cats, kittens, dogs, frogs, hoptoads, rabbits, a salamander with a short tail, or large mice. I make no comment except to remark that at least he doesn't think they're mine.

As traps are taboo (too many fingers and toes—260$^1/_2$ to be exact, counting everyone) I left nightly saucers of milk for the loolies. Cookies. The latest issue of *House Beautiful*. I tried appealing to their sense of fun with a rubber lizard and a Hallowe'en nose. Please be informed that hope will get you nowhere. Our cat produced a litter of seven female kittens, and litter is the one right word, believe me. Our dog had an encounter with a skunk and, subsequently, terrorized the whole neighborhood by acting like an animal out of Mythical Beasts. We went through measles, mumps, green apples, a rash of dents and blown fuses and more baby rabbits and vacuum cleaner trouble. And have you ever, when getting the wash ready, emptied a child's *sock* and found yourself holding something terrible with a bite out of it?

Next, I "hexed." If you must know, I wrote "loolies" in pig Latin on the inside of a peanut-butter sandwich and ate it for lunch. It tasted clean, and good, and true. Yet, within twenty-four hours I was back on the *s'wahoo ol' buddy* circuit, and there was a whole quartet of the aforementioned s.o.b.s and one of them had a guitar. If you think I put up with this hootenanny nonsense you win first prize, two pounds of beckon and a dozen eggsh.

And then, out of the Slough of Despond, came the midnight storm. It was a doozy. One of those torrential, lightning-ripped, rumble, BLAM things, black as cats one second and livid fluorescent green the next. Did the children rouse, frightened and seeking comfort? No. Did milord awaken to batten down the hatches and protect his nearest and dearest from loose electricity? No. 'Twas I, Minnie the Mermaid (no Ho-Daddy, she!) who crossed the Rubicon without so much as a flashlight (the battery was dead).

Oh, pioneers! I used to think I'd have made a splendid settler woman.

Brave. Intrepid. Dauntless. The Indians would have named me Little Bright Rattlesnake. I know, now, I'd have been a dud. For, when I pussyfooted into the bathroom for a towel to mop wet windowsills with and, BLAM, saw the loolie . . . had an Indian been handy he could have lifted my scalp right off my head, slick as a whistle, without benefit of tomahawk—that's how high my hair rose and how loose I was all the way up from my knees . . . as I vainly flicked the light switch.

From my knees down I was pure steel piston and I was out in the kitchen in nothing flat, desperately trying light switches en route and making thin keening noises as I snatched up suitable weapons.

Armed, I took a deep breath and started back, an inch at a time, keeping close to the walls like they do in the movies. Quietly. Quietly. The storm slammed and glittered about the house but Little Bright Rattlesnake slipped silently—the lights came on suddenly and I screamed.

Milord appeared in the hallway, sleepy and disheveled. "What—" he began, and stopped. I think at that moment he'd have traded me in for a used Edsel.

Behind him the bathroom was brilliantly lit, and empty. The note on the mirror was gone. He'd never believe me. Never in the wide world.

"I . . . uh . . . thought I heard something," I explained, lamely.

"You did," he said, eyeing my broom, and long-handled barbecue fork, and me. "Thunder."

Let us, for politeness' sake, lower the curtain here and raise it again the following morning. *This* morning, to be exact. Visualize, if you will, the sunny kitchen with its limp rained-on curtains, and me staring bug-eyed and whopper-jawed at the name *Chauncey* written in strawberry jam on the refrigerator door.

I realize *why* the loolie's strange attire. I wonder numbly what *else* he may have pocketed. The note on the mirror arises Phoenix-like in my mind.

> Dearest *Chauncey*:
> Someone who uses barbershop hair tonic used my hairbrush. Pray tell, could it be you? How would you like to be snatched baldheaded?
>
>> Love and kisses,
>> Guess Who

As you have no doubt surmised, Chauncey is milord's middle name which he keeps under such careful guard that even Agent 007 couldn't spring it. Well, I thought, it was out now. I could almost see the graffiti on the sidewalk, the locker room floor at the club, the office bulletin board . . .

Hastily, I soaped a sponge and wiped the refrigerator door, and none too soon, for milord burst into the kitchen as if shot from guns. His expression was deathly, his voice a knell.

"Honey," he intoned in accents of DOOM, "I'm . . . I'm getting bald!"

G. P. Putnam's Sons, the trade publisher which had recently acquired Berkley Publishing Corp. as a wholly-owned subsidiary, wanted to publish *Orbit* under a "young adult" label, arguing that that would double its sales. This meant, however, that the manuscript of the first volume fell into the hands of a juvenile editor who routinely altered a couple of words that he thought might offend librarians. The words, for the record, were "breasts" and "heterosexuality." The second of these changes made hash of a key sentence in James Blish's "How Beautiful With Banners." I found out about the changes after they had been set in type, and made such a beautiful stink that Putnam agreed to restore the text. Subsequent volumes have been published as adult books, which indeed they are. (Incidentally, the second volume sold better than the first.)

To Ted Thomas, November 24, 1965:

> Dear Ted,
> . . . So much for the time machine. Assume this is all accounted for, and your guy is marooned in the past; when the story opens, he's been there ten years and has a wife and kid. What's he been doing all that time? How come he's still living in a cave and has no tools but a stone ax? How come no house, no calendar, no attempt to leave a permanent record, no attempt at agriculture (not even medicinal herbs, for Chrissake), no stethoscope (a roll of bark would be better than nothing), no smokehouse, no nothing? No spear, no bow, nothing salvaged from the wreck; no pottery to cook in; not a chair or table, or a door to close the mouth of the cave; not so much as a grass hat. In ten years?
> Now we come to the cave people, and they are good and believable; you make your one good strong point—that these cave

22

types wouldn't necessarily make a demigod out of your guy as soon as he set a bone or handed out an aspirin. But is this really all there is to them? . . . . Has this guy really been here for ten years without learning any of their names or recognizing them as individuals? They come on stage just as "a man," or "a woman," as if he'd never seen any of them before. How come?

Finally, what is he up to? This is the crucial point, and the story hits or misses on it. Is he looking forward beyond his own life span and hoping to accomplish something permanent, or is he just doctoring because he's a doctor? Does he hope to have a successor? If so, why doesn't he take the kid on his rounds? Is he hoping his own genes will improve the race? If so, why hasn't he been impregnating every female he could catch? I suspect your point is that he *is* just doctoring because he's a doctor, and this turns me off a little (I mean, suppose they'd sent back a plumber: would he just plumb?), but I don't want to try to talk you out of it, just to say that you should not leave the reader (me) in doubt.

From Thomas, December 3, 1965:

Dear Damon,

We have a nice issue here on "The Doctor," one that may even be significant. I think you are wrong. Here's why.

. . . . This is most emphatically NOT a story about time machine hardware and processes, yet you want it to be. You or I or any of 50 of us could on a half hour's reflection come up with several plausible answers to each of the questions you raise about the details of the time travel and the accident that left him there and the lack of rescue. But these are mere trappings to the story of a man doing all he knows how to do in an effort to adjust as a man of integrity.

As it happens, I know all the answers to your questions because I thought them out, at least far enough to see they were not important. For example, he can't use the remnants of the ship since it is made of an intractable molybdenum alloy, the one that is in diver's tanks; he can't get off even a piece of it; it erodes and splinters flint.

Now, if you are right on what you think this story should have, and you may be, I think we may be on to what's different between an SF story and a general story. The intelligent SF reader demands these SF trappings and will not go without them. . . . The reader

23

of a general story does this to a much greater extent except in those stories where the scenery *is* the story. So if you are right—and I hope you're not—the twain may never meet. But even you see something in this story, and what knocked me on my ear was spotting that the kid is going to get killed.

I sat down to write this one with a very vivid scene in mind of the killing of the kid as an act of revenge by one of the creatures for the doctor's treatment. It was in the front of my mind all the way through, but it would not write. When I finished it, I went over it carefully to try to find a place to stuff it in, but it would not stuff. . . .

To Thomas, May 10, 1966:

Dear Ted,

Here is "The Doctor" with some suggested changes for your approval.

It suddenly struck me last night, after I finished copy-editing this, that maybe these people don't have language. I had hold of the wrong end of it. Of course he doesn't know their names—they haven't got any. When Gant uses pantomime with the woman about her infected tooth, & when his wife pats him silently on the shoulder, it feels exactly right. If you can take out the few instances when Gant talks to them, I think the whole thing will fall into place.

I took out most of the junk I talked you into putting in.

THE DOCTOR

by Ted Thomas

When Gant first opened his eyes he thought for an instant he was back in his home in Pennsylvania. He sat up suddenly and looked wildly around in the dark of the cave, and then he remembered where he was. The noise he made frightened his wife and his son, Dun, and they rolled to their feet, crouched, ready to leap. Gant grunted reassuringly at them and climbed off the moss-packed platform he had built for a bed. The barest glimmerings of dawn filtered into the cave, and the remnants of the fire glowed at the mouth. Gant went to the fire and poked it and put some chips on it and blew on them. It had been a long time since he had had such a vivid memory of his old life half a million years away. He looked at the wall of the cave, at the place where he kept his calendar, painfully scratched into the rock. It had been ten years ago today when he had stepped into that molybdenum-steel cylinder in the Bancroft Building at Pennsylvania State University. What was it he had said? "Sure, I'll try it. You ought to have a medical doctor in it on the first trial run. You physicists could not learn anything about the physiological effects of time travel. Besides, this will make history, and I want to be in on it."

Gant stepped over the fire and listened carefully at the mouth of the cave, near the log barrier. Outside he heard the sound of rustling brush and heavy breathing, and he knew he could not leave now. He drank some water from a gourd and ate some dried bison with his wife and son. They all ate quietly.

Dawn came, and he stepped to the mouth of the cave and listened. The great animal had left. He waved to his wife and Dun, dragged aside the barrier, and went out.

He went along the face of the cliff, staying away from the heavy underbrush at its foot. He would go into it when he returned, and he would look for food.

In the marsh that lay beyond the underbrush was one of the many monuments to his failures. In the rocks and tree stumps there, he had tried to grow penicillium molds on the sweet juices of some of the berries that abounded in the region. He had crushed the berries and placed the juices in a hundred different kinds of receptacles. For three years he had tried to raise the green mold, but all he ever produced was a slimy gray mass that quickly rotted when the sun struck it.

He hefted the heavy stone ax in his right hand. As he approached the cave he was looking for, he grunted loudly and then went in. The people inside held their weapons in their hands, and he was glad he had called ahead. He ignored them and went to a back corner to see the little girl.

She sat on the bare stone, leaning against the rock with her mouth open, staring dully at him as he came up to her, her eyes black against the thick blond hair that grew on her face. Gant whirled at the others and snarled at them, and snatched a bearhide from the bed of the man and carried it to the girl. He wrapped her in it and then felt the part of her forehead where there was no hair. It was burning hot, must be about 105 degrees, possibly a little

25

more. He put her down on the rock and thumped her chest and heard the solid, hard sound of filled lungs. It was full-blown pneumonia, no longer any doubt. She gasped for breath, and there was no breath. Gant picked her up again and held her. He sat with her for over an hour, changing her position frequently in his arms, trying to make her comfortable as she gasped. He held a handful of wet leaves to her forehead to try to cool her burning face, but it did not seem to help. She went into convulsions at the end.

He laid the body on a rock ledge and pulled the mother over to see it. The mother bent and touched the girl gently on the face and then straightened and looked at Gant helplessly. He picked up the body and walked out of the cave and down into the woods. It took several hours to dig a hole deep enough with a stick.

He hunted on the way back to the caves, and he killed a short, heavy-bodied animal that hung upside down from the lower branches of a tree. It emitted a foul odor as he killed it, but it would make a good meal. He found a large rock outcropping with a tiny spring coming out from under it. A mass of newly sprouted shoots grew in the soggy ground. He picked them all, and headed back to his cave. His wife and Dun were there and their faces brightened when they saw what he brought. His wife immediately laid out the animal and skinned it with a fragment of sharp, shiny rock. Dun watched her intently, leaning over while it cooked to smell the fragrant smoke. Gant looked at the short, thick, hairy woman tending the cooking, and he looked at the boy. He could easily see himself in the thin-limbed boy. Both his wife and his son had the heavy brows and the jutting jaw of the cave people. But Dun's body was lean and his eyes were blue and sparkling, and he often sat close to Gant and tried to go with him when he went out of the cave. And once, when the lightning blazed and the thunder roared, Gant had seen the boy standing at the mouth of the cave staring at the sky in puzzlement, not fear, and Gant had put a hand on his shoulder and tried to find the words that told of electrical discharges and the roar of air rushing into a void, but there were no words.

The meat was done and the shoots were softened, and the three of them squatted at the fire and reached for the food. Outside the cave they heard the sound of movement in the gravel, and Gant leaped for his club while his wife and Dun retreated to the rear of the cave. Two men appeared, one supporting the other, both empty-handed. Gant waited until he could see that one of them was injured; he could not place his right foot on the ground. Then Gant came forward and helped the injured man to a sitting position at the mouth of the cave. He leaned over to inspect the foot. The region just above the ankle was discolored and badly swollen, and the foot was at a slight angle to the rest of the leg. Both the fibula and the tibia seemed to be broken, and Gant

26

stood up and looked around for splints. The man would probably die; there was no one to take care of him during the weeks needed for his leg to heal, no one to hunt for him and give him food and put up with his almost complete inactivity.

Gant found two chips from logs and two short branches and some strips from a cured hide. He knelt in front of the man and carefully held his hands near the swollen leg so the man could see he was going to touch it.

The man's great muscles were knotted in pain and his face was gray beneath the hair. Gant waved the second man around to one side where he could keep an eye on him, and then he took the broken leg and began to apply tension. The injured man stood it for a moment and then roared in pain and instinctively lashed out with his good leg. Gant ducked the kick, but he could not duck the blow from the second man. It hit him on the side of the head and knocked him out of the mouth of the cave. He rolled to his feet and came back in. The second man stood protectively in front of the injured man, but Gant pushed him aside and knelt down again. The foot was straight, so Gant placed the chips and branches on the leg and bound them in place with the leather thongs. Weak and helpless, the injured man did not resist. Gant stood up and showed the second man how to carry the injured man. He helped them on their way.

When they left, Gant returned to his food. It was cold, but he was content. For the first time they had come to him. They were learning. He hurt his teeth on the hard meat and he gagged on the spongy shoots, but he squatted in his cave and he smiled. There had been a time long ago when he had thought that these people would be grateful to him for his work, that he would become known by some such name as The Healer. Yet here he was, years later, happy that at last one of them had come to him with an injury. Yet Gant knew them too well by now to be misled. These people did not have even the concept of medical treatment, and the day would probably come when one of them would kill him as he worked.

He sighed, picked up his club and went out of the cave. A mile away was a man with a long gash in the calf of his left leg. Gant had cleaned it and packed it with moss and tied it tight with a hide strip. It was time to check the wound, so he walked the mile carefully, on the lookout for the large creatures that roamed the forests. The man was chipping rock in front of his cave, and he nodded his head and waved and showed his teeth in a friendly gesture when he saw Gant. Gant showed his teeth in turn and looked at the leg. He saw that the man had removed the moss and bandage, and had rubbed the great wound with dung. Gant bent to inspect the wound and immediately smelled the foul smell of corruption. Near the top of the wound, just beneath the knee, was a mass of black, wet tissues. Gangrene. Gant

27

straightened and looked around at some of the others near the cave. He went to them and tried to make them understand what he wanted to do, but they did not pay much attention. Gant returned and looked down at the wounded man, noting that his movements were still quick and coordinated, and that he was as powerfully built as the rest of them. Gant shook his head; he could not perform the amputation unaided, and there was no help to be had. He tried again to show them that the man would die unless they helped him, but it was no use. He left.

He walked along the foot of the cliffs, looking in on the caves. In one he found a woman with a swollen jaw, in pain. She let him look in her mouth, and he saw a rotted molar. He sat down with her and with gestures tried to explain that it would be painful at first if he removed the tooth, but that it would soon be better. The woman seemed to understand. Gant took up a fresh branch and scraped a rounded point on one end. He picked up a rock twice the size of his fist, and placed the woman in a sitting position with her head resting on his thigh. He placed the end of the stick low on the gum to make sure he got the root. Carefully he raised the rock, knowing he would have but one try. He smashed the rock down and felt the tooth give way and saw blood spout from her mouth. She screamed and leaped to her feet and turned on Gant, but he jumped away. Then something struck him from behind and he found himself pinned to the ground with two men sitting on him. They growled at him and one picked up a rock and the stick and smashed a front tooth from Gant's mouth. Then they threw him out of the cave. He rolled down through the gravel and came up short against a bush. He leaped to his feet and charged back into the cave. One of the men swung a club at him, but he ducked and slammed the rock against the side of the man's head. The other ran. Gant went over to the woman, picking as he went a half handful of moss from the wall of the cave. He stood in front of her and packed some of the moss in the wound in his front jaw, and leaned over to show her the bleeding had stopped. He held out the moss to her, and she quickly took some and put it in the proper place in her jaw. She nodded to him and patted his arm and rubbed the blood out of the hair on her chin. He left the cave, without looking at the unconscious man.

Some day they would kill him. His jaw throbbed as he walked along the gravel shelf and headed for home. There would be no more stops today, and so he threaded his way along the foot of the cliff. He heard sounds of activity in several of the caves, and in one of the largest of them he heard excited voices yelling. He stopped, but his jaw hurt too much to go in. The noise increased and Gant thought they might be carving up a large kill. He was always on the lookout for meat, so he changed his mind and went in. Inside

28

was a boy about the age of Dun, lying on his back, gasping for air. His face had a bluish tinge, and at each intake of air his muscles tensed and his back arched with the effort to breathe. Gant pushed to his side and forced his mouth open. The throat and uvula were greatly swollen, the air passage almost shut. He quickly examined the boy, but there was no sign of injury or disease. Gant was puzzled, but then he concluded the boy must have chewed or eaten a substance to which he was sensitive. He looked at the throat again. The swelling was continuing. The boy's jutting jaws made mouth-to-mouth resuscitation impossible. A tracheotomy was indicated. He went over to the fire and smashed one piece of flint chopping stone on another, and quickly picked over the pieces. He chose a short, sharp fragment and stooped over the boy. He touched the point of the fragment against the skin just beneath the larynx, squeezed his thumb and forefinger on the fragment to measure a distance a little over half an inch from the point, and than thrust down and into the boy's throat until his thumb and forefinger just touched the skin. Behind him he heard a struggle, and he looked up in time to see several people restrain a woman with an ax. He watched to see that they kept her out of the cave and away from him before he turned back to the boy. By gently turning the piece of flint he made an opening in the windpipe. He turned the boy on his side to prevent the tiny trickle of blood from running into the opening. The result was dramatic. The boy's struggles stopped, and the rush of air around the piece of flint sounded loud in the still of the cave. The boy lay back and relaxed and breathed deeply, and even the people in the cave could tell he was now much better. They gathered around and watched silently, and Gant could see the interest in their faces. The boy's mother had not come back.

For half an hour Gant sat holding the flint in the necessary position. The boy stirred restlessly a time or two, but Gant quieted him. The people drifted back to their activities in the cave, and Gant sat and tended his patient.

He leaned over the boy. He could hear the air beginning to pass through his throat once again. In another fifteen minutes the boy's throat was open enough, and Gant withdrew the flint in one swift movement. The boy began to sit up, but Gant held him down and pressed the wound closed. It stayed closed, and Gant got up. No one paid any attention when he left.

He went along the gravel shelf, ignoring the sounds of life that came out of the caves as he went by. He rounded a boulder and saw his own cave ahead.

The log barrier was displaced and he could hear snarls and grunts as he ran into the semidarkness inside. Two bodies writhed on the floor of the cave. He ran closer and saw that his wife and another woman were struggling there, raking each other's skin with thick, sharp nails, groping for each other's jugular vein with long, yellow teeth. Gant drove his heel into the side of the woman's body, just above the kidney. The air exploded from her lungs and she went limp. He twisted a hand in her hair and yanked her limp body away from his wife's teeth and ran for the entrance of the cave, dragging her after him. Outside, he threw the limp body down the slope. He turned and caught his wife as she came charging out. She fought him, trying to get to the woman down the slope, and it was only because she was no longer trying to kill that he was able to force her back into the cave.

Inside, she quickly stopped fighting him. She went and knelt over something lying on the foot of his bed. He rubbed his sore jaw and went over to see what it was. He stared down in the dim light of the cave. It was Dun, and he was dead. His head had been crushed. Gant cried out and leaned against the wall. He knelt and hugged Dun's warm body to him, pushing his wife aside. He pressed his face into the boy's neck and thought of the years that he had planned to spend in teaching Dun the healing arts. He felt a heavy pat on his shoulder and looked up. His wife was there, awkwardly patting him on the shoulder, trying to comfort him. Then he remembered the woman who had killed his son.

He ran out of the cave and looked down the slope. She was not there, but he caught a flash of movement down the gravel shelf and he could see her staggering toward her cave. He began to run after her, but stopped. His anger was gone, and he felt no emotion save a terrible emptiness. He turned and went back into the cave for Dun's body. In the forest he slowly dug a deep hole. He felt numb as he dug, but when it was done and he had rolled a large stone on top of the grave, he kneeled down near it, held his face in his hands and cried. Afterward, he followed the stream bed to a flat table of solid rock. At the edge of the rock table, where the wall of rock began to rise to the cliffs above, half hidden in the shrub pine, was a mass of twisted metal wreckage. He looked down on it and thought again of that day ten years ago. Here, on the site of Pennsylvania State University, at College Park, Pennsylvania, was where he started and where he ended. But a difference of half a million years lay between the start and the end.

Once tears had come to his eyes when he looked at the wreckage, but no longer. There was work to do here and he was the only one who could do it. He nodded and turned to climb to his cave. There was cold meat and shoots there, and a wife, and perhaps there could be another son. And this day, for the first time, an injured man had come to see him.

To a writer whose name I suppress, December 20, 1965:

> Dear Mr.——,
> . . . This is a minor objection, in the sense that it could be
> repaired by changing a few phrases, but I was bothered by the
> vagueness about astronomical distances & locations, & even the
> distinction between stars and planets.

The following story derives from a story of mine called "Semper Fi,"
with whose point of view Kate Wilhelm disagreed. In a sense, "Baby, You
Were Great" is the same story with an entirely different plot, setting, and
cast of characters. The funny thing is that in these respects it closely parallels
a story I once meant to write, called "Public Figure," which I had never
mentioned to Kate or anybody.

BABY, YOU WERE GREAT

by Kate Wilhelm

John Lewisohn thought that if one more door slammed, or one more bell
rang, or one more voice asked if he was all right, his head would explode.
Leaving his laboratories, he walked through the carpeted hall to the elevator
that slid wide to admit him noiselessly, was lowered, gently, two floors,
where there were more carpeted halls. The door he shoved open bore a neat
sign, AUDITIONING STUDIO. Inside, he was waved on through the reception
room by three girls who knew better than to speak to him unless he spoke
first. They were surprised to see him; it was his first visit there in seven or
eight months. The inner room where he stopped was darkened, at first glance
appearing empty, revealing another occupant only after his eyes had time to
adjust to the dim lighting.

John sat in the chair next to Herb Javits, still without speaking. Herb was
wearing the helmet and gazing at a wide screen that was actually a one-way
glass panel permitting him to view the audition going on in the next room.
John lowered a second helmet to his head. It fit snugly and immediately

31

made contact with the eight prepared spots on his skull. As soon as he turned it on, the helmet itself was forgotten.

A girl had entered the other room. She was breathtakingly lovely, a long-legged honey blonde with slanting green eyes and apricot skin. The room was furnished as a sitting room with two couches, some chairs, end tables and a coffee table, all tasteful and lifeless, like an ad in a furniture trade publication. The girl stopped at the doorway and John felt her indecision, heavily tempered with nervousness and fear. Outwardly she appeared poised and expectant, her smooth face betraying none of her emotions. She took a hesitant step toward the couch, and a wire showed trailing behind her. It was attached to her head. At the same time a second door opened. A young man ran inside, slamming the door behind him; he looked wild and frantic. The girl registered surprise, mounting nervousness; she felt behind her for the door handle, found it and tried to open the door again. It was locked. John could hear nothing that was being said in the room; he only felt the girl's reaction to the unexpected interruption. The wild-eyed man was approaching her, his hands slashing through the air, his eyes darting glances all about them constantly. Suddenly he pounced on her and pulled her to him, kissing her face and neck roughly. She seemed paralyzed with fear for several seconds, then there was something else, a bland nothing kind of feeling that accompanied boredom sometimes, or too-complete self-assurance. As the man's hands fastened on her blouse in the back and ripped it, she threw her arms about him, her face showing passion that was not felt anywhere in her mind or in her blood.

"Cut!" Herb Javits said quietly.

The man stepped back from the girl and left her without a word. She looked about blankly, her torn blouse hanging about her hips, one shoulder strap gone. She was very beautiful. The audition manager entered, followed by a dresser with a gown that he threw about her shoulders. She looked startled; waves of anger mounted to fury as she was drawn from the room, leaving it empty. The two watching men removed their helmets.

"Fourth one so far," Herb grunted. "Sixteen yesterday; twenty the day before . . . All nothing." He gave John a curious look. "What's got you stirred out of your lab?"

"Anne's had it this time," John said. "She's been on the phone all night and all morning."

"What now?"

"Those damn sharks! I told you that was too much on top of the airplane crash last week. She can't take much more of it."

"Hold it a minute, Johnny," Herb said. "Let's finish off the next three

32

girls and then talk.'' He pressed a button on the arm of his chair and the room beyond the screen took their attention again.

This time the girl was slightly less beautiful, shorter, a dimply sort of brunette with laughing blue eyes and an upturned nose. John liked her. He adjusted his helmet and felt with her.

She was excited; the audition always excited them. There was some fear and nervousness, not too much. Curious about how the audition would go, probably. The wild young man ran into the room, and her face paled. Nothing else changed. Her nervousness increased, not uncomfortably. When he grabbed her, the only emotion she registered was the nervousness.

''Cut,'' Herb said.

The next girl was also brunette, with gorgeously elongated legs. She was very cool, a real professional. Her mobile face reflected the range of emotions to be expected as the scene played through again, but nothing inside her was touched. She was a million miles away from it all.

The next one caught John with a slam. She entered the room slowly, looking about with curiosity, nervous, as they all were. She was younger than the other girls, less poised. She had pale gold hair piled in an elaborate mound of waves on top of her head. Her eyes were brown, her skin nicely tanned. When the man entered, her emotions changed quickly to fear, then to terror. John didn't know when he closed his eyes. He was the girl, filled with unspeakable terror; his heart pounded, adrenalin pumped into his system; he wanted to scream but could not. From the dim unreachable depths of his psyche there came something else, in waves, so mixed with terror that the two merged and became one emotion that pulsed and throbbed and demanded. With a jerk he opened his eyes and stared at the window. The girl had been thrown down to one of the couches, and the man was kneeling on the floor beside her, his hands playing over her bare body, his face pressed against her skin.

''Cut!'' Herb said. His voice was shaken. ''Hire her,'' he said. The man rose, glanced at the girl, sobbing now, and then quickly bent over and kissed her cheek. Her sobs increased. Her golden hair was down, framing her face; she looked like a child. John tore off the helmet. He was perspiring.

Herb got up, turned on the lights in the room, and the window blanked out, blending with the wall. He didn't look at John. When he wiped his face, his hand was shaking. He rammed it in his pocket.

''When did you start auditions like that?'' John asked, after a few moments of silence.

''Couple of months ago. I told you about it. Hell, we had to, Johnny.

33

That's the six hundred nineteenth girl we've tried out! Six hundred nineteen! All phonies but one! Dead from the neck up. Do you have any idea how long it was taking us to find that out? Hours for each one. Now it's a matter of minutes."

John Lewisohn sighed. He knew. He had suggested it, actually, when he had said, "Find a basic anxiety situation for the test." He hadn't wanted to know what Herb had come up with.

He said, "Okay, but she's only a kid. What about her parents, legal rights, all that?"

"We'll fix it. Don't worry. What about Anne?"

"She's called me five times since yesterday. The sharks were too much. She wants to see us, both of us, this afternoon."

"You're kidding! I can't leave here now!"

"Nope. Kidding I'm not. She says no plug-up if we don't show. She'll take pills and sleep until we get there."

"Good Lord! She wouldn't dare!"

"I've booked seats. We take off at twelve-thirty-five." They stared at one another silently for another moment, then Herb shrugged. He was a short man, not heavy but solid. John was over six feet, muscular, with a temper that he knew he had to control. Others suspected that when he did let it go, there would be bodies lying around afterward, but he controlled it.

Once it had been a physical act, an effort of body and will to master that temper; now it was done so automatically that he couldn't recall occasions when it even threatened to flare anymore.

"Look, Johnny, when we see Anne, let me handle it. Right? I'll make it short."

"What are you going to do?"

"Give her an earful. If she's going to start pulling temperament on me, I'll slap her down so hard she'll bounce a week." He grinned. "She's had it all her way up to now. She knew there wasn't a replacement if she got bitchy. Let her try it now. Just let her try." Herb was pacing back and forth with quick, jerky steps.

John realized with a shock that he hated the stocky, red-faced man. The feeling was new; it was almost as if he could taste the hatred he felt, and the taste was unfamiliar and pleasant.

Herb stopped pacing and stared at him for a moment. "Why'd she call you? Why does she want you down, too? She knows you're not mixed up with this end of it."

"She knows I'm a full partner, anyway," John said.

"Yeah, but that's not it." Herb's face twisted in a grin. "She thinks you're still hot for her, doesn't she? She knows you tumbled once, in the

34

beginning, when you were working on her, getting the gimmick working right." The grin reflected no humor then. "Is she right, Johnny, baby? Is that it?"

"We made a deal," John said. "You run your end, I run mine. She wants me along because she doesn't trust you, or believe anything you tell her anymore. She wants a witness."

"Yeah, Johnny. But you be sure you remember our agreement." Suddenly Herb laughed. "You know what it was like, Johnny, seeing you and her? Like a flame trying to snuggle up to an icicle."

At three-thirty they were in Anne's suite in the Skyline Hotel in Grand Bahama. Herb had a reservation to fly back to New York on the 6 P.M. flight. Anne would not be off until four, so they made themselves comfortable in her rooms and waited. Herb turned her screen on, offered a helmet to John, who shook his head, and they both seated themselves. John watched the screen for several minutes; then he, too, put on a helmet.

Anne was looking at the waves far out at sea where they were long, green, undulating; then she brought her gaze in closer, to the blue-green and quick seas, and finally in to where they stumbled on the sandbars, breaking into foam that looked solid enough to walk on. She was peaceful, swaying with the motion of the boat, the sun hot on her back, the fishing rod heavy in her hands. It was like being an indolent animal at peace with its world, at home in the world, being one with it. After a few seconds she put down the rod and turned, looking at a tall smiling man in swimming trunks. He held out his hand and she took it. They entered the cabin of the boat where drinks were waiting. Her mood of serenity and happiness ended abruptly, to be replaced by shocked disbelief, and a start of fear.

"What the hell . . . ?" John muttered, adjusting the audio. You seldom needed audio when Anne was on.

". . . Captain Brothers had to let them go. After all, they've done nothing yet—" the man was saying soberly.

"But why do you think they'll try to rob me?"

"Who else is here with a million dollars' worth of jewels?"

John turned it off and said, "You're a fool! You can't get away with something like that!"

Herb stood up and crossed to the window wall that was open to the stretch of glistening blue ocean beyond the brilliant white beaches. "You know what every woman wants? To own something worth stealing." He chuckled, a sound without mirth. "Among other things, that is. They want to be roughed up once or twice, and forced to kneel. . . . Our new psychologist is pretty good, you know? Hasn't steered us wrong yet. Anne might kick some, but it'll go over great."

"She won't stand for an actual robbery." Louder, emphatically, he added, "I won't stand for that."

"We can dub it," Herb said. "That's all we need, Johnny, plant the idea, and then dub the rest."

John stared at his back. He wanted to believe that. He needed to believe it. His voice was calm when he said, "It didn't start like this, Herb. What happened?"

Herb turned then. His face was dark against the glare of light behind him. "Okay, Johnny, it didn't start like this. Things accelerate, that's all. You thought of a gimmick, and the way we planned it, it sounded great, but it didn't last. We gave them the feeling of gambling, or learning to ski, of automobile racing, everything we could dream up, and it wasn't enough. How many times can you take the first ski jump of your life? After a while you want new thrills, you know? For you it's been great, hasn't it? You bought yourself a shiny new lab and closed the door. You bought yourself time and equipment and when things didn't go right, you could toss it out and start over, and nobody gave a damn. Think of what it's been like for me, kid! I gotta keep coming up with something new, something that'll give Anne a jolt and through her all those nice little people who aren't even alive unless they're plugged in. You think it's been easy? Anne was a green kid. For her everything was new and exciting, but it isn't like that now, boy. You better believe it is *not* like that now. You know what she told me last month? She's sick and tired of men. Our little hot-box Annie! Tired of men!"

John crossed to him and pulled him around toward the light. "Why didn't you tell me?"

"Why, Johnny? What would you have done that I didn't do? *I* looked harder for the right guy. What would you do for a new thrill for her? I worked for them, kid. Right from the start you said for me to leave you alone. Okay. I left you alone. You ever read any of the memos I sent? You initialed them, kiddo. Everything that's been done, we both signed. Don't give me any of that why didn't I tell you stuff. It won't work!" His face was ugly red and a vein bulged in his neck. John wondered if he had high blood pressure, if he would die of a stroke during one of his flash rages.

John left him at the window. He had read the memos. Herb was right; all he had wanted was to be left alone. It had been his idea; after twelve years of work in a laboratory on prototypes he had shown his—gimmick—to Herb Javits. Herb had been one of the biggest producers on television then; now he was the biggest producer in the world.

The gimmick was simple enough. A person fitted with electrodes in his brain could transmit his emotions, which in turn could be broadcast and picked up by the helmets to be felt by the audience. No words, or thoughts

36

went out, only basic emotions—fear, love, anger, hatred . . . That, tied in with a camera showing what the person saw, with a voice dubbed in, and you were the person having the experience, with one important difference—you could turn it off if it got to be too much. The "actor" couldn't. A simple gimmick. You didn't really need the camera and the sound track; many users never turned them on at all, but let their own imaginations fill in the emotional broadcast.

The helmets were not sold, only leased or rented after a short, easy fitting session. A year's lease cost fifty dollars, and there were over thirty-seven million subscribers. Herb had created his own network when the demand for more hours squeezed him out of regular television. From a one-hour weekly show, it had gone to one hour nightly, and now it was on the air eight hours a day live, with another eight hours of taped programming.

What had started out as A DAY IN THE LIFE OF ANNE BEAUMONT was now a life in the life of Anne Beaumont, and the audience was insatiable.

Anne came in then, surrounded by the throng of hangers-on that mobbed her daily—hairdressers, masseurs, fitters, script men . . . She looked tired. She waved the crowd out when she saw John and Herb were there. "Hello, John," she said, "Herb."

"Anne, baby, you're looking great!" Herb said. He took her in his arms and kissed her solidly. She stood still, her hands at her sides.

She was tall, very slender, with wheat-colored hair and gray eyes. Her cheekbones were wide and high, her mouth firm and almost too large. Against her deep red-gold suntan her teeth looked whiter than John remembered. Although too firm and strong ever to be thought of as pretty, she was a very beautiful woman. After Herb released her, she turned to John, hesitated only a moment, then extended a slim, sun-browned hand. It was cool and dry in his.

"How have you been, John? It's been a long time."

He was very glad she didn't kiss him, or call him darling. She smiled only slightly and gently removed her hand from his. He moved to the bar as she turned to Herb.

"I'm through, Herb." Her voice was too quiet. She accepted a whiskey sour from John, but kept her gaze on Herb.

"What's the matter, honey? I was just watching you, baby. You were great today, like always. You've still got it, kid. It's coming through like always."

"What about this robbery? You must be out of your mind . . ."

"Yeah, that. Listen, Anne baby, I swear to you I don't know a thing about it. Laughton must have been giving you the straight goods on that. You

37

know we agreed that the rest of this week you just have a good time, remember? That comes over too, baby. When you have a good time and relax, thirty-seven million people are enjoying life and relaxing. That's good. They can't be stimulated all the time. They like the variety." Wordlessly John held out a glass, scotch and water. Herb took it without looking.

Anne was watching him coldly. Suddenly she laughed. It was a cynical, bitter sound. "You're not a damn fool, Herb. Don't try to act like one." She sipped her drink again, staring at him over the rim of the glass. "I'm warning you, if anyone shows up here to rob me, I'm going to treat him like a real burglar. I bought a gun after today's broadcast, and I learned how to shoot when I was ten. I still know how. I'll kill him, Herb, whoever it is."

"Baby," Herb started, but she cut him short.

"And this is my last week. As of Saturday, I'm through."

"You can't do that, Anne," Herb said. John watched him closely, searching for a sign of weakness; he saw nothing. Herb exuded confidence. "Look around, Anne, at this room, your clothes, everything. . . . You are the richest woman in the world, having the time of your life, able to go anywhere, do anything . . ."

"While the whole world watches—"

"So what? It doesn't stop you, does it?" Herb started to pace, his steps jerky and quick. "You knew that when you signed the contract. You're a rare girl, Anne, beautiful, emotional, intelligent. Think of all those women who've got nothing but you. If you quit them, what do they do? Die? They might, you know. For the first time in their lives they're able to feel like they're living. You're giving them what no one ever did before, what was only hinted at in books and films in the old days. Suddenly they know what it feels like to face excitement, to experience love, to feel contented and peaceful. Think of them, Anne, empty, with nothing in their lives but you, what you're able to give them. Thirty-seven million drabs, Anne, who never felt anything but boredom and frustration until you gave them life. What do they have? Work, kids, bills. You've given them the world, baby! Without you they wouldn't even want to live anymore."

She wasn't listening. Almost dreamily she said, "I talked to my lawyers, Herb, and the contract is meaningless. You've already broken it over and over. I agreed to learn a lot of new things. I did. My God! I've climbed mountains, hunted lions, learned to ski and water-ski, but now you want me to die a little bit each week . . . That airplane crash, not bad, just enough to terrify me. Then the sharks. I really do think it was having sharks brought in when I was skiing that did it, Herb. You see, you will kill me. It will happen, and you won't be able to top it, Herb. Not ever."

There was a hard, waiting silence following her words. *No!* John shouted soundlessly. He was looking at Herb. He had stopped pacing when she started to talk. Something flicked across his face—surprise, fear, something not readily identifiable. Then his face went blank and he raised his glass and finished the scotch and water, replacing the glass on the bar. When he turned again, he was smiling with disbelief.

"What's really bugging you, Anne? There have been plants before. You knew about them. Those lions didn't just happen by, you know. And the avalanche needed a nudge from someone. You know that. What else is bugging you?"

"I'm in love, Herb."

Herb waved that aside impatiently. "Have you ever watched your own show, Anne?" She shook her head. "I thought not. So you wouldn't know about the expansion that took place last month, after we planted that new transmitter in your head. Johnny boy's been busy, Anne. You know these scientist types, never satisfied, always improving, changing. Where's the camera, Anne? Do you ever know where it is anymore? Have you ever seen a camera in the past couple of weeks, or a recorder of any sort? You have not, and you won't again. You're on now, honey." His voice was quite low, amused almost. "In fact the only time you aren't on is when you're sleeping. I know you're in love. I know who he is. I know how he makes you feel. I even know how much money he makes a week. I should know, Anne baby. I pay him." He had come closer to her with each word, finishing with his face only inches from hers. He didn't have a chance to duck the flashing slap that jerked his head around, and before either of them realized it, he had hit her back, knocking her into a chair.

The silence grew, became something ugly and heavy, as if words were being born and dying without utterance because they were too brutal for the human spirit to bear. There was a spot of blood on Herb's mouth where Anne's diamond ring had cut him. He touched it and looked at his finger. "It's all being taped now, honey, even this," he said. He turned his back on her and went to the bar.

There was a large red print on her cheek. Her gray eyes had turned black with rage.

"Honey, relax," Herb said after a moment. "It won't make any difference to you, in what you do, or anything like that. You know we can't use most of the stuff, but it gives the editors a bigger variety to pick from. It was getting to the point where most of the interesting stuff was going on after you were off. Like buying the gun. That's great stuff there, baby. You weren't blanketing a single thing, and it'll all come through like pure gold." He finished mixing his drink, tasted it, and then swallowed half of it. "How many women have to go out and buy a gun to protect themselves? Think of them all, feeling that gun, feeling the things you felt when you picked it up, looked at it . . ."

"How long have you been tuning in all the time?" she asked. John felt a stirring along his spine, a tingle of excitement. He knew what was going out over the miniature transmitter, the rising crests of emotion she was feeling. Only a trace of them showed on her smooth face, but the raging interior torment was being recorded faithfully. Her quiet voice and quiet body were lies; the tapes never lied.

Herb felt it too. He put his glass down and went to her, kneeling by the chair, taking her hand in both of his. "Anne, please, don't be that angry with me. I was desperate for new material. When Johnny got this last wrinkle out, and we knew we could record around the clock, we had to try it, and it wouldn't have been any good if you'd known. That's no way to test anything. You knew we were planting the transmitter . . ."

"How long?"

"Not quite a month."

"And Stuart? He's one of your men? He is transmitting also? You hired him to . . . to make love to me? Is that right?"

Herb nodded. She pulled her hand free and averted her face. He got up then and went to the window. "But what difference does it make?" he shouted. "If I introduced the two of you at a party, you wouldn't think anything of it. What difference if I did it this way? I knew you'd like each other. He's bright, like you, likes the same sort of things you do. Comes from a poor family, like yours . . . Everything said you'd get along."

"Oh, yes," she said almost absently. "We get along." She was feeling in her hair, her fingers searching for the scars.

"It's all healed by now," John said. She looked at him as if she had forgotten he was there.

"I'll find a surgeon," she said, standing up, her fingers white on her glass. "A brain surgeon—"

"It's a new process," John said slowly. "It would be dangerous to go in after them."

She looked at him for a long time. "Dangerous?"

He nodded.

"You could take it back out."

He remembered the beginning, how he had quieted her fear of the electrodes and wires. Her fear was that of a child for the unknown and the unknowable. Time and again he had proved to her that she could trust him, that he wouldn't lie to her. He hadn't lied to her, then. There was the same trust in her eyes, the same unshakable faith. She would believe him. She

40

would accept without question whatever he said. Herb had called him an icicle, but that was wrong. An icicle would have melted in her fires. More like a stalactite, shaped by centuries of civilization, layer by layer he had been formed until he had forgotten how to bend, forgotten how to find release for the stirrings he felt somewhere in the hollow, rigid core of himself. She had tried and, frustrated, she had turned from him, hurt, but unable not to trust one she had loved. Now she waited. He could free her, and lose her again, this time irrevocably. Or he could hold her as long as she lived.

Her lovely gray eyes were shadowed with fear, and the trust that he had given to her. Slowly he shook his head.

"I can't," he said. "No one can."

"I see," she murmured, the black filling her eyes. "I'd die, wouldn't I? Then you'd have a lovely sequence, wouldn't you, Herb?" She swung around, away from John. "You'd have to fake the story line, of course, but you are so good at that. An accident, emergency brain surgery needed, everything I feel going out to the poor little drabs who never will have brain surgery done. It's very good," she said admiringly. Her eyes were black. "In fact, anything I do from now on, you'll use, won't you? If I kill you, that will simply be material for your editors to pick over. Trial, prison, very dramatic . . . On the other hand, if I kill myself . . ."

John felt chilled; a cold, hard weight seemed to be filling him. Herb laughed. "The story line will be something like this," he said. "Anne has fallen in love with a stranger, deeply, sincerely in love with him. Everyone knows how deep that love is, they've all felt it, too, you know. She finds him raping a child, a lovely little girl in her early teens. Stuart tells her they're through. He loves the little nymphet. In a passion she kills herself. You are broadcasting a real storm of passion, right now, aren't you, honey? Never mind, when I run through this scene, I'll find out." She hurled her glass at him, ice cubes and orange slices flying across the room. Herb ducked, grinning.

"That's awfully good, baby. Corny, but after all, they can't get too much corn, can they? They'll love it, after they get over the shock of losing you. And they will get over it, you know. They always do. Wonder if it's true about what happens to someone experiencing a violent death?" Anne's teeth bit down on her lip, and slowly she sat down again, her eyes closed tight. Herb watched her for a moment, then said, even more cheerfully, "We've got the kid already. If you give them a death, you've got to give them a new life. Finish one with a bang. Start one with a bang. We'll name the kid Cindy, a real Cinderella story after that. They'll love her, too."

Anne opened her eyes, black, dulled now; she was so full of tension that

John felt his own muscles contract. He wondered if he would be able to stand the tape she was transmitting. A wave of excitement swept him and he knew he would play it all, feel it all, the incredibly contained rage, fear, the horror of giving a death to them to gloat over, and finally, anguish. He would know it all. Watching Anne, he wished she would break now. She didn't. She stood up stiffly, her back rigid, a muscle hard and ridged in her jaw. Her voice was flat when she said, "Stuart is due in half an hour. I have to dress." She left them without looking back.

Herb winked at John and motioned toward the door. "Want to take me to the plane, kid?" In the cab he said, "Stick close to her for a couple of days, Johnny. There might be an even bigger reaction later when she really understands just how hooked she is." He chuckled again. "By God! It's a good thing she trusts you, Johnny boy!"

As they waited in the chrome and marble terminal for the liner to unload its passengers, John said, "Do you think she'll be any good after this?"

"She can't help herself. She's too life-oriented to deliberately choose to die. She's like a jungle inside, raw, wild, untouched by that smooth layer of civilization she shows on the outside. It's a thin layer, kid, real thin. She'll fight to stay alive. She'll become more wary, more alert to danger, more excited and exciting . . . She'll really go to pieces when he touches her tonight. She's primed real good. Might even have to do some editing, tone it down a little." His voice was very happy. "He touches her where she lives, and she reacts. A real wild one. She's one; the new kid's one; Stuart . . . They're few and far between, Johnny. It's up to us to find them. God knows we're going to need all of them we can get." His expression became thoughtful and withdrawn. "You know, that really wasn't such a bad idea of mine about rape and the kid. Who ever dreamed we'd get that kind of a reaction from her? With the right sort of buildup . . ." He had to run to catch his plane.

John hurried back to the hotel, to be near Anne if she needed him. But he hoped she would leave him alone. His fingers shook as he turned on his screen; suddenly he had a clear memory of the child who had wept, and he hoped Stuart would hurt Anne just a little. The tremor in his fingers increased; Stuart was on from six until twelve, and he already had missed almost an hour of the show. He adjusted the helmet and sank back into a deep chair. He left the audio off, letting his own words form, letting his own thoughts fill in the spaces.

Anne was leaning toward him, sparkling champagne raised to her lips, her eyes large and soft. She was speaking, talking to him, John, calling him by name. He felt a tingle start somewhere deep inside him, and his glance was lowered to rest on her tanned hand in his, sending electricity through him.

42

Her hand trembled when he ran his fingers up her palm, to her wrist where a blue vein throbbed. The slight throb became a pounding that grew, and when he looked again into her eyes, they were dark and very deep. They danced and he felt her body against his, yielding, pleading. The room darkened and she was an outline against the window, her gown floating down about her. The darkness grew denser, or he closed his eyes, and this time when her body pressed against his, there was nothing between them, and the pounding was everywhere.

In the deep chair, with the helmet on his head, John's hands clenched, opened, clenched, again and again.

To R. A. Lafferty, December 20, 1965:

Dear Mr. Lafferty,

I return these two stories with reluctance & regret; I think they are both too short for their own good. Either one, if it had some plot, would make a memorable story; as it is, it seems to me that you have dropped them too soon. The theme is stated but not developed. We get the major premise of a syllogism, and then you stop. These stories leave me fascinated but unsatisfied because they never advance more than an inch from where they begin. What would happen *if* somebody tried to make the Perfect Place, or if a man became the Emperor of the Spiders? "Aranea" begs the question by having the guy hauled off to a loony-bin, and "Jones" simply by freezing the story in time. These are dreams, authentic dreams, but not stories. In a story or a play, something must happen, acts must have consequences. Dreams are essential but they are not enough.

To Robert Silverberg, January 16, 1966:

Dear Bob,

. . . I have a feeling which is hard to put into words that the trouble with this thing is just that you did not reach down far enough when you wrote it. I come back to the feeling that everybody in the damn story is too nice. We are all trying to be nice guys, but we all have resources of shame, guilt, rage, fear, resentment, hatred & despair that can be tapped for writing. (And love, pity, worship & tenderness, but I am beating on you about the dark side because I miss it in your work.) People who start from the gut end of the scale, like Harlan, don't have to worry about this; people who start from a cerebral position, like you, like me & Jim Blish, have to work at it. It is not easy for a reserved & inhibited writer to turn around and look at this part of himself, but if you can do it, it will make a hell of a difference to you. I believe you can, & am pulling for you.

To R. A. Lafferty, February 10, 1966:

Dear Mr. Lafferty,
That's the one. . . . I laughed like an idiot while reading it, disturbing a roomful of people, dogs and children. It's a lovely story, completely & consistently insane.

From Lafferty, February 15, 1966:

Dear Mr. Knight:
It was a pleasant letter from you, especially that you were taking my piece for Orbit 2. Anything else can be faked, but buying a story is one of the really friendly things an editor does. . . . Something I read in one of the writers' magazines gave me the idea that science fiction would be easy to write. It isn't, for me. I wasn't raised on the stuff like most of the Science Fiction writers seem to have been. The only things I had read in it were the Modern Library anthology and H. G. Wells. I got a copy of every science fiction [magazine] on the news-stands (there were more of them then than now) and tried to figure out just what field it covered; I still don't know.

THE HOLE ON THE CORNER

by R. A. Lafferty

Homer Hoose came home that evening to the golden cliché: the unnoble dog who was a personal friend of his; the perfect house where just to live was a happy riot; the loving and unpredictable wife; and the five children—the perfect number (four more would have been too many, four less would have been too few).

The dog howled in terror and bristled up like a hedgehog. Then it got a whiff of Homer and recognized him; it licked his heels and gnawed his knuckles and made him welcome. A good dog, though a fool. Who wants a smart dog!

Homer had a little trouble with the doorknob. They don't have them in all the recensions, you know; and he had that off-the-track feeling tonight. But he figured it out (you don't pull it, you turn it), and opened the door.

"Did you remember to bring what I asked you to bring this morning, Homer?" the loving wife Regina inquired.

"What did you ask me to bring this morning, quick-heat blueberry biscuit of my heart?" Homer asked.

"If *I'd* remembered, I'd have phrased it different when I asked if you remembered," Regina explained. "But I know I told you to bring something, old ketchup of my soul. Homer! Look at me, Homer! You look different tonight! DIFFERENT!! *You're not my Homer, are you!* Help! Help! There's a monster in my house!! Help, help! Shriek!"

"It's always nice to be married to a wife who doesn't understand you," Homer said. He enfolded her affectionately, bore her down, trod on her with large friendly hooves, and began (as it seemed) to devour her.

"Where'd you get the monster, mama?" son Robert asked as he came in. "What's he got your whole head in his mouth for? Can I have one of the apples in the kitchen? What's he going to do, kill you, mama?"

"Shriek, shriek," said mama Regina. "Just one apple, Robert, there's just enough to go around. Yes, I think he's going to kill me. Shriek!"

Son Robert got an apple and went outdoors.

"Hi, papa, what's you doing to mama?" Daughter Fregona asked as she came in. She was fourteen, but stupid for her age. "Looks to me like you're going to kill her that way. I thought they peeled people before they swallowed them. Why! You're not papa at all, are you? You're some

45

monster. I thought at first you were my papa. You look just like him except for the way you look."

"Shriek, shriek," said mama Regina, but her voice was muffled.

They had a lot of fun at their house.

Homer Hoose came home that evening to the golden cliché: the u.n.d.; the p.h.; the l. and u.w.; and the f.c. (four more would have been too many).

The dog waggled all over him happily, and son Robert was chewing an apple core on the front lawn.

"Hi, Robert," Homer said, "what's new today?"

"Nothing, papa. Nothing ever happens here. Oh yeah, there's a monster in the house. He looks kind of like you. He's killing mama and eating her up."

"Eating her up, you say, son? How do you mean?"

"He's got her whole head in his mouth."

"Droll, Robert, mighty droll," said Homer, and he went in the house.

One thing about the Hoose children: a lot of times they told the bald-headed truth. There *was* a monster there. He *was* killing and eating the wife Regina. This was no mere evening antic. It was something serious.

Homer the man was a powerful and quick-moving fellow. He fell on the monster with judo chops and solid body punches; and the monster let the woman go and confronted the man.

"What's with it, you silly oaf?" the monster snapped. "If you've got a delivery, go to the back door. Come punching people in here, will you? Regina, do you know who this silly simpleton is?"

"Wow, that was a pretty good one, wasn't it, Homer?" Regina gasped as she came from under, glowing and gulping. "Oh, him? Gee, Homer, I think he's my husband. But how can he be, if you are? Now the two of you have got me so mixed up that I don't know which one of you is my Homer."

"Great goofy Gestalten! You don't mean I look like him?" howled Homer the monster, near popping.

"My brain reels," moaned Homer the man. "Reality melts away. Regina! Exorcise this nightmare if you have in some manner called it up! I knew you shouldn't have been fooling around with that book."

"Listen, mister reely-brains," wife Regina began on Homer the man. "You learn to kiss like he does before you tell me which one to exorcise. All I ask is a little affection. And this I didn't find in a book."

"How we going to know which one is papa? They look just alike," daughters Clara-Belle, Anna-Belle, and Maudie-Belle came in like three little chimes.

46

"Hell-hopping horrors!" roared Homer the man. "How are you going to know—? He's got green skin."

"There's nothing wrong with green skin as long as it's kept neat and oiled," Regina defended.

"He's got tentacles instead of hands," said Homer the man.

"Oh boy, I'll say!" Regina sang out.

"How we going to know which one is papa when they look just alike?" the five Hoose children asked in chorus.

"I'm sure there's a simple explanation to this, old chap," said Homer the monster. "If I were you, Homer—and there's some argument whether I am or not—I believe I'd go to a doctor. I don't believe we both need to go, since our problem's the same. Here's the name of a good one," said Homer the monster, writing it out.

"Oh, I know him," said Homer the man when he read it. "But how did you know him? He isn't an animal doctor. Regina, I'm going over to the doctor to see what's the matter with me, or you. Try to have this nightmare back in whatever corner of your under-id it belongs in when I come back."

"Ask him if I keep taking my pink medicine," Regina said.

"No, not him. It's the head doctor I'm going to."

"Ask him if I have to keep on dreaming those pleasant dreams," Regina said. "I sure do get tired of them. I want to get back to the other kind. Homer, leave the coriander seed when you go." And she took the package out of his pocket. "You did remember to bring it. My other Homer forgot."

"No. I didn't," said Homer the monster. "You couldn't remember what you told me to get. Here, Regina."

"I'll be back in a little while," said Homer the man. "The doctor lives on the corner. And you, fellow, if you're real, keep your plankton-picking polypusses off my wife till I get back."

Homer Hoose went up the street to the house of Dr. Corte on the corner. He knocked on the door, and then opened it and went in without waiting for an answer. The doctor was sitting there, but he seemed a little bit dazed.

"I've got a problem, Dr. Corte," said Homer the man. "I came home this evening, and I found a monster eating my wife—as I thought."

"Yes, I know," said Dr. Corte. "Homer, we got to fix that hole on the corner."

"I didn't know there was a hole there, doctor. As it happened, the fellow wasn't really swallowing my wife, it was just his way of showing affection.

Everybody thought the monster looked like me, and doctor, it has green skin and tentacles. When I began to think it looked like me too, then I came here to see what was wrong with me, or with everybody else.''

"I can't help you, Hoose. I'm a psychologist, not a contingent-physicist. Only one thing to do; we got to fix that hole on the corner.''

"Doctor, there's no hole in the street on this corner.''

"Wasn't talking about a hole in the street. Homer, I just got back from a visit of my own that shook me up. I went to an analyst who analyzes analysts. 'I've had a dozen people come to see me with the same sort of story,' I told him. 'They all come home in the evening; and everything is different, or themselves are different; or they find that they are already there when they get there. What do you do when a dozen people come in with the same nonsense story, Dr. Diebel?' I asked him.

" 'I don't know, Corte,' he said to me. 'What do I do when *one* man comes in a dozen times with the same nonsense story, all within one hour, and he a doctor too?' Dr. Diebel asked me.

" 'Why, Dr. Diebel?' I asked. 'What doctor came to you like that?'

" 'You,' he said. 'You've come in here twelve times in the last hour with the same dish of balderhash; you've come in each time looking a little bit different; and each time you act as if you hadn't seen me for a month. Dammit, man,' he said, 'you must have passed yourself going out when you come in.'

" 'Yes, that *was* me, wasn't it?' I said. 'I was trying to think who he reminded me of. Well, it's a problem, Dr. Diebel,' I said. 'What are you going to do about it?'

" 'I'm going to the analyst who analyzes the analysts who analyze the analysts,' he said. 'He's tops in the field.' Dr. Diebel rushed out then; and I came back to my office here. You came in just after that. I'm not the one to help you. But, Homer, we got to do something about that hole on the corner!''

"I don't understand the bit about the hole, doctor," Homer said. "But—has a bunch of people been here with stories like mine?''

"Yes, every man in this block has been in with an idiot story, Homer, except— Why, everybody except old double-domed Diogenes himself! Homer, that man who knows everything has a finger in this up to the humerus. I saw him up on the power poles the other night, but I didn't think anything of it. He likes to tap the lines before they come to his meter. Saves a lot on power that way, and he uses a lot of it in his laboratory. But he was setting up the hole on the corner. That's what he was doing. Let's get him and bring him to your house and make him straighten it out.''

"Sure, a man that knows everything ought to know about a hole on the

48

corner, doctor. But I sure don't see any hole anywhere on this corner.''

The man who knew everything was named Diogenes Pontifex. He lived next door to Homer Hoose, and they found him in his backyard wrestling with his anaconda.

"Diogenes, come over to Homer's with us," Dr. Corte insisted. "We've got a couple of questions that might be too much even for you."

"You touch my pride there," Diogenes sang out. "When psychologists start using psychology on you, it's time to give in. Wait a minute till I pin this fellow."

Diogenes put a chancery on the anaconda, punched the thing's face a few times, then pinned it with a double bar-arm and body lock, and left it writhing there. He followed them into the house.

"Hi, Homer," Diogenes said to Homer the monster when they had come into the house. "I see there's two of you here at the same time now. No doubt that's what's puzzling you."

"Doctor Corte, did Homer ask you if I could stop dreaming those pleasant dreams?" wife Regina asked. "I sure do get tired of them. I want to go back to the old flesh-crawlers."

"You should be able to do so tonight, Regina," said Dr. Corte. "Now then, I'm trying to bait Diogenes here into telling us what's going on. I'm sure he knows. And if you would skip the first part, Diogenes, about all the other scientists in the world being like little boys alongside of you, it would speed things up. I believe that this is another of your experiments like— Oh no! Let's not even think about the last one!

"Tell us, Diogenes, about the hole on the corner, and what falls through it. Tell us how some people come home two or three times within as many minutes, and find themselves already there when they get there. Tell us how a creature that staggers the imagination can seem so like an old acquaintance after a moment or two that one might not know which is which. I am not now sure which of these Homers it was who came to my office several moments ago, and with whom I returned to this house. They look just alike in one way, and in another they do not."

"My Homer always was funny looking," Regina said.

"They appear quite different if you go by the visual index," Diogenes explained. "But nobody goes by the visual index except momentarily. Our impression of a person or a thing is much more complex, and the visual element in our appraisal is small. Well, one of them is Homer in gestalt two, and the other is Homer in gestalt nine. But they are quite distinct. Don't ever get the idea that such are the same persons. That would be silly."

"And Lord spare us that!" said Homer the man. "All right, go into your act, Diogenes."

''First, look at me closely, all of you,'' Diogenes said. ''Handsome, what? But note my clothing and my complexion and my aspect.

''Then to the explanations: It begins with my Corollary to Phelan's Corollary on Gravity. I take the opposite alternate of it. Phelan puzzled that gravity should be so weak on all worlds but one. He said that the gravity of that one remote world was typical, and that the gravity of all other worlds was atypical and the result of a mathematical error. But I, from the same data, deduce that the gravity of our own world is not too weak, but too strong. It is about a hundred times as strong as it should be.''

''What do you compare it to when you decide it is too strong?'' Dr. Corte wanted to know.

''There's nothing I can compare it to, doctor. The gravity of *every* body that I am able to examine is from eighty to a hundred times too strong. There are two possible explanations: either my calculations or theories are somehow in error—unlikely—or there are, in every case, about a hundred bodies, solid and weighted, occupying the same place at the same time. *Old Ice Cream Store Chairs! Tennis Shoes in October! The Smell of Slippery Elm! County-Fair Barkers with Warts on Their Noses! Horned Toads in June!*''

''I was following you pretty good up to the Ice Cream Store Chairs,'' said Homer the monster.

''Oh, I tied that part in, and the tennis shoes too,'' said Homer the man. ''I'm pretty good at following this cosmic theory business. What threw me was the slippery elm. I can't see how it especially illustrates a contingent theory of gravity.''

''The last part was an incantation,'' said Diogenes. ''Do you remark anything different about me now?''

''You're wearing a different suit now, of course,'' said Regina, ''but there's nothing remarkable about that. Lots of people change to different clothes in the evening.''

''You're darker and stringier,'' said Dr. Corte. ''But I wouldn't have noticed any change if you hadn't told us to look for it. Actually, if I didn't know that you were Diogenes, there wouldn't be any sane way to identify Diogenes in you. You don't look a thing like you, but still I'd know you anywhere.''

''I was first a gestalt two. Now I'm a gestalt three for a while,'' said Diogenes. ''Well, first we have the true case that a hundred or so solid and weighty bodies are occupying the same space that our earth occupies, and at the same time. This in itself does violence to conventional physics. But now let us consider the characteristics of all these cohabiting bodies. Are they occupied and peopled? Will it then mean that a hundred or so persons are occupying at all times the same space that each person occupies? Might not

50

this idea do violence to conventional psychology? Well, I have proved that there are at least eight other persons occupying the same space occupied by each of us, and I have scarcely begun proving. *Stark White Sycamore Branches! New-Harrowed Earth! (New harrow, old earth.) Cow Dung Between Your Toes in July! Pitchers'-Mound Clay in the Old Three-Eye League! Sparrow Hawks in August!*"

"I fell off the harrow," said wife Regina. "I got the sycamore branches bit, though."

"I got clear down to the sparrow hawks," said Homer the monster.

"Do you remark anything different about me this time?" Diogenes asked.

"You have little feathers on the backs of your hands where you used to have little hairs," said Homer the man, "and on your toes. You're barefoot now. But I wouldn't have noticed any of it if I hadn't been looking for something funny."

"I'm a gestalt four now," said Diogenes. "My conduct is likely to become a little extravagant."

"It always was," said Dr. Corte.

"But not so much as if I were a gestalt five," said Diogenes. "As a five, I might take a Pan-like leap onto the shoulders of young Fregona here, or literally walk barefoot through the hair of the beautiful Regina as she stands there. Many normal gestalt twos become gestalt fours or fives in their dreams. It seems that Regina does.

"I found the shadow, but not the substance, of the whole situation in the psychology of Jung. Jung served me as the second element in this, for it was the errors of Phelan and Jung in widely different fields that set me on the trail of the truth. What Jung really says is that each of us is a number of persons in depth. This I consider silly. There is something about such far-out theories that repels me. The truth is that our counterparts enter into our unconsciousness and dreams only by accident, as being most of the time in the same space that we occupy. But we are all separate and independent persons. And we may, two or more of us, be present in the same frame at the same time, and then in a near, but not the same, place. Witness the gestalt two and the gestalt nine Homers present.

"I've been experimenting to see how far I can go with it, and the gestalt nine is the furthest I have brought it so far. I do not number the gestalten in the order of their strangeness to our own norm, but in the order in which I discovered them. I'm convinced that the concentric and congravitic worlds and people complexes number near a hundred, however."

"Well, there *is* a hole on the corner, isn't there?" Dr. Corte asked.

"Yes, I set it up there by the bus stop as a convenient evening point of entry for the people of this block," said Diogenes. "I've had lots of opportunity to study the results these last two days."

"Well, just how *do* you set up a hole on the corner?" Dr. Corte persisted.

"Believe me, Corte, it took a lot of imagination," Diogenes said. "I mean it literally. I drew so deeply on my own psychic store to construct the thing that it left me shaken, and I have the most manifold supply of psychic images of any person I know. I've also set up magnetic amplifiers on both sides of the street, but it is my original imagery that they amplify. I see a never-ending field of study in this."

"Just what is the incantation stuff that takes you from one gestalt to another?" Homer the monster asked.

"It is only one of dozens of possible modes of entry, but I sometimes find it the easiest," said Diogenes. "It is Immediacy Remembered, or the Verbal Ramble. It is the Evocation—an intuitive or charismatic entry. I often use it in the Bradmont Motif—named by me from two as-aff writers in the twentieth century."

"You speak of it as it—well—isn't *this* the twentieth century?" Regina asked.

"This the twentieth? Why, you're right! I guess it is," Diogenes agreed. "You see, I carry on experiments in other fields also, and sometimes I get my times mixed. All of you, I believe, do sometimes have moments of peculiar immediacy and vividness. It seems then as if the world were somehow fresher in that moment, as though it were a new world. And the explanation is that, to you, it *is* a new world. You have moved, for a moment, into a different gestalt. There are many accidental holes or modes of entry, but mine is the only contrived one I know of."

"There's a discrepancy here," said Dr. Corte. "If the persons are separate, how can you change from one to another?"

"I do not change from one person to another," said Diogenes. "There have been three different Diogenes' lecturing you here in series. Fortunately, my colleagues and I, being of like scientific mind, work together in close concert. We have made a successful experiment in substitution acceptance on you here this evening. Oh, the ramifications of this thing! The aspects to be studied. I will take you out of your narrow gestalt-two world and show you worlds upon worlds."

"You talk about the gestalt-two complex that we normally belong to," said wife Regina, "and about others up to gestalt nine, and maybe a hundred. Isn't there a gestalt one? Lots of people start counting at one."

"There is a number one, Regina," said Diogenes. "I discovered it first and named it, before I realized that the common world of most of you was of a similar category. But I do not intend to visit gestalt one again. It is turgid and dreary beyond tolerating. One instance of its mediocrity will serve. The people of gestalt one refer to their world as the 'everyday world.' Retch quietly, please. May the lowest of us never fall so low! *Persimmons After First Frost! Old Barbershop Chairs! Pink Dogwood Blossoms in the Third Week of November! Murad Cigarette Advertisements!!*'

Diogenes cried out the last in mild panic, and he seemed disturbed. He changed into another fellow a little bit different, but the new Diogenes didn't like what he saw either.

"*Smell of Wet Sweet Clover!*" he cried out. "*St. Mary's Street in San Antonio! Model Airplane Glue! Moon Crabs in March!* It won't work! The rats have run out on me! Homer and Homer, grab that other Homer there! I believe he's a gestalt six, and they sure are mean."

Homer Hoose wasn't particularly mean. He had just come home a few minutes late and had found two other fellows who looked like him jazzing his wife Regina. And those two mouth men, Dr. Corte and Diogenes Pontifex, didn't have any business in his house when he was gone either.

He started to swing. You'd have done it too.

Those three Homers were all powerful and quick-moving fellows, and they had a lot of blood in them. It was soon flowing, amid the crashing and breaking-up of furniture and people—ocher-colored blood, pearl-gray blood, one of the Homers even had blood of a sort of red color. Those boys threw a real riot!

"Give me that package of coriander seed, Homer," wife Regina said to the latest Homer as she took it from his pocket. "It won't hurt to have three of them. Homer! Homer! Homer! All three of you! Stop bleeding on the rug!"

Homer was always a battler. So was Homer. And Homer.

"*Stethoscopes and Moonlight and Memory—*ah—*in Late March,*" Dr. Corte chanted. "Didn't work, did it? I'll get out of here a regular way. Homers, boys, come up to my place, one at a time, and get patched up when you're finished. I have to do a little regular medicine on the side nowadays."

Dr. Corte went out the door with the loopy run of a man not in very good condition.

"*Old Hairbreadth Harry Comic Strips! Congress Street in Houston! Light Street in Baltimore! Elizabeth Street in Sydney! Varnish on Old Bar-Room Pianos! B-Girls Named Dotty!* I believe it's easier just to make a dash for my house next door," Diogenes rattled off. And he did dash out with the easy run of a man who is in good condition.

"I've had it!" boomed one of the Homers—and we don't know which

53

one—as he was flung free from the donnybrook and smashed into a wall. "Peace and quiet is what a man wants when he comes home in the evening, not this. Folks, I'm going to come home all over again. I'm going to wipe my mind clear of all this. When I turn back from the corner I'll be whistling Dixie and I'll be the most peaceful man in the world. But when I get home, I bet neither of you guys had better have happened at all."

And Homer dashed up to the corner.

Homer Hoose came home that evening to the g.c.—everything as it should be. He found his house in order and his wife Regina alone.

"Did you remember to bring the coriander seed, Homer, little gossamer of my fusus?" Regina asked him.

"Ah, I remembered to get it, Regina, but I don't seem to have it in my pocket now. I'd rather you didn't ask me where I lost it. There's something I'm trying to forget. Regina, I didn't come home this evening before this, did I?"

"Not that I remember, little dolomedes sexpunctatus."

"And there weren't a couple other guys here who looked just like me only different?"

"No, no, little cobby. I love you and all that, but nothing else could look like you. Nobody has been here but you. Kids! Get ready for supper! Papa's home!"

"Then it's all right," Homer said. "I was just daydreaming on my way home, and all that stuff never happened. Here I am in the perfect house with my wife Regina, and the kids'll be underfoot in just a second. I never realized how wonderful it was. AHHHHNNN!!! YOU'RE NOT REGINA!!"

"But of course I am, Homer. Lycosa Regina is my species name. Well, come, come, you know how I enjoy our evenings together."

She picked him up, lovingly broke his arms and legs for easier handling, spread him out on the floor, and began to devour him.

"No, no, you're not Regina," Homer sobbed. "You look just like her, but you also look like a giant monstrous arachnid. Dr. Corte was right, we got to fix that hole on the corner."

"That Dr. Corte doesn't know what he's talking about," Regina munched. "He says I'm a compulsive eater."

"What's you eating papa again for, mama?" daughter Fregona asked as she came in. "You know what the doctor said."

"It's the spider in me," said mama Regina. "I wish you'd brought the coriander seed with you, Homer. It goes so good with you."

"But the doctor says you got to show a little restraint, mama," daughter

Fregona cut back in. "He says it becomes harder and harder for papa to grow back new limbs so often at his age. He says it's going to end up by making him nervous."

"Help, help!" Homer screamed. "My wife is a giant spider and is eating me up. My legs and arms are already gone. If only I could change back to the first nightmare! *Night-Charleys under the Beds at Grandpa's House on the Farm! Rosined Cord to Make Bull-Roarers on Hallowe'en! Pig Mush in February! Cobwebs on Fruit Jars in the Cellar!* No, no, not that! Things never work when you need them. That Diogenes fools around with too much funny stuff."

"All I want is a little affection," said Regina, talking with her mouth full.

"Help, help," said Homer as she ate him clear up to his head. "Shriek, shriek!"

To Joanna Russ, May 15, 1966:

Dear Joanna,

Thanks for letting me see "Bluestocking" and "The Barbarian" again. I like them both, and am putting through a contract. . . . I have a notion I would like to run the first two stories in *Orbit 2*, "The Barbarian" in *Orbit 3*, & I trust there will be more to follow. Will it disappoint you if I run them in their natural order? It seems to me their cumulative effect is better than if we ran them ass-backwards.

Glad to settle for "I Gave Her Sack and Sherry" as a title for #1. Not sure I see the aptness of "Bluestocking" for #2; does it have any, & if not, can you think of another title?

. . . I think these are charming stories, & hope you will write more. It is just as well that you did not consult me before beginning this series, because I would have said nobody could bring off a series of heroic fantasies built around a woman.

I am afraid I had forgotten C. L. Moore's Jirel of Joiry stories when I said this; but then Jirel was a sort of Joan of Arc type and I never could believe in her, whereas Joanna's Alyx is by God a woman.

I GAVE HER SACK AND SHERRY

by Joanna Russ

Many years ago, long before the world got into the state it is in today, young women were supposed to obey their husbands; but nobody knows if they did nor not. In those days they wore their hair piled foot upon foot on top of their heads. Along with such weights they would also carry water in two buckets at the ends of a long pole; this often makes you slip. One did; but she kept her mouth shut. She put the buckets down on the ground and with two sideward kicks—like two dance steps, flirt with the left foot, flirt with the right—she emptied the both of them. She watched the water settle into the ground. Then she swung the pole upon her shoulder and carried them home. She was only just seventeen. Her husband had made her do it. She swung the farm door open with her shoulder and said:

SHE: Here is your damned water.

HE: Where?

SHE: It is beneath my social class to do it and you know it.

HE: You have no social class; only I do, because I am a man.

SHE: *I* wouldn't do it if you were a—

(Here follows something very unpleasant.)

HE: Woman, go back with those pails. Someone is coming tonight.

SHE: Who?

HE: That's not your business.

SHE: Smugglers.

HE: Go!

SHE: Go to hell.

Perhaps he was somewhat afraid of his tough little wife. She watched him from the stairs or the doorway, always with unvarying hatred; that is what comes of marrying a wild hill girl without a proper education. Beatings made her sullen. She went to the water and back, dissecting him every step of the way, separating blond hair from blond hair and cracking and sorting his long limbs. She loved that. She filled the farm water barrel, rooted the maid-servant out of the hay and slapped her, and went indoors with her head full of pirates. She spun, she sewed, she shelled, ground, washed, dusted, swept, built fires all that day and once, so full of her thoughts was she that she savagely wrung and broke the neck of an already dead chicken.

Near certain towns, if you walk down to the beach at night, you may see a very queer sight: lights springing up like drifting insects over the water and others answering from the land, and then something bobbing over the black waves to a blacker huddle drawn up at the very margin of the sand. They are at their revenues. The young wife watched her husband sweat in the kitchen. It made her gay to see him bargain so desperately and lose. The maid complained that one of the men had tried to do something indecent to her. Her mistress watched silently from the shadows near the big hearth and more and more of what she saw was to her liking. When the last man was gone she sent the maid to bed, and while collecting and cleaning the glasses and the plates like a proper wife, she said:

"They rooked you, didn't they!"

"Hold your tongue," said her husband over his shoulder. He was laboriously figuring his book of accounts with strings of circles and crosses and licking his finger to turn the page.

"The big one," she said, "what's his name?"

"What's it to you?" he said sharply. She stood drying her hands in a towel and looking at him. She took off her apron, her jacket and her rings; then she pulled the pins out of her black hair. It fell below her waist and she stood for the last time in this history within a straight black cloud.

She dropped a cup from her fingers, smiling at him as it smashed. They say actions speak louder. He jumped to his feet; he cried, "What are you doing!" again and again in the silent kitchen; he shook her until her teeth rattled.

"Leaving you," she said.

He struck her. She got up, holding her jaw. She said, "You don't see anything. You don't know anything."

"Get upstairs," he said.

"You're an animal," she cried, "you're a fool," and she twisted about as he grasped her wrist, trying to free herself. They insist, these women, on crying, on making demands, and on disagreeing about everything. They fight from one side of the room to the other. She bit his hand and he howled and brought it down on the side of her head. He called her a little whore. He stood blocking the doorway and glowered, nursing his hand. Her head was spinning. She leaned against the wall and held her head in both hands. Then she said:

"So you won't let me go."

He said nothing.

"You can't keep me," she said, and then she laughed; "no, no, you can't," she added, shaking her head, "you just can't." She looked before her and smiled absently, turning this fact over and over. Her husband was rubbing his knuckles.

"What do you think you're up to?" he muttered.

"If you lock me up, I can't work," said his wife and then, with the knife she had used for the past half year to pare vegetables, this woman began to saw at her length of hair. She took the whole sheaf in one hand and hacked at it. Her husband started forward. She stood arrested with her hands involved in her hair, regarding him seriously, while without taking his eyes off her, running the tip of his tongue across his teeth, he groped behind the door—he knew there is one thing you can always do. His wife changed color. Her hands dropped with a tumbled rush of hair, she moved slowly to one side, and when he took out from behind the door the length of braided hide he used to herd cattle, when he swung it high in the air and down in a snapping arc to where she—not where she was; where she had been—this extraordinary young woman had leapt half the distance between them and wrested the stock of the whip from him a foot from his hand. He was off balance and fell; with a vicious grimace she brought the stock down short and hard on the top of his head. She had all her wits about her as she stood over him.

But she didn't believe it. She leaned over him, her cut black hair swinging over her face; she called him a liar; she told him he wasn't bleeding. Slowly she straightened up, with a swagger, with a certain awe. *Good lord!* she thought, looking at her hands. She slapped him, called his name impatiently, but when the fallen man moved a little—or she fancied he did—a thrill ran up her spine to the top of her head, a kind of soundless chill, and snatching the vegetable knife from the floor where she had dropped it, she sprang like an arrow from the bow into the night that waited, all around the house, to devour.

Trees do not pull up their roots and walk abroad, nor is the night ringed with eyes. Stones can't speak. Novelty tosses the world upside down, however. She was terrified, exalted, and helpless with laughter. The tree on either side of the path saw her appear for an instant out of the darkness, wild with hurry, straining like a statue. Then she zigzagged between the tree trunks and flashed over the lip of the cliff into the sea.

In all the wide headland there was no light. The ship still rode at anchor, but far out, and clinging to the line where the water met the air like a limpet or a moray eel under a rock, she saw a trail of yellow points appear on the face of the sea: one, two, three, four. They had finished their business. Hasty and out of breath, she dove under the shadow of that black hull, and treading the shifting seas that fetched her up now and again against the ship's side that was too flat and hard to grasp, she listened to the noises overhead: creaking, groans, voices, the sound of feet. Everything was hollow and loud, mixed with the gurgle of the ripples. She thought, *I am going to give them a surprise.* She felt something form within her, something queer, dark, and hard, like the strangeness of strange customs, or the blackened face of the goddess Chance, whose image set up at crossroads looks three ways at once to signify the crossing of influences. Silently this young woman took off her leather belt and wrapped the buckleless end around her right hand. With her left she struck out for the ship's rope ladder, sinking into the water under a mass of bubbles and crosscurrents eddying like hairs drawn across the surface. She rose some ten feet farther on. Dripping seawater like one come back from the dead, with eighteen inches of leather crowned with a heavy brass buckle in her right hand, her left gripping the rope and her knife between her teeth (where else?) she began to climb.

The watch—who saw her first—saw somebody entirely undistinguished. She was wringing the water out of her skirt. She sprang erect as she caught sight of him, burying both hands in the heavy folds of her dress.

"We-ell!" said he.

She said nothing, only crouched down a little by the rail. The leather belt, hidden in her right—her stronger—hand, began to stir. He came closer—he stared—he leaned forward—he tapped his teeth with his forefinger. "Eh, a pussycat!" he said. She didn't move. He stepped back a pace, clapped his hands and shouted; and all at once she was surrounded by men who had come crack! out of nothing, sprung in from the right, from the left, shot up from the deck as if on springs, even tumbling down out of the air. She did not know if she liked it.

"Look!" said the watch, grinning as if he had made her up.

Perhaps they had never seen a woman before, or perhaps they had never seen one bare-armed, or with her hair cut off, or sopping wet. They stared as if they hadn't. One whistled, indrawn between his teeth, long and low. "What does she want?" said someone. The watch took hold of her arm and the sailor who had whistled raised both hands over his head and clasped them, at which the crowd laughed.

"She thinks we're hot!"

"She wants some, don't you, honey?"

"Ooh, kiss me, kiss me, dearie!"

"I want the captain!" she managed to get out. All around crowded men's faces: some old, some young, all very peculiar to her eyes with their unaccustomed whiskers, their chins, their noses, their loose collars. It occurred to her that she did not like them a bit. She did not exactly think they were behaving badly, as she was not sure how they ought to behave, but they reminded her uncannily of her husband, of whom she was no longer at all afraid. So when the nearest winked and reached out two hands even huger than the shadow of hands cast on the deck boards, she kicked him excruciatingly in the left knee (he fell down), the watch got the belt buckle round in a circle from underneath (up, always up, especially if you're short), which gave him a cut across the cheek and a black eye; this leaves her left hand still armed and her teeth, which she used. It's good to be able to do several things at once. Forward, halfway from horizon to zenith, still and clear above the black mass of the rigging and the highest mast, burned the constellation of the Hunter, and under that—by way of descent down a monumental fellow who had just that moment sprung on board—frothed and foamed a truly fabulous black beard. She had just unkindly set someone howling by trampling on a tender part (they were in good spirits, most of them, and fighting one another in a heap; she never did admit later to all the things she did in that melee) when the beard bent down over her, curled and glossy as a piece of the sea. Children never could resist that beard. Big one looked at little one. Little one looked at big one. Stars shone over his head. He recognized her at once, of course, and her look, and the pummeling she had left behind her, and the cracked knee, and all the rest of it. "So," he said, "you're a fighter, are you!" He took her hands in his and crushed them, good and hard; she smiled brilliantly, involuntarily.

"I'll take you on," he said. "You've got style."

When she fenced with him (she insisted on fencing with him) she worked with a hard, dry persistence that surprised him. "Well, I have got your —— and you have got my teaching," he said philosophically at first, "whatever you may want with *that*," but on the second day out she slipped on soapsuds on the tilting deck ("Give it up, girl, give it up!"), grabbed the fellow who was scrubbing away by the ankles, and brought him down —screaming—on top of the captain. Blackbeard was not surprised that she had tried to do this, but he was very surprised that she had actually brought it off. "Get up," he told her (she was sitting where she fell and grinning). She pulled up her stockings. He chose for her a heavier and longer blade, almost as tall as she ("Huh!" she said, "it's about time"), and held out the blade and the scabbard, one in each hand, both at the same time. She took them, one in each hand, both at the same time.

"By God, you're ambidextrous!" he exclaimed.

"Come on!" she said.

That was a blade that was a blade! She spent the night more or less tangled up in it, as she never yet had with him. Things were still unsettled between them. Thus she slept alone in his bed, in his cabin; thus she woke alone, figuring she still had the best of it. Thus she spurned a heap of his possessions with her foot (the fact that she did not clean the place up in womanly fashion put him to great distress), writhed, stretched, turned over and jumped as a crash came from outside. There was a shuttered window above the bed that gave on the deck. Someone—here she slipped on her shift and swung open the shutter—was bubbling, shouting, singing, sending mountains of water lolloping across the boards. Someone (here she leaned out and twisted her head about to see) naked to the waist in a barrel was taking a bath. Like Poseidon. He turned, presenting her with the black patches under his armpits streaming water, with his hair and beard running like black ink.

"Halloooo!" he roared. She grunted and drew back, closing the shutter. She had made no motion to get dressed when he came in, but lay with her arms under her head. He stood in the doorway, tucking his shirt into his trousers; then this cunning man said, "I came to get something" (looking at her sidewise), and diffidently carried his wet, tightly curled beard past her into a corner of the cabin. He knelt down and burrowed diligently.

"Get what?" she said. He didn't answer. He was rummaging in a chest he had dragged from the wall; now he took out of it—with great tenderness and care—a woman's nightdress, worked all in white lace, which he held up to her, saying:

"Do you want this?"

"No," she said, and meant it.

"But it's expensive," he said earnestly, "it is, look," and coming over to sit on the edge of the bed, he showed the dress to her, for the truth was it was so expensive that he hadn't meant to give it to her at all, and only offered it out of—well, out of—

"I don't want it," she said, a little sharply.

"Do you like jewelry?" he suggested hopefully. He had not got thoroughly dried and water was dripping unobtrusively from the ends of his hair onto the bed; he sat patiently holding the nightgown out by the sleeves to show it off. He said ingenuously, "Why don't you try it on?"

Silence.

"It would look good on you," he said. She said nothing. He laid down the nightgown and looked at her, bemused and wondering; then he reached out and tenderly touched her hair where it hung down to the point of her small, grim jaw.

"My, aren't you little," he said.

She laughed. Perhaps it was being called little, or perhaps it was being touched so very lightly, but this farm girl threw back her head and laughed until she cried, as the saying is, and then:

"Tcha! It's a bargain, isn't it!" said this cynical girl. He lowered himself onto the floor on his heels; then tenderly folded the nightgown into a lacy bundle, which he smoothed, troubled.

"No, give it to me," she demanded sharply. He looked up, surprised.

"Give it!" she repeated, and scrambling across the bed she snatched it out

61

of his hands, stripped off her shirt, and slid the gown over her bare skin. She was compact but not stocky and the dress became her; she walked about the cabin, admiring her sleeves, carrying the train over one arm while he sat back on his heels and blinked at her.

"Well," she said philosophically, "come on." He was not at all pleased. He rose (her eyes followed him), towering over her, his arms folded. He looked at the nightgown, at the train she held, at her arched neck (she had to look up to meet his gaze), at her free arm curved to her throat in a gesture of totally unconscious femininity. He had been thinking, a process that with him was slow but often profound; now he said solemnly:

"Woman, what man have you ever been with before?"

"Oh!" said she startled, "my husband," and backed off a little.

"And where is he?"

"Dead." She could not help a grin.

"How?" She held up a fist. Blackbeard sighed heavily.

Throwing the loose bedclothes onto the bed, he strode to his precious chest (she padded inquisitively behind him), dropped heavily to his knees, and came up with a heap of merchandise: bottles, rings, jingles, coins, scarves, handkerchiefs, boots, toys, half of which he put back. Then, catching her by one arm, he threw her over his shoulder in a somewhat casual or moody fashion (the breath was knocked out of her) and carried her to the center of the cabin, where he dropped her—half next to and half over a small table, the only other part of the cabin's furnishings besides the bed. She was trembling all over. With the same kind of solemn preoccupation he dumped his merchandise on the table, sorted out a bottle and two glasses, a bracelet, which he put on her arm, earrings similarly, and a few other things that he studied and then placed on the floor. She was amazed to see that there were tears in his eyes.

"Now, why don't you fight me!" he said emotionally.

She looked at the table, then at her hands.

"Ah!" he said, sighing again, pouring out a glassful and gulping it, drumming the glass on the table. He shook his head. He held out his arms and she circled the table carefully, taking his hands, embarrassed to look him in the face. "Come," he said, "up here," patting his knees, so she climbed awkwardly onto his lap, still considerably wary. He poured out another glass and put it in her hand. He sighed, and put nothing into words; only she felt on her back what felt like a hand and arched a little—like a cat—with pleasure; then she stirred on his knees to settle herself and immediately froze. He did nothing. He was looking into the distance, into nothing. He might have been remembering his past. She put one arm around his neck to steady herself, but her arm felt his neck most exquisitely and she did not like that, so she gave it up and put one hand on his shoulder. Then she could not help but feel his shoulder. It was quite provoking. He mused into the distance. Sitting on his lap, she could feel his breath stirring about her bare face, about her neck—she turned to look at him and shut her eyes; she thought, *What am I doing?* and the blood came to her face harder and harder until her cheeks blazed. She felt him sigh, felt that sigh travel from her side to her stomach to the back of her head, and with a soft, hopeless, exasperated cry ("I don't expect to enjoy this!") she turned and sank, both hands firstmost, into Blackbeard's oceanic beard.

And he, the villain, was even willing to cooperate.

Time passes, even (as they say) on the sea. What with moping about while he visited farmhouses and villages, watching the stars wheel and change overhead as they crept down the coast, with time making and unmaking the days, bringing dinnertime (as it does) and time to get up and what-not— Well, there you are. She spent her time learning to play cards. But gambling and prophecy are very closely allied—in fact they are one thing—and when he saw his woman squatting on deck on the balls of her feet, a sliver of wood in her teeth, dealing out the cards to tell fortunes (cards and money appeared in the East at exactly the same time in the old days) he thought—or thought he saw—or recollected—that goddess who was driven out by the other gods when the world was made and who hangs about still on the fringes of things (at crossroads, at the entrance to towns) to throw a little shady trouble into life and set up a few crosscurrents and undercurrents of her own in what ought to be a regular and predictable business. She herself did not believe in gods and goddesses. She told the fortunes of the crew quite obligingly, as he had taught her, but was much more interested in learning the probabilities of the appearance of any particular card in one of the five suits*—she had begun to evolve what she thought was a rather elegant little theory—when late one day he told her, "Look, I am going into a town tonight, but you can't come." They were lying anchored on the coast, facing west, just too far away to see the lights at night. She said, "Wha'?"

"I am going to town tonight," he said (he was a very patient man), "and you can't come."

"Why not?" said the woman. She threw down her cards and stood up, facing into the sunset. The pupils of her eyes shrank to pinpoints. To her he was a big, blind rock, a kind of outline; she said again, "Why not?" and her whole face lifted and became sharper as one's face does when one stares against the sun.

"Because you can't," he said. She bent to pick up her cards as if she had

*ones, tens, hundreds, myriads, tens of myriads

made some mistake in listening, but there he was saying, "I won't be able to take care of you."

"You won't have to," said she. He shook his head. "You won't come."

"Of course I'll come," she said.

"You won't," said he.

"The devil I won't!" said she.

He put both arms on her shoulders, powerfully, seriously, with utmost heaviness and she pulled away at once, at once transformed into a mystery with a closed face; she stared at him without expression, shifting her cards from hand to hand. He said, "Look, my girl—" and for this got the entire fortunes of the whole world for the next twenty centuries right in his face.

"Well, well," he said, "I see," ponderously, "I see," and stalked away down the curve of the ship, thus passing around the cabin, into the darkening eastern sky, and out of the picture.

But she did go with him. She appeared, dripping wet and triumphantly smiling, at the door of the little place of business he had chosen to discuss business in and walked directly to his table, raising two fingers in greeting, a gesture that had taken her fancy when she saw it done by someone in the street. She then uttered a word Blackbeard thought she did not understand (she did). She looked with interest around the room—at the smoke from the torches—and the patrons—and a Great Horned Owl somewhat the worse for wear that had been chained by one leg to the bar (an ancient invention)—and the stuffed blowfish that hung from the ceiling on a string: lazy, consumptive, puffed-up, with half its spines broken off. Then she sat down.

"Huh!" she said, dismissing the tavern. Blackbeard was losing his temper. His face suffused with blood, he put both enormous fists on the table to emphasize that fact; she nodded civilly, leaned back on her part of the wall (causing the bench to rock), crossed her knees, and swung one foot back and forth, back and forth, under the noses of both gentlemen. It was not exactly rude but it was certainly disconcerting.

"You. Get out," said the other gentleman.

"I'm not dry yet," said she in a soft, reasonable voice, like a bravo trying to pick a quarrel, and she laid both arms across the table, where they left two dark stains. She stared him in the face as if trying to memorize it—hard enough with a man who made it his business to look like nobody in particular—and the *other gentleman* was about to rise and was reaching for something or other under the table when her gentleman said:

"She's crazy." He cleared his throat. "You sit down," he said. "My apologies. *You* behave," and social stability thus reestablished, they plunged into a discussion she understood pretty well but did not pay much attention to, as she was too busy looking about. The owl blinked, turned his head completely around, and stood on one foot. The blowfish rotated lazily. Across the room stood a row of casks and a mortared wall; next to that a face in the dimness—a handsome face—that smiled at her across the saltpeter, a wise, nasty, irresponsible, trouble-making smile, at which the handsome face winked. She laughed out loud.

"Shut up," said Blackbeard, not turning round.

He was in a tight place.

She watched him insist and prevaricate and sweat, building all kinds of earnest, openhearted, irresistible arguments with the gestures of his big hands, trying to bully the insignificant other gentleman—and failing—and not knowing it—until finally at the same moment the owl screeched like a rusty file, a singer at the end of the bar burst into wailing quartertones, and Blackbeard—wiping his forehead—said, "All right."

"No, dammit," she cried, "you're ten percent off!"

He slapped her. The other gentleman cleared his throat.

"All right," Blackbeard repeated. The other man nodded. Finishing his wine, drawing on his gloves, already a little bored perhaps, he turned and left. In his place, as if by a compensation of nature, there suddenly appeared, jackrabbited between the tables, the handsome young owner of the face who was not so handsome at close range but dressed fit to kill all the same with a gold earring, a red scarf tucked into his shirt, and a satanic resemblance to her late husband. She looked rapidly from one man to the other, almost malevolently; then she stood rigid, staring at the floor.

"Well, baby," said the intruder.

Blackbeard turned his back on his girl.

The intruder took hold of her by the nape of the neck but she did not move; he talked to her in a low voice; finally she blurted out, "Oh yes! Go on!" (fixing her eyes on the progress of Blackbeard's monolithic back towards the door) and stumbled aside as the latter all but vaulted over a table to retrieve his lost property. She followed him, her head bent, violently flushed. Two streets off he stopped, saying, "Look, my dear, can I please not take you ashore again?" but she would not answer, no, not a word, and all this time the singer back at the tavern was singing away about the Princess Oriana who traveled to meet her betrothed but was stolen by bandits, and how she prayed, and how the bandits cursed, and how she begged to be returned to her prince, and how the bandits said, "Not likely," and how she finally ended it all by jumping into the Bosphorus—in short, art in the good old style with plenty of solid vocal technique, a truly Oriental expressiveness, and innumerable verses.

(She always remembered the incident and maintained for the rest of her life that small producers should combine in trading with middlemen so as not to lower prices by competing against each other.)

In the first, faint hint of dawn, as Blackbeard lay snoring and damp in the bedclothes, his beard spread out like a fan, his woman prodded him in the ribs with the handle of his sword; she said, "Wake up! Something's happening.

"I am," she added. She watched him as he tried to sit up, tangled in the sheets, pale, enormous, the black hair on his chest forming with unusual distinctness the shape of a flying eagle. "Wha'?" he said.

"I am," she repeated. Still half asleep, he held out his arms to her, indicating that she might happen all over the place, might happen now, particularly in bed, *he* did not care. *"Wake up!"* she said. He nearly leapt out of bed, but then perceived her standing leaning on his sword, the corners of her mouth turned down. No one was being killed. He blinked, shivered, and shook his head. "Don't do that," he said thickly. She let the sword fall with a clatter. He winced.

"I'm going away," she said very distinctly, "that's all," and thrusting her face near his, she seized him by the arms and shook him violently, leaping back when he vaulted out of the bed and whirling around with one hand on the table—ready to throw it. That made him smile. He sat down and scratched his chest, giving himself every now and then a kind of shake to wake himself up, until he could look at her directly in the eyes and ask:

"Haven't I treated you well?"

She said nothing. He dangled one arm between his knees moodily and rubbed the back of his neck with the other, so enormous, so perfect, so relaxed, and in every way so like real life that she could only shrug and fold her arms across her breast. He examined his feet and rubbed, for comfort, the ankle and the arch, the heel and the instep, stretching his feet, stretching his back, rubbing his fingers over and over and over.

"Damn it, I am cleverer than you!" she exclaimed.

He sighed, meaning perhaps "no," meaning perhaps "I suppose so"; he said, "You've been up all night, haven't you?" and then he said, "My dear, you must understand—" but at that moment a terrific battering shook the ship, propelling the master of it outside, naked as he was, from which position he locked his woman in.

(In those days craft were high, square and slow, like barrels or boxes put out to sea; but everything is relative, and as they crept up on each other, throwing fits every now and again when headed into the wind, creaking and straining at every joist, ships bore skippers who remembered craft braced with twisted rope from stem to stern, craft manned exclusively by rowers,

66

above all craft that invariably—or usually—sank, and they enjoyed the keen sensation of modernity while standing on a deck large enough for a party of ten to dine on comfortably and steering by use of a rudder that no longer required a pole for leverage or broke a man's wrist. Things were getting better. With great skill a man could sail as fast as other men could run. Still, in this infancy of the world, one ship wallowed after another; like cunning sloths one feebly stole up on another; and when they closed—without fire (do you want us to burn ourselves *up*?)—the toothless, ineffectual creatures clung together, sawing dully at each other's grappling ropes, until the fellows over there got over here or the fellows over here got over there and then—on a slippery floor humped like the back of an elephant and just about as small, amid rails, boxes, pots, peaks, tar, slants, steps, ropes, coils, masts, falls, chests, sails and God knows what—they hacked at each other until most of them died. That they did very efficiently.

And the sea was full of robbers.)

Left alone, she moved passively with the motion of the ship; then she picked up very slowly and looked into very slowly the hand mirror he had taken for her out of his chest, brass-backed and decorated with metal rosewreaths, the kind of object she had never in her life seen before. There she was, oddly tilted, looking out of the mirror, and behind her the room as if seen from above, as if one could climb down into the mirror to those odd objects, bright and reversed, as if one could fall into the mirror, become tiny, clamber away, and looking back see one's own enormous eyes staring out of a window set high in the wall. Women do not always look in mirrors to admire themselves, popular belief to the contrary. Sometimes they look only to slip off their rings and their bracelets, to pluck off their earrings, to unfasten their necklaces, to drop their brilliant gowns, to take the color off their faces until the bones stand out like spears and to wipe the hues from around their eyes until they can look and look at merely naked human faces, at eyes no longer brilliant and aqueous like the eyes of angels or goddesses but hard and small as human eyes are, little control points that are always a little disquieting, always a little peculiar, because they are not meant to be looked at but to look, and then—with a shudder, a shiver—to recover themselves and once again to shimmer, to glow. But some don't care. This one stumbled away, dropped the mirror, fell over the table (she passed her hand over her eyes) and grasped—more by feeling than by sight—the handle of the sword he had given her, thirty or forty—or was it seventy?—years before. The blade had not yet the ironical motto it was to bear some years later: *Good Manners Are Not Enough*, but she lifted it high all the same, and grasping with her left hand the bronze chain Blackbeard used to fasten his treasure chest, broke the lock of the door in one blow.

67

Such was the strength of iron in the old days.

There is talent and then there is the other thing. Blackbeard had never seen the other thing. He found her after the battle was over with her foot planted on the back of a dead enemy, trying to free the sword he had given her. She did so in one jerky pull and rolled the man overboard with her foot without bothering about him further; she was looking at an ornamented dagger in her left hand, a beautiful weapon with a jeweled handle and a slender blade engraved with scrolls and leaves. She admired it very much. She held it out to him, saying, "Isn't that a beauty?" There was a long gash on her left arm, the result of trying to stop a downward blow with nothing but the bronze chain wrapped around her knuckles. The chain was gone; she had only used it as long as it had surprise value and had lost it somewhere, somehow (she did not quite remember how). He took the dagger and she sat down suddenly on the deck, dropping the sword and running both hands over her hair to smooth it again and again, unaware that her palms left long red streaks. The deck looked as if a tribe of monkeys had been painting on it or as if everyone—living and dead—had smeared himself ritually with red paint. The sun was coming up. He sat down next to her, too winded to speak. With the intent watchfulness (but this will be a millennium or two later) of someone focusing the lens of a microscope, with the noble, arrogant carriage of a tennis star, she looked first around the deck—and then at him—and then straight up into the blue sky.

"So," she said, and shut her eyes.

He put his arm around her; he wiped her face. He stroked the nape of her neck and then her shoulder, but now his woman began to laugh, more and more, leaning against him and laughing and laughing until she was convulsed and he thought she had gone out of her mind. "What the devil!" he cried, almost weeping, "what the devil!" She stopped at that place in the scale where a woman's laughter turns into a shriek; her shoulders shook spasmodically, but soon she controlled that too. He thought she might be hysterical so he said, "Are you frightened? You won't have to go through this again."

"No?" she said.

"Never."

"Well," she said, "perhaps I will all the same," and in pure good humor she put her arms about his neck. There were tears in her eyes—perhaps they were tears of laughter—and in the light of the rising sun the deck showed ever more ruddy and grotesque. *What a mess*, she thought. She said, "It's all right; don't you worry," which was, all in all and in the light of things, a fairly kind good-bye.

"Why the devil," she said with sudden interest, "don't doctors cut up the bodies of dead people in the schools to find out how they're put together?''

But he didn't know.

Six weeks later she arrived—alone—at that queen among cities, that moon among stars, that noble, despicable, profound, simpleminded and altogether exasperating capital of the world: Ourdh. Some of us know it. She materialized so quietly and expertly out of the dark that the gatekeeper found himself looking into her face without the slightest warning: a young, gray-eyed countrywoman, silent, shadowy, self-assured. She was hugely amused. "My name," she said, "is Alyx."

"Never heard of it," said the gatekeeper, a little annoyed.

"Good heavens," said Alyx, "not yet," and vanished through the gate before he could admit her, with the curious slight smile one sees on the lips of very old statues: inexpressive, simple, classic.

She was to become a classic, in time.

But that's another story.

To Richard Wilson, July 5, 1966:

Dear Dick,

I don't think the world has been waiting for another last-man-last-woman story, but this one is so good I can't bear to pass it up. Can I talk you into making some revisions?

Item, the solvent. What you want here is just some way of cleaning out the human population without leaving a lot of rotting corpses, and without affecting other forms of life. I think you are crossing yourself up by trying to explain it so specifically that the reader can easily see whether it would work or not. Since nobody actually knows what was done anyhow, how would you feel about just leaving this a mystery?

Item, length. I think this version is too long, & should be trimmed by at least a thousand words, preferably two thousand. Will you look through it and see if you think you can get that much out of it? Some of the journal entries could go, maybe, where they are repetitive, and perhaps some of Rolfe's soliloquies. (Do not on any account take out the tree or the mined road!)

Item, the ending. The story is so poignant elsewhere that I think a flat ending like this is bound to disappoint others as it did me. Can you think of a way to strengthen it?

To Wilson, July 27, 1966:

Dear Dick,
    You did it, you son of a gun. New ending is beautiful & perfect, made me want to bawl.

To James Blish, August 9, 1966:

Dear Jim,
    . . . Stories on hand include two long ones, one by Dick Wilson, who astonished me; if it does not get a Hugo or Nebula, there is no justice. . . . Meanwhile, back at the ranch, I am telling Dardis that there should be two *Orbits* a year, and he is not fighting me very hard, but even this is not that simple, because it also depends on Putnam, with whom you remember I had a real brannigan last time; Putnam at this writing has not seen *Orbit 2*, & depending on whether or not they are able to face the fact that this is not a juvenile collection, they may or may not decide to do it in hardcover at all.

From Richard Wilson, August 8, 1966:

Dear Damon:
    . . . You might be interested in what one of your fellow editors said of "Mother to the World" just last May (now that the die is cast): ". . . standard and unexciting setting . . . uneven dialog . . . rough transitions between the diary and the third person narration . . . rather uninteresting storyline . . ."

MOTHER TO THE WORLD

by *Richard Wilson*

(Nebula Award, Best Novelette, 1968)

His name was Martin Rolfe. She called him Mr. Ralph.

She was Cecelia Beamer, called Siss.

He was a vigorous, intelligent, lean and wiry forty-two, a shade under six feet tall. His hair, black, was thinning but still covered all of his head; and all his teeth were his own. His health was excellent. He'd never had a cavity or an operation and he fervently hoped he never would.

She was a slender, strong young woman of twenty-eight, five feet four. Her eyes, nose and mouth were regular and well-spaced, but the combination fell short of beauty. She wore her hair, which was dark blonde, not quite brown, straight back and long in two pigtails which she braided daily, after a ritualistic hundred brushings. Her figure was better than average for her age and therefore good, but she did nothing to emphasize it. Her disposition was cheerful when she was with someone; when alone her tendency was to work hard at the job at hand, giving it her serious attention. Whatever she was doing was the most important thing in the world to her just then and she had a compulsion to do it absolutely right. She was indefatigable but she liked, almost demanded, to be praised for what she did well.

Her amusements were simple ones. She liked to talk to people, but most people quickly became bored with what she had to say—she was inclined to be repetitive. Fortunately for her, she also liked to talk to animals, birds included.

She was a retarded person with the mentality of an eight-year-old.

Eight can be a delightful age. Rolfe remembered his son at eight—bright, inquiring, beginning to emerge from childhood but not so fast as to lose any of his innocent charm; a refreshing, uninhibited conversationalist with an original viewpoint on life. The boy had been a challenge to him and a constant delight. He held on to that memory, drawing sustenance from it, for her.

Young Rolfe was dead now, along with his mother and three billion other people.

Rolfe and Siss were the only ones left in all the world.

It was M.R. that had done it, he told her. Massive Retaliation; from the Other Side.

71

When American bombs rained down from long-range jets and rocket carriers, nobody'd known the Chinese had what they had. Nobody'd suspected it of that relatively backward country which the United States had believed it was softening up, in a brushfire war, for enforced diplomacy.

Rolfe hadn't been aware of any speculation that Peking's scientists were concentrating their search not on weapons but on biochemistry. Germ warfare, sure. There'd been propaganda from both sides about that, but nothing had been hinted about a biological agent, as it must have been, that could break down human cells and release the water.

"M.R.," he told her. "Better than nerve gas or the neutron bomb." Like those, it left the buildings and equipment intact. Unlike them, it didn't leave any messy corpses—only the bones, which crumbled and blew away. Except the bone dust trapped inside the pathetic mounds of clothing that lay everywhere in the city.

"Are they coming over now that they beat us?"

"I'm sure they intended to. But there can't be any of them left. They outsmarted themselves, I guess. The wind must have blown it right back at them. I don't really know what happened, Siss. All I know is that everybody's gone now, except you and me."

"But the animals—"

Rolfe had found it best in trying to explain something to Siss to keep it simple, especially when he didn't understand it himself. Just as he had learned long ago that if he didn't know how to pronounce a word he should say it loud and confidently.

So all he told Siss was that the bad people had got hold of a terrible weapon called M.R.—she'd heard of that—and used it on the good people and that nearly everybody had died. Not the animals, though, and damned if he knew why.

"Animals don't sin," Siss told him.

"That's as good an explanation as any I can think of," he said. She was silent for a while. Then she said: "Your name—initials—are M.R., aren't they?"

He'd never considered it before, but she was right. Martin Rolfe —Massive Retaliation. I hope she doesn't blame everything on me, he thought. But then she spoke again. "M.R. That's short for Mister. What I call you. Your name that I have for you. Mister Ralph."

"Tell me again how we were saved, Mr. Ralph."

She used the expression in an almost evangelical sense, making him uncomfortable. Rolfe was a practical man, a realist and freethinker.

"You know as well as I do, Siss," he said. "It's because Professor

72

Cantwell was doing government research and because he was having a party. You certainly remember; Cantwell was your boss."

"I know that. But you tell it so good and I like to hear it."

"All right. Bill Cantwell was an old friend of mine from the army and when I came to New York I gave him a call at the University. It was the first time I'd talked to him in years; I had no idea he'd married again and had set up housekeeping in Manhattan."

"And had a working girl named Siss," she put in.

"The very same," he agreed. Siss never referred to herself as a maid, which was what she had been. "And so when I asked Bill if he could put me up, I thought it would be in his old bachelor apartment. He said sure, just like that, and I didn't find out till I got there, late in the evening, that he had a new wife and was having a house-party and had invited two couples from out of town to stay over."

"I gave my room to Mr. and Mrs. Glenn, from Columbus," Siss said.

"And the Torquemadas, of Seville, had the regular guest room." Whoever they were; he didn't remember names the way she did. "So that left two displaced persons, you and me."

"Except for the Nassers."

The Nassers, as she pronounced it, were the two self-contained rooms in the Cantwell basement. The NASAs, or the Nasas, was what Cantwell called them because the National Aeronautics and Space Administration had given him a contract to study the behavior of human beings in a closed system.

Actually the money had gone to Columbia University, where Cantwell was a professor of mechanical and aerospace engineering.

"A sealed-off environment," Rolfe said. "But because Columbia didn't have the space just at that time, and because the work was vital, NASA gave Cantwell permission to build the rooms in his own home. They were—still are—in his basement, and that's where you and I slept that fateful night when the world ended."

"I still don't understand."

"We were completely sealed off in there," Rolfe said. "We weren't breathing Earth air and we weren't connected in any way to the rest of the world. We might as well have been out in space or on the moon. So when it happened to everybody else—to Professor and Mrs. Cantwell, and to the Glenns and the Torquemadas and to the Nassers in Egypt and the Joneses in Jones Beach and all the people at Columbia, and in Washington and Moscow and Pretoria and London and Peoria and Medicine Hat and La Jolla and all those places all over—it didn't happen to us. That's because Professor Cantwell was a smart man and his closed systems worked."

"And we were saved."

"That's one way of looking at it."

"What's the other way?"

"We were doomed."

From his notebooks:

Siss asked why I'm so sure there's nobody but us left in the whole world. A fair question. Of course I'm not absolutely positively cross-my-heart-and-hope-to-die, swear-on-a-Bible convinced that there isn't a poor live slob hidden away in some remote corner. Other people besides Bill must have been working with closed systems; certainly any country with a space program would be, and maybe some of *their* nassers were inhabited, too. I hadn't heard that any astronauts or cosmonauts were in orbit that day but if they were, and got down safely, I guess they could be alive somewhere.

But I've listened to the rest of the world on some of the finest radio equipment ever put together and there hasn't been a peep out of it. I've listened and signaled and listened and signaled and listened. Nothing. Nil. Short wave, long wave. AM, FM, UHF, marine band, everywhere. Naught. Not a thing. Lots of automatic signals from unmanned satellites, of course, and the quasars are still being heard from, but nothing human.

I've sent out messages on every piece of equipment connected to Con Ed's EE net. RCA, American Cable & Radio, the Bell System, Western Union, The Associated Press, UPI, Reuters' world news network, *The New York Times'* multifarious teletypes, even the Hilton Hotels' international reservations system. Nothing. By this time I'd become fairly expert at communications and I'd found the Pentagon network at AT&T. Silent. Ditto the hot line to the Kremlin. I read the monitor teletype and saw the final message from Washington to Moscow. Strictly routine. No hint that anything was amiss anywhere. Just as it must have been at the Army message center at Pearl Harbor on another Sunday morning a generation ago.

This is for posterity, these facts. My evidence is circumstantial. But to Siss I say: "There's nobody left but us. I know. You'll have to take my word for it that the rest of the world is as empty as New York."

Nobody here but us chickens, boss. Us poor flightless birds. One middle-aged rooster and one sad little hen, somewhat deficient in the upper story. What do you want us to do, boss? What's the next step in the great cosmic scheme? Tell us: where do we go from here?

But don't tell me; tell Siss. I don't expect an answer; she does. She's the one who went into the first church she found open that Sunday morning (some of them were locked, you know) and said all the prayers she knew, and asked for mercy for her relatives, and her friends, and her employers, and for me, and for all the dead people who had been alive only yesterday, and finally for herself; and then she asked why. She was in there for an hour and when she came out I don't think she'd had an answer.

Nobody here but us chickens, boss. What do you want us to do now, fricassee ourselves?

Late on the morning of doomsday they had taken a walk down Broadway, starting from Cantwell's house near the Columbia campus.

There were a number of laughs to be had from cars in comical positions, if anybody was in a laughing mood. Some were standing obediently behind white lines at intersections, and obviously their drivers had been overtaken during a red light. With its driver gone, each such car had simply stood there, its engine dutifully using up all the gas in its tank and then coughing to a stop. Others had nosed gently into shop windows, or less gently into other cars or trucks. One truck, loaded with New Jersey eggs, had overturned and its cargo was dripping in a yellowy-white puddle. Rolfe, his nose twitching as if in anticipation of a warm day next week, made a mental note never to return to that particular spot.

Several times he found a car which had been run up upon from behind by another. It was as if, knowing they would never again be manufactured, they were trying copulation.

While Siss was in church Rolfe found a car that had not idled away all its gas and he made a dry run through the streets. He discovered that he could navigate pretty well around the stalled or wrecked cars, though occasionally he had to drive up on the sidewalk or make a three-block detour to get back to Broadway.

Then he and Siss, subdued after church, went downtown.

"Whose car is this, Mr. Ralph?" she asked him.

"My car, Siss. Would you like one, too?"

"I can't drive."

"I'll teach you. It may come in handy."

"I was the only one in church," she said. It hadn't got through to her yet, he thought; not completely.

"Who were you expecting?" he asked kindly

"God, maybe."

She was gazing straight ahead, clutching her purse in her lap. She had the expression of a person who had been let down.

At 72nd Street a beer truck had demolished the box office of the Trans-Lux movie house and foamy liquid was still trickling out of it, across the

75

sidewalk and along the gutter and into a sewer. Rolfe stopped the car and got out. An aluminum barrel had been punctured. The beer leaking from it was cool. He leaned over and let it run into his mouth for a while.

The Trans-Lux had been having a Fellini festival; the picture was *8-1/2*. On impulse he went inside and came back to the car with the reels of film in a black tin box. He remembered the way the movie had opened, with all the cars stalled in traffic. Like Broadway, except that the Italian cars had people in them. He put the box in the rear of the car and said: "We'll go to the movies sometime." Siss looked at him blankly.

At Columbus Circle a Broadway bus had locked horns with a big van carrying furniture from North Carolina. At 50th Street a Mustang had nosed gently into the front of a steak house, as if someone had led it to a hitching post.

He made an illegal left turn at 42nd Street, noting what was playing at the Rialto: two naughty, daring, sexy, nudie pix, including a re-run of "My Bare Lady." He didn't stop for that one.

At the old Newsweek Building east of Broadway, an Impala had butted into the ground-floor liquor store. The plate glass lay smashed but the bottles in the window were intact. He made a mental note. Across the street, one flight up, was the Keppel Folding Boat Company, which had long intrigued him. Soon it might be useful to unfold one and sail off to a better place. He marked it in his mind.

Bookstores, 42nd Street style. Dirty books and magazines. Girly books. Deviant, flagellant, homosexual, Lesbian, sadistic books. Pornographic classics restored to the common man—*Memoirs of a Woman of Pleasure*. *The Kama Sutra*, quaint but lasciviously advertised. Books of nudes for the serious artist (no retoucher's airbrush here, men!).

Nudie pix in packets, wrapped in pliofilm, at a buck and a half the set. Large girls in successive states of undress. How big can a breast be before it disgusts? What is the optimum bosom size? A cup? D cup? It would depend on the number to be fed, wouldn't it? And how hungry they were? Or was that criterion passé?

He looked over at Siss, who wasn't looking at him or the bookstores or the dirty-movie houses but straight ahead. She had a nice figure. About a C.

But it was never the body alone; it was the mind that went with it and the voice with which it spoke.

"What are you thinking, Siss?" he asked.

"Nothing," she said. It was probably true. "What are *you* thinking?"

Riposte. How could he tell her?

He improvised. They were passing Bryant Park. "Pigeons in the park," he said. "I'm thinking of the pigeons. Hungrier than yesterday because

76

nobody's buying peanuts for them, bringing slices of bread from home; there's no bread lady buying bagfuls for them at Horn & Hardart's day-old bakery shop.''

"It's a sad time, isn't it, Mr. Ralph?''

"Yes, Siss; a sad time.''

They got to First Avenue and the U.N. There wasn't anybody there, either.

Notes for a History of the World was what he wrote on page one of his notebook.

On page two he had alternate titles, some facetious:

The True History of the Martin Rolfe Family on the Planet Earth; or, *Two for Tomorrow.*

Recollections of a World Well Lost.

How the Population Crisis Was Solved.

What Next? or, if *You* Don't Do It, Marty, Who the Hell Will?

From his notebooks:

Thank God for movies. We'd be outen our minds by now if I hadn't taught myself to be a projectionist.

Radio City Music Hall apparently's only movie on Con Ed's EE list. Bit roomy for Siss and me but getting used to it. Sometimes she sits way down front, I in mezzanine, and we shout to each other when Gregory Peck does heroic things.

Collected first runs to add to *8-1/2* from all major Manhattan houses —Capitol, Criterion, Cinema I & II, State, etc.—so we have good backlog. Also, if Siss likes, we run it again right away or next night. I don't mind. Then there are the 42nd St. houses and the art houses and the nabes & Mod. Museum film library. Shouldn't run out for a long time.

Days are for exploring and shopping. I go armed because of the animals. Siss stays home at the hotel.

(*Why* are there animals? Find out. *Where* find out; how?)

The dogs in packs are worst. So far they haven't attacked and a shot fired in the air scares them off. So far.

Later they left the city. It had been too great a strain to live a life half primitive, half luxurious. The contrast was too much. And the rats were getting bolder. The rats and the dogs.

They had lived there at first for the convenience. He picked a hotel on Park Avenue. He put Siss in a single room and took a suite down the hall for himself.

He guessed correctly that there'd be huge refrigerators and freezers stocked with food enough for years.

The hotel, with its world-famous name, was one of the places the Consolidated Edison Company had boasted was on its Emergency Electricity net, along with City Hall, the Empire State Building, the tunnels and bridges, Governors Island and other key installations. The EE net, worked out for Civil Defense (what had ever become of Civil Defense?), guaranteed uninterrupted electricity to selected customers through the use of deep underground grids and conduits, despite flood, fire, pestilence or war. A promotional piece claimed that only total annihilation could knock out the system.

There was a hint of the way it worked in a slogan that Con Ed considered using before the government censors decided it would have given too much away: ". . . as long as the Hudson flows."

Whatever the secret, he and Siss had electricity, from which so many blessings flowed, for as long as they stayed in the city.

From his notebooks:

I've renamed our hotel The Living End. Siss calls it our house, or maybe Our House.

I won't let her go out by herself but she has the run of the hotel. She won't use the self-service elevators. Doesn't trust them. Don't blame her. She cooks in the hotel kitchen and carries our meals up two flights on a tray.

Garbage disposal no problem. There's an incinerator that must work by electricity. So far it's taken everything I've dumped down it. I can't feel any heat but it doesn't stink.

We're getting some outdoor stinks, though. Animal excrement that nobody cleans up (I'd be doing nothing else if I started). Uncollected garbage. Rotting food in supermarkets and other places without EE.

There are certain streets I avoid now. Whole sections, when the wind is wrong.

Bad night at the Living End. Had a nightmare.

I dreamed that Siss and I, home from the Music Hall (Cary Grant and Audrey Hepburn in something from the sixties), were having a fight. I don't know about what but we were shouting and I was calling her unforgivable names and she was saying she was going to clinb up to the 20th floor and jump, when the phone rang . . .

I woke up, seeming to hear the echo of the last ring. The phone was there on the floor, under the night table.

I didn't dare pick it up.

78

It must have happened just before dawn, when Manhattan was as deserted as it ever got.

I took a chance on the EE and went up in the elevators to the top of the Empire State Bldg. First time I'd ever been up—also the last, probably. What a sight. Plenty of cars, cabs, trucks, buses rammed into each other & sides of bldgs but lots more just came to natural (!) stop in midstreet or near curb. Very feasible to drive around and out of town, tho probably not thru tunnels. GW Bridge shd be okay, with its 8 lanes. Have to get out of town one day anyhow, so best explore in advance.

Planes. No sign that any crashed but bet lots did somewhere. Everything looks orderly at NY airports.

Fires. Few black spots—signs of recent fires. Nothing major.

Harbor & rivers. Some ships, lots of boats drifting around loose. No sign of collisions; nothing big capsized.

Animals. Dog packs here and there. Sound of their barking rises high. *Nasty* sound. Birds, all kinds.

Air very dry.

Down in the street again, Rolfe began to think about the animals other than the dogs that ran in packs. How long would it be until the bigger ones—the wolves and bears and mountain lions—found their way into the city? He decided to visit Abercrombie & Fitch and arm himself with something heavier than the pistol he carried. Big-bore stuff, whatever they called it.

Rolfe was admiring an elephant gun in the fantastic store (Hemingway had shopped here, and probably Martin and Osa Johnson and Frank Buck and others from the lost past) when he remembered another sound he'd heard from the top of the Empire State Building. It had puzzled him, but now he could identify it. It had been the trumpeting of an elephant. An elephant in Manhattan? The circus wasn't in town— He knew then, but for the moment he pushed aside the thought and its implications.

After he had picked out the guns, and a wicked gas-operated underwater javelin for good measure, he outfitted himself in safari clothes. Khaki shorts and high socks, a big-pocketed bush jacket, a sun helmet. Hurrah for Captain Spalding! He looked a true Marxman, he thought, humming the song Groucho had sung and admiring himself in a full-length mirror.

He took a cartridge belt and boxes of shells and first-aid and water-purification kits and a trapper's knife and a light-weight trail ax and a compass and binoculars and snowshoes and deerskin gloves and a tough pair of boots. He staggered out into Madison Avenue and dumped everything

79

into the back of the cream-colored Lincoln convertible he was driving that day.

The trumpeting of the elephant had come from the Central Park Zoo, of course. He drove in from Fifth Avenue and parked near the restaurant opposite the sea lions' pool. He could see three of them lying quietly on a stone ledge, just above the water, watching him. He wondered when they'd last been fed.

First, though, he went to the administration building and let himself in with lock-picking tools. He had become adept at the burglary trade. He found a set of what seemed to be master keys and tried them first at the aviary. They worked.

The names of the birds, on the faded wooden plaques, were as colorful as their plumage. There was a Papuan lory, a sulphur-crested cockatoo, the chiffchaff and kookaburra bird, laughing jackass and motmot, chachalaca, drongo and poor old puffin. He opened their cages and watched their tentative, gaudy passage to freedom.

A pelican waddled out comically, suspicion in its round eyes. He ducked a hawk and cowered from a swift, fierce eagle. An owl lingered, blinking, until he shooed it toward the doors. He left to the last two brooding vultures, hesitating to free creatures so vile. But there was a role for scavengers, too. He opened their cage and ran, to get outdoors before they did.

After the cacophony of the aviary, he was surprised at the silence as he neared the monkey house. He'd have to be damned careful about the gorilla, which obviously had to be shot. The big chimps were nothing to fool around with, either. But the monkey house was empty. The signs were there and the smell remained but the apes, big and little, were not. Could they have freed themselves? But all the cages were locked.

Puzzled, he went on to the smaller mammals, freeing the harmless ones, the raccoons, the mongooses, the deflowered skunks, the weasels and prairie dogs—even the spiny porcupine, which looked over its shoulder at him as it shuffled toward the doors.

He freed the foxes, too, and they bounded off as if to complete an interrupted mission. "Go get the rats," Rolfe yelled after them.

He marked the location of the wolves and the big cats. He'd come back to them with his guns.

Last of all he freed the lone elephant, scarcely grown, whose trumpet call had summoned him. The elephant—an unofficial sign said it was a female, Geraldine—followed him at a distance almost to the car, then broke into a clumsy trot and drank from the sea lions' pool.

As Rolfe was returning to the cages with the guns he knew why there weren't any monkeys. The big and little apes were hominids, like man. Their evolutionary climb had doomed them, too.

He killed the beasts of prey. It was an awful business. He was not a good shot even at close range and the executions took many bullets. A sinuous, snarling black panther took six before he was sure. The caged beasts, refusing to stand still for the mercy killings, made it hot, bloody, stinking work. He guessed it was necessary.

Finally he was done. Quivering and sweating, he returned to the car. The sea lions honked and swam across to his side of the pool. He could see now that there were three babies and two adults.

What was he to do with them? He couldn't bring himself to a final butchery. And what was he to do about all the other captive animals—in the Bronx Zoo uptown, in zoos all over the world? He couldn't be a one-man Animal Rescue League.

Rolfe had a momentary fantasy in which he enticed the sea lions into the car (four in the back, one in the front) and drove them to the East River, where they flopped into the water and swam toward the sea, honking with gratitude.

But he knew that in his present state of exhaustion he couldn't lift even the babies, and there was no way for them to get out of their enclosure unaided. Maybe he could come back with a truck and plank and fish to tempt them with. He left the problem, and that of the Bronx and Prospect Parks Zoos and the Aquarium (not to get too far afield) and started the car.

Geraldine looked after him. He would have liked a little trumpet of farewell but she had found some long grass and was eating.

As he drove back to the Living End through the wider streets, weaving carefully around the stalled cars, his mind was full of the other trapped beasts, great and small, starving and soon to go mad from thirst, as if in punishment for having outlived man.

Only then did the other thought crash into his consciousness—what of the millions of pets, trapped in the houses of their vanished owners? Dogs and cats, unable to open the refrigerators or the cans in the pantries. Some would have the craft to tear open packages of dried food and would learn to drink from leaking faucets or from toilet bowls. But at best they could prolong their miserable existence for only a few more days.

What was he to do about the pets? What could he do? Run around the city freeing them? Where would he start? Should he free all those on the north sides of odd-numbered streets? Or those on the ground floors of houses in named streets beginning with consonants? What were the rules? How did you play God?

He resolved not to talk to Siss about it. He wouldn't have her breaking her heart over a billion doomed animals; she had enough to mourn.

From his notebooks:
What should I call today? Rolfeday? Sissuary the 13th? Year Zero?

Shd hav kept track but don't really know how many days it's been since I walked out of Bill's storage vault and found myself 1/2 the human pop. of the whole furshlugginer world.

Asked Siss. *She* remembers. It has been exactly 11 days since the holocaust. She accounted for every one of them. Moren I cld do: they started to run together for me after the first three.

OK, so it's Sissuary the 11th, Year One, Anno Rolfe. *Some*body's got to keep a record.

How many days in Sissuary? We'll see. Got to name the second month before closing out the first.

It was difficult for him to look back and remember exactly when he had first realized with certainty that this was the woman with whom he was fated to spend the rest of his life, when it had dawned on him that this moron was to be his bosom companion, that he had to take care of her, provide for her, *talk* to her (and *listen* to her), answer her stupid questions, *sleep* with her!

The realization must have come about the time he began to experience his stomachaches. They weren't pains; they were more like a gnawing at the vitals of his well-being, a pincers movement by the enemy that was trapping him where he didn't want to be, with someone he didn't want to be with, a leaden weight that was smothering his freedom.

Some of her traits nearly drove him out of his mind. He was oversensitive, he supposed, but he had to wince and tried to close his ears every time she converted a sneeze into a clearly-enunciated "Ah *choo!*" and waited for him to bless her.

Worse because more frequent was her way of grunting audibly when she was picking up something, or pushing something or moving something around. This was to let him know that she was hard at work, for him. After a while he forced himself to praise her while she was at it—her diligence, her strength, her unselfishness—and she stopped making so much noise. He hated himself for being a hypocrite and felt sure she would see through him, but she never did and in the end his exaggerated praise became a way of life. It stood him in good stead later, when he had to tell her white lies about the degree of his affection for her and the great esteem in which he held her.

82

From his notebooks:

Asked Siss if she'd ever read a book and she said oh yes the Good Book, Parts of it. It used to comfort her a lot more in the old days, apparently. She's read two books all the way thru—Uncle Wiggily and Japanese Fairy Tales, and parts of a Tarzan book. She sometimes used to look at the paper—read the comics, the horoscope, picture captions, the TV listings. Lord save us from ever having to hold a literary conversation.

To be fair I've tried to remember the last 10 books I read before doom. Probably be a pretty stupid list if I was following my usual random reading pattern—off on an Erle Stanley Gardner or James Bond kick and reading everything available all at once.

Aside from his obligation to humanity to sire a new race, what was there for him to do? Rolfe considered the possibilities, dividing them into two groups: necessities (duties or obligations) and pastimes (including frivolities).

Under necessities he put:

Keep a journal for posterity, if any. He was already doing that.

Give Siss the equivalent of a grammar school education; more if she could take it.

Try to elevate her taste for the sake of the unborn children she would one day influence.

Keep his family fed and sheltered. Would it be necessary to clothe them, except for warmth in the winter? Nudity might be more practical, as well as healthier.

Then he jotted down on a separate piece of paper "Obligation to self paramount" and looked at it. He felt that he had to come first, with his duty to Siss a little lower (on the paper and in his estimation) because he was smarter than she was and therefore more worth saving.

Then he had another look and amended it. Siss was more worth saving because she was a woman and able to reproduce her kind.

But not without his help, of course.

Finally he put himself and Siss together at the top of the list. No good saving one without the other.

Pastimes. Take up a sport to keep fit. What one-man sports were there? Woodchopping? Fat chance. Too blister-prone, he. Hiking? Maybe he and Siss should hike around the world to make absolutely positively sure there was nobody else. Or around the eastern United States, anyhow. Or just up and down the Hudson River Valley? Somehow walking didn't seem to be his sport, either.

83

He might take up cooking. Men had always been the best chefs and now ingenuity would be needed to make nourishing and palatable meals from what was available to them. They couldn't depend on canned and preserved food forever. Okay, he'd be a cook. Of course that was a sport that tended to put pounds on, not take them off. He'd better find an antidote, like swimming or handball.

How about collecting? What—money? Diamonds? Great art? Neither money nor diamonds, obviously; neither had any intrinsic value in a World of Two—and then art was best left where it was, as well-protected as anything in the poor old world. If he wanted Siss to see a Rembrandt or an Andrew Wyeth, he'd take her to it.

From his notebooks:

Collecting old-fashioned windup phonographs against the day when no elec. Also old-fashioned 78 records. Got to keep so many things I can't reproduce.

Music. Good; Siss likes. She enjoys Tchaikowsky, Wagner and Beethoven (what wildness must stir within her poor head sometimes!) She'll sit still for Bach. I can't complain.

We're both crazy about Cole Porter, she for the music, I for the words, those great words, so much more ironic now than he had ever meant them to be.

"It's All Right With Me," for instance.

We've found a place. We— Is that the first time I've used the word?

It's far enough away from the city to be really country; beyond the stink and the reminders of dead glory; yet close enough so I can get in for supplies if I need them. I've stored up enough good gassed-up cars so that travel is no problem, but I think I'll try to stay here as much as I can. I used to be a fair woodsman. Let's see how much I remember.

It's peaceful here. My stomachache is better, all of a sudden.

He insisted on thinking of her as a person who had come into his custody and for whom he was responsible. For a long time all he felt toward her was pity; no desire. And for that reason he also pitied himself.

Because she was what she was, it would be unthinkable for her to touch him in any but the most innocent of ways, as she would one of her animal friends.

And when she called him anything but Mr. Ralph, using a word like honey, he was not flattered because he had heard her apply it also to a squirrel, a bluejay and a field mouse.

"Mr. Ralph, can I ask you a favor? Would you mind if you took me for a ride?"

It wasn't that she particularly wanted to go anywhere; apparently her enjoyment lay in sharing the front seat with him; he noticed that she sat very close to him, in almost the exact center of the seat and did not, as he had speculated she might, sit at the far right, next to the window.

For her ride she chose an ornate costume which included a hat, a silk scarf, dark glasses, jacket, blouse and skirt, stockings and half-heel shoes.

She picked the costume at what she called the Monkey Ward store while he shopped down the block for a fairly clean convertible with sound tires and a fair amount of gas in the tank.

They rode out past the quarry. Long ago he had stored away the fact that Quarry Road was the highway probably least littered with debris.

There was one bad place where he had to get off into a field to skirt what looked as if it had been a 50-car chain-reaction smashup. Otherwise, it was good driving all the way to the lake.

He parked near the old boat-launching site and automatically scanned the watery horizon for any sign of sail or smoke. He had never entirely abandoned hopes of finding other people.

He had brought from the liquor store (catty-corner from Monkey Ward's) a fifth of a high-priced Scotch and as they sat looking out over the lake he carefully opened it, preserving the tinfoil for her.

Then he ceremoniously offered her a drink. She declined, as he knew she would, saying:

"Not now, thanks. Maybe some other time." Apparently a piece of etiquette she'd learned was that it was bad manners to refuse anything outright—especially something to eat or drink.

Rolfe said: "I'll have one, though, if you don't mind." And she replied, in what must have been a half-remembered witticism, "Take two, they're small."

He took two in succession, neither small.

The lake was serene, the sun was warm but not hot, a breeze blew from the east and the bugs were infrequent.

"Doesn't it bother you that there's nobody else?" he asked her. "Don't you get *lonesome?*"

But she said: "I'm always lonesome. I was. Now I'm less lonesome than I was. Thanks to you, Mr. Ralph."

Now what could he say to that? So he sat there, touched but scowling out at the horizon, and then he reached for the very old Scotch (the world had still lived when it was bottled) and took a very big swallow. Only later did he think to offer her one.

"Some other time, maybe," she said. "Not right now."

There came a day when her last brassiere lost its hooks and she obtained his dispensation to stop wearing it. And another when her blouses lost their buttons and refused to stay closed by the mere tucking of their tails into her skirts, and he told her it didn't matter in the least; until finally her last rags fell from her.

She said to him: "You're my Mr. Ralph, honey, and it's not wrong to be this way with you, is it, Mr. Ralph?"

This touched him so that he took her naked, innocent body in his arms and kissed the top of her clean, sweet head and he said:

"You're my big little girl and you couldn't do anything wrong if you tried."

And only then, for the first time, he felt a desire for this waif—this innocent in whom the seeds of the whole human race were locked.

She gave him a quick daring kiss on the cheek and ran off, saying: "It's time I started supper now. My gosh, we have to get you fed."

He remembered with shame a pathetic scene early in their life together. They had gone to Monkey Ward's and dressed from the skin out in brand-new evening clothes. He'd had to help her cancel some tasteless combinations but at last she stood before him like an angel. Or, as he'd said: "Damned if you don't look like a Madison Avenue model."

"You shouldn't swear, Mr. Ralph," she said. "But thanks anyhow."

"And you shouldn't talk. You're welcome. Look, we're going to play a game. We're going to a fancy night club. We're going to make believe you're a mute—that you can't talk. No matter what, you must not say a word. Not a word."

"All right, Mr. Ralph."

"Starting right now, damn it! I'm sorry. I mean starting right now. All you can do is nod or smile. You can touch me if you want to. But you can't talk at all. That's part of the game. Do you understand?"

She started to say yes, then caught herself and nodded.

The silent nod from this beautifully gowned woman immediately made her ten times more attractive. Pleased with himself and with her, he gave her his arm and bowed her into the front seat of the Bentley he had searched out for their evening.

The night club had once been a major one, with a resident big-name band. Changing fashion had turned it into a discotheque, so that it had a juke box. He fed it a handful of coins to pay his way into a night of illusion. But the tables were bare and therefore wrong. He found a linen closet and set them with tablecloths and silverware, glasses, candlesticks.

The illusion grew. He found a switch that set in motion a set of colored lights which played on multi-faceted colored globes which hung from the ceiling. Another switch set them spinning slowly.

"What do you do in your spare time?" he asked her, knowing she wouldn't reply but wanting to see how she would react.

She shrugged, smiled a little and shook her head in what he tried to imagine was an attitude that said she had so little spare time that it was negligible.

She was carrying out her part of the bargain. She did it extremely well. She listened without a word to his conversation, looking into his eyes as he pretended they were two among hundreds of elegant diners. He reconstructed talk from pre-holocaust nights out. He pretended she was a girl he had once been engaged to and told her extravagant things. She looked back at him and smiled, as if mockingly, as the old girl would have done. He pretended it was a later time, with the engagement in ruins and him solacing himself with the wife of his best friend, with the best friend's knowledge and consent, and the girl across from him gave him silent looks of profound sympathy. He pretended he had hired a call girl and spoke foully to her. She smiled bravely, her lips quivering, saying nothing.

Angered by the illusion which he had created and which mocked him, he drank too much and continued to abuse her—for herself, now; for doing as he had asked, for remaining silent.

The juke box was playing "Begin the Beguine" and ghostly dancers danced inside the circle of tables, under the soft colored lights. He saw them and cursed them for their nonexistence. He got up, knocking his chair over backwards, and shouted at her.

"Speak!" he said. "I release you from your muteness."

She shook her head, no longer smiling.

"Speak! you misbegotten halfwit! You monstrous bird-brained imposter! You scullery maid in a Schiaparelli gown. Speak, you—mental case."

But still she said nothing; merely looked at him with those deep eyes that seemed to understand and forgive.

Only at the very end of their evening out, when he had drunk himself into a stupor and stared across the room over her right shoulder, as if transfixed by his misery, did she speak. And then she said only:

"We better go home, Mr. Ralph, honey."

Then with a strength greater than his she half carried him there to the car and drove him home and put him to bed. It was a good thing he'd taught her to drive.

He woke up contrite, half remembering that he'd behaved unforgivably.

87

But she forgave him, as perhaps no one else ever would have, using these words:

"I forgive you, Mr. Ralph. You knewd not what you dood."

He was delighted. "Do not what I would," he said. "Had I but dood what I could, who knew what would have been dood?"

"I don't think that's very nice, Mr. Ralph. I said I forgive you. You're supposed to say thank you and say you're sorry, even if you're not sorry."

He was still laughing at her, even after the realization that he had a hangover.

"Okay. I'm sorry even if I'm not sorry and it's very good of you to forgive me for my insufferable behavior, even if nobody asked you to."

"Thank you for saying that, Mr. Ralph. Now I'll fix you a hangover remedy."

"Where did you learn to concoct a hangover remedy, for God's sake?"

"I was a working girl once for a poor man who got intoxicated and his wife. I learned it there."

She gave him no magic potion but an ordinary tomatoey thing laced with pepper and Worcestershire sauce. He drank it down but stubbornly declined to feel better for a full hour. By then he had persuaded Siss he needed a cold beer and she'd brought him one—disapproving but proud of her ingenuity in having produced it, since they kept no store of alcoholic beverages. She must have made an ingenious search to find a cold beer; he was suddenly proud of her.

But, remembering his performance of the night before, he hated himself.

From the holding of hands to the kiss is not so far a thing as from the not holding of hands to the holding.

One thinks of the innocence of holding hands (children do it; men shake hands) but it is a vast journey from a platonic handclasp, over which there is no lingering, to the clasp which is so intense and telegraphic (accompanied, as it may be, by ardent gazing) that it would be a great surprise if the kiss to which it soon led were rebuffed.

And a kiss may lead anywhere. This he knew. He wondered how much she knew, or felt or surmised.

Dared he take her hand to help her across a stream or a rocky place? So far he had taken her arm, holding her firmly just above the elbow as if she were an elderly woman and he a large Boy Scout. He had no wish yet for anything more intimate.

It was a hesitant, tentative beginning to their romance.

"Do you mind my touching you?" he asked. Lately he had found that it

88

gave him pleasure to touch her hair or trace the outline of her ear, or run his finger along her breastbone. Nothing carnal.

"No; I enjoy it."

And so they married. He arranged a ceremony, not only for her sense of propriety but to satisfy his demand for a kind of stability amid chaos.

He made it as elaborate as possible. He found a big flat rock to be the altar. He picked flowers and garlanded them into a headpiece for her. Let her head be covered, though her body was not.

She surprised him with a piece of writing. Crudely written in pencil on a sheet from a lined pad, it said:

"To my Mr. Ralph—

"This is our day to mary to-gether. My day and your day. I feel real good about it even if nobody else cant come. I'll try and make you a good wife with all my heart.

"I know you do the same thing for me because you are kind and good dear Mr. Ralph.

"Your freind and wife
"Cecelia Beamer"

It was the first time he knew what Siss was the nickname for.

Never before a sentimental man, Martin took his wife, Cecelia Beamer Rolfe, in his arms and kissed her with tenderness and affection.

He put her wedding-letter, as he thought of it, away in his desk, where it would be safe.

He wanted to consummate the marriage outdoors. It was a perfect June day, the sun warm, the grass soft, a breeze gentle. Lord knew they could not have asked for greater privacy than that of their own planet. But he felt Siss would have been, if not shocked, embarrassed unless four walls surrounded them.

Therefore he took her indoors, where she removed her flowery hat and put it in water, in a bowl.

Then she turned to him and said: "Tell me what to do, Mr. Ralph. I don't know what to do for you."

"For us, child," he said. "What we do—whatever we do from now on, is for us. Together."

"I like you saying that. Tell me what I should do."

"You don't have to do anything except be loved and love back in whatever way you feel. Anything you feel and do is right because you're my wife and I'm your husband."

"Would it be wrong for me to want you to hold me—here?" she asked. Eyes cast down, she touched her breasts. "I feel as if I'm bursting, I'm so full of love for my Mr. Ralph. I never thought—back then, that—"

He had to stop her talking and kissed her.

For a ring he had made a circlet of grass. When it broke apart or fell to pieces he made her another. In a way, he thought sometimes, it was like renewing the vows.

Once, years later, when he was looking for a pencil he found in the back of her drawer a collection of hundreds of wisps or strands of dried grass. She had saved each of the worn-out rings, obviously. She had kept them in a cheaply-manufactured container of plastic masquerading as leather which said in gaudy lettering "My Jewel Box." These were her gems, her only treasure.

He sometimes asked Siss, suddenly, intently: "Are you my friend?" And she would reply: "Yes, I am. Didn't you think so?" And he would be ashamed, but also gratified, and his heart would swell because she had said more than just Yes.

A woman is a race apart, a friend had told him once. "But," Rolfe added to himself, "this is ridiculous." He and Siss could not have been more unlike mentally.

Well, of course. That could have been true even if he'd had the whole world to choose from. Suppose she had been a selfish, empty-headed teenager; how long could he have stood someone like that? Or she could have been a crone, a hag; work-worn, fat, diseased, crippled. You're a pretty lucky guy, Martin Rolfe; Mr. Ralph, sir!

Sexually they were complementary, for instance. But was that enough? Except for little bits of time, no. But those are very important little bits of time, aren't they, Marty? Precious even. Each a potential conception, a possible person.

But aside from that, no; it was not enough.

But because her entire existence was one of trying to please him, she learned eventually to make acceptable verbal responses and their mating became more satisfactory to him. His stomach ached less frequently.

By trial and error and by diligence, as she learned any task, she learned to speak to him in bed with an approximation of high intelligence, murmuring words of sympathy, approval, surprise, delight, playfulness, even shock at appropriate times. She learned to modulate her laughter, once coarse and raucous. She learned that a few words, sincerely but carefully expressed, did more for their mutual happiness than a babble, or an ungrammatical gush.

Her physical responses, as of a slave to a beloved master, had always been gratifying to him, except for her one unbreakable habit—her tendency to say "Oh, praise God!" whenever she achieved orgasm, or whenever she thought he had.

Once she had asked him to tell her about his life.

"What about it?" he had asked.

"All about it," she'd said.

"That would be a lot to tell."

"As much as you want to, then, Mr. Ralph."

Without a word of introduction he would start: "I was sixteen when I first kissed a girl. Awfully old . . ."

He'd always thought it shameful that he'd been unkissed so long and had never confessed it before. It was years later before Siss got up the courage to say: "Mr. Ralph, you told me once you didn't get a kiss till you were sixteen and that's too bad, but do you know how old I was?"

And he had said No, he didn't and she'd said:

"Twenty-eight, Mr. Ralph: that's how old. So don't you feel so bad."

And he'd asked her, though he was practically certain: "You mean I was the first one ever to kiss you?"

"The first man, except my father, yes, sir, Mr. Ralph. And do you know what? I'm awfully glad it was you that was the first, and that now nobody else ever will. I'm glad of that."

And so he had to postpone his confession. He had been on the point of telling Siss about his previous marriage—how he had chosen his wife from those available for matrimony among the fairly large number of women he had known.

What a fantastically wide choice he had had! The irony of now, with no choice at all, made him marvel to think that he could have picked from among millions, had he known doom was to come and that he and his mate, if she too were saved, would be parents to the entire human race. With what care he would have searched, what exacting tests he would have applied, to screen the mass of womanhood for a fitting mate for the last man!

But because he had expected all life to continue he had chosen from an extremely small sample. Nevertheless he had chosen well.

Later he would tell Siss; not now. He would not hurt her at this time with talk about what, by hindsight, had been a perfect marriage; nor did he feel like hurting himself by contrasting a happy past marriage to an intelligent woman with what he had now.

Now he would tell Siss about another time in his adult past, a sad interlude during which he and his perfect wife had separated and he was living alone.

91

How foolish to have had that quarrel with his dead perfect wife, he thought. How senseless to have lost all the time that they might have had together.

Yet he had achieved a certain peace in his solitude. And their marriage had been stronger when he returned to her.

"I'm going to tell you about a time I was living all alone in a little trailer in the woods," he told Siss.'

He had been a free-lance editor in those days, doctoring doddering magazines, doing articles for his editor friends, and reading for a publishing house, and so was able to avoid the frenzied daily commute. He used the mails and phone and got into the city a couple of times a month.

He enjoyed an occasional dinner or cocktail party in his exurb; but he valued his privacy enough to decline many invitations and to withdraw to his trailer.

Rolfe himself never entertained. His truck-back trailer home was unsuited for anything but the shortest of visits. He'd have the mailman in for a drink of bourbon on Christmas Eve, or chat with the man who came around to collect for the volunteer ambulance corps, or play ten-second-move chess with the route man who delivered the only food Rolfe ate at home—eggs, and the butter he fried them in.

The truck-back home normally sat in the middle of Rolfe's eighteen acres—far enough out of town so that there were woods to surround him and a dammed-up stream in which to swim, but close enough for an electric power line to be run in.

If Rolfe's choice of this way to live during his separation was an eccentricity, then he was eccentric. One other thing about him was a little odd. He had nailed a sign to a tree at the beginning of the track which led off the country road to his place. It said:

PRIVATE ROAD
MINED

The police came around after he put up the sign, which he'd burned into the end of an egg crate with an electric pen. The policemen, a lieutenant and a sergeant, left their car at the county road and walked carefully along the edge of Rolfe's track to the pickup truck in the clearing near the dammed-up stream. A pheasant moved without haste into some undergrowth as they came up to the door over the tailgate.

Rolfe invited them in, making room for them to sit down by lifting a manuscript off the one easy chair and motioning the sergeant to the camp chair in front of the typewriter on the bracket that folded down from the wall.

Rolfe sat on the single bunk along the driver's side, having first got cokes out of the tiny refrigerator. He knew better than to offer liquor to policemen on duty. They chatted for a while before the lieutenant said: "About your sign, Mr. Rolfe; we've had some complaints."

"Call me Martin. Complaints? I like my privacy, that's all."

"My name's Sol," the lieutenant said, "and this is Eric." They shook hands all round again, now that the first-name basis had been established, and Sol said: "About the road being mined. Sure it's private property and nobody respects the principle of that more than I do, but somebody might get hurt. Somebody who couldn't read, maybe, or who wandered in after dark—not relly meaning to trespass, you know."

"Sure," Rolfe said. "I can understand that."

"Besides," the sergeant—Eric—said, "anybody with war surplus ammunition was supposed to have turned it in years ago. It's the law."

"I don't know what you mean," Rolfe said. "I haven't booby-trapped the road. I wouldn't hurt a rabbit, much less a human being. Why, I'm so soft-hearted I don't even fish the stream."

Sol said: "I get it. You just put up the sign to keep people away—like 'Beware of the Dog,' even if you don't have a dog."

"And there really aren't any bouncing Bettys out there then?" Eric said. "I'm relieved. Believe me, we walked mighty easy along the edge."

Martin Rolfe grinned. "Gentlemen, I think I begin to understand. And it's all my fault because I'm such a poor speller. What I was trying to do was to call attention to the fact that it isn't a public road or a hiking trail or a place for young vandals to go if they have a hankering to break windows or set fires in out-of-the-way places. I believe there've been a few such incidents around town."

"Too many," Sol said. "But I still don't know what you mean about being a poor speller."

"What I intended to say on the sign, I guess, was 'Mind you, this is a private road.' It's a kind of New England expression."

"I've heard it," Eric said. "They have signs like that in London, where my wife's from—she was a war bride, you know, lieutenant—that say 'Mind the step.' "

"That's m-i-n-d, not m-i-n-e-d," Sol said.

"Is that right?" Rolfe asked with a grin. "I told you I wasn't much of a speller. I'd better change the sign, then, hadn't I?"

Instead of replying directly, Sol asked: "Ever have trouble with kids back in here?"

"Kids and grown-ups both," Rolfe said. "Different kinds of trouble. Kids broke a window one night. I was asleep and got a shower of broken glass all over my face. Another time a big brave man with a gun shot the hell out of a mother partridge and her brood and left them flopping around. He wasn't even planning to eat them. Did you ever put a living thing out of its misery with your bare hands, Sol? That same day I put up the sign. The partridges and I haven't been bothered since.''

Sol got up and let himself out into the clearing. ''I had to kill a doe once that some mighty hunter put a hole into but didn't think worth following into the brush.'' Eric went out with Martin Rolfe behind him and all three walked along the middle of the track to the county road. Birds chirped at them and a leisurely rabbit hopped away.

At the blacktopped road Martin Rolfe went to his sign. He took a pencil out of his shirt pocket and scratched a vertical line through the *E* in *mined*. Then he joined the *N* and *D* with a copyreader's mark.

The sergeant said, ''I don't know that that's too highly visible. Besides, a couple of rains'll wash it off.''

''Oh, come on, Eric,'' the lieutenant said, getting into the car. ''It's as plain as day.''

''Thanks, lieutenant,'' Martin said, going over to the police car to say goodbye. ''I never could spell worth a damn.''

''Oh yeah?'' Eric said. ''I'll bet you can outspell both of us any day.'' He was looking back at the sign as he got into the car and he tripped, so that he had to grab for the door to steady himself.

''Mind the step,'' Martin said.

It was achingly poignant for him to leaf through the pages of a copy he'd saved of *The New York Times Magazine.*

How lovable and childlike seemed the people doing the weird things fashion advertising demanded of them! How earnest were the statements made in the articles and the letter pages. For example, there was the ironic, the heart-breakingly laughable article about the population explosion— about the insupportable hundreds of millions there soon would be in India, or the six billion there'd be on Earth in just a few more years.

Would that there were only as many people as had read that particular Sunday issue of the *Times.* A million and a half? World enough. Or even if there existed on Earth only the few hundred people it had taken to write, edit and print that particular issue of *The New York Times Magazine.* Even if there were only *one* other than Siss and himself. One man to play chess with, or to philosophize with.

He thrust away from him the thought that the third person on Earth might be another woman. It was too dangerous, too explosive a thought. Would he betray Siss for a normal woman? Certainly he would never abandon her, but betrayal was certain—she would be so easy to fool. What form, other than an intellectual one, would it take? Would he take the new woman blatantly as his mate, with a facile explanation to Siss? Would the new one try to banish Siss (he'd never stand for that—would he?), or decree a demeaning role for her in a reorganized household—something he might rationalize himself into accepting? (He could hear the new one saying: "You want our children—Earth's only children—to be intelligent, don't you? You don't want the new world peopled with feeble-minded brats, do you?")

His thoughts went back to the possible consequences if a third person were male. Suppose the man were not a chess player? Suppose he were a mere brute, with brutish instincts? Would Martin have to share Siss with him, Eskimo style? Even if he could bring himself (or Siss) to accept such an arrangement, how long could it continue without an explosion?

No—as long as he was fantasizing it would be simpler to dream up two other people, a man and a woman who had already arranged their own lives, who had made the adjustment.

Still—how long could two couples—and only two—live side by side without something boiling over? Wife-swapping was too prevalent an institution in the bad old days, when there was all kinds of other entertainment, not to be a daily temptation in an all-but-depopulated world.

No—it would be best to have no third or fourth person—not unless there could be an infinity of others besides . . .

Ah, but he was so *lonely!*

"I'm going to the city," he told Siss.

They had done without the city for a long time. They had made do with the things they had, or could make; they'd let their clothing drop away and hadn't replaced it; they'd grown their own food; made their country house the center of their universe. But now he wanted to go back.

She must have seen something in his eyes. "Let me go for you," she said. "Just tell me what you want."

Sometimes she chose such an ironic way of saying things that he fleetingly suspected her of having not only intelligence but wit.

"Just tell you what I want! As if—" He stopped. As if he could tell her. As if he knew.

He knew only that he had to get away for a little while. He wanted to be alone, with his own memories of a populated Earth.

He also wanted a drink.

Long ago he had made it a rule never to have liquor in the house. It would be too great a temptation to have it handy. He could see himself degenerating into a drunken bum. With an unlimited supply close at hand and a devoted woman to do all the work that needed to be done, he could easily slip into an animalistic role—become a creature with a whiskey-sodden, atrophied brain.

A fitting father and mother to the world such a pair would be!

And so he had made his rule: drink all you want when you have to—in the city—but never bring it home.

And so he had told Siss: "I don't know what I want, exactly. I just want to go to the city."

And she had said: "All right, Mr. Ralph, if you have to."

There was her perception again, if that's what it was. "If you have to," she'd said, though he'd talked of want, not need.

"I do," he said. "But I'll come back. Is there anything I can bring you?" She looked around the kitchen and began to say something, then stopped and said instead: "Nothing we really need. You just go, Mr. Ralph, and take as long as you have to. It'll give me a chance to go do that berry-picking I been wanting to."

She was so sweet that he almost decided not to go. But then he kissed her—very thankful, just then, that she was his Siss and not some too-bright shrew of a problem wife—and went. He drove in, naked in a Cadillac.

He had rolled the swivel chair out of the store onto the sidewalk and was sitting in it in the afternoon sunshine. Beside him on the pavement were half a dozen bottles, each uncapped. He was talking to himself.

"As the afternoon sun, blood-red through the haze of the remnants of a once overpopulated world, imperceptibly glides to its bed, one of the two known survivors becomes quietly plastered." He had a drink on that, then went on:

"What thoughts pass through the mind of this pitiful creature, this naked relic of a man left to eke out the rest of his days on a ruined planet?

"Does he ever recall the glory that once was his and that of his fellows? Or is he so sunk in misery—in the mere scratching of a bare existence from an arid soil—that he has forgotten the heights to which his kind once had risen? Subject pauses in thought and reaches for bottle. Drinks deeply from bottle, but not so deeply as to induce drunken sickenness. Aim of subject is quiet plasterization, happy drunkdom, a nonceness of Nirvana, with harm to none and bitterness never. Sicken drunkenness?

"A respite of reverie, perhaps, as subject casts mind back to happy past. Mr. Martin Rolfe in Happier Days."

He picked up his *New York Times Magazine* and leafed through it. It was almost as good as having another drink. There they were—they couldn't have been more than 17—leaping in their panty girdles to show the freedom

96

of action and the elasticity of the crotch. He remembered once having heard a newsman, waiting in the rain for the arrival of a President, say: "Being a reporter is essentially an undignified occupation." So had been being a model, obviously.

Things of the past . . . He thought: "A title for my memoirs—*Things of the Past*." He took up the *Times* again and turned to an ad of a debonair young man in a revolving door holding a copy of the *Wall Street Journal*. "I dreamt I was trapped in a revolving door in my Arcticweave tropical worsted," Rolfe said, summing up the situation. He looked like the 28-year-old Larchmont type; five years out of college, with a Master's, two kids, wife beginning to drink a little bit too much. "If he's trapped there long enough he may read the paper right through to the shipping pages and ship out to the islands."

Rolfe looked pityingly at the trapped Larchmont type, armed against his predicament only with his Arcticweave suit, his *Wall Street Journal* and, presumably, a wallet full of wife-and-baby pictures, credit cards and a commutation ticket issued by a railroad company petitioning to suspend passenger service.

"You poor bastard," Rolfe said.

Of course he was saying it to himself, too. He said it all the way home: "You poor bastard. You poor bastard."

Siss was waiting for him in the cool garden. Gently she led him indoors. She said, with only the slightest hint of reproach (he could stand that much—he deserved more): "You been drinking too much again, Mr. Ralph. You know it's bad for you."

"You're right, Siss. Absolutely right."

"You got to take care of yourself. I try to, but you got to try, too."

Tenderly she put him to bed. He knew then, among other times, how much he needed her, and he struggled to say something nice to her before he dropped off to sleep. Finally he said: "You know, Siss, you're nicer than all those crazy leaping girls in the York Times." That's what she called it, the York Times. "You got a lot more sense, too, than they look as if they had."

From his notebooks:

Got drunk saft. Downtown. Dangerous. Not fair to Siss. Liable get et up by dogs while stinko. Bad show.

Can't bring bottle home, tho. Too great a temptation to get sozzled daily and twice on Sunday.

Why is Sunday worse than other days? I tried to rename it but Siss insisted we keep it. She also demanded it come every seven days, just like in good old days. Had to give in. So much for calendar reform.

97

He sought other ways of escaping. He hiked and climbed and explored.

Once he found a spot on the brow of a hill from which one (that is, he) could see for miles but from which no work of man was visible except the top of a silo at the top of a similar hill across a wide valley.

Having found the spot, he cleared wild strawberry plants from beneath a young maple tree, leaving the ferns and the cushiony moss, and lay down to rest. It had been a strenuous climb, and hot, and now the insects were upon him. But though the flies buzzed they did not often land and the mosquitoes were torpid and easily slapped. After a while—it was almost noon (as if the hour mattered)—he had a couple of swallows from the flask he carried in his rucksack and ate some cheese. He thought of the flask as his iron rations.

As he rummaged in the rucksack he found a roll of plastic tape he'd brought along to help him blaze a trail. He hadn't needed it; instead he'd marked his way by cutting branches with a long-handled pruning tool.

But as he lay in the solitude he had sought out and found (how odd to seek solitude in an empty world!), under one of the myriad of trees, where the only sounds were of buzzing insects, chirping birds, the soughing of trees in a soft wind—he knew what to do with the plastic tape. He printed something on a little square of paper, small but legible, and, with the tape, attached it to the lowest bough of his young maple. Now he lay under it, savoring what he had done.

The little sign said: THIS TREE RESERVED.

One June night it rained in great, warm, wind-driven sheets. He had not experienced such a storm since a visit a decade earlier to the tropics.

The pleasure he took in the soaking, bath-temperature rain was enhanced by the danger from the lightning. It stabbed down from the sky as if seeking him out, destroying and burning only yards away, as if it would be a great cosmic joke to strike that one spot on the surface of the Earth and kill the last man.

He defied it, prancing wildly, then halting deliberately as if transfixed when it flashed, posing with outthrust or upthrust arms, yelling, defying the thing or Being that had sent the storm, loosing his pent-up frustrations, his disappointments and hates in the elemental power of the storm.

He had trapped the beast in a pit, unfairly. It had nearly exhausted itself in attempts to leap the sheer walls. At least he hadn't lined the bottom with spikes.

Rolfe could have killed it from above, poisoned it, let it starve. Instead he jumped into the pit, armed with two knives, to risk mauling and death.

He realized his folly instantly. The creature was far from helpless. Its claws were sharp, though its movements were clumsy in the cramped pit-bottom, and its fetid breath was as much a weapon as its fangs.

Only by the sheerest of luck, he felt, did he avoid the claws and fangs long enough to plunge first one knife then the other into the beast's heart.

As its death struggles subsided he lay there, his face buried in the back of its neck, hugging the thing he'd killed, a sadness coming over him as he felt the fading heartbeat.

Later he skinned the beast. He and Siss ate the meat and slept under the pelt. But first he had buried the head, in tribute to a worthy antagonist, a kind of salute to another male.

And unto them was born a son.

Siss seemed to know just what to do, by instinct. Clumsily he helped. He cut the umbilical with a boiled pair of scissors. Made a knot. Washed the red little thing.

Eventually Siss lay quiet, dry, serene, holding her swaddled child. He sat on the floor next to the bed and looked and looked at the mother and child. A holy picture, he thought. He sat for hours, staring, wondering. She looked back at him, silent, wondering.

The new human being slept, serene.

It could not have been more perfect.

His son. His boy. His and hers but, he felt it fair enough to say, mostly his.

His son Adam. What else had there been to name him? Adam. Trite but noble. He had considered calling him Ralph, but only briefly. It would be too comical to have his mother go around introducing him to their near circle of friends—relatives all, come to think of it—as Ralph Ralph.

There'd be no need for introductions for many years, of course, in a closed society such as theirs. The years did pass.

There was his son, tall for his age, straight, brown, good with his hands . . .

But bright? Intelligent? How was a father to know? A prejudiced parent sees only the good, ignores what he doesn't want to accept, can be oblivious to faults obvious to anyone else.

He talked to him and got gratifying responses. But wouldn't almost any response be gratifying to a parent? Parents are easily satisfied. Especially fathers of sons.

Had he conditioned himself to the point where he would be satisfied if his son showed more than animal intelligence? The conditioning encompassed an agony of watching as his son grew—watching for signs of mental retardation, of idiocy, of dullness, or bigheadedness, of torpor.

And then they had a daughter.

From his notebooks:

My son. Brown as a penny. Naked as a jaybird. Slender, muscled, handsome, active, good with his hands.

Bright? Seems so. Obviously too soon to really tell.

Five years old and just made his first kill. Wild dog, attacking our goat. Got him in the right eye with a .30-30 at————yards (measure and fill in).

Strong and brave and skilled and good looking.

Let's hope intelligent, too.

Please, God.

My daughter. My precious, my beauty. What a delight you are, with your serene smile and your loving way of wrapping your arms around my leg and looking up at Old Daddy. You're your mother's child, aren't you? So good, so quiet. But you're quick on your feet and your reflexes (I've tested them) are sound. I think we're all right.

The Diary of Siss

(Siss was not very faithful about her diary. The printed word was not her medium. Although her intentions were obviously good, there are fewer than a dozen entries in all, and they are reproduced below. She did not date them. The handwriting in the last entry is slightly better than that of the first, but maybe only because she was using a sharper pencil. A more revealing diary probably would be found in her heart, if that could be read, or in her children.)

Mr. Ralph told me write things down when they big & inportant I will start now. Today Mr. Ralph married me.

Very happy today. Learning to please my husband.

Very very happy. Today moved to our country house I like it better than the big city.

Today I had a baby, a boy.

My word for today is contentment. I have to spell it and tell what it means. Mr. Ralph says I need an eddukaton, he will eddukate me.

My word for today is education. Mr. Ralph seen what I wrote in my dairy yestdy.

I have 2 words for today diary & yesterday. Also saw not seen.

Today I had a baby, a girl. Ralph said now everything is going to be alright.

And presumably it was. Having doubled the population, the human race seemed to be on a firm footing. There was love in the world; a growing, proud family, and a new self-assurance in Siss—note that he was Ralph now, not Mr. Ralph. We may be sure, though, that the strict if loving father gave her two words for tomorrow: all right. A father, a mother, a son, a daughter. A little learning, a lot of love.

In the summer of his eighth year Adam and his father were in the woods back of the pasture, in the little clearing at the side of the stream that ran pure and sparkling before it broadened into the shallow muddy pond the livestock used. Martin and the boy were eating lunch after a morning of woodcutting and conversation.

Adam, naked like his father, had asked: "Am I going to grow some more hair, like you?"

And Martin said: "Sure, when you get bigger. When you begin to be a man."

And Adam had compared his smooth skin with his father's hard, muscled, hairy body and said: "Mom's got hair in that place, too, but she's different."

So Martin explained, sweating even though he was sitting still now, and his son took it all in, nodding, just as if it were no more important than knowing why the cow had her calf. It was obvious that until now Adam had not connected the function of the bull with the dropping of the calf. Martin explained, in human terms.

"That's pretty neat," Adam said. "When do I get to do it?"

Martin tried to keep his voice matter-of-fact. How do you instruct your son in incest?

The explanation was completed, finally, and it was Martin's turn to ask a question. "Think carefully about this, son. If you could save the life of one person—your mother or me but not the other—which would you save?"

Adam answered without hesitation. "I'd save Mother, of course."

Martin looked hard at his strong, handsome son and asked the second part of the question. "Why?"

Adam said: "I didn't mean to hurt your feelings, Dad. I'd save both of you if I could—"

"I know you would. You've been a crack shot since you were five. But there might be only one chance. Your answer is the only possible one, but I have to know why you gave it."

The boy frowned as he struggled to reason out the reply he had made instinctively. "Because—if necessary—she and I could—" Then it came out in a rush: "Because she could be the mother to the world and I could be the father."

Martin shuddered as if a long chill had just passed. It was all right. He embraced his fine, strong, *intelligent* son and wept.

After a little while Siss appeared, walking the path beside the stream, naked as the two of them but different, as Adam had said, and riding the naked baby on her hip.

"Thought we'd join the menfolks for lunch," she said. "I picked some berries for dessert." She carried the blackberries in a mesh bag and some had been bruised, staining the tanned skin a delicate blue just below her slim waist.

Martin said: "You sure make a good-looking picture, you two. Come here and give me a kiss."

The baby kissed him first, then toddled off to smooch up for Adam, who gave her a dutiful peck.

Their father held open his arms and Siss sat beside him, putting the berries aside. She rested her head on his shoulder, serene. Martin folded her to him and kissed her eyes and cheeks and hair and neck and finally her lips, there in the sunshine, by the side of the pure stream, in the presence of all the world.

"Do you think—" she started to say, but Martin said "Hush, now. It's all right. Everything's all right, Siss darling." She sighed and relaxed against him. He had never called her darling before. He kissed her again for a long time and she gradually lay back on the soft ground and raised one knee and bent the other to accommodate her husband.

The baby lost interest and went to wade in the stream but Adam watched, his elbow on his knee, and once he said, "Don't crush the blackberries," and reached out to get them. He ate a handful, slowly.

Then he heard his mother gasp, "Oh, praise God!" and after a moment both his parents became still. And after a little while longer he looked to see that the baby was okay and then went to the intertwined, gently-breathing bodies, which were more beautiful than anything he had ever seen.

Adam knelt beside them and kissed his father's neck and his mother's lips. Siss opened her arms and enfolded her son, too.

And Adam asked, with his face against his mother's cheek, which was wet and warm, "Is this what love is?"

And his mother answered, "Yes, honey," and his father said, in a muffled kind of way, "It's everything there is, son."

Adam reached out for the berries and put one in his mother's mouth and one in his father's and one in his. Then he got up to give one to the baby.

To Philip José Farmer, August 1, 1966:

> Dear Phil,
> I like "Don't Wash the Carats" and am putting through a contract . . . but am not sure I understand it. Did the patient's wife leave in disgust when his diamonds turned back into hemorrhoids? Or did she leave with them while they were still diamonds, & in this case, should the line perhaps read " 'She took off for parts unknown with my surgeon just after my hemorrhoid operation' "? Please advise.

If you think this is raunchy, you should have seen the next one he sent me.

To Robert P. Mills, January 2, 1967:

> Dear Bob,
> Thank you for letting me see these. . . . As I told you on the phone, I am entranced by the idea of a spaceship flying into a girl's goona, but don't think Phil has done anything with it here, or made the preparations for it terribly convincing.

DON'T WASH THE CARATS

by Philip José Farmer

The knife slices the skin. The saw rips into bone. Gray dust flies. The plumber's helper (the surgeon is economical) clamps its vacuum onto the plug of bone. Ploop! Out comes the section of skull. The masked doctor, Van Mesgeluk, directs a beam of light into the cavern of cranium.

He swears a large oath by Hippocrates, Aesculapius and the Mayo Brothers. The patient doesn't have a brain tumor. He's got a diamond.

The assistant surgeon, Beinschneider, peers into the well and, after him, the nurses.

"Amazing!" Van Mesgeluk says. "The diamond's not in the rough. It's cut!"

"Looks like a 58-facet brilliant, 127.1 carats," says Beinschneider, who has a brother-in-law in the jewelry trade. He sways the light at the end of the drop cord back and forth. Stars shine; shadows run.

"Of course, it's half-buried. Maybe the lower part isn't diamond. Even so . . ."

"Is he married?" a nurse says.

Van Mesgeluk rolls his eyes. "Miss Lustig, don't you ever think of anything but marriage?"

"Everything reminds me of wedding bells," she replies, thrusting out her hips.

"Shall we remove the growth?" Beinschneider says.

"It's malignant," Van Mesgeluk says. "Of course, we remove it."

He thrusts and parries with a fire and skill that bring cries of admiration and a clapping of hands from the nurses and even cause Beinschneider to groan a bravo, not unmingled with jealousy. Van Mesgeluk then starts to insert the tongs but pulls them back when the first lightning bolt flashes beneath and across the opening in the skull. There is a small but sharp crack and, very faint, the roll of thunder.

"Looks like rain," Beinschneider says. "One of my brothers-in-law is a meteorologist."

"No. It's heat lightning," Van Mesgeluk says.

"With thunder?" says Beinschneider. He eyes the diamond with a lust his wife would give diamonds for. His mouth waters; his scalp turns cold. Who owns the jewel? The patient? He has no rights under this roof. Finders keepers? Eminent domain? Internal Revenue Service?

104

"It's mathematically improbable, this phenomenon," he says. "What's California law say about mineral rights in a case like this?"

"You can't stake out a claim!" Van Mesgeluk roars. "My God, this is a human being, not a piece of land!"

More lightning cranks whitely across the opening, and there is a rumble as of a bowling ball on its way to a strike.

"I said it wasn't heat lightning," Van Mesgeluk growls.

Beinschneider is speechless.

"No wonder the e.e.g. machine burned up when we were diagnosing him," Van Mesgeluk says. "There must be several thousand volts, maybe a hundred thousand, playing around down there. But I don't detect much warmth. Is the brain a heat sink?"

"You shouldn't have fired that technician because the machine burned up," Beinschneider says. "It wasn't her fault, after all."

"She jumped out of her apartment window the next day," Nurse Lustig says reproachfully. "I wept like a broken faucet at her funeral. And almost got engaged to the undertaker." Lustig rolls her hips.

"Broke every bone in her body, yet there wasn't a single break in her skin," Van Mesgeluk says. "Remarkable phenomenon."

"She was a human being, not a phenomenon!" Beinschneider says.

"But psychotic," Van Mesgeluk replies. "Besides, that's my line. She was 33 years old but hadn't had a period in ten years."

"It was that plastic intra-uterine device," Beinschneider says. "It was clogged with dust. Which was bad enough, but the dust was radioactive. All those tests . . ."

"Yes," the chief surgeon says. "Proof enough of her psychosis. I did the autopsy, you know. It broke my heart to cut into that skin. Beautiful. Like Carrara marble. In fact, I snapped the knife at the first pass. Had to call in an expert from Italy. He had a diamond-tipped chisel. The hospital raised hell about the expense, and Blue Cross refused to pay."

"Maybe she was making a diamond," says Nurse Lustig. "All that tension and nervous energy had to go somewhere."

"I always wondered where the radioactivity came from," Van Mesgeluk says. "Please confine your remarks to the business at hand, Miss Lustig. Leave the medical opinions to your superiors."

He peers into the hole. Somewhere between heaven of skull and earth of brain, on the horizon, lightning flickers.

"Maybe we ought to call in a geologist. Beinschneider, you know anything about electronics?"

"I got a brother-in-law who runs a radio and TV store."

"Good. Hook up a step-down transformer to the probe, please. Wouldn't want to burn up another machine."

"An e.e.g. now?" Beinschneider says. "It'd take too long to get a transformer. My brother-in-law lives clear across town. Besides, he'd charge double if he had to reopen the store at this time of the evening."

"Discharge him, anyway," the chief surgeon says. "Ground the voltage. Very well. We'll get that growth out before it kills him and worry about scientific research later."

He puts on two extra pairs of gloves.

"Do you think he'll grow another?" Nurse Lustig says. "He's not a bad-looking guy. I can tell he'd be simpatico."

"How the hell would I know?" says Van Mesgeluk. "I may be a doctor, but I'm not quite God."

"God who?" says Beinschneider, the orthodox atheist. He drops the ground wire into the hole; blue sparks spurt out. Van Mesgeluk lifts out the diamond with the tongs. Nurse Lustig takes it from him and begins to wash it off with tap water.

"Let's call in your brother-in-law," Van Mesgeluk says. "The jewel merchant, I mean."

"He's in Amsterdam. But I could phone him. However, he'd insist on splitting the fee, you know."

"He doesn't even have a degree!" Van Mesgeluk cries. "But call him. How is he on legal aspects of mineralogy?"

"Not bad. But I don't think he'll come. Actually, the jewel business is just a front. He gets his big bread by smuggling in chocolate-covered LSD drops."

"Is that ethical?"

"It's top-quality Dutch chocolate," Beinschneider says stiffly.

"Sorry. I think I'll put in a plastic window over the hole. We can observe any regrowth."

"Do you think it's psychosomatic in origin?"

"Everything is, even the sex urge. Ask Miss Lustig."

The patient opens his eyes. "I had a dream," he says. "This dirty old man with a long white beard . . ."

"A typical archetype," Van Mesgeluk says. "Symbol of the wisdom of the unconscious. A warning . . ."

". . . his name was Plato," the patient says. "He was the illegitimate son of Socrates. Plato, the old man, staggers out of a dark cave at one end of which is a bright klieg light. He's holding a huge diamond in his hand; his fingernails are broken and dirty. The old man cries, 'The Ideal is Physical!

106

The Universal is the Specific Concrete! Carbon, actually. Eureka! I'm rich! I'll buy all of Athens, invest in apartment buildings, Great Basin, COMSAT!

" 'Screw the mind!' the old man screams. 'It's all mine!' "

"Would you care to dream about King Midas?" Van Mesgeluk says.

Nurse Lustig shrieks. A lump of sloppy grayish matter is in her hands. "The water changed it back into a tumor!"

"Beinschneider, cancel that call to Amsterdam!"

"Maybe he'll have a relapse," Beinschneider says.

Nurse Lustig turns savagely upon the patient. "The engagement's off!"

"I don't think you loved the real me," the patient says, "whoever you are. Anyway, I'm glad you changed your mind. My last wife left me, but we haven't been divorced yet. I got enough trouble without a bigamy charge.

"She took off with my surgeon for parts unknown just after my hemorrhoid operation. I never found out why."

From James Sallis, November 15, 1966:

> Dear Mr. Knight—
> . . . I want to get at a new kind of sf, I want to evade the
> mock-epic and -dramatic that comes so easily to it, I want to write
> sf using what I've learned from contemporary poetry. I want to
> focus on moments of stillness ("instants of desertion, instances of
> silence"), the quiet soft sigh that comes before a thing breaks up
> or changes. . . .

To Sallis, November 19, 1966:

> Dear Jim,
> . . . Literary s.f. is just what I am after in *Orbit*, although I
> sometimes feel the damn thing is going a hell of a lot more literary
> than I intended, & that everybody had better hang on tight on the
> curves; but I am letting it go its own way, since I don't see any
> alternative except to bounce the best stories I get.

To Thomas A. Dardis, November 21, 1966:

Dear Tom,
Herewith some suggested front and back jacket copy for *Orbit 2*.

I think it would be a mistake to de-emphasize the title or to introduce any subtitle patterned on Judith Merril's annual; first, we would be competing in a field which I think is already over-crowded, with Miss Merril's annual series, the Nebula Award annuals, the Wollheim-Carr annuals, and the annual volumes of stories from *Analog, Galaxy, If* and *Fantasy & Science Fiction*; second, we would be throwing away what we really have to sell—a series of collections of *new* science fiction. . . .

I do understand Putnam's concern, however, and I agree that there should be something on the jacket to indicate to librarians and booksellers just what this book is, why it's important and so on. I've tried to take care of this in the back jacket copy, as well as in a line or two of the front copy.

To Norman Spinrad, November 28, 1966:

Dear Norm,
I like "An Act of Love," but not enough to buy it for *Orbit*; you will no doubt think this is a shame, but I am relieved, because I am not quite ready for that kind of trouble with Putnam yet.

I was a little disappointed that the chocolate syrup turned out to be a disappointment—well, yeah, cold and sticky; but anyhow, I think your guy went at it backward, if you don't mind my saying so; the idea is to lick the syrup off and *then* ball the chick. I am told it has been done with peanut butter, but I think this shows a lack of imagination. Chicken soup, maybe.

THE PLANNERS

by Kate Wilhelm

(Nebula Award, Best Short Story, 1968)

Rae stopped before the one-way glass, stooped and peered at the gibbon infant in the cage. Darin watched her bitterly. She straightened after a moment, hands in smock pockets, face innocent of any expression what-so-goddam-ever, and continued to saunter toward him through the aisle between the cages.

"You still think it is cruel, and worthless?"

"Do you, Dr. Darin?"

"Why do you always do that? Answer my question with one of your own?"

"Does it infuriate you?"

He shrugged and turned away. His lab coat was on the chair where he had tossed it. He pulled it on over his sky-blue sport shirt.

"How is the Driscoll boy?" Rae asked.

He stiffened, then relaxed again. Still not facing her, he said, "Same as last week, last year. Same as he'll be until he dies."

The hall door opened and a very large, very homely face appeared. Stu Evers looked past Darin, down the aisle. "You alone? Thought I heard voices."

"Talking to myself," Darin said. "The committee ready yet?"

"Just about. Dr. Jacobsen is stalling with his nose-throat spray routine, as usual." He hesitated a moment, glancing again down the row of cages, then at Darin. "Wouldn't you think a guy allergic to monkeys would find some other line of research?"

Darin looked, but Rae was gone. What had it been this time: the Driscoll boy, the trend of the project itself? He wondered if she had a life of her own when she was away. "I'll be out at the compound," he said. He passed Stu in the doorway and headed toward the vivid greenery of Florida forests.

The cacophony hit him at the door. There were four hundred sixty-nine monkeys on the thirty-six acres of wooded ground the research department was using. Each monkey was screeching, howling, singing, cursing, or otherwise making its presence known. Darin grunted and headed toward the compound. The Happiest Monkeys in the World, a newspaper article had called them. Singing Monkeys, a subhead announced. MONKEYS GIVEN

109

SMARTNESS PILLS, the most enterprising paper had proclaimed. *Cruelty Charged*, added another in subdued, sorrowful tones.

The compound was three acres of carefully planned and maintained wilderness, completely enclosed with thirty-foot-high, smooth plastic walls. A transparent dome covered the area. There were one-way windows at intervals along the wall. A small group stood before one of the windows: the committee.

Darin stopped and gazed over the interior of the compound through one of the windows. He saw Heloise and Skitter contentedly picking nonexistent fleas from one another. Adam was munching on a banana; Homer was lying on his back idly touching his feet to his nose. A couple of the chimps were at the water fountain, not drinking, merely pressing the pedal and watching the fountain, now and then immersing a head or hand in the bowl of cold water. Dr. Jacobsen appeared and Darin joined the group.

"Good morning, Mrs. Bellbottom," Darin said politely. "Did you know your skirt has fallen off?" He turned from her to Major Dormouse. "Ah, Major, and how many of the enemy have you swatted to death today with your pretty little yellow rag?" He smiled pleasantly at a pimply young man with a camera. "Major, you've brought a professional peeping tom. More stories in the paper, with pictures this time?" The pimply young man shifted his position, fidgeted with the camera. The major was fiery; Mrs. Bellbottom was on her knees peering under a bush, looking for her skirt. Darin blinked. None of them had on any clothing. He turned toward the window. The chimps were drawing up a table, laden with tea things, silver, china, tiny finger sandwiches. The chimps were all wearing flowered shirts and dresses. Hortense had on a ridiculous flop-brimmed sun hat of pale green straw. Darin leaned against the fence to control his laughter.

"Soluble ribonucleic acid," Dr. Jacobsen was saying when Darin recovered, "sRNA for short. So from the gross beginnings when entire worms were trained and fed to other worms that seemed to benefit from the original training, we have come to these more refined methods. We now extract the sRNA molecule from the trained animals and feed it, the sRNA molecules in solution, to untrained specimens and observe the results."

The young man was snapping pictures as Jacobsen talked. Mrs. Whoosis was making notes, her mouth a lipless line, the sun hat tinging her skin with green. The sun on her patterned red and yellow dress made it appear to jiggle, giving her fleshy hips a constant rippling motion. Darin watched, fascinated. She was about sixty.

". . . my colleague, who proposed this line of experimentation, Dr. Darin," Jacobsen said finally, and Darin bowed slightly. He wondered what

110

Jacobsen had said about him, decided to wait for any questions before he said anything.

"Dr. Darin, is it true that you also extract this substance from people?"

"Every time you scratch yourself, you lose this substance," Darin said. "Every time you lose a drop of blood, you lose it. It is in every cell of your body. Sometimes we take a sample of human blood for study, yes."

"And inject it into those animals?"

"Sometimes we do that," Darin said. He waited for the next, the inevitable question, wondering how he would answer it. Jacobsen had briefed them on what to answer, but he couldn't remember what Jacobsen had said. The question didn't come. Mrs. Whoosis stepped forward, staring at the window.

Darin turned his attention to her; she averted her eyes, quickly fixed her stare again on the chimps in the compound. "Yes, Mrs. uh . . . Ma'am?" Darin prompted her. She didn't look at him.

"Why? What is the purpose of all this?" she asked. Her voice sounded strangled. The pimpled young man was inching toward the next window.

"Well," Darin said, "our theory is simple. We believe that learning ability can be improved drastically in nearly every species. The learning curve is the normal, expected bell-shaped curve, with a few at one end who have the ability to learn quite rapidly, with the majority in the center who learn at an average rate, and a few at the other end who learn quite slowly. With our experiments we are able to increase the ability of those in the broad middle, as well as those in the deficient end of the curve so that their learning abilities match those of the fastest learners of any given group. . . ."

No one was listening to him. It didn't matter. They would be given the press release he had prepared for them, written in simple language, no polysyllables, no complicated sentences. They were all watching the chimps through the windows. He said, "So we gabbled the gazooka three times wretchedly until the spirit of camping fired the girls." One of the committee members glanced at him. "Whether intravenously or orally, it seems to be equally effective," Darin said, and the perspiring man turned again to the window. "Injections every morning . . . rejections, planned diet, planned parenthood, planned plans planning plans." Jacobsen eyed him suspiciously. Darin stopped talking and lighted a cigarette. The woman with the unquiet hips turned from the window, her face very red. "I've seen enough," she said. "This sun is too hot out here. May we see the inside laboratories now?"

Darin turned them over to Stu Evers inside the building. He walked back slowly to the compound. There was a grin on his lips when he spotted Adam

111

on the far side, swaggering triumphantly, paying no attention to Hortense who was rocking back and forth on her haunches, looking very dazed. Darin saluted Adam, then, whistling, returned to his office. Mrs. Driscoll was due with Sonny at 1 P.M.

Sonny Driscoll was fourteen. He was five feet nine inches, weighed one hundred sixty pounds. His male nurse was six feet two inches and weighed two hundred twenty-seven pounds. Sonny had broken his mother's arm when he was twelve; he had broken his father's arm and leg when he was thirteen. So far the male nurse was intact. Every morning Mrs. Driscoll lovingly washed and dressed her baby, fed him, walked him in the yard, spoke happily to him of plans for the coming months, or sang nursery songs to him. He never seemed to see her. The male nurse, Johnny, was never farther than three feet from his charge when he was on duty.

Mrs. Driscoll refused to think of the day when she would have to turn her child over to an institution. Instead she placed her faith and hope in Darin.

They arrived at two-fifteen, earlier than he had expected them, later than they had promised to be there.

"The kid kept taking his clothes off," Johnny said morosely. The kid was taking them off again in the office. Johnny started toward him, but Darin shook his head. It didn't matter. Darin got his blood sample from one of the muscular arms, shot the injection into the other one. Sonny didn't seem to notice what he was doing. He never seemed to notice. Sonny refused to be tested. They got him to the chair and table, but he sat staring at nothing, ignoring the blocks, the bright balls, the crayons, the candy. Nothing Darin did or said had any discernible effect. Finally the time was up. Mrs. Driscoll and Johnny got him dressed once more and left. Mrs. Driscoll thanked Darin for helping her boy.

Stu and Darin held class from four to five daily. Kelly O'Grady had the monkeys tagged and ready for them when they showed up at the schoolroom. Kelly was very tall, very slender and red-haired. Stu shivered if she accidentally brushed him in passing; Darin hoped one day Stu would pull an Adam on her. She sat primly on her high stool with her notebook on her knee, unaware of the change that came over Stu during school hours, or, if aware, uncaring. Darin wondered if she was really a Barbie doll fully programmed to perform laboratory duties, and nothing else.

He thought of the Finishing School for Barbies where long-legged, high-breasted, stomachless girls went to get shaved clean, get their toenails painted pink, their nipples removed, and all body openings sewn shut, except for their mouths, which curved in perpetual smiles and led nowhere.

The class consisted of six black spider-monkeys who had not been fed yet. They had to do six tasks in order: 1) pull a rope; 2) cross the cage and get a stick that was released by the rope; 3) pull the rope again; 4) get the second stick that would fit into the first; 5) join the sticks together; 6) using the lengthened stick, pull a bunch of bananas close enough to the bars of the cage to reach them and take them inside where they could eat them. At five the monkeys were returned to Kelly, who wheeled them away one by one back to the stockroom. None of them had performed all the tasks, although two had gone through part of them before the time ran out.

Waiting for the last of the monkeys to be taken back to its quarters, Stu asked, "What did you do to that bunch of idiots this morning? By the time I got them, they all acted dazed."

Darin told him about Adam's performance; they were both laughing when Kelly returned. Stu's laugh turned to something that sounded almost like a sob. Darin wanted to tell him about the school Kelly must have attended, thought better of it, and walked away instead.

His drive home was through the darkening forests of interior Florida for sixteen miles on a narrow straight road.

"Of course, I don't mind living here," Lea had said once, nine years ago when the Florida appointment had come through. And she didn't mind. The house was air-conditioned; the family car, Lea's car, was air-conditioned; the back yard had a swimming pool big enough to float the Queen Mary. A frightened, large-eyed Florida girl did the housework, and Lea gained weight and painted sporadically, wrote sporadically—poetry—and entertained faculty wives regularly. Darin suspected that sometimes she entertained faculty husbands also.

"Oh, Professor Dimples, one hour this evening? That will be fifteen dollars, you know." He jotted down the appointment and turned to Lea. "Just two more today and you will have your car payment. How about that!" She twined slinky arms about his neck, pressing tight high breasts hard against him. She had to tilt her head slightly for his kiss. "Then your turn, darling. For free." He tried to kiss her; something stopped his tongue, and he realized that the smile was on the outside only, that the opening didn't really exist at all.

He parked next to an MG, not Lea's, and went inside the house where the martinis were always snapping cold.

"Darling, you remember Greta, don't you? She is going to give me lessons twice a week. Isn't that exciting?"

"But you already graduated," Darin murmured. Greta was not tall and not long-legged. She was a little bit of a thing. He thought probably he did remember her from somewhere or other, vaguely. Her hand was cool in his.

"Greta has moved in; she is going to lecture on modern art for the spring semester. I asked her for private lessons and she said yes."

"Greta Farrel," Darin said, still holding her small hand. They moved away from Lea and wandered through the open windows to the patio where the scent of orange blossoms was heavy in the air.

"Greta thinks it must be heavenly to be married to a psychologist." Lea's voice followed them. "Where are you two?"

"What makes you say a thing like that?" Darin asked.

"Oh, when I think of how you must understand a woman, know her moods and the reasons for them. You must know just what to do and when, and when to do something else . . . Yes, just like that."

His hands on her body were hot, her skin cool. Lea's petulant voice drew closer. He held Greta in his arms and stepped into the pool where they sank to the bottom, still together. She hadn't gone to the Barbie school. His hands learned her body; then his body learned hers. After they made love, Greta drew back from him regretfully.

"I do have to go now. You are a lucky man, Dr. Darin. No doubts about yourself, complete understanding of what makes you tick."

He lay back on the leather couch staring at the ceiling. "It's always that way, Doctor. Fantasies, dreams, illusions. I know it is because this investigation is hanging over us right now, but even when things are going relatively well, I still go off on a tangent like that for no real reason." He stopped talking.

In his chair Darin stirred slightly, his fingers drumming softly on the arm, his gaze on the clock whose hands were stuck. He said, "Before this recent pressure, did you have such intense fantasies?"

"I don't think so," Darin said thoughtfully, trying to remember.

The other didn't give him time. He asked, "And can you break out of them now when you have to, or want to?"

"Oh, sure," Darin said.

Laughing, he got out of his car, patted the MG, and walked into his house. He could hear voices from the living room and he remembered that on Thursdays Lea really did have her painting lesson.

Dr. Lacey left five minutes after Darin arrived. Lacey said vague things about Lea's great promise and untapped talent, and Darin nodded sober agreement. If she had talent, it certainly was untapped so far. He didn't say so.

Lea was wearing a hostess suit, flowing sheer panels of pale blue net over a skin-tight leotard that was midnight blue. Darin wondered if she realized that she had gained weight in the past few years. He thought not.

"Oh, that man is getting impossible," she said when the MG blasted away from their house. "Two years now, and he still doesn't want to put my things on show."

Looking at her, Darin wondered how much more her things could be on show.

"Don't dawdle too long with your martini," she said. "We're due at the Ritters' at seven for clams."

The telephone rang for him while he was showering. It was Stu Evers. Darin stood dripping water while he listened.

"Have you seen the evening paper yet? That broad made the statement that conditions are extreme at the station, that our animals are made to suffer unnecessarily."

Darin groaned softly. Stu went on, "She is bringing her entire women's group out tomorrow to show proof of her claims. She's a bigwig in the SPCA, or something."

Darin began to laugh then. Mrs. Whoosis had her face pressed against one of the windows, other fat women in flowered dresses had their faces against the rest. None of them breathed or moved. Inside the compound Adam laid Hortense, then moved on to Esmeralda, to Hilda . . .

"God damn it, Darin, it isn't funny!" Stu said.

"But it is. It is."

Clams at the Ritters' were delicious. Clams, hammers, buckets of butter, a mountainous salad, beer, and finally coffee liberally laced with brandy. Darin felt cheerful and contented when the evening was over. Ritter was in Med. Eng. Lit. but he didn't talk about it, which was merciful. He was sympathetic about the stink with the SPCA. He thought scientists had no imagination. Darin agreed with him and soon he and Lea were on their way home.

"I am so glad that you didn't decide to stay late," Lea said, passing over the yellow line with a blast of the horn. "There is a movie on tonight that I am dying to see."

She talked, but he didn't listen, training of twelve years' drawing out an occasional grunt at what must have been appropriate times. "Ritter is such a bore," she said. They were nearly home. "As if you had anything to do with that incredible statement in tonight's paper."

"What statement?"

"Didn't you even read the article? For heaven's sake, why not? Everyone will be talking about it . . ." She sighed theatrically. "Someone quoted a reliable source who said that within the foreseeable future, simply by developing the leads you now have, you will be able to produce monkeys that are as smart as normal human beings." She laughed, a brittle meaningless sound.

"I'll read the article when we get home," he said. She didn't ask about the statement, didn't care if it was true or false, if he had made it or not. He read the article while she settled down before the television. Then he went for a swim. The water was warm, the breeze cool on his skin. Mosquitoes found him as soon as he got out of the pool, so he sat behind the screening of the verandah. The bluish light from the living room went off after a time and there was only the dark night. Lea didn't call him when she went to bed. He knew she went very softly, closing the door with care so that the click of the latch wouldn't disturb him if he was dozing on the verandah.

He knew why he didn't break it off. Pity. The most corrosive emotion endogenous to man. She was the product of the doll school that taught that the trip down the aisle was the end, the fulfillment of a maiden's dreams; shocked and horrified to learn that it was another beginning, some of them never recovered. Lea never had. Never would. At sixty she would purse her lips at the sexual display of uncivilized animals, whether human or not, and she would be disgusted and help formulate laws to ban such activities. Long ago he had hoped a child would be the answer, but the school did something to them on the inside too. They didn't conceive, or if conception took place, they didn't carry the fruit, and if they carried it, the birth was of a stillborn thing. The ones that did live were usually the ones to be pitied more than those who fought and were defeated *in utero*.

A bat swooped low over the quiet pool and was gone again against the black of the azaleas. Soon the moon would appear, and the chimps would stir restlessly for a while, then return to deep untroubled slumber. The chimps slept companionably close to one another, without thought of sex. Only the nocturnal creatures, and the human creatures, performed coitus in the dark. He wondered if Adam remembered his human captors. The colony in the compound had been started almost twenty years ago, and since then none of the chimps had seen a human being. When it was necessary to enter the grounds, the chimps were fed narcotics in the evening to insure against their waking. Props were changed then, new obstacles added to the old conquered ones. Now and then a chimp was removed for study, usually ending up in dissection. But not Adam. He was father of the world. Darin grinned in the darkness.

Adam took his bride aside from the other beasts and knew that she was lovely. She was his own true bride, created for him, intelligence to match his own burning intelligence. Together they scaled the smooth walls and glimpsed the great world that lay beyond their garden. Together they found the opening that led to the world that was to be theirs, and they left behind them the lesser beings. And the god searched for them and finding them not, cursed them and sealed the opening so that none of the others could follow. So it was that Adam and his bride became the first man and woman and from them flowed the progeny that was to inhabit the entire world. And one day

116

Adam said, for shame woman, seest thou that thou art naked? And the woman answered, so are you, big boy, so are you. So they covered their nakedness with leaves from the trees, and thereafter they performed their sexual act in the dark of night so that man could not look on his woman, nor she on him. And they were thus cleansed of shame. Forever and ever. Amen. Hallelujah.

Darin shivered. He had drowsed after all, and the night wind had grown chill. He went to bed. Lea drew away from him in her sleep. She felt hot to his touch. He turned to his left side, his back to her, and he slept.

"There is potential x," Darin said to Lea the next morning at breakfast. "We don't know where x is actually. It represents the highest intellectual achievement possible for the monkeys, for example. We test each new batch of monkeys that we get and sort them—x-1, x-2, x-3, suppose, and then we breed for more x-1's. Also we feed the other two groups the sRNA that we extract from the original x-1's. Eventually we get a monkey that is higher than our original x-1, and we reclassify right down the line and start over, using his sRNA to bring the others up to his level. We make constant checks to make sure we aren't allowing inferior strains to mingle with our highest achievers, and we keep control groups that are given the same training, the same food, the same sorting process, but no sRNA. We test them against each other."

Lea was watching his face with some interest as he talked. He thought he had got through, until she said, "Did you realize that your hair is almost solid white at the temples? All at once it is turning white."

Carefully he put his cup back on the saucer. He smiled at her and got up. "See you tonight," he said.

They also had two separate compounds of chimps that had started out identically. Neither had received any training whatever through the years; they had been kept isolated from each other and from man. Adam's group had been fed sRNA daily from the most intelligent chimps they had found. The control group had been fed none. The control-group chimps had yet to master the intricacies of the fountain with its ice-cold water; they used the small stream that flowed through the compound. The control group had yet to learn that fruit on the high, fragile branches could be had, if one used the telescoping sticks to knock them down. The control group huddled without protection, or under the scant cover of palm-trees when it rained and the dome was opened. Adam long ago had led his group in the construction of a rude but functional hut where they gathered when it rained.

Darin saw the women's committee filing past the compound when he parked his car. He went straight to the console in his office, flicked on a switch and manipulated buttons and dials, leading the group through the paths, opening one, closing another to them, until he led them to the newest of the compounds, where he opened the gate and let them inside. Quickly he closed the gate again and watched their frantic efforts to get out. Later he turned the chimps loose on them, and his grin grew broader as he watched the new-men ravage the old women. Some of the offspring were black and hairy, others pink and hairless, some intermediate. They grew rapidly, lined up with arms extended to receive their daily doses, stood before a machine that tested them instantaneously, and were sorted. Some of them went into a disintegration room, others out into the world.

A car horn blasted in his ears. He switched off his ignition and got out as Stu Evers parked next to his car. "I see the old bats got here," Stu said. He walked toward the lab with Darin. "How's the Driscoll kid coming along?"

"Negative," Darin said. Stu knew they had tried using human sRNA on the boy, and failed consistently. It was too big a step for his body to cope with. "So far he has shown total intolerance to A-127. Throws it off almost instantly."

Stuart was sympathetic and noncommittal. No one else had any faith whatever in Darin's own experiment. A-127 might be too great a step upward, Darin thought. The *Ateles* spider monkey from Brazil was too bright.

He called Kelly from his office and asked about the newly arrived spider monkeys they had tested the day before. Blood had been processed; a sample was available. He looked over his notes and chose one that had shown interest in the tasks without finishing any of them. Kelly promised him the prepared syringe by 1 P.M.

What no one connected with the project could any longer doubt was that those simians, and the men that had been injected with sRNA from the Driscoll boy, had actually had their learning capacities inhibited, some of them apparently permanently.

Darin didn't want to think about Mrs. Driscoll's reaction if ever she learned how they had been using her boy. Rae sat at the corner of his desk and drawled insolently, "I might tell her myself, Dr. Darin. I'll say, Sorry, Ma'am, you'll have to keep your idiot out of here; you're damaging the brains of our monkeys with his polluted blood. Okay, Darin?"

"My God, what are you doing back again?"

"Testing," she said. "That's all, just testing."

Stu called him to observe the latest challenge to Adam's group, to take place in forty minutes. Darin had forgotten that he was to be present. During the night a tree had been felled in each compound, its trunk crossing the small stream, damming it. At eleven the water fountains were to be turned off for the rest of the day. The tree had been felled at the far end of the

118

compound, close to the wall where the stream entered, so that the trickle of water that flowed past the hut was cut off. Already the group not taking sRNA was showing signs of thirst. Adam's group was unaware of the interrupted flow.

Darin met Stu and they walked together to the far side where they would have a good view of the entire compound. The women had left by then. "It was too quiet for them this morning," Stu said. "Adam was making his rounds; he squatted on the felled tree for nearly an hour before he left it and went back to the others."

They could see the spreading pool of water. It was muddy, uninviting looking. At eleven-ten it was generally known within the compound that the water supply had failed. Some of the old chimps tried the fountain; Adam tried it several times. He hit it with a stick and tried it again. Then he sat on his haunches and stared at it. One of the young chimps whimpered pitiably. He wasn't thirsty yet, merely puzzled and perhaps frightened. Adam scowled at him. The chimp cowered behind Hortense, who bared her fangs at Adam. He waved menacingly at her, and she began picking fleas from her offspring. When he whimpered again, she cuffed him. The young chimp looked from her to Adam, stuck his forefinger in his mouth and ambled away. Adam continued to stare at the useless fountain. An hour passed. At last Adam rose and wandered nonchalantly toward the drying stream. Here and there a shrinking pool of muddy water steamed in the sun. The other chimps followed Adam. He followed the stream through the compound toward the wall that was its source. When he came to the pool he squatted again. One of the young chimps circled the pool cautiously, reached down and touched the dirty water, drew back, reached for it again, and then drank. Several of the others drank also. Adam continued to squat. At twelve-forty Adam moved again. Grunting and gesturing to several younger males, he approached the tree-trunk. With much noise and meaningless gestures, they shifted the trunk. They strained, shifted it again. The water was released and poured over the heaving chimps. Two of them dropped the trunk and ran. Adam and the other two held. The two returned.

They were still working when Darin had to leave, to keep his appointment with Mrs. Driscoll and Sonny. They arrived at one-ten. Kelly had left the syringe with the new formula in Darin's small refrigerator. He injected Sonny, took his sample, and started the tests. Sometimes Sonny cooperated to the extent of lifting one of the articles from the table and throwing it. Today he cleaned the table within ten minutes. Darin put a piece of candy in his hand; Sonny threw it from him. Patiently Darin put another piece in the boy's hand. He managed to keep the eighth piece in the clenched hand long enough to guide the hand to Sonny's mouth. When it was gone, Sonny opened his mouth for more. His hands lay idly on the table. He didn't seem to relate the hands to the candy with the pleasant taste. Darin tried to guide a second to his mouth, but Sonny refused to hold a piece a second time.

When the hour was over and Sonny was showing definite signs of fatigue, Mrs. Driscoll clutched Darin's hands in hers. Tears stood in her eyes. "You actually got him to feed himself a little bit," she said brokenly. "God bless you, Dr. Darin. God bless you!" She kissed his hand and turned away as the tears started to spill down her cheeks.

Kelly was waiting for him when the group left. She collected the new sample of blood to be processed. "Did you hear about the excitement down at the compound? Adam's building a dam of his own."

Darin stared at her for a moment. The breakthrough? He ran back to the compound. The near side this time was where the windows were being used. It seemed that the entire staff was there, watching silently. He saw Stu and edged in by him. The stream twisted and curved through the compound, less than ten inches deep, not over two feet anywhere. At one spot stones lay under it; elsewhere the bottom was of hard-packed sand. Adam and his crew were piling up stones at the one suitable place for their dam, very near their hut. The dam they were building was two feet thick. It was less than five feet from the wall, fifteen feet from where Darin and Stu shared the window. When the dam was completed, Adam looked along the wall. Darin thought the chimp's eyes paused momentarily on his own. Later he heard that nearly every other person watching felt the same momentary pause as those black, intelligent eyes sought out and held other intelligence.

". . . next thunderstorm. Adam and the flood . . ."

". . . eventually seeds instead of food . . ."

". . . his brain. Convolutions as complex as any man's."

Darin walked away from them, snatches of future plans in his ears. There was a memo on his desk. Jacobsen was turning over the SPCA investigatory committee to him. He was to meet with the university representatives, the local SPCA group, and the legal representatives of all concerned on Monday next at 10 A.M. He wrote out his daily report on Sonny Driscoll. Sonny had been on too-good behavior for too long. Would this last injection give him just the spark of determination he needed to go on a rampage? Darin had alerted Johnny, the bodyguard, whoops, male nurse, for just such a possibility, but he knew Johnny didn't think there was any danger from the kid. He hoped Sonny wouldn't kill Johnny, then turn on his mother and father. He'd probably rape his mother, if that much goal-directedness ever flowed through him. And the three men who had volunteered for the injections from Sonny's blood? He didn't want to think of them at all, therefore couldn't get them out of his mind as he sat at his desk staring at nothing. Three convicts. That's all, just convicts hoping to get a parole for

120

helping science along. He laughed abruptly. They weren't planning anything now. Not that trio. Not planning for a thing. Sitting, waiting for something to happen, not thinking about what it might be, or when, or how they would be affected. Not thinking. Period.

"But you can always console yourself that your motives were pure, that it was all for Science, can't you, Dr. Darin?" Rae asked mockingly.

He looked at her. "Go to hell," he said.

It was late when he turned off his light. Kelly met him in the corridor that led to the main entrance. "Hard day, Dr. Darin?"

He nodded. Her hand lingered momentarily on his arm. "Good night," she said, turning in to her own office. He stared at the door for a long time before he let himself out and started toward his car. Lea would be furious with him for not calling. Probably she wouldn't speak at all until nearly bedtime, when she would explode into tears and accusations. He could see the time when her tears and accusations would strike home, when Kelly's body would still be a tangible memory, her words lingering in his ears. And he would lie to Lea, not because he would care actually if she knew, but because it would be expected. She wouldn't know how to cope with the truth. It would entangle her to the point where she would have to try an abortive suicide, a screaming-for-attention attempt that would ultimately tie him in tear-soaked knots that would never be loosened. No, he would lie, and she would know he was lying, and they would get by. He started the car, aimed down the long sixteen miles that lay before him. He wondered where Kelly lived. What it would do to Stu when he realized. What it would do to his job if Kelly should get nasty, eventually. He shrugged. Barbie dolls never got nasty. It wasn't built in.

Lea met him at the door, dressed only in a sheer gown, her hair loose and unsprayed. Her body flowed into his, so that he didn't need Kelly at all. And he was best man when Stu and Kelly were married. He called to Rae, "Would that satisfy you?" but she didn't answer. Maybe she was gone for good this time. He parked the car outside his darkened house and leaned his head on the steering wheel for a moment before getting out. If not gone for good, at least for a long time. He hoped she would stay away for a long time.

To Thomas A. Dardis, December 6, 1966:

Dear Tom,

I have been mulling over the question of the *Orbit* subtitle some more, and I do not see any way to jazz this up without misrepresenting the book. In particular, the suggestion that the subtitle should read "H. G. Wells Awards" would involve us in a transparent fraud. Since we are the original publishers of the stories in *Orbit*, we would in effect be giving the awards to ourselves. A ploy of this kind would deceive nobody, least of all the librarians.

It should be remembered that *Orbit* is not a selection from the year's published s.f. stories like the Merril anthology and other annuals; it is not an award collection like *Nebula Award Stories*. If we try to disguise *Orbit* as one of these, we are going to get clobbered, because we will be putting up a fake against the real thing. *Orbit* is a collection of new science fiction stories, edited by me. These two things, and the merits of the collections themselves, are the only selling points we have, and it would be disastrous to kick them under the rug.

At this point I feel somewhat like a chef who has created a new dish for a restaurant proprietor who thinks its flavors are too subtle, and wants to smother it with ketchup.

Dardis told me later that he had read this letter in an editorial meeting, and that the last paragraph had got a laugh.

To Dardis, December 9, 1966:

Dear Tom,

. . . I hope it is understood all around that the title of the book is *Orbit 2*, and that *The Best Science Fiction Stories of the Year* is a subtitle. If the latter were adopted as the title, *Orbit 2* would become an appendage, impossible to classify, and would give an undesirable suggestion of confusion on the part of the publishers.

To R. A. Lafferty, December 19, 1966:

Dear Raphael,

. . . "Past Master" is science fiction, all right, but I think it is the wrong length. The feeling I got when I was reading it was that

122

the lightness & detachment of your short-story style are inappropriate in a longer story—we expect more involvement, expect to care more about what happens in a novelette. But I have been learning lately that many stories that seem too long are really too short, & maybe that's the case here. Maybe the story ought to be longer so that you would have room to fill in more of Astrobe & bring more of the people to life. I tell you all this for what it is worth, probably very little.

To Harry Harrison, February 1, 1967:

Dear Harry,

Glad to get a look at this, & it has some striking moments, but I am a little uneasy about stories in which the whole thing turns out to be a test simulation, & try not to buy them any oftener than I can help; they are a little too much like the "it was all a dream" or "I was only kidding" plot. I may as well admit now, since you will find out eventually, that I have just bought one from Katie. If there were any justice, I would buy yours too, but there isn't.

To Gene Wolfe, November 19, 1966:

Dear Gene,

I have read "Changeling" again, and still can't sort it out into any one consistent, linear, daylight-logic pattern, but have concluded that I am not supposed to, so I had better just shut up and buy it. It seems to mean something to me, although I would hate to have to explain what, & the whole thing hangs together so tightly that I can't imagine wanting you to change a word. Incidentally, I'm in the process of buying a story from a guy named Jim Sallis, a new writer, awfully good, and hungry for company. Write to him if you feel like it: his address is RD 3, Iowa City, Iowa. . . .

Years later, during a slightly drunken party in Madeira Beach, Gene whispered to me, "The old man is dead, you know." And then I understood it.

THE CHANGELING

by Gene Wolfe

I suppose whoever finds these papers will be amazed at the simplicity of their author, who put them under a stone instead of into a mailbox or a filing cabinet or even a cornerstone—these being the places where most think it wise to store up their writings. But consider, is it not wiser to put papers like these into the gut of a dry cave as I have done?

For if a building is all it should be, the future will spare it for a shrine; and if your children's sons think it not worth keeping, will they think the letters of the builders worth reading? Yet that would be a surer way than a filing cabinet. Answer truly: Did you ever know of papers to be read again once they entered one of these, save when some clerk drew them out by number? And who would seek for these?

There is a great, stone-beaked, hook-billed snapping turtle living under the bank here, and in the spring, when the waterfowl have nested and brooded, he swims beneath their chicks more softly than any shadow. Sometimes they peep once when he takes their legs, and so they have more of life than these sheets would have once the clacking cast iron jaw of a mailbox closed on them.

Have you ever noted how eager it is to close when you have pulled out your hand? You cannot write *The Future* on the outside of an envelope; the box would cross that out and stamp *Dead Letter Office* in its place.

Still, I have a tale to tell; and a tale untold is one sort of crime:

I was in the army, serving in Korea, when my father died. That was before the North invaded, and I was supposed to be helping a captain teach demolition to the ROK soldiers. The army gave me compassionate leave when the hospital in Buffalo sent a telegram saying how sick he was. I suppose everyone moved as fast as they could, I know I did, but he died while I was flying across the Pacific. I looked into his coffin where the blue silk lining came up to his hard, brown cheeks and crowded his working shoulders; and went back to Korea. He was the last family I had, and things changed for me then.

There isn't much use in my making a long story of what happened afterward; you can read it all in the court-martial proceedings. I was one of the ones who stayed behind in China, neither the first nor the last to change his mind a second time and come home. I was also one of the ones who had to stand trial; let's say that some of the men who had been in the prison camp with me remembered things differently. You don't have to like it.

124

While I was in Ft. Leavenworth I started thinking about how it was before my mother died, how my father could bend a big nail with his fingers when we lived in Cassonsville and I went to the Immaculate Conception School five days a week. We left the month before I was supposed to start the fifth grade, I think.

When I got out I decided to go back there and look around before I tried to get a job. I had four hundred dollars I had put in Soldier's Deposit before the war, and I knew a lot about living cheap. You learn that in China.

I wanted to see if the Kanakessee River still looked as smooth as it used to, and if the kids I had played softball with had married each other, and what they were like now. Somehow the old part of my life seemed to have broken away, and I wanted to go back and look at that piece. There was a fat boy who was tongue-tied and laughed at everything, but I had forgotten his name. I remembered our pitcher, Ernie Cotha, who was in my grade at school and had buck teeth and freckles; his sister played center field for us when we couldn't get anybody else, and closed her eyes until the ball thumped the ground in front of her. Peter Palmieri always wanted to play Vikings or something like that, and pretty often made the rest of us want to too. His big sister Maria bossed and mothered us all from the towering dignity of thirteen. Somewhere in the background another Palmieri, a baby brother named Paul, followed us around watching everything we did with big, brown eyes. He must have been about four then; he never talked, but we thought he was an awful pest.

I was lucky in my rides and moved out of Kansas pretty well. After a couple of days I figured I would be spending the next night in Cassonsville, but it seemed as though I had run out of welcomes outside a little hamburger joint where the state route branched off the federal highway. I had been holding out my thumb nearly three hours before a guy in an old Ford station wagon offered me a lift. I'd mumbled, "Thanks," and tossed my AWOL bag in back before I ever got a good look at him. It was Ernie Cotha, and I knew him right away—even though a dentist had done something to his teeth so they didn't push his lip out any more. I had a little fun with him before he got me placed, and then we got into a regular school reunion mood talking about the old times.

I remember we passed a little barefoot kid standing alongside the road, and Ernie said, "You recollect how Paul always got in the way, and one time we rubbed his hair with a cow pile? You told me next day how you caught blazes from Mama Palmieri about it."

I'd forgotten, but it all came back as soon as he mentioned it. "You know," I said, "it was a shame the way we treated that boy. He thought we were big shots, and we made him suffer for it."

125

"It didn't hurt him any," Ernie said. "Wait till you see him; I bet he could lick us both."

"The family still live in town?"

"Oh sure." Ernie let the car drift off the blacktop a little, and it threw up a spurt of dust and gravel before he got it back on. "Nobody leaves Cassonsville." He took his eyes from the road for a moment to look at me. "You knew Maria's old Doc Witte's nurse now? And the old people have a little motel on the edge of the fairgrounds. You want me to drop you there, Pete?"

I asked him how the rates were, and he said they were low enough, so, since I'd have to bunk down somewhere, I told him that would be all right. We were quiet then for five or six miles, before Ernie started up again.

"Say, you remember the big fight you two had? Down by the river. You wanted to tie a rock to a frog and throw him in, and Maria wouldn't let you. That was a real scrap."

"It wasn't Maria," I told him, "that was Peter."

"You're nuts," Ernie said. "That must have been twenty years ago. Peter wasn't even born then."

"You must be thinking of another Peter," I said. "I mean Peter Palmieri, Maria's brother."

Ernie stared at me until I thought he was going to run us into the ditch. "That's who I mean too," he said, "but little Peter's only a kid eight, maybe nine." He glanced back at the road. "You're thinking of Paul, only it was Maria you had the fight with; Paul was just a toddler."

We were quiet again for a few minutes after that, and it gave me time to remember that tussle on the river bank. I recalled that four or five of us had walked up to the point where we always tied the skiff we used to cross over to our rocky, useless island in the middle of the channel. We meant to play pirates or something, but the skiff had dragged loose from its moorings and was gone. Peter had tried to get the rest of us to search downstream for it, but everyone was too lazy. It was one of those hot, still summer days when the dust floats in the air; the days that make you think of threshing. I caught a frog somehow and hit upon the idea for an experiment.

Then I remembered that Ernie was at least partially right. Maria had tried to stop me and I had hit her in the eye with a stone. But that wasn't the big fight. It was Peter who came to avenge Maria then, Peter with whom I rolled snarling and scratching, trying to get a grip on his sweat-slick body in the prickly weeds. Ernie was right about Paul's being no more than an infant, and there had been a scrap with Maria; but it was Peter who'd finally made me cut the string from the frog's leg and let it go. Side by side we had watched the little green animal hop back toward the water, and then, when it

126

was only one jump away from dear safety, I had lashed out and suddenly, swiftly, driven the broad blade of my scout knife through him and pinned him to the mud.

The Palmieris' place was called The Cassonsville Tourist Lodge. There were ten white cottages and a house with a café jutting out of the front to support a big sign that said *EAT* like Buddha commanding the grasshopper.

Mama Palmieri surprised me by recognizing me at once and smothering me with kisses. She herself had hardly changed at all. Her hair had gone gray at the temples, but most of it was still the glossy black it had been; and while she had always been fat, she was no fatter now. Maybe not quite so solid looking. I don't think Papa really remembered me, but he gave me one of his rare smiles.

He was a small, dark, philosophical man who seldom spoke, and I suppose people meeting the two of them for the first time would assume that Mama dominated her husband. The truth was that she regarded him as infallible in every crisis. And for practical purposes Mama was almost right; he had the inexhaustible patience and rock-bound common sense of a Sicilian burro—all the qualities that have made that tough, diminutive animal the traditional companion of wandering friars and desert rats.

The Palmieris wanted me to stay in Maria's room (she had gone to Chicago to attend some sort of nurses' convention and was not due back until the end of the week) as a guest, and insisted that I eat with the family. I made them rent me a cabin instead at five dollars a night—which they swore was the full rate—but I gave in on the eating. We were still talking in that disjointed way people do on these occasions when Paul came in.

I would not have recognized him if I'd met him on the street, but I liked him at first sight; a big, dark, solemn kid with a handsome profile he had never discovered and probably never would.

After Mama made the introductions she started worrying about dinner and wondering when Peter would get home. Paul reassured her by saying he'd driven past Peter walking with a gang of kids as he'd come out from town. He said he'd offered his brother a lift but had been turned down.

Something about the way he said it gave me the willies. I remembered what Ernie had said about Peter being younger than Paul, and somehow Paul gave the same impression. He was wearing a college sweater and had the half cocky, half unsure mannerisms of a boy trying to be a man, yet he seemed to be talking about somone much younger.

After a while we heard the screen door slam and light, quick steps coming in. When I saw him I knew I had been expecting it all along. It was Peter, and he was perhaps eight years old. Not just another Italian-looking kid; but Peter, with his sharp chin and black eyes. He didn't seem to recall me at all, and Mama bragged about how not many women could bear healthy sons at fifty like she had. I went to bed early that night.

Naturally I had been keyed up all evening waiting to hear something that would show they knew about me; but when I fell asleep I was thinking about Peter, and I hadn't been thinking about anything else for a long time.

The next day was Saturday, and since Paul had the day off from his summer job he offered to drive me around town. He had a '54 Chevy he had pretty much rebuilt himself, and he was very proud of it.

After we had seen all the usual things, which didn't take long in Cassonsville, I asked him to take me to the island in the river where we had played as boys. We had to walk about a mile because the road doesn't come close to the river at that point, but there was a path the kids had made. Grasshoppers fled in waves before us through the dry grass.

When we got to the water Paul said, "That's funny, there's usually a little boat here the kids use to get out to the island."

I was looking at the island, and I saw the skiff tied to a bush at the edge of the water. It looked like the same one we had used when I was a kid myself, and who knows, maybe it was. The island itself interested me more. It was a good deal closer to shore—in fact, the Kanakessee was a good deal narrower—than I had remembered, but I had expected that since everything in Cassonsville was smaller including the town itself. What surprised me was that the island was bigger, if anything. There was a high point, almost a hill, in the center that sloped down and then up to a bluff on the upstream end, and trailed a long piece of wasteland downstream. Altogether it must have covered four or five acres.

In a few minutes we saw a boy on the island, and Paul yelled across the water for him to row the boat over to us. He did, and Paul rowed the three of us back. I remember I was afraid the little skiff would founder under the load; the silent water was no more than an inch from pouring over the sides, despite the boy's bailing with a rusty can to lighten the boat of its bilge.

On the island we found three more boys, including Peter. There were some wooden swords, made by nailing a short slat crosswise to a longer, thrust into the ground; but none of the boys were holding them. Seeing Peter there, just as he used to be when I was a kid myself, made me search the faces of the other boys to see if I could find someone else I had known among them. I couldn't; they were just ordinary kids. What I am trying to say is that I felt too tall out here to be a real person, and out of place in the only place where I really wanted to be. Maybe it was because the boys were sulky, angry at having their game interrupted and afraid of being laughed at. Maybe it was because every tree and rock and bush and berry tangle was familiar and unaltered—but unremembered before I saw it.

128

From the bank the island had seemed nearer, though larger, than I recalled. Now, somehow, there was much more water between it and the shore. The illusion was so odd that I tapped Paul on the shoulder and said, "I'll bet you can't throw a rock from here to the other side."

He grinned at me and said, "What'll you bet?"

Peter said, "He can't do it. Nobody can." It was the first time any of the boys had spoken above a mumble.

I had been planning to pay for Paul's gasoline anyway, so I said that if he did it I'd get his tank filled at the first station we came to on the way home.

The stone arced out and out until it seemed more like an arrow than a pebble, and at last dropped into the water with a splash. As nearly as I could judge it was still about thirty feet from the bank.

"There," Paul said, "I told you I could do it."

"I thought it dropped short," I said.

"The sun must have been in your eyes." Paul sounded positive. "It dropped four foot up the bank." Picking up another rock, he tossed it confidently from one hand to the other. "If you want me to, I'll do it over."

For a second I couldn't believe my ears. Paul hadn't struck me as someone who would try to collect a bet he hadn't won. I looked at the four boys. Usually there's nothing that will fire up a boy like a bet or the offer of a prize, but these still resented our intrusion too much to talk. All of them were looking at Paul, however, with the deep contempt a normal kid feels for a welcher.

I said, "O.K., you won," to Paul and got a boy to come with us in the skiff so he could row it back.

When we reached the car, Paul mentioned that there was a baseball game that afternoon, Class "A" ball, at the county seat; so we drove over and watched the game. That is, I sat and stared at the field, but when it was over I couldn't have told you whether the final score was nothing to nothing or twenty to five. On the way home I bought Paul's gas.

It was suppertime when we got back, and after supper Paul and Papa Palmieri and I sat out on the porch and drank cans of beer. We talked baseball for a little while, then Paul left. I told Papa a few stories about Paul hanging around with us older kids when he was small, then about me fighting with Peter over the frog, and waited for him to correct me.

He sat without speaking for a long time. Finally I said, "What's the matter?"

He re-lit his cigar and said, "You know all about it." It wasn't a question.

I told him I didn't really know anything about it, but that up to that minute I was beginning to think I was losing my mind.

129

He said, "You want to hear?" His voice was completely mechanical except for the trace of Italian accent. I said I did.

"Mama and me came here from Chicago when Maria was just a little baby, you know?"

I told him I had heard something about it.

"I have a good job, that's why we come to this town. Foreman at the brick works."

I said I knew that too. He had held that job while I was a kid in Cassonsville.

"We rented a little white house down on Front Street, and unpacked our stuff. Even bought some new. Everybody knew I had a good job; my credit was good. We'd been in the town couple months, I guess, when I came home from work one night and find Mama and the baby with this strange boy. Mama's holding little Maria in her lap and saying. 'Look there, Maria, that's-a your big brother.' I think maybe Mama's gone crazy, or playing a joke on me, or something. That night the kids eat with us like there was nothing strange at all."

"What did you do?" I asked him.

"I didn't do nothing. Nine times outa ten that's the best thing you can do. I wait and keep my eyes open. Night time comes and the boy goes to a little room upstairs we weren't going to use and goes to sleep. He's got an army cot there, clothes in the closet, school books, everything. Mama says we ought to get him a real bed soon when she sees me looking in there."

"Was Mama the only one . . . ?"

Papa lit a fresh cigar and I realized that it was growing dark and that both of us had been pitching our voices lower than usual.

"Everybody," Papa said. "The next day after work I go to the nuns at the school. I think I'll tell them what he looks like; maybe they know who he is."

"What did they say?" I asked him.

"They say 'Oh, you're Peter Palmieri's papa, he's such a nice boy,' soon's I tell them who I am. Everybody's like that." He was silent for a long time, then he added, "When *my* Papa writes next from the old country he says, 'How's my little Peter?' "

"That was all there was to it?"

The old man nodded. "He stays with us, and he's a good boy—better than Paul or Maria. But he never grows up. First he's Maria's big brother. Then he's her twin brother. Then little brother. Now he's Paul's little brother. Pretty soon he'll be too young to belong to Mama and me and then he'll leave, I think. You're the only one besides me who ever noticed. You played with them when you're a kid, huh?"

I told him, "Yes."

We sat on the porch for a half hour or so longer, but neither of us wanted to talk any more. When I got up to leave Papa said, "One thing. Three times I get holy water from the priest an' pour it on him while he sleeps. Nothing happens, no blisters, no screaming, nothing."

The next day was Sunday. I put on my best clothes, a clean sport shirt and good slacks, and hitched a ride to town with a truck driver who'd stopped for an early coffee at the café. I knew the nuns at Immaculate Conception would all go to the first couple of masses at the church, but since I had wanted to get away from the motel before the Palmieris grabbed me to go with them I had to leave early. I spent three hours loafing about the town—everything was closed—then went to the little convent and rang the bell.

A young nun I had never seen before answered and took me to see the Mother Superior, and it turned out to be Sister Leona, who had taught the third grade. She hadn't changed much; nuns don't, it's the covered hair and never wearing makeup, I think. Anyway, as soon as I saw her I remembered her as though I had just left her class, but I don't think she placed me, even though I told her who I was. When I was through explaining I asked her to let me see the records on Peter Palmieri, and she wouldn't. I'd wanted to see if they could possibly have a whole file drawer of cards and reports going back twenty years or more on one boy, but though I pleaded and yelled and finally threatened she kept saying that each student's records were confidential and could be shown only with the parent's permission.

Then I changed my tactics. I remembered perfectly well that when we were in the fourth grade a class picture had been taken. I could even recall the day, how hot it was, and how the photographer had ducked in and out of his cloth, looking like a bent-over nun when he was aiming the camera. I asked Sister Leona if I could look at that. She hesitated a minute and then agreed and had the young sister bring a big album that she told me had all the class pictures since the school was founded. I asked for the fourth grade of nineteen forty-four and after some shuffling she found it.

We were ranged in alternate columns of boys and girls, just as I had remembered. Each boy had a girl on either side of him but another boy in front and in back. Peter, I was certain, had stood directly behind me one step higher on the school steps, and though I couldn't think of their names I recalled the faces of the girls to my right and left perfectly.

The picture was a little dim and faded now, and having seen the school building on my way to the convent I was surprised at how much newer it had looked then. I found the spot where I had stood, second row from the back and about three spaces over from our teacher Sister Therese, but my face wasn't there. Between the two girls, tiny in the photograph, was the sharp,

131

dark face of Peter Palmieri. No one stood behind him, and the boy in front was Ernie Cotha. I ran my eyes over the list of names at the bottom of the picture and his name was there, but mine was not.

I don't know what I said to Sister Leona or how I got out of the convent. I only remember walking very fast through the almost empty Sunday-morning streets until the sign in front of the newspaper office caught my eye. The sun was reflected from the gilded lettering and the plate glass window in a blinding glare, but I could see dimly the figures of two men moving about inside. I kicked the door until one of them opened it and let me into the ink-scented room. I didn't recognize either of them, yet the expectancy of the silent, oiled presses in back was as familiar as anything in Cassonsville, unchanged since I had come in with my father to buy the ad to sell our place.

I was too tired to fence with them. Something had been taken out of me in the convent and I could feel my empty belly with a little sour coffee in it. I said, "Listen to me please, sir. There was a boy named Pete Palmer; he was born in this town. He stayed behind when the prisoners were exchanged at Panmunjom and went to Red China and worked in a textile mill there. They sent him to prison when he came back. He'd changed his name after he left here, but that wouldn't make any difference; there'll be a lot about him because he was a local boy. Can I look in your files under August and September of 1959? Please?"

They looked at each other and then at me. One was an old man with badly fitting false teeth and a green eyeshade like a movie newspaperman; the other was fat and tough looking with dull, stupid eyes. Finally the old man said, "There wasn't no Cassonsville boy stayed with the Communists. I'da remembered a thing like that."

I said, "Can I look, please?"

He shrugged his shoulders. "It's fifty cents an hour to use them files, and you can't tear nothing or take nothing out with you, understand?"

I gave him two quarters and he led me back to the morgue. There was nothing, nothing at all. There was nothing for 1953 when the exchange had taken place either. I tried to look up my birth announcement then, but there were no files before 1945; the old man out front said they'd been "burnt up when the old shop burned."

I went outside then and stood in the sun awhile. Then I went back to the motel and got my bag and went out to the island. There were no kids this time; it was very lonely and very peaceful. I poked around a bit and found this cave on the south side, then lay down on the grass and smoked my last two cigarettes and listened to the river and looked up at the sky. Before I knew it, it had started to get dark and I knew I'd better begin the trip home.

When it was too dark to see the bank across the river I went into this cave to sleep.

I think I had really known from the first that I was never going to leave the island again. The next morning I untied the skiff and let it drift away on the current, though I knew the boys would find it hung up on some snag and bring it back.

How do I live? People bring me things, and I do a good deal of fishing—even through the ice in winter. Then there are blackberries and walnuts here on the island. I think a lot, and if you do that right it's better than the things people who come to see me sometimes tell me they couldn't do without.

You'd be surprised at how many do come to talk to me. One or two almost every week. They bring me fishhooks and sometimes a blanket or a sack of potatoes and some of them tell me they wish to God they were me.

The boys still come, of course. I wasn't counting them when I said one or two people. Papa was wrong. Peter still has the same last name as always and I guess now he always will, but the boys don't call him by it much.

From Wolfe, undated, 1967:

Dear Damon,

. . . I cannot thank you adequately for what you said about "The Changeling," you can't imagine how happy I was to sell that story. And the best story is waste paper if no editor likes it well enough to publish it. Any published piece of writing half belongs to the man who said, "*This* one." . . .

Why don't more people like "Fiddler's Green?" I think I know, but I don't know what the hell to do about it. Let me put it this way. To enjoy a story like "Fiddler's Green" the reader must have a belief in a world larger than that perceived by the senses without being terrified by it. In the conventional fantastic novel somebody falls through a gibble-gabosh and finds himself in some author's idea of Avalon, by that name or some other. This kind of

133

thing at its best can be great, *e.g.* Tolkien, but it is 100% fiction. We *know* there never was and never could be a Tolkien Middle Earth or E.R.B.'s Mars. We are not so sure, late at night, about "Fiddler's Green" or Dante's Hell. Therefore most readers, I think, keep telling themselves, "It's crap. Shut up, down there." And when someone asks, "How did you like it?" they say, "Crap." I read Budrys' review. He said, if I remember, something like, "McKenna's bones should be allowed to rest undisturbed." Dig?

To Robert Silverberg, January 16, 1967:

Dear Bob,
I can't fault this one technically in any way, & it is certainly dark & nasty enough to suit anybody, but I have a nagging feeling that there's something missing, and I'm not sure I can put my finger on it. If I had to try, I guess I would point to the meeting with the girl, pp. 11-15, which goes so quickly and smoothly that I think it gives the impression of a casual pickup, & the effort to give it more meaning by the intensity of the narrator's language does not work (for me) and is unconvincing.

From Silverberg, January 26, 1967:

Dear Damon,
You and your *Orbit* are a great tribulation to me. I suppose I could take "Passengers" and ship it off to Fred Pohl and collect my $120 and start all over trying to sell one to you, but I don't want to do that, because I believe this story represents just about the best I have in me, and if I can't get you to take it it's futile to go on submitting others.

To Silverberg, March 22, 1967:

Dear Bob,
God help us both, I am going to ask you to revise this one more time. The love story now has every necessary element, but it seems to me it's an empty jug. Now I want you to put the love into it. I say this with a feeling of helplessness, because I don't know how to tell you how to do it. I believe that when the writer feels it,

134

it sometimes somehow gets onto the paper, but I don't know how. I think you have to con yourself into thinking *you* are in love with this girl, long enough to write those scenes, and deeply enough to con the reader in turn. The reason I ask you to do this difficult thing is that without it, the reader is an observer—he sees the girl remotely and dispassionately. He's got to see her as the hero, a man in love, sees her: she has got to get her hooks into him, so that there will be a wrench and a rip when they pull loose. This is a cruel story; it's got to hurt the reader, or it fails.

PASSENGERS

by Robert Silverberg

(Nebula Award, Best Short Story, 1969)

There are only fragments of me left now. Chunks of memory have broken free and drifted away like calved glaciers. It is always like that when a Passenger leaves us. We can never be sure of all the things our borrowed bodies did. We have only the lingering traces, the imprints.

Like sand clinging to an ocean-tossed bottle. Like the throbbings of amputated legs.

I rise. I collect myself. My hair is rumpled; I comb it. My face is creased from too little sleep. There is sourness in my mouth. Has my Passenger been eating dung with my mouth? They do that. They do anything.

It is morning.

A gray, uncertain morning. I stare at it awhile, and then, shuddering, I opaque the window and confront instead the gray, uncertain surface of the inner panel. My room looks untidy. Did I have a woman here? There are ashes in the trays. Searching for butts, I find several with lipstick stains. Yes, a woman was here.

I touch the bedsheets. Still warm with shared warmth. Both pillows tousled. She has gone, though, and the Passenger is gone, and I am alone.

How long did it last, this time?

I pick up the phone and ring Central. "What is the date?"

The computer's bland feminine voice replies, "Friday, December fourth, nineteen eighty-seven."

"The time?"

"Nine fifty-one, Eastern Standard Time."

"The weather forecast?"

"Predicted temperature range for today thirty to thirty-eight. Current temperature, thirty-one. Wind from the north, sixteen miles an hour. Chances of precipitation slight."

"What do you recommend for a hangover?"

"Food or medication?"

"Anything you like," I say.

The computer mulls that one over for a while. Then it decides on both, and activates my kitchen. The spigot yields cold tomato juice. Eggs begin to fry. From the medicine slot comes a purplish liquid. The Central Computer is always so thoughtful. Do the Passengers ever ride it, I wonder? What thrills could that hold for them? Surely it must be more exciting to borrow the million minds of Central than to live a while in the faulty, short-circuited soul of a corroding human being!

December 4, Central said. Friday. So the Passenger had me for three nights.

I drink the purplish stuff and probe my memories in a gingerly way, as one might probe a festering sore.

I remember Tuesday morning. A bad time at work. None of the charts will come out right. The section manager irritable; he has been taken by Passengers three times in five weeks, and his section is in disarray as a result, and his Christmas bonus is jeopardized. Even though it is customary not to penalize a person for lapses due to Passengers, according to the system, the section manager seems to feel he will be treated unfairly. So he treats us unfairly. We have a hard time. Revise the charts, fiddle with the program, check the fundamentals ten times over. Out they come: the detailed forecasts for price variations of public utility securities, February-April 1988. That afternoon we are to meet and discuss the charts and what they tell us.

I do not remember Tuesday afternoon.

That must have been when the Passenger took me. Perhaps at work; perhaps in the mahogany-paneled boardroom itself, during the conference. Pink concerned faces all about me; I cough, I lurch, I stumble from my seat. They shake their heads sadly. No one reaches for me. No one stops me. It is too dangerous to interfere with one who has a Passenger. The chances are great that a second Passenger lurks nearby in the discorporate state, looking for a mount. So I am avoided. I leave the building.

136

After that, what?

Sitting in my room on bleak Friday morning, I eat my scrambled eggs and try to reconstruct the three lost nights.

Of course it is impossible. The conscious mind functions during the period of captivity, but upon withdrawal of the Passenger nearly every recollection goes too. There is only a slight residue, a gritty film of faint and ghostly memories. The mount is never precisely the same person afterwards; though he cannot recall the details of his experience, he is subtly changed by it.

I try to recall.

A girl? Yes: lipstick on the butts. Sex, then, here in my room. Young? Old? Blonde? Dark? Everything is hazy. How did my borrowed body behave? Was I a good lover? I try to be, when I am myself. I keep in shape. At 38, I can handle three sets of tennis on a summer afternoon without collapsing. I can make a woman glow as a woman is meant to glow. Not boasting: just categorizing. We have our skills. These are mine.

But Passengers, I am told, take wry amusement in controverting our skills. So would it have given my rider a kind of delight to find me a woman and force me to fail repeatedly with her?

I dislike that thought.

The fog is going from my mind now. The medicine prescribed by Central works rapidly. I eat, I shave, I stand under the vibrator until my skin is clean. I do my exercises. Did the Passenger exercise my body Wednesday and Thursday mornings? Probably not. I must make up for that. I am close to middle age, now; tonus lost is not easily regained.

I touch my toes twenty times, knees stiff.

I kick my legs in the air.

I lie flat and lift myself on pumping elbows.

The body responds, maltreated though it has been. It is the first bright moment of my awakening: to feel the inner tingling, to know that I still have vigor.

Fresh air is what I want next. Quickly I slip into my clothes and leave. There is no need for me to report to work today. They are aware that since Tuesday afternoon I have had a Passenger; they need not be aware that before dawn on Friday the Passenger departed. I will have a free day. I will walk the city's streets, stretching my limbs, repaying my body for the abuse it has suffered.

I enter the elevator. I drop fifty stories to the ground. I step out into the December dreariness.

The towers of New York rise about me.

In the street the cars stream forward. Drivers sit edgily at their wheels.

137

One never knows when the driver of a nearby car will be borrowed, and there is always a moment of lapsed coordination as the Passenger takes over. Many lives are lost that way on our streets and highways; but never the life of a Passenger.

I begin to walk without purpose. I cross Fourteenth Street, heading north, listening to the soft violent purr of the electric engines. I see a boy jigging in the street and know he is being ridden. At Fifth and Twenty-second a prosperous-looking paunchy man approaches, his necktie askew, this morning's *Wall Street Journal* jutting from an overcoat pocket. He giggles. He thrusts out his tongue. Ridden. Ridden. I avoid him. Moving briskly, I come to the underpass that carries traffic below Thirty-fourth Street toward Queens, and pause for a moment to watch two adolescent girls quarreling at the rim of the pedestrian walk. One is a Negro. Her eyes are rolling in terror. The other pushes her closer to the railing. Ridden. But the Passenger does not have murder on its mind, merely pleasure. The Negro girl is released and falls in a huddled heap, trembling. Then she rises and runs. The other girl draws a long strand of gleaming hair into her mouth, chews on it, seems to awaken. She looks dazed.

I avert my eyes. One does not watch while a fellow sufferer is awakening. There is a morality of the ridden; we have so many new tribal mores in these dark days.

I hurry on.

Where am I going so hurriedly? Already I have walked more than a mile. I seem to be moving toward some goal, as though my Passenger still hunches in my skull, urging me about. But I know that is not so. For the moment, at least, I am free.

Can I be sure of that?

Cogito ergo sum no longer applies. We go on thinking even while we are ridden, and we live in quiet desperation, unable to halt our courses no matter how ghastly, no matter how self-destructive. I am certain that I can distinguish between the condition of bearing a Passenger and the condition of being free. But perhaps not. Perhaps I bear a particularly devilish Passenger which has not quitted me at all, but which merely has receded to the cerebellum, leaving me the illusion of freedom while all the time surreptitiously driving me onward to some purpose of its own.

Did we ever have more that that: the illusion of freedom?

But this is disturbing, the thought that I may be ridden without realizing it. I burst out in heavy perspiration, not merely from the exertion of walking. Stop. Stop here. Why must you walk? You are at Forty-second Street. There is the library. Nothing forces you onward. Stop a while, I tell myself. Rest on the library steps.

138

I sit on the cold stone and tell myself that I have made this decision for myself.

Have I? It is the old problem, free will versus determinism, translated into the foulest of forms. Determinism is no longer a philosopher's abstraction; it is cold alien tendrils sliding between the cranial sutures. The Passengers arrived three years ago. I have been ridden five times since then. Our world is quite different now. But we have adjusted even to this. We have adjusted. We have our mores. Life goes on. Our governments rule, our legislatures meet, our stock exchanges transact business as usual, and we have methods for compensating for the random havoc. It is the only way. What else can we do? Shrivel in defeat? We have an enemy we cannot fight; at best we can resist through endurance. So we endure.

The stone steps are cold against my body. In December few people sit here.

I tell myself that I made this long walk of my own free will, that I halted of my own free will, that no Passenger rides my brain now. Perhaps. Perhaps. I cannot let myself believe that I am not free.

Can it be, I wonder, that the Passenger left some lingering command in me? Walk to this place, halt at this place? That is possible too.

I look about me at the others on the library steps.

An old man, eyes vacant, sitting on newspaper. A boy of thirteen or so with flaring nostrils. A plump woman. Are all of them ridden? Passengers seem to cluster about me today. The more I study the ridden ones, the more convinced I become that I am, for the moment, free. The last time, I had three months of freedom between rides. Some people, they say, are scarcely ever free. Their bodies are in great demand, and they know only scattered bursts of freedom, a day here, a week there, an hour. We have never been able to determine how many Passengers infest our world. Millions, maybe. Or maybe five. Who can tell?

A wisp of snow curls down out of the gray sky. Central had said the chance of precipitation was slight. Are they riding Central this morning too?

I see the girl.

She sits diagonally across from me, five steps up and a hundred feet away, her black skirt pulled up on her knees to reveal handsome legs. She is young. Her hair is deep, rich auburn. Her eyes are pale; at this distance, I cannot make out the precise color. She is dressed simply. She is younger than thirty. She wears a dark green coat and her lipstick has a purplish tinge. Her lips are full, her nose slender, high-bridged, her eyebrows carefully plucked.

I know her.

I have spent the past three nights with her in my room. She is the one.

139

Ridden, she came to me, and ridden, I slept with her. I am certain of this. The veil of memory opens; I see her slim body naked on my bed.

How can it be that I remember this?

It is too strong to be an illusion. Clearly this is something that I have been *permitted* to remember for reasons I cannot comprehend. And I remember more. I remember her soft gasping sounds of pleasure. I know that my own body did not betray me those three nights, nor did I fail her need.

And there is more. A memory of sinuous music; a scent of youth in her hair; the rustle of winter trees. Somehow she brings back to me a time of innocence, a time when I am young and girls are mysterious, a time of parties and dances and warmth and secrets.

I am drawn to her now.

There is an etiquette about such things, too. It is in poor taste to approach someone you have met while being ridden. Such an encounter gives you no privilege; a stranger remains a stranger, no matter what you and she may have done and said during your involuntary time together.

Yet I am drawn to her.

Why this violation of taboo? Why this raw breach of etiquette? I have never done this before. I have been scrupulous.

But I get to my feet and walk along the step on which I have been sitting, until I am below her, and I look up, and automatically she folds her ankles together and angles her knees as if in awareness that her position is not a modest one. I know from that gesture that she is not ridden now. My eyes meet hers. Her eyes are hazy green. She is beautiful, and I rack my memory for more details of our passion.

I climb step by step until I stand before her.

"Hello," I say.

She gives me a neutral look. She does not seem to recognize me. Her eyes are veiled, as one's eyes often are, just after the Passenger has gone. She purses her lips and appraises me in a distant way.

"Hello," she replies coolly. "I don't think I know you."

"No. You don't. But I have the feeling you don't want to be alone just now. And I know I don't." I try to persuade her with my eyes that my motives are decent. "There's snow in the air," I say. "We can find a warmer place. I'd like to talk to you."

"About what?"

"Let's go elsewhere, and I'll tell you. I'm Charles Roth."

"Helen Martin."

She gets to her feet. She still has not cast aside her cool neutrality; she is suspicious, ill at ease. But at least she is willing to go with me. A good sign.

"Is it too early in the day for a drink?" I ask.

140

"I'm not sure. I hardly know what time it is."

"Before noon."

"Let's have a drink anyway," she says, and we both smile.

We go to a cocktail lounge across the street. Sitting face to face in the darkness, we sip drinks, daiquiri for her, bloody mary for me. She relaxes a little. I ask myself what it is I want from her. The pleasure of her company, yes. Her company in bed? But I have already had that pleasure, three nights of it, though she does not know that. I want something more. Something more. What?

Her eyes are bloodshot. She has had little sleep these past three nights.

I say, "Was it very unpleasant for you?"

"What?"

"The Passenger."

A whiplash of reaction crosses her face. "How did you know I've had a Passenger?"

"I know."

"We aren't supposed to talk about it."

"I'm broadminded," I tell her. "My Passenger left me some time during the night. I was ridden since Tuesday afternoon."

"Mine left me about two hours ago, I think." Her cheeks color. She is doing something daring, talking like this. "I was ridden since Monday night. This was my fifth time."

"Mine also."

We toy with our drinks. Rapport is growing, almost without the need of words. Our recent experiences with Passengers give us something in common, although Helen does not realize how imtimately we shared those experiences.

We talk. She is a designer of display windows. She has a small apartment several blocks from here. She lives alone. She asks me what I do. "Securities analyst," I tell her. She smiles. Her teeth are flawless. We have a second round of drinks. I am positive, now, that this is the girl who was in my room when I was ridden.

A seed of hope grows in me. It was a happy chance that brought us together again, so soon after we parted as dreamers. A happy chance, too, that some vestige of the dream lingered in my mind.

We have shared something, who knows what, and it must have been good to leave such a vivid imprint on me, and now I want to come to her conscious, aware, my own master, and renew that relationship, making it a real one this time. It is not proper, for I am trespassing on a privilege that is not mine except by virtue of our Passengers' brief presence in us. Yet I need her. I want her.

She seems to need me, too, without realizing who I am. But fear holds her back.

I am frightened of frightening her, and I do not try to press my advantage too quickly. Perhaps she would take me to her apartment with her now, perhaps not, but I do not ask. We finish our drinks. We arrange to meet by the library steps again tomorrow. My hand momentarily brushes hers. Then she is gone.

I fill three ashtrays that night. Over and over I debate the wisdom of what I am doing. But why not leave her alone? I have no right to follow her. In the place our world has become, we are wisest to remain apart.

And yet—there is that stab of half-memory when I think of her. The blurred lights of lost chances behind the stairs, of girlish laughter in second-floor corridors, of stolen kisses, of tea and cake. I remember the girl with the orchid in her hair, and the one in the spangled dress, and the one with the child's face and the woman's eyes, all so long ago, all lost, all gone, and I tell myself that this one I will not lose, I will not permit her to be taken from me.

Morning comes, a quiet Saturday. I return to the library, hardly expecting to find her there, but she is there, on the steps, and the sight of her is like a reprieve. She looks wary, troubled; obviously she has done much thinking, little sleeping. Together we walk along Fifth Avenue. She is quite close to me, but she does not take my arm. Her steps are brisk, short, nervous.

I want to suggest that we go to her apartment instead of to the cocktail lounge. In these days we must move swiftly while we are free. But I know it would be a mistake to think of this as a matter of tactics. Coarse haste would be fatal, bringing me perhaps an ordinary victory, a numbing defeat within it. In any event her mood hardly seems promising. I look at her, thinking of string music and new snowfalls, and she looks toward the gray sky.

She says, "I can feel them watching me all the time. Like vultures swooping overhead, waiting, waiting. Ready to pounce."

"But there's a way of beating them. We can grab little scraps of life when they're not looking."

"They're *always* looking."

"No," I tell her. "There can't be enough of them for that. Sometimes they're looking the other way. And while they are, two people can come together and try to share warmth."

"But what's the use?"

"You're too pessimistic, Helen. They ignore us for months at a time. We have a chance. We have a chance."

But I cannot break through her shell of fear. She is paralyzed by the nearness of the Passengers, unwilling to begin anything for fear it will be

142

snatched away by our tormentors. We reach the building where she lives, and I hope she will relent and invite me in. For an instant she wavers, but only for an instant: she takes my hand in both of hers, and smiles, and the smile fades, and she is gone, leaving me only with the words, "Let's meet at the library again tomorrow. Noon."

I make the long chilling walk home alone.

Some of her pessimism seeps into me that night. It seems futile for us to try to salvage anything. More than that: wicked for me to seek her out, shameful to offer a hesitant love when I am not free. In this world, I tell myself, we should keep well clear of others, so that we do not harm anyone when we are seized and ridden.

I do not go to meet her in the morning.

It is best this way, I insist. I have no business trifling with her. I imagine her at the library, wondering why I am late, growing tense, impatient, then annoyed. She will be angry with me for breaking our date, but her anger will ebb, and she will forget me quickly enough.

Monday comes. I return to work.

Naturally, no one discusses my absence. It is as though I have never been away. The market is strong that morning. The work is challenging; it is mid-morning before I think of Helen at all. But once I think of her, I can think of nothing else. My cowardice in standing her up. The childishness of Saturday night's dark thoughts. Why accept fate so passively? Why give in? I want to fight, now, to carve out a pocket of security despite the odds. I feel a deep conviction that it can be done. The Passengers may never bother the two of us again, after all. And that flickering smile of hers outside her building Saturday, that momentary glow—it should have told me that behind her wall of fear she felt the same hopes. She was waiting for me to lead the way. And I stayed home instead.

At lunchtime I go to the library, convinced it is futile.

But she is there. She paces along the steps; the wind slices at her slender figure. I go to her.

She is silent a moment. "Hello," she says finally.

"I'm sorry about yesterday."

"I waited a long time for you."

I shrug. "I made up my mind that it was no use to come. But then I changed my mind again."

She tries to look angry. But I know she is pleased to see me again—else why did she come here today? She cannot hide her inner pleasure. Nor can I. I point across the street to the cocktail lounge.

"A daiquiri?" I say. "As a peace offering?"

"All right."

143

Today the lounge is crowded, but we find a booth somehow. There is a brightness in her eyes that I have not seen before. I sense that a barrier is crumbling within her.

"You're less afraid of me, Helen," I say.

"I've never been afraid of you. I'm afraid of what could happen if we take the risks."

"Don't be. Don't be."

"I'm trying not to be afraid. But sometimes it seems so hopeless. Since *they* came here—"

"We can still try to live our own lives."

"Maybe."

"We have to. Let's make a pact, Helen. No more gloom. No more worrying about the terrible things that might just maybe happen. All right?"

A pause. Then a cool hand against mine.

"All right."

We finish our drinks, and I present my Credit Central to pay for them, and we go outside. I want her to tell me to forget about this afternoon's work and come home with her. It is inevitable, now, that she will ask me, and better sooner than later.

We walk a block. She does not offer the invitation. I sense the struggle inside her, and I wait, letting that struggle reach its own resolution without interference from me. We walk a second block. Her arm is through mine, but she talks only of her work, of the weather, and it is a remote, arm's-length conversation. At the next corner she swings around, away from her apartment, back toward the cocktail lounge. I try to be patient with her.

I have no need to rush things now, I tell myself. Her body is not a secret to me. We have begun our relationship topsy-turvy, with the physical part first; now it will take time to work backward to the more difficult part that some people call love.

But of course she is not aware that we have known each other that way. The wind blows swirling snowflakes in our faces, and somehow the cold sting awakens honesty in me. I know what I must say. I must relinquish my unfair advantage.

I tell her, "While I was ridden last week, Helen, I had a girl in my room."

"Why talk of such things now?"

"I have to, Helen. You were the girl."

She halts. She turns to me. People hurry past us in the street. Her face is very pale, with dark red spots growing in her cheeks.

"That's not funny, Charles."

"It wasn't meant to be. You were with me from Tuesday night to early Friday morning."

"How can you possibly know that?"

"I do. I do. The memory is clear. Somehow it remains, Helen. I see your whole body."

"Stop it, Charles."

"We were very good together," I say. "We must have pleased our Passengers because we were so good. To see you again—it was like waking from a dream, and finding that the dream was real, the girl right there—"

"No!"

"Let's go to your apartment and begin again."

She says, "You're being deliberately filthy, and I don't know why, but there wasn't any reason for you to spoil things. Maybe I was with you and maybe I wasn't, but you wouldn't know it, and if you did know it you should keep your mouth shut about it, and—"

"You have a birthmark the size of a dime," I say, "about three inches below your left breast."

She sobs and hurls herself at me, there in the street. Her long silvery nails rake my cheeks. She pummels me. I seize her. Her knees assail me. No one pays attention; those who pass by assume we are ridden, and turn their heads. She is all fury, but I have my arms around hers like metal bands, so that she can only stamp and snort, and her body is close against mine. She is rigid, anguished.

In a low, urgent voice I say, "We'll defeat them, Helen. We'll finish what they started. Don't fight me. There's no reason to fight me. I know, it's a fluke that I remember you, but let me go with you and I'll prove that we belong together."

"Let—go—"

"Please. Please. Why should we be enemies? I don't mean you any harm. I love you, Helen. Do you remember, when we were kids, we could play at being in love? I did; you must have done it too. Sixteen, seventeen years old. The whispers, the conspiracies—all a big game and we knew it. But the game's over. We can't afford to tease and run. We have so little time, when we're free—we have to trust, to open ourselves—"

"It's wrong."

"No. Just because it's the stupid custom for two people brought together by Passengers to avoid one another, that doesn't mean we have to follow it. Helen—Helen—"

Something in my tone registers with her. She ceases to struggle. Her rigid body softens. She looks up at me, her tearstreaked face thawing, her eyes blurred.

"Trust me," I say. "Trust me, Helen!"

She hesitates. Then she smiles.

145

In that moment I feel the chill at the back of my skull, the sensation as of a steel needle driven deep through bone. I stiffen. My arms drop away from her. For an instant, I lose touch, and when the mists clear all is different.

"Charles?" she says. *"Charles?"*

Her knuckles are against her teeth. I turn, ignoring her, and go back into the cocktail lounge. A young man sits in one of the front booths. His dark hair gleams with pomade; his cheeks are smooth. His eyes meet mine.

I sit down. He orders drinks. We do not talk.

My hand falls on his wrist, and remains there. The bartender, serving the drinks, scowls but says nothing. We sip our cocktails and put the drained glasses down.

"Let's go," the young man says.

I follow him out.

To Thomas A. Dardis, June 16, 1967:

Dear Tom,

. . . If we are going to have our usual hassle with Putnam over the contents of *Orbit 3*, I'd like to have it now and get it over with. As I've told you, I remain opposed to any censorship of *Orbit*; I continue to insist that it is an adult book and should not be emasculated. I am unwilling to shuffle the contents of *Orbit 3* and *4* in order to make *Orbit 3* innocuous, first because this would mean taking out the best stories in *Orbit 3** and lowering its quality; second because this would merely postpone the problem.

The following story has no correspondence attached to it because the author handed it to me at dinner (at the Tom Quick Inn in Milford, during a Milford Conference) and I read it and bought it on the spot. This is not the way most writers submit stories; but Harlan Ellison is not like any other writer.

---

i.e., "Mother to the World" and "The Planners."

SHATTERED LIKE A
GLASS GOBLIN

by Harlan Ellison

So it was there, eight months later, that Rudy found her; in that huge and ugly house off Western Avenue in Los Angeles; living with them, all of them, not just Jonah, but all of them.

It was November in Los Angeles, near sundown, and unaccountably chill even for the fall in that place always near the sun. He came down the sidewalk and stopped in front of the place. It was gothic hideous, with the grass half-cut and the rusted lawnmower sitting in the middle of an unfinished swath. Grass cut as if in a placating gesture to the outraged tenants of the two lanai apartment houses that loomed over the squat structure on either side. (Yet how strange . . . the apartment buildings were taller, the old house hunched down between them, but *it* seemed to dominate *them*. How odd.)

Cardboard covered the upstairs windows.

A baby carriage was overturned on the front walk.

The front door was ornately carved.

Darkness seemed to breathe heavily.

Rudy shifted the duffel bag slightly on his shoulder. He was afraid of the house. He was breathing more heavily as he stood there, and a panic he could never have described tightened his fat muscles on either side of his shoulderblades. He looked up into the corners of the darkening sky, seeking a way out, but he could only go forward. Kristina was in there.

Another girl answered the door.

She looked at him without speaking, her long blond hair half-obscuring her face; peering out from inside the veil of Clairol and dirt.

When he asked a second time for Kris, she wet her lips in the corners, and a tic made her cheek jump. Rudy set down the duffel bag with a whump. "Kris, please," he said urgently.

The blonde girl turned away and walked into the dim hallways of the terrible old house. Rudy stood in the open doorway, and suddenly, as if the blonde girl had been a barrier to it, and her departure had released it, he was assaulted like a smack in the face, by a wall of pungent scent. It was marijuana.

He reflexively inhaled, and his head reeled. He took a step back, into the

147

last inches of sunlight coming over the lanai apartment building, and then it was gone, and he was still buzzing, and moved forward, dragging the duffel bag behind him.

He did not remember closing the front door, but when he looked, some time later, it was closed behind him.

He found Kris on the third floor, lying against the wall of a dark closet, her left hand stroking a faded pink rag rabbit, her right hand at her mouth, the little finger crooked, the thumb-ring roach holder half-obscured as she sucked up the last wonders of the joint. The closet held an infinitude of odors—dirty sweat socks as pungent as stew, fleece jackets on which the rain had dried to mildew, a mop gracious with its scent of old dust hardened to dirt, the overriding weed smell of what she had been at no one knew how long—and it held her. As pretty as pretty could be.

"Kris?"

Slowly her head came up, and she saw him. Much later, she tracked and focused and she began to cry. "Go away."

In the limpid silences of the whispering house, back and above him in the darkness, Rudy heard the sudden sound of leather wings beating furiously for a second, then nothing.

Rudy crouched down beside her, his heart grown twice its size in his chest. He wanted so desperately to reach her, to talk to her. "Kris . . . please . . ." She turned her head away, and with the hand that had been stroking the rabbit she slapped at him awkwardly, missing him.

For an instant, Rudy could have sworn he heard the sound of someone counting heavy gold pieces, somewhere off to his right, down a passageway of the third floor. But when he half-turned, and looked out through the closet door, and tried to focus his hearing on it, there was no sound.

Kris was trying to crawl back further into the closet. She was trying to smile.

He turned back, on hands and knees moved into the closet after her.

"The rabbit," she said, languorously. "You're crushing the rabbit." He looked down, his right knee was lying on the soft matted-fur head of the pink rabbit. He pulled it out from under his knee and threw it into a corner of the closet. She looked at him with disgust. "You haven't changed, Rudy. Go away."

"I'm outta the army, Kris," Rudy said gently. "They let me out on a medical. I want you to come back, Kris, please."

She would not listen, but pulled herself away from him, deep into the closet, and closed her eyes. He moved his lips several times, as though trying to recall words he had already spoken, but there was no sound, and he lit a cigarette, and sat in the open doorway of the closet, smoking and waiting for her to come back to him. He had waited eight months for her to come back to him, since he had been inducted and she had written him telling him, *Rudy, I'm going to live with Jonah at the house.*

There was the sound of something very tiny, lurking in the infinitely black shadow where the top step of the stairs from the second floor met the landing. It giggled in a glass harpsichord trilling. Rudy knew it was giggling at him, but he could make out no movement from that corner.

Kris opened her eyes and stared at him with distaste. "Why did you come here?"

"Because we're gonna be married."

"Get out of here."

"I love you, Kris. Please."

She kicked out at him. It didn't hurt, but it was meant to. He backed out of the closet slowly.

Jonah was down in the living room. The blonde girl who had answered the door was trying to get his pants off him. He kept shaking his head no, and trying to fend her off with a weak-wristed hand. The record player under the brick-and-board bookshelves was playing Simon & Garfunkel, "The Big Bright Green Pleasure Machine."

"Melting," Jonah said gently. "Melting," and he pointed toward the big, foggy mirror over the fireplace mantel. The fireplace was crammed with unburned wax milk cartons, candy bar wrappers, newspapers from the underground press, and kitty litter. The mirror was dim and chill. "Melting!" Jonah yelled suddenly, covering his eyes.

"Oh shit!" the blonde girl said, and threw him down, giving up at last. She came toward Rudy.

"What's wrong with him?" Rudy asked.

"He's freaking out again. Christ, what a drag he can be."

"Yeah, but what's *happening* to him?"

She shrugged. "He sees his face melting, that's what he says."

"Is he on marijuana?"

The blonde girl looked at him with sudden distrust. "Hey, who are you?"

"I'm a friend of Kris's."

The blonde girl assayed him for a moment more, then by the way her shoulders dropped and her posture relaxed, she accepted him. "I thought you might've just walked in, you know, maybe the Laws. You know?"

There was a Middle Earth poster on the wall behind her, with its brightness faded in a long straight swath where the sun caught it every morning. He looked around uneasily. He didn't know what to do.

"I was supposed to marry Kris. Eight months ago," he said.

"You want to fuck?" asked the blonde girl. "When Jonah trips he turns

149

off. I been drinking Coca-Cola all morning and all day, and I'm really horny."

Another record dropped onto the turntable and Little Stevie Wonder blew hard into his harmonica and started singing, "I Was Born To Love Her."

"I was engaged to Kris," Rudy said, feeling sad. "We were going to be married when I got out of basic. But she decided to come over here with Jonah, and I didn't want to push her. So I waited eight months, but I'm out of the army now."

"Well, do you or don't you?"

Under the dining-room table. She put a satin pillow under her. It said: *Souvenir of Niagara Falls, New York.*

When he went back into the living room, Jonah was sitting up on the sofa, reading Hesse's *Magister Ludi.*

"Jonah?" Rudy said. Jonah looked up. It took him a while to recognize Rudy.

When he did, he patted the sofa beside him, and Rudy came and sat down.

"Hey, Rudy, where y'been?"

"I've been in the army."

"Wow."

"Yeah, it was awful."

"You out now? I mean for good?"

Rudy nodded. "Uh-huh. Medical."

"Hey, that's good."

They sat quietly for a while. Jonah started to nod, and then said to himself, "You're not very tired."

Rudy said, "Jonah, hey listen, what's the story with Kris? You know, we was supposed to get married about eight months ago."

"She's around someplace," Jonah answered.

Out of the kitchen, through the dining room where the blonde girl lay sleeping under the table, came the sound of something wild, tearing at meat. It went on for a long time, but Rudy was looking out the front window, the big bay window. There was a man in a dark gray suit standing talking to two policemen on the sidewalk at the edge of the front walk leading up to the front door.

"Jonah, can Kris come away now?"

Jonah looked angry. "Hey, listen, man, nobody's *keeping* her here. She's been grooving with all of us and she likes it. Go ask her. Christ, don't bug *me!*"

The two cops were walking up the front door.

Rudy got up and went to answer the doorbell.

150

They smiled at him when they saw his uniform.

"May I help you?" Rudy asked them.

The first cop said, "Do you live here?"

"Yes," said Rudy. "My name is Rudolph Boekel. May I help you?"

"We'd like to come inside and talk to you."

"Do you have a search warrant?"

"We don't want to search, we only want to talk to you. Are you in the army?"

"Just discharged. I came home to see my family."

"Can we come in?"

"No, sir."

The second cop looked troubled. "Is this the place they call 'The Hill'?"

"Who?" Rudy asked, looking perplexed.

"Well, the neighbors said this was 'The Hill' and there were some pretty wild parties going on here."

"Do you hear any partying?"

The cops looked at each other. Rudy added, "It's always very quiet here. My mother is dying of cancer of the stomach."

They let Rudy move in, because he was able to talk to people who came to the door from the outside. Aside from Rudy, who went out to get food, and the weekly trips to the Unemployment Line, no one left The Hill. It was usually very quiet.

Except sometimes there was the sound of growling in the back hall leading up to what had been a maid's room; and the splashing from the basement, the sound of wet things on bricks.

It was a self-contained little universe, bordered on the north by acid and mescaline, on the south by pot and peyote, on the east by speed and redballs, on the west by downers and amphetamines. There were eleven people living in The Hill. Eleven, and Rudy.

He walked through the halls, and sometimes found Kris, who would not talk to him, save once, when she asked him if he'd ever been heavy behind anything except love. He didn't know what to answer her, so he only said, "Please," and she called him a square and walked off toward the stairway leading to the dormered attic.

Rudy had heard squeaking from the attic. It had sounded to him like the shrieking of mice being torn to pieces. There were cats in the house.

He did not know why he was there, except that he didn't understand why she wanted to stay. His head always buzzed and he sometimes felt that if he just said the right thing, the right way, Kris would come away with him. He began to dislike the light. It hurt his eyes.

151

No one talked to anyone else very much. There was always a struggle to keep high, to keep the group-high as elevated as possible. In that way they cared for each other.

And Rudy became their one link with the outside. He had written to someone—his parents, a friend, a bank, someone—and now there was money coming in. Not much, but enough to keep the food stocked, and the rent paid. But he insisted Kris be nice to him.

They all made her be nice to him, and she slept with him in the little room on the second floor where Rudy had put his newspapers and his duffel bag. He lay there most of the day, when he was not out on errands for The Hill, and he read the smaller items about train wrecks and molestations in the suburbs. And Kris came to him and they made love of a sort.

One night she convinced him he should ''make it, heavy behind acid'' and he swallowed fifteen hundred mikes in two big gel caps, and she was stretched out like taffy for six miles. He was a fine copper wire charged with electricity, and he pierced her flesh. She wriggled with the current that flowed through him, and became softer yet. He sank down through the softness, and carefully observed the intricate wood-grain effect her teardrops made as they rose in the mist around him. He was downdrifting slowly, turning and turning, held by a whisper of blue that came out of his body like a spiderweb. The sound of her breathing in the moist crystal pillared cavity that went down and down was the sound of the very walls themselves, and when he touched them with his warm metal fingertips she drew in breath heavily, forcing the air up around him as he sank down, twisting slowly in a veil of musky looseness.

There was an insistent pulsing somewhere below him, and he was afraid of it as he descended, the high-pitched whining of something threatening to shatter. He felt panic. Panic gripped him, flailed at him, his throat constricted, he tried to grasp the veil and it tore away in his hands; then he was falling, faster now, much faster, and afraid afraid!

Violet explosions all around him and the shrieking of something that wanted him, that was seeking him, pulsing deeply in the throat of an animal he could not name, and he heard her shouting, heard her wail and pitch beneath him and a terrible crushing feeling in him . . .

And then there was silence.

That lasted for a moment.

And then there was soft music that demanded nothing but inattention. So they lay there, fitted together, in the heat of the tiny room, and they slept for hours.

After that, Rudy seldom went out into the light. He did the shopping at night, wearing shades. He emptied the garbage at night, and he swept down the front walk, and did the front lawn with scissors because the lawnmower would have annoyed the residents of the lanai apartments, who no longer complained, because there was seldom a sound from The Hill.

He began to realize he had not seen some of the eleven young people who lived in The Hill for a long time. But the sounds from above and below and around him in the house grew more frequent.

Rudy's clothes were too large for him now. He wore only underpants. His hands and feet hurt. The knuckles of his fingers were larger, from cracking them, and they were always an angry crimson.

His head always buzzed. The thin perpetual odor of weed was saturated in the wood walls and the rafters. He read newspapers all the time, old newspapers whose items were imbedded in his memory. He remembered a job he had once held as a garage mechanic, but that seemed a very long time ago. When they cut off the electricity in The Hill, it didn't bother Rudy, because he preferred the dark. But he went to tell the eleven.

He could not find them.

They were all gone. Even Kris, who should have been there somewhere.

He heard the moist sounds from the basement and went down with fur and silence into the darkness. The basement had been flooded. One of the eleven named Teddy was there. He was attached to the slime-coated upper wall of the basement, hanging close to the stone, pulsing softly and giving off a thin green light. He dropped a rubbery arm into the water, and let it hang there moving idly with the tideless tide. Then something came near it, and he made a sharp movement, and brought the thing up still writhing in his rubbery grip, and inched it up the wall to a dark, moist spot on his upper surface, near the veins that covered its length, and pushed the thing at the dark-blood spot, where it shrieked with a terrible sound, and went in and there was a sucking noise, then a swallowing sound.

Rudy went back upstairs. On the first floor he found the one who was the blonde girl, whose name was Adrianne. She lay out thin and white as a tablecloth on the dining-room table as three of the others put their teeth into her, and through their hollow sharp teeth they drank up the yellow fluid from the bloated pus-pockets that had been her breasts and buttocks. Their faces were very white and their eyes were like soot-smudges.

Climbing to the second floor, Rudy was almost knocked down by the passage of something that had been Victor, flying on heavily ribbed leather wings. It was carrying a cat in its jaws.

He found Kris in the attic, in a corner breaking the skull and sucking out the moist brains of a thing that giggled like a harpsichord.

153

"Kris, we have to go away," he told her. She reached out and touched him, snapping her long, pointed, dirty fingernails against him. He rang like crystal.

In the rafters of the attic Jonah crouched, gargoyled and sleeping. There was a green stain on his jaws, and something stringy in his claws.

"Kris, please," he said urgently.

His head buzzed.

His ears itched.

Kris sucked out the last of the mellow good things in the skull of the silent little creature, and scraped idly at the flaccid body with hairy hands. She settled back on her haunches, and her long, hairy muzzle came up.

Rudy scuttled away.

He ran loping, his knuckles brushing the attic floor as he scampered for safety. Behind him, Kris was growling. He got down to the second floor and then to the first, and tried to climb up on the Morris chair to the mantel, so he could see himself in the mirror, in the light from the moon through the flyblown window. But Naomi was on the window, lapping up the flies with her tongue.

He climbed with desperation, wanting to see himself. And when he stood before the mirror, he saw that he was transparent, that there was nothing inside him, that his ears had grown pointed and had hair on their tips; his eyes were as huge as a tarsier's, and the reflection of the light hurt him.

Then he heard the growling behind and below him.

The little glass goblin turned, and the werewolf rose up on its hind legs and touched him till he rang like fine crystal.

And the werewolf said with very little concern, "Have you ever grooved heavy behind anything except love?"

"Please!" the little glass goblin begged, just as the great hairy paw slapped him into a million coruscating rainbow fragments all expanding consciously into the tight little enclosed universe that was The Hill, all buzzing highly contracted and tingling off into a darkness that began to seep out through the silent wooden walls . . .

From Langdon Jones, November 23, 1967:

Dear Mr. Knight,

On his return from the States, Mike Moorcock mentioned to me that you had expressed interest in seeing my story "The Time Machine." Doubleday have had a copy which is now free, and I have asked them to forward it on to you.

Although this is a proof copy (it was originally to have been published in *New Worlds*) it has not yet been published anywhere, as the printer decided that it wasn't fit to be read by a decent-minded public.

To Lawrence P. Ashmead, November 29, 1967:

Dear Larry,

Thanx for sending me Lang Jones' "The Time Machine." I bought it like a shot, though not positive the world is ready on this side of the Atlantic, either. It will be interesting to see what Putnam's printers say.

From Langdon Jones, September 21, 1968:

Dear Damon,

I herewith return the Xerox copy of "The Time Machine" (which arrived yesterday), with my corrections of the copyediting. Those alterations which I authorise I have marked "o.k.," those I do not, "no." Any alterations not marked you may take as having my approval.

I must say that I felt many of the changes were entirely arbitrary, and reflected the taste of the editor rather than any kind of fidelity to the story, and I am very glad that I had the opportunity of correcting them. . . .

I trust that there is no possibility of my corrections not being incorporated in the printed story, and if this is not the case, would like to withdraw my story forthwith.

I request most urgently that if you publish other works of mine I am consulted about all alterations that you wish to make.

From Michael Moorcock and James Sallis, undated:

Damon,
    [In Moorcock's handwriting] These changes are barbaric. Maybe you don't want more stories from the U.K. [In Sallis's writing] (Or U.S.)

To Langdon Jones, September 24, 1968:

    Dear Lang,
    Got the corrected Xeroxes, & will restore all the changes you have marked "no," even the hyphens. I think you are wrong about some of these, but after all it is your story. I want to compliment you on the temperate tone of your letters, by the way; it must have been a rude shock to find out that any changes had been made in the story without consulting you, and I never would have done it if I hadn't been in such a bleeding hurry to get away from Milford. To avoid hassles like this in the future I plan to send out Xeroxes of copyedited mss. routinely whenever there are changes of anything more than spelling & grammar.
    On one point you have me dead to rights—"coach" is commonly used to mean a car in a train, & when I came to it I changed it automatically and without thinking. (Bus companies often call themselves "coach systems," but nobody pays any attention.)

THE TIME MACHINE

by Langdon Jones

The cell is not large. There is just room for a small bunk along one wall, and a small table on the other side, a stool in front of it. The table and the stool have once been painted a glossy red, but their finish has long been spoiled by time, and now light wood shows through the streaks of paint. The floor is flagged, and the walls are made of large blocks of stone. The stone has streaks of dampness across its surface, and in the air is a sweet smell of decay. There is a window high in the far wall, set with bars of rusted iron, and through it can be seen a patch of blue sky, and a wisp of yellow cloud. Sometimes, not very often, a bird flashes across the space like a brief hallucination. In the opposite wall there is a large metal door, with a grille set into its surface. Behind the grille is a shutter, so that those outside may, when they wish, observe the prisoner from a safe distance.

The bunk is made of metal, and is fixed permanently to one wall. It is painted green, and this color is interrupted only where the rusty nuts and bolts extrude. On one side the bunk is bolted to the wall, and on the other it is supported by two metal legs, which have worn little depressions in the stone floor. Above the bunk, crudely scratched into the wall, are various drawings and messages. There are initials, dates, obscenities and phallic drawings. Set a little apart from the others is the only one which does not make immediate sense. It is engraved deeply into the wall, and consists of two words, set one above the other. The engraving obviously took a great deal of time to complete. The upper of these words is "TIME," the lower, "SOLID."

The bunk is covered by rumpled gray blankets, which smell of the sweat of generations of prisoners. Sitting at the foot of the bunk is the prisoner. He is leaning over, his elbows on his knees, his back hunched, looking at a photograph in his hands.

The photograph is of a girl. It is just a little larger than two inches square, and is in black and white. It is a close-up, and the lower part of her arms, and her body below the waist are not revealed. Her head is not directly facing the camera, and she appears to be looking at something to one side, revealing a three-quarter view of her face. Behind her is a brick wall—a decorative wall in Holland Park on that day after the hotel and after the morning in the coffee shop; soon they were to part again at the railway station.

Her dark hair was drawn back, and she had a calm but emotional expression on her face. Her face was fairly round, but her high cheekbones caused a slight concavity of her cheeks, giving her always a slightly drawn look which he had always found immensely attractive, ever since he had first known her. Her features were somewhat negroid—"a touch of the tar brush, as my mother used to put it," she had said in one of her letters—large dark eyes, and large lips which, when she smiled, gave her a look of ironic sadness. Occasionally she also had the practical look of a Northern housewife, and her energy was expressed in her face and her body. Her body was very slim, and her flesh felt like the flesh of no other woman on earth. When he had first seen her she had been wearing a black dress at a party, a dress which did nothing to conceal the smallness of her breasts, and which proudly proclaimed her slightness. This had captivated him immediately. It was something which accented her femininity, although doubtless she had not considered it in this way, and he saw her that first time as the most beautiful thing on earth.

He would meet her in Leicester. He would set off early on Sunday and take a train to Victoria, and walk among the few people about at this time on a Sunday morning to the coach station. He could never understand why it was—as he sat in the cafeteria with a cup of coffee—that the people all about appeared so ugly. The only people that morning who were at all pleasing to the eye were a family of Indians who had sat near him—the women in saris, and the men bewhiskered and proud in turbans. Perhaps it was all subjective, and everyone appeared ugly because he knew that this morning, in little more than three hours, he would be meeting her again. The weather was not impossibly cold—they wanted to make love, and many things were against it that week. At nine-fifteen he would walk over, past the coaches for Lympne airport and France, to the far corner of the yard, where the Leicester coach would be waiting.

He got in the coach. There were never more than eight or nine people who wanted to go to Leicester early on a Sunday morning, and he would walk down to the back of the coach and sit on the left-hand side. Why always the left, he didn't know. At nine thirty-five the vehicle would set off, pouring out clouds of diesel smoke, emerging from its home like a mechanical dragon. As they passed Marble Arch, Swiss Cottage, and headed for the M1, he was conscious of a mounting tension. Partly sexual—partly the knowledge that soon he would see her again, and partly because he knew that *he* knew. What was going to happen this time? He could visualize that one morning she wouldn't come, but he would, and instead of loving there would be hatred and fighting. She had told him during the week, and he had been very upset. But he wanted her to continue, for he knew what it would do to her to have to stop now. What had been set into action was a series of circumstances that had to run a certain course until it was possible to break it. And the breaking would be hard—was hard.

The sun was shining, and the fields that they passed became transformed, as they always did, by her proximity in time. Everything around him was beautiful. It was as if he could see the scene through the coach window with an intensity that would not be possible normally. It was as if together they were one being, and that apart from her he was less than half a person. But there were four other people who depended on her as well. Two little boys, one little girl and one adult man. A family is a complete entity as well. Later he would go to her home in West Cutford, and see her with her children, and feel himself to be a malevolent force, a wildly destructive element that didn't

158

belong here, and yet, seeing at the same time an image of what might have been; how close was this reality to the one he wanted.

When the coach left the motorway, it was only half an hour before he would be in Leicester, and three quarters before they would be together, their proximity having an astronomical rightness, as implacably correct as the orbit of the earth. The watery January sun shone onto the brown brick buildings that told him that soon he would be at their meeting-place—the coach station in Southgate Street. This place had a special significance for him; it was like the scene of some great historical event. But most of the places were; not the hotel, where the coming and going of other people obscured the significance of their own, but their little shed at Groby Pond, their room at the top of a house in West London. All these places deserved some kind of immortality.

Now the tension was very strong; his muscles were clenched all over his body and his hands were shaking. The coach approached some traffic lights, turned left, bumping over a rough road surface, and went down a grim street, full of half-demolished buildings. Further down were some other buildings composed of reddish-brown brick, except for a modern pub which was opposite a large flat area surrounded by metal railings. The coach turned into this concrete area, for this was Southgate Street. As the coach slowed up the few people inside began to rise, putting on overcoats and collecting their luggage. He looked intently through the windows to see if she had arrived. She wasn't here yet. The coach was early; it was only quarter-past twelve. There was six and a half hours of the day left. This was always the most difficult part. Before he had felt that he was going toward her; that he could feel the distance between them lessening. But now all the movement was up to her and he could no longer be directly aware of it.

He climbed down from the coach and went to the other side of the road, waiting for her car to arrive. Looking across at the coach station, he knew that he would remember this place for the rest of his life whatever happened. In one month, seventeen days and six hours they would say good-bye for the last time.

Cars were passing in groups; there would be a time when nothing was on the road at all, then later twenty cars would come along together, and his eyes would move as he looked at first one, then the next. A cold wind was blowing, and he was shivering uncontrollably. A couple of girls walked past on the other side of the street, talking and laughing together. A car came along that looked like hers, but inside it was a large, white-haired man. This was impossible. He turned and walked round to the entrance of the pub. This was The Shakespeare, the same name as another pub that had featured in

159

their lives; it was as if their whole existence was marked out by common-place things that were all cryptograms, that all had hidden significance. Their love made everything more real, and at the same time turned the world into a devious collection of symbols.

He pushed through the doors of the pub and went into the lounge bar. He ordered a drink, and then went to sit by one of the windows. If he stood up and looked through the net curtains he could just see part of the coach station. Parked outside was a car, but from here it did not look like hers. He sat down, and regarded the shiny surface of the table in front of him.

Things were obviously bad for her at home. Her letters had told him what had been going on. She could not get away from this situation; she would part from him and then go back to a person who was being hurt, a person whose life was being threatened by their love—a love that seemed innocent and inevitable. That first night, when they suddenly found themselves in bed together, when a few hours before they had been little more than friendly strangers, it had all seemed so right. They both knew that life was now going to become difficult, but still wanted it to happen. He stood up, and peered through the window. The parked car was still there, and she was not in sight. He sat down again. But how much stress could one stand? How much could this man stand? He understood the situation, but how long would it be before his control broke down, and he came with nothing in his brain but an urge to destroy? How would he react to this? How could he possibly try to physical-ly hurt a man he had hurt so much already? He stood up and looked through the window again. Suddenly finding it impossible to wait in the pub any longer, he abruptly walked toward the door and went outside in the cold again. The parked car was not hers. It was nearly half-past twelve. He crossed the road and went back inside the coach station. He sat down on a bench with his back to the road. In his bag was a book, and he took it out. It was very cold. He began to read.

The sun has passed the point at which it shines directly into the cell. Now dark shadows are creeping across the floor, and it is becoming colder. The prisoner lifts his feet from the floor and lies back on his bunk, holding the photograph above him. At the time the photograph had been taken they had spent two days in a room in a hotel in London, doing little but making love, going out occasionally for food. It had been a fairly cheap hotel, and the room had looked, at first, rather bare. But in two hours it had become transformed into a jeweled palace. The red bed-cover had glowed with the mystical luminosity of a robe in a Flemish painting. When they had left the hotel, they had gone to Holland Park, aching to make love again, full of an insatiable desire to repeat an experience so good it should have been unrepeatable. He felt vaguely surprised that the exposed flesh of her face and

160

neck did not show any signs of his love. He felt that his hands and lips and tongue should have left visible tracks on her skin and would show that this woman was loved. Perhaps there was a gentleness in her eyes, a quirk of her lips; but perhaps he was imagining these signs.

He held the photograph close to his eyes so that he could see the grain, and the slight fuzziness of her individual hairs. Now he was conscious of the photograph as a record only. A piece of paper that was not even there at the time. Recorded tracks of light that had reflected from her at that time into the lens of a camera. This contact with her was so nebulous, and yet the photograph somehow solidified the events, gave them a concrete reality, as if at some time or some place they were together in Holland Park, she in front of him, apologizing for her tiredness and the untidiness of her hair, saying "Just after making love is not the best time for taking a picture of me," and then being quiet and looking to one side, and the shutter opening, slowly, slower, and then freezing, wide open, this "time" a tangible material like film going through a camera, that can be wound on, stopped and taken out.

Their love affair was now like a piece of sculpture, an object that plainly begins at one point and ends at another, but which may be seen as a single object in space, which may be looked at closely, details expanding, may be examined from different angles, touched, embraced, wept upon.

The last time in the hotel had been good, so good that he could now remember nothing but an ecstatic feeling of life and death and her cries regularly punctuating the quiet of the room, and his own gasped sounds joining hers in a complex of rhythm, and then nothing but his own engulfment in a torrent of whiteness.

Caroline Howard. First just a name, and then a name that was a woman, and then a name that was so intertwined with his own existence it became a million things, was a part of him. Just the sound of her name, reflected softly from the stone walls, was enough to bring back a whole series of memories and associations; it must be like the lifetime's memories of a drowning man. In a fraction of a second it was all there to be seen, touched, tasted, smelled. Caroline Howard Caroline Howard Caroline Howard—a bright orgasm in morning sunlight.

The time machine operates on an organic, electrochemical basis, with mineral connections. It is operated by means of a circulating substance that is sometimes fluid and sometimes gaseous, passing through an infinite number of stages of creation. This substance becomes finer and finer in form, eventually phasing from the limits of existence to great solidity and density, beginning the cycle again. The implications of this cycle, with the relative nature of its stages, provide the basic crystallizing power of the machine. The apparatus is also provided with gross mechanical parts, cogs, motors and chains, which are essential to the smooth transport of its medium through all the stages of metamorphosis. The machine deals with relationships, patterns and similarities. Some of the implications of the time machine are almost metaphysical in nature.

It may easily be seen that the machine is not like any other of the mechanical constructions that have been made up to now. While the operation of the machine may be analyzed in detail, the reader of such a description will not be able to understand at all the functions of its cycles. Also the mechanically-minded reader will notice immediately that there are components which he would deem unnecessary and uneconomic, and he will undoubtedly comment too that more components seem to be essential for the machine to work at all, and that in its present state if would be capable of doing absolutely nothing. The time machine is capable, in fact, of operation in a number of different ways. On the other hand it may work in a more general sense for one, or any number of separate observers. Also, the machine may, and does, operate entirely on its own, unobserved; it does this constantly, the separate parts of the construction existing at different and all points of time.

It is to be understood that time is not a moving stream. Time is a minor quality of the continuum, common only to living creatures, and consists of an involuntary change of attention. The consciousness of a creature is an infinitely restricted series of sense-impressions, operating in three dimensions only. The universe consists of a four-dimensional geometric form, which, in cross-section, contains all the physical facts of matter, and is curved so that it eventually rejoins itself, forming a four-dimensional ring shape. Thus, a cross-section of any part of this ring will produce the universe at any particular point in "time." This "time" is merely the attention of the creature observing the shape about him, and is due to his being able to be aware of only one infinitely small part of the shape. His attention is constantly and involuntarily operating on a different part of the ring, giving the impression of movement and animation to what is in fact a static object, and also giving him the false impression of temporal extension. If one draws a wavy line, and follows this line with one's eyes, it will appear to move up and down, whereas with a widening of attention the line can immediately be appreciated as an unmoving and complete object. The time that each of us experiences is common only to us, and is an internal psychic operation rather than a measurable physical fact.

If we stand at one end of a room and walk across to the other, this restricted attention is all that gives the impression of movement. In fact

162

movement is an aspect of time, and to someone lacking this restriction of attention, it would be obvious that the movement was only an impression in the mind of the person concerned and that his body, as it crossed the room, was merely a solid and static object.

We can see now that time is not the barrier it was once thought to be, and that as a psychic mechanism it may be radically altered, or completely destroyed. It is surprising that this was not realized before; the time-dilation or time-destruction observed by takers of the "mind-expanding" hallucinogenic drugs has been often noted, as well as the more usual distortions of time during various common mental states.

The time machine, by operating in terms of relationships of pattern, is able to crystallize the attention of the observer, producing a concrete *déjà vu*, and in the solidity of its wheels and pistons we find reflected the tangibility of the universe, in all its states of being.

He looked up from the book. And saw her. She was talking to two bus men, asking them if they knew whether the London bus had arrived yet. He hurriedly put the book away, and as he stood she saw him. She was wearing her black fur coat, and her face, as she came toward him, was his own face, as familiar as the face he shaved each morning, a face that was more than the sum of all the faces he knew; his own, his parents', his friends', more than anything else he would ever find. Her face was troubled. They approached each other slowly, not running with joyful exuberance as they had the last time they had met here, or moving quickly with desperation to clasp each other, to shut off the world in the closeness of each other's arms as they would later. He took her gently in his arms, and they kissed softly, and then embraced, holding each other tightly. She exhaled his name in a sigh, a drooping inflection that suggested pressure that had been building up suddenly released. Now was right; everything was infinitely right. His face was pressed against her neck, the scent of her hair was filling his nostrils, her body was warm in his arms. Now he was alive, and he did not want to move from this position ever again. His hands ran over her back, and he felt her lips at his neck; he was melting into a state of complete being, a state that had intolerable tensions and unformulated desires, that caused his breath to be exhaled explosively, hearing the sounds he made, they both made, to be like miniature versions of the sounds crushed from their bodies by the dazzling pressure of orgasm. Waves of pressure ran round his body; his head moved, lips brushing her cheek, her ear, her neck. Their heads drew apart, and he looked into her eyes. He felt his head moving with the impossible surging of communication of emotions impossible to communicate. His eyes moved as he tried to take in all the details of her face at once. He smiled, and saw an answering smile on her face, a reflection of his own feelings. They kissed for a long time, and then slowly drew apart.

"How have things been at home?"

"Not too good. Difficult."

They began to walk out of the coach station, their arms round each other.

"Do you mind if we go for a drink first? I do feel that I need it."

"Of course not."

They walk across the road, and into The Shakespeare. They sit at the table with drinks, and she opens her coat to reveal her gray dress. He tells her that he is very fond of the dress, and they tell each other "I love you," a universal reassurance, always needed. Soft lips against his. Unhappiness in her eyes. In memory, not much is said. A letter is discussed, and one or two sentences are actually verbalized, although in a constantly varying way. "He can accept the whole thing intellectually, and he doesn't want to stop it, for my sake. He knows I'm seeing you."

"I know."

"No, I mean today. He saw me off, and watched me drive away in the car." A feeling of mute horror that stays the same, despite the changing pattern of the words. "What with my period and everything, all my energies are at a low ebb. I'm in the most schizophrenic state. There's part of me that can't bear the thought of having an affair, and the rest of me wants nothing but you." He says nothing. There is nothing but the sound of her voice, and he watches her lips moving, sees the flecks of mascara on her cheeks, feels terror at his innocent power of inflicting pain.

Later they leave the pub, at one o'clock, and drive off to Groby Pond, the place at which they arrived the last time, his first trip to Leicester, after driving off twelve miles in the wrong direction, laughing at the confusion into which they were both plunged by their mutual proximity. They take a wrong turning this time, and the next time. At Groby Pond was a disused quarry where they had come before, to be alone under an enormous sky, a sky that made no judgments, condemned no one, and was content to be.

The city is devoted to the appreciation of beauty—Rolling architecture is spread out in autumn sunlight—The city has patterned trees set out among the plazas—High towers pillars for the sky—Spotlights are situated along the kerbs to show the human bodies on the pavements to their best advantage—Last year a man was found wearing clothes and was executed—Soft winds blow scents of musk into the market—In the main square is a gigantic golden representation of a single testicle—the sounds of the people are the muted voice of summer holidaymakers—laughter on a tennis court—Parks are rolling grassland with bowers supplied for making love, which must be made aesthetically—the main crime is committing offenses against the soul, for which the penalty is instant, and beautiful, decapitation—Birds shriek into the sun, protesting at the loss of their virgin cruelty—Sleek, fat cats assume poses in the gutters—Men urinate only from the tops of high buildings—The government headquarters consists of five red towers, standing up in the city like the fingers of a bloody hand—All the pubs have yards where one may sit with one's love and drink together for the last time—the courtyards are like seas—there are no lavatories—illness is forbidden by state decree—Sculptures are designed to be orgasms in steel—In a park in the center of the city is a large brick shed with a light on its side—Serious musicians play only some Mozart and some Berg—Beaches and pavilions glisten like mirrors in the sun—The city beats like a bird's wing—People float in aerial choreography, like the sinking drowned—Metal is woven in great garlands and shines throughout the city—Capsules of mescalin are set in trays at every point—The city is the city of time—the city knows no time—the city is the city of soft people—the city of flags and paintings that move—the city is the city of the afternoon—mown grass falls from the sky like rain—the city is the city of beautiful decay, where all is young—the city is the city of the sky—the city of eternal surprise— the city of long dark hair—the city of eggs with marble shells—the city is a diffraction grating, and from a height of three hundred feet can be seen only as a blaze of color—it is the city of high parabolas—the city of impossible waterfalls—the city of melting silver blades—the city is the city of brooks—they weave their way everywhere—all the time is the sound of bubbling water. . . .

The time machine utilizes certain objects for its various operations: a skull cap with electrodes attached to a machine designed for the artificial production of sexual orgasm; the miniature score of Messiaen's *Chronochromie;* a magnetic tape, two thousand, four hundred feet long, containing nothing but the voice of a man repeating the world "time"; a reproduction of Dali's landscape, *Persistence of Memory;* a bracket clock by Joseph Knibb.

He enters the time machine, giving himself up to its embrace, feeling his normal consciousness changing, the widening of his perceptions. Colors flow over his body like a smooth sheet of water—blue sparks ignite in his brain—he is conscious of the pattern his body makes in space-time—He moves his finger and sees the resultant wiggling shape, his finger like an electroencephalograph pen—Words float in his mind, picked out in violet fire—Long steel fingers fiddle about in his brain like the legs of robot spiders—he falls asleep and wakes up three hundred times a second—His feet are removed by steel hands and placed neatly under his bed—His arms are broken off with mechanical deftness—his body is taken completely apart by the mechanical fingers, and he slides in pieces through the conveyor belts of the machine.

They pulled up at the pond, with the front of the car only a few yards from the water's edge. There were several other cars parked here too; this was a fairly popular beauty spot. A few people were outside their cars, braving the January weather, throwing pieces of bread to the ducks on the water. They sat for a while, he with his arm around her, his face pressed to her hair, stroking her with slow fingers, their voices low as they spoke to each other, both of them weighed down by circumstances so vast that they could not be seen all at one time. She had brought along a bottle of wine, cheap red wine with brandy added, a box of sandwiches, and also a thermos flask of coffee. They filled the cup of the flask with wine, and took it in turns to sip from it. "You realize that these are only delaying tactics on my part? I feel so low. If I really wanted to make love, I wouldn't want food or anything." He nodded, for he knew. It was up to her to make the move today. She offered him a small sandwich, but at the moment he was unable to eat; his stomach was locked with tension. But he watched her eating, looking at her as if looking could lock her forever within him, knowing that in time the outlines of her features would fade, until one day, alone, he would remember only a composite picture of her face, not looking as she looked on this day at any time. But still he looked at her intensely, watching the movements of her hands, her glances and her dark eyes.

They packed away the food, and she came into his arms again. "In a minute we can go and make love."

"Do you want a cigarette first?" She took a cigarette, and they stayed smoking for a moment, now and then drinking from the cup.

Now was the time to leave the car, and they went round to the boot, where she had stored an enormous bundle of blankets, wrapped in a grey oilcloth. She had smuggled these blankets out of the house so that they should at least be comfortable. As he helped her with the bundle, he was very conscious of the people about, as if they knew that it was full of blankets. Last time they had climbed over a wide green gate that led to the quarry, but now they could see a car parked by the gate, full of people looking out at the sheet of silver that was Groby Pond. This time, they decided, they should go over a stile a little further down, set into a low stone wall. They walked along, he with one arm clasping the bundle, the other round her, his fingers buried in the fur of her collar. The last time they had been here they had gone over the green gate, ignored a small path leading to the left towards a brick shed and some other buildings in a little dip, and had taken the right-hand path up to the top of the quarry, and had lain in the brambles in this incredibly open place, in which it seemed there was nothing but a huge sky and great vistas of grey stone cliffs. Later they would go through the gate and would turn left, down the small path, and they would never go over this stile again. He pushed the blankets under the bottom rung and climbed over, helping her as she followed. There was a tortuous path leading downwards through the trees and undergrowth, in the direction of a brook. They began to go down the path, he leading the way and holding onto her hand, sliding, being whipped by branches and circumnavigating patches of mud, and clambered across it. Now the way ahead looked even more impenetrable, and even less likely to lead up the the top of the quarry. He suggested that she wait here, while he would go on to see what was ahead.

His perspective changes—He rushes along corridors of people, the same people, in quanta of time, each one slightly different from the last, like a cine film—A mad express, lights reflecting from the walls of life.

The time machine poses problems.

Why? Why did they take this path, that second time, when later they would find a much easier way to get to their little shed? Why did they not brave the stares of the people in the car, and avoid this tortuous journey? Why, the first time, did they go over the green gate but completely ignore the path that led to their refuge? The shed at Groby Pond was so important to them. They even called it their "den." It was a little enclosed world of three sides, in which they could shut out the knowledge of pain and the niceties of balance that were necessary for them to stay whole. They could observe this world outside through an open fourth side, only partly masked by stringy bushes, and could hear its water bubbling nearby. Why did they, then, choose not to go down the small path on these two occasions? It is not only in love, but in all life that people often act with the blind illogicality of the insane. What is this quality called "time" that makes them act so? How can one assess an adulterous love affair seen now in terms of shape?

He emerged into a clearing. There were some brick buildings to the right, a couple of sheds and a cottage with boarded-up windows. He went over to try the doors but found them locked. He found that he was concentrating on this moment of being alone, living it with a perverse kind of enjoyment, like

167

the enjoyment of being cold just before stepping into a warm bath. He turned. Behind him was a shed with three sides. It was about five feet high and very roomy. The front was half-concealed by straggly bushes and the darkness inside should hide the glimmer of two bodies, unless someone got too close. He walked across to the shed, and went inside. He was rather disappointed by the interior, which was gloomy and damp. He came out of the shed again, wondering whether or not it would be suitable. He decided to use the opportunity of this solitude to urinate, smiling, as he unzipped his fly, at this unexpected modesty of his, and feeling rather ashamed of it at the same time. Hearing her coming, he forced the process even faster and barely finished before she appeared from behind the buildings. Feeling a little like a guilty schoolboy, he zipped up his trousers and went towards her. "I've found a place," he said, "but you may find it a bit sordid." She walked across to the shed and looked inside. "Why, it's perfect. But will we be seen from the road?" He stepped back until he was a long way away. He could see her now only as a vague patch of lightness in the shed. "No," he called, "it's fine!" He came back, and picking up the bundle of blankets he carried it inside the shed. He put the bundle down, and then took her in his arms. They kissed, their bodies pressed together, and his general tension was suddenly transformed into sexual desire, his body responding to hers with a swiftness that spoke of their long absence. They drew apart, and she squatted on the floor and began to unroll the bundle. Inside were two large blankets, and he was amused to see that she had even had the forethought to bring a red towel with her. They spread out the groundsheet, and arranged the blankets into an improvised double bed. He took off his sweater and arranged it to serve as a pillow. Now when they spoke their voices were hushed, and quietly they both took off their shoes, lifted the blankets, and slid side by side into their bed in the shed at Groby Pond, while outside the brook bubbled past.

The time machine caresses with soft winds—it deafens the mind with brave light—slow blind worms stretch their bodies through time—straight files of fingers tap on miles of desks—grey vines are shrined in fog and kick and scream like young horses—wings are torn from my *back!*

Gas springs from eight star-formed arms
Which revolve like pink wheels
"Ghost" gas is leaked off into the spandrels
Pressuring a container which explodes
Pulling a chain which pulls a claw
Which plucks the tine of a tuning fork

Sounding a clear A
Which reorganizes the constituents of the gas
Stars wheels and spandrels
Form a double hexagon of mystical significance
And the gas throbs with the deep blue glow
Of an unnatural agency
The shapes of the spandrels—
Cherubs' faces with foliage—
Reform the organization of the gas
Which rings and metamorphoses
Into lead

The time machine taps his body with a thousand fingers which play over his skin like a row of pianists. The fingers have little needles in the tips, which are feeding a special electrically conductive ink. This ink is tattooed into his body in a complex pattern, and soon the whirls and curlicues will flow with an electrical force. Time drips from a faucet like dark green treacle.

Later they were going to lie together naked in this shed, but this time the coldness and the likelihood of detection made them agree beforehand to keep on as many clothes as possible. Their bodies twisted together, her hands running over him, he kissing her ear, her neck, her throat. They whimper together with the delight of this long-delayed contact. He slides his leg between hers, pressing it high, and feels the muscles of her thighs clenching in response. He unzips her dress behind, and lowers his face to the flesh of her shoulders and back, this feeling of her flesh against his coming as an actual physical relief, as if, for the rest of his life, when not with her, he would always miss the feel of her body. He slid the dress down, exposing the soft dark skin of her chest and arms, and the little brassiere. His mouth found the sweetness of her shoulders, and his lips lingered there. Her hands were on his thighs, and then his shirt was unbuttoned, and her lips were against his stomach. He helped her hands with his belt and trousers, sliding his clothes from his legs completely, and shuddering under the ecstatic pressure of her hands. He felt that their lovemaking could never become banal; each time they came together it was a mutual exploration of pleasure. Each possible contact of their bodies could be repeated a million times. Her dress was now round her neck, and his hands ran over the smooth warm flesh. This time of lovemaking was all times of lovemaking, the little soft mounds of her breasts, her arching stomach, always receiving the caresses of his hands and mouth, never any other. The afternoon was the afternoon of her body; there was nothing else in time or space, nothing but her limbs and her flesh, nothing but the pressure of her hands on his skin. They kissed as if their mouths were drawn together magnetically, until their faces were covered with saliva, and there was nothing but a wide wet world of voluptuous love. Their arms around each other, their bodies surged together at the hips. He slid her pants down over her legs, caressing the smooth skin of her limbs, until the scrap of silk disappeared into the blankets. And now their bodies pressed together with nothing between them, the feel of their naked flesh making their kisses even more urgent. His hand circled, running over her skin, her belly, her thighs, running through a nest of hair between her legs, circling smaller until it found puckered flesh, moving up and down slowly, pressing deeper, until his finger finally entered a soft dark electrical place, and she gasped, and arched her body still more. He was vaguely expecting to find a string in the way, but he could feel none, and then forgot about it. This was Caroline; now she could understand, and so could he. Time passed, and none was comprehended. Nothing mattered but the feel of her body. He slid two fingers inside her, and she caught her breath. His tongue ran over her stomach, and he rotated his wrist, his fingers moving in a soft wet place, curves of muscle pressing them. Her hands were on him, driving everything from his mind but the consciousness of her and of this exquisite pressure. He felt a different quality in the wetness of her vagina, and a long time later realized that there was a profuse flow of blood. When he finally withdrew his hand, he slowly moved it up, arching his wrist so that his fingers did not touch the bedclothes and brought his hand to the light. His first two fingers were covered from top to bottom in thick, bright red blood. She was watching his hand too; it had suddenly assumed a position of paramount importance, like an object framed by perspective lines in a photograph. What had been an unobtrusive movement had become a dramatic gesture. He felt as though he had just been probing a terrible wound in her body, and he had a brief moment of horror. "Have you got a piece of rag?" She indicated a packet of sanitary pads that he hadn't noticed before, and he took one, and quickly wiped the blood from his fingers. She felt his erection beginning to subside, and asked, "Are you sure you want to make love?" He nodded, not thinking of asking her the same question, thinking of nothing but loving her. His hands ran over her again, and soon his body found itself moving over her, now above her, now sliding into the dampness of her.

Now there was a pause.

Now they were together.

He looked down at her face, and kissed her slowly on the lips, running his hands in little repetitive caresses over her bare shoulders. Slow movements began, like the movements of glaciers, years of time translated into flashes of fire. Then faster, now a rhythm. A single strand of bright steel, a long rod that flashed brightly, twirling in the bright electrical air, wider and wider, filling the world with silver. And then he paused, looking down at her face, raising his eyebrows slightly. She smiled. "We haven't seen each other often enough, have we?" He began to move again, feeling the focus of their bodies damply sliding together, the warmth of her flesh next to his. The world revolved about him. He lifted his head, feeling the movement like a ritual of intense importance. And thin strands of wire string out, joining together, forming thicker strands, ropes of wire, less and less, until there is only one rod, gleaming brightly, shining and glittering, twisting and coruscating, growing wider and wider . . . He stopped his movements again, and then started, slowly. Moving in her he could feel his skin all over his body, his limbs warm, and a nostalgic, dropping emptiness in his stomach. He concentrated on these feelings, trying to blot out the other feeling from his mind—the feeling of sharpness, a diffused sweet whiteness that was even now making itself more manifest, becoming more and more powerful, almost overwhelming. He stopped again, suddenly. He kissed her gently on the lips and spoke. "It's obviously going to be like this all the time. Will you mind us pausing like this?" "No, no, that's all right." They kissed again, their tongues trembling together, damp surfaces all over their bodies in contact. And he felt his body moving again.

The city is the city of broken festivals—city of changing carpets and the August moon—spires dance in the squares—in the city the night is velvet—instead of drains, set along the gutters are bowls of wild flowers—cats sing among headstones—drunken women in bright flared skirts dance among piles of petals—the city is full of soft waters that fall slowly from the moon—in the center of the city is a tall steel rod that grows wider and wider, opening out at the top into an enormous white umbrella—colored banners are set from building to building, covering the city in bursts of flame—skeletons dance in the city's lights—the festival is a jubilee of eternity—vendors of violet shadows move in a concourse through the streets—crowds of people move like slow pink phantoms—long white worms coil about the lamp standards—the city revolves in the fire of night—stainless steel fingers spread to receive the dawn—festivities ring out among the spider struts—all the people are spread with daffodils. . . .

Their bodies lay together. They were now one being, neither male nor female, but just a complete body of a strange, lethargic creature that twitched, regularly contracting itself under some blankets. He moved in her, feeling her soft moisture, feeling the folds of voluptuous muscle holding him. When they stopped again, they lay over to one side. Now he could caress her, and his hand moved over her back, along her thighs, feeling acres of flesh, fields that he could explore at leisure, feeling too the damp blows at his hips, the feeling of the underside of her body against his abdomen, his testicles rolling back and forth and bumping her. His hand probed beneath her, feeling the wetness that had run from her and the pucker of her anus, trying to ingest the whole of her body, his stomach sinking and his body melting into hers, pausing, moving again. Once he had to stop suddenly, and all his muscles became rigid with the effort of shutting off, his arms shaking, feeling a spurt of semen, and then the feelings receding, and now moving vigorously, knowing that they would not return for a long time, looking down at her face, her swollen lips, her mouth half-open, her breath exhaled in little sighs, each movement of his body echoed by hers, a shuddering over the whole of her.

The city shimmers like glass—waltzes fade in dark alcoves—the sun shatters and falls to the sea like tumbling drops of blood—wire springs nod in the morning air—grass dies in profuse movements—fountains are spurting, their water viscous in death—skulls rattle on pavements—the city is brown, and the stones crack—flowers are growing from genitals—the pavements are littered with dying blooms—the air is sweet with the death of flowers—dye drips from the banners, bleaching them to pure white. . . .

A sound of water, dim light, and leaves and stones on the ground. It was as if he was seeing everything with a preternatural clarity, watching the stones to keep his mind away from the mass of physical sensations in which he was floating. Their bodies writhed together on the ground, and he felt that this movement, this strange dance, had been going on for eternity, that there had never been any other life, that he had been born in this woman and would die in her embrace. His body was floating, he was conscious of vast chemical reactions going on in the universe. Her breath was coming in loud gasps now, and he knew that it wouldn't be long. But he might have to stop, and it might escape again. A white wedge inserted itself, growing more and more prominent, and his body began to erupt in a silver anguish. He stopped. He was breathless and covered with sweat. Lying still in her he looked at her face. She was breathing heavily, and as he watched her face changed, moving from side to side, all the marks of normal human life dropping away, her head going back, her mouth open. Her cries began, slow regular cries, and he began to move again, letting the feelings blossom, opening the floodgates, dropping, dropping, a silver line blooming inside him, higher, higher, but not quite high enough, and then breaking, their movements

172

frenzied, resignation, dimly hearing his own voice, feeling his head dropping, and then only a world of whiteness.

The city implodes, the towers, spires and struts of metal raining to the center like a waterfall—liquid pours in on the dead city—whirlpools of vegetation—dead people dance in the water—all that is left is a floating mass of flowers and machines.

They lay together quietly, and he kissed her, feeling his body warm and relaxed, with no tension in him anywhere. She opened her eyes, looking worried. "I wanted to give you something you could remember, like that time in the hotel . . ." "It's all right; nothing went wrong. It was good for me." She smiled at him. "That sometimes happens. It just starts when I am relaxed." They lay together some more, and smoked a cigarette. He slowly withdrew from her, and she handed him the towel as he kneeled upright. He rubbed the towel over the front of his body, suddenly realizing that it was pitch dark. He could feel clots of blood on his flesh, and rubbed energetically. He lit a match to see how much blood there was on him. There were a few stains left, and he wiped at them. In the dim light of the match he could see the pallid skin of his body, and looking at his half-erect penis he suddenly felt a revulsion for his own flesh, and shook out the match. There was congealed blood all over his hairs, feeling uncomfortable, but he realized that it would have to stay there until he had time to wash. They began to search for their clothes by match-light. "We said we were going to keep on our clothes, but I managed to lose all mine except my dress, and that was round my neck!" They laughed together as they searched. While they were dressing they were quiet, and he wondered if she too felt this strange melancholy that had settled on him. He lit another match, and looked at his watch. "It's half-past five; we were quite a long time. It gives us just long enough to sit in the car for a while and then get back to Leicester." They gathered together their possessions, re-bundled the blankets, and emerged from the little shed, walking slowly past the line of buildings, holding hands, up toward the road.

They moved carefully through the blackness, seeing nothing but the dark shapes of trees against the dim sky. A car briefly flooded the road above with light. As they got to the higher ground there was a large black shed, with a single light on the side. The ground was yellow in this light, which shone onto the surrounding trees, making them look like pale ghosts. They stood together watching this light, conscious of the smallness of their bodies and feeling a strong and inexplicable sadness. The light made everything cold and unreal, an analytical light that transformed familiar trees into symbols of unconsummated love and inevitable death. Her hand tightened round his, and they stood watching the light for a long time. He knew that one day he would find the events of this day quite amusing, but at the moment he felt only a sadness fed by the yellow light. They turned, and walked quickly to the green gate, climbing over hurriedly. The lake was dark as they walked past, and all was quiet but for the sound of water lapping at the shore. There was a car parked near hers, and as they passed they saw a couple kissing. "Let's tell them that we know a much better place!" she said, and he laughed as he helped her squeeze the bundle into the boot.

They could both keenly feel the cold, and he shivered as she got in the car and unlocked his door. Inside the car she switched on the light, and then got out the box of sandwiches. Now he felt hungry, and he ate quickly. There was congealed blood round his fingernails, but he didn't want to clean it off, wanting to carry her substances as long as he could. They sat and talked lethargically, kissing each other gently. In each other's eyes they could read the urgent question: "What are we to *do?*" Now there was very little of the day left. At quarter to six, one hour before they were due to part again, the car backed out and turned onto the road, leaving Groby Pond behind it.

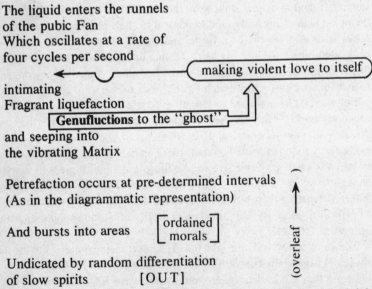

The car drew up outside the coach station. The London coach, a bright looming monster, was ready to leave, and would shortly be drawing out of the station on its way to the M1. As the car pulled up outside The Shakespeare, they turned and fell into each other's arms. Her lips were frantic on his, and they pressed tightly to each other, wanting to make love again, wanting to hold each other and never to let go. Soon, very soon, they would leave, and the distance between them would expand rapidly, at a combined rate of one hundred and twenty miles an hour. His right hand was under her coat, running over her shoulder and back, trying to impress the feel of her on his mind forever. She pulls the front of her sweater out of her skirt and thrusts his cold hand up against the warmth of her body. They meet for polite conversation in a pub. She sits over an armchair, her legs dangling over one arm, listening to Messiaen's *Trois Petites Liturgies*. They talk together in the yard of Henekey's in Portobello Road on a bright sunny day, thinking that time was more crucial to them then than ever before, their words measured now only in hundreds. Cogs turn, and the time machine performs a ritual osculation at the foot of a metal apparition. The city swirls in autumn tides, its drowned coiling like ropes, the bodies illuminated by the sunny greenness of the water, hair forming moving curves, skin shredding off in twisting rinds, fixed by the sun above in a moment of coiling, gentle—beauty. They meet again, hurriedly taking off their clothes and making love on a living room carpet. They die. They are born. The birds of night flap through years, their large black wings dripping yellow drops of poison. The universe rolls through the aether like a dead whale. They kiss, trying to merge into each other, tongues searching for this union which will bind them forever. The car door opens. He leaps out and walks quickly across to the coach. He sits by a window, and a girl sits beside him. As the coach moves off he watches her car, and sees her sitting inside in the darkness, watching the coach.

They do not wave to each other.

The prisoner feels in the right-hand pocket of his denim suit. He pulls out a small leather wallet, and puts the photograph into one of the compartments, transferring it back to the pocket. Now it is evening; the stone walls are touched with gold. He lies on his back on the bunk, watching the ceiling, and the rippling spider webs. A little while later there is a rattling sound at the door. Soon it opens, and his warder walks in. He turns his head on the bunk and looks at the warder.

The man clears his throat and then begins to speak, as if speaking is an effort.

"There has been a general decree. All the prisoners are to be released. You are free to go."

The atmosphere of the Milford Conference was so intense and it went on so long that writers' wives sitting in the kitchen caught the fever and went home seething with self-expression. This happened regularly to Jim Blish's artist wife Judith, and she complained about it bitterly—"I don't even *want* to write!" Another spouse it happened to is Terry Carr's wife Carol, who looks something like Sophia Loren. To everyone's surprise, however, it turned out that she really is a writer, and a good one. No one was more surprised than Carol herself, who left this story half-finished for months and showed it to me only on Terry's urging. I thought it was great and said so; she finished it, and then we went around a little about the ending.

To Carol Carr, June 7, 1968:

Dear Carol,
    I love the story dearly, but I think it needs a new punchline. Could it be something like, "At least he isn't a goy?" Pls. advise. Meanwhile I will put through a contract. . . .
    Could you think of another title?
    Please come all week to Conference whether your fink husband can or not; who needs him?

LOOK, YOU THINK YOU'VE GOT TROUBLES

by *Carol Carr*

To tell you the truth, in the old days we would have sat shivah for the whole week. My so-called daughter gets married, my own flesh and blood, and not only he doesn't look Jewish, he's not even human.

"Papa," she says to me, two seconds after I refuse to speak to her again in my entire life, "if you know him you'll love him, I promise." So what can I answer—the truth, like I always tell her: "If I know him I'll vomit, that's how he affects me. I can help it? He makes me want to throw up on him."

With silk gloves you have to handle the girl, just like her mother. I tell her

176

what I feel, from the heart, and right away her face collapses into a hundred cracks and water from the Atlantic Ocean makes a soggy mess out of her paper sheath. And that's how I remember her after six months—standing in front of me, sopping wet from the tears and making me feel like a monster—me—when all the time it's her you-should-excuse-the-expression husband who's the monster.

After she's gone to live with him (New Horizon Village, Crag City, Mars), I try to tell myself it's not me who has to—how can I put it?—deal with him intimately; if she can stand it, why should I complain? It's not like I need somebody to carry on the business; my business is to enjoy myself in my retirement. But who can enjoy? Sadie doesn't leave me alone for a minute. She calls me a criminal, a worthless no-good with gallstones for a heart.

"Hector, where's your brains?" she says, having finally given up on my emotions. I can't answer her. I just lost my daughter, I should worry about my brains too? I'm silent as the grave. I can't eat a thing. I'm empty—drained. It's as though I'm waiting for something to happen but I don't know what. I sit in a chair that folds me up like a bee in a flower and rocks me to sleep with electronic rhythms when I feel like sleeping, but who can sleep? I look at my wife and I see Lady Macbeth. Once I caught her whistling as she pushed the button for her bath. I fixed her with a look like an icicle tipped with arsenic.

"What are you so happy about? Thinking of your grandchildren with the twelve toes?"

She doesn't flinch. An iron woman.

When I close my eyes, which is rarely, I see our daughter when she was fourteen years old, with skin just beginning to go pimply and no expression yet on her face. I see her walking up to Sadie and asking her what she should do with her life now she's filling out, and my darling Sadie, my life's mate, telling her why not marry a freak; you got to be a beauty to find a man here, but on Mars you shouldn't know from so many fish. "I knew I could count on you, Mama," she says, and goes ahead and marries a plant with legs.

Things go on like this—impossible—for months. I lose twenty pounds, my nerves, three teeth and I'm on the verge of losing Sadie, when one day the mailchute goes ding-dong and it's a letter from my late daughter. I take it by the tips of two fingers and bring it in to where my wife is punching ingredients for the gravy I won't eat tonight.

"It's a communication from one of your relatives."

"Oh-oh-oh." My wife makes a grab for it, meanwhile punching CREAM-TOMATO-SAUCE-BEEF DRIPPINGS. No wonder I have no appetite.

"I'll give it to you on one condition only," I tell her, holding it out of her

177

trembling reach. "Take it into the bedroom and read it to yourself. Don't even move your lips for once; I don't want to know. If she's God forbid dead, I'll send him a sympathy card."

Sadie has a variety of expressions but the one thing they have in common is they all wish me misfortune in my present and future life.

While she's reading the letter I find suddenly I have nothing to do. The magazines I read already. Breakfast I ate (like a bird). I'm all dressed to go out if I felt like, but there's nothing outside I don't have inside. Frankly, I don't feel like myself—I'm nervous. I say a lot of things I don't really intend and now maybe this letter comes to tell me I've got to pay for my meanness. Maybe she got sick up there; God knows what they eat, the kind of water they drink, the creatures they run around with. Not wanting to think about it too much, I go over to my chair and turn it on to brisk massage. It doesn't take long till I'm dreaming (fitfully).

I'm someplace surrounded by sand, sitting in a baby's crib and bouncing a diapered kangaroo on my knee. It gurgles up at me and calls me grandpa and I don't know what I should do. I don't want to hurt its feelings, but if I'm a grandpa to a kangaroo, I want no part of it; I only want it should go away. I pull out a dime from my pocket and put it into its pouch. The pouch is full of tiny insects which bite my fingers. I wake up in a sweat.

"Sadie! Are you reading, or rearranging the sentences? Bring it here and I'll see what she wants. If it's a divorce, I know a lawyer."

Sadie comes into the room with her I-told-you-so waddle and gives me a small wet kiss on the cheek—a gold star for acting like a mensch. So I start to read it, in a loud monotone so she shouldn't get the impression I give a damn:

"Dear Daddy, I'm sorry for not writing sooner. I suppose I wanted to give you a chance to simmer down first." (Ingrate! Does the sun simmer down?) "I know it would have been inconvenient for you to come to the wedding, but Mor and I hoped you would maybe send us a letter just to let us know you're okay and still love me, in spite of everything."

Right at this point I feel a hot sigh followed by a short but wrenching moan.

"Sadie, get away from my neck. I'm warning you . . ."

Her eyes are going flick-a-fleck over my shoulder, from the piece of paper I'm holding to my face, back to the page, flick-a-fleck, flick-a-fleck.

"All right, already," she shoo-shoos me. "I read it, I know what's in it. Now it's your turn to see what kind of a lousy father you turned out to be." And she waddles back into the bedroom, shutting the door extra careful, like she's handling a piece of snow-white velvet.

When I'm certain she's gone, I sit myself down on the slab of woven dental floss my wife calls a couch and press a button on the arm that reads

178

Semi-Cl.: Feldman To Friml. The music starts to slither out from the speaker under my left armpit. The right speaker is dead and buried and the long narrow one at the base years ago got drowned from the dog, who to this day hasn't learned to control himself when he hears "Desert Song."

This time I'm lucky; it's a piece by Feldman that comes on. I continue to read, calmed by the music.

"I might as well get to the point, Papa, because for all I know you're so mad you tore up this letter without even reading it. The point is that Mor and I are going to have a baby. Please, please don't throw this into the disintegrator. It's due in July, which gives you over three months to plan the trip up here. We have a lovely house, with a guest room that you and Mama can stay in for as long as you want."

I have to stop here to interject a couple of questions, since my daughter never had a head for logic and it's my strong point.

First of all, if she were in front of me in person right now I would ask right off what means "Mor and I are going to have a baby." Which? Or both? The second thing is, when she refers to it as "it" is she being literal or just uncertain? And just how lovely can a guest room be that has all the air piped in and you can't even see the sky or take a walk on the grass because there is no grass, only simulated this and substituted that?

All the above notwithstanding, I continue to read:

"By the way, Papa, there's something I'm not sure you understand. Mor, you may or may not know, is as human as you and me, in all the important ways—and frankly a bit more intelligent."

I put down the letter for a minute just to give the goosebumps a chance to fly out of my stomach ulcers before I go on with her love and best and kisses and hopes for seeing us soon, Lorinda.

I don't know how she manages it, but the second I'm finished, Sadie is out of the bedroom and breathing hard.

"Well, do I start packing or do I start packing? And when I start packing, do I pack for us or do I pack for me?"

"Never. I should die three thousand deaths, each one with a worse prognosis."

It's a shame a company like Interplanetary Aviation can't afford, with the fares they charge, to give you a comfortable seat. Don't ask how I ever got there in the first place. Ask my wife—she's the one with the mouth. First of all, they only allow you three pounds of luggage, which if you're only bringing clothes is plenty, but we had a few gifts with us. We were only planning to stay a few days and to sublet the house was Sadie's idea, not mine.

179

The whole trip was supposed to take a month, each way. This is one reason Sadie thought it was impractical to stay for the weekend and then go home, which was the condition on which I'd agreed to go.

But now that we're on our way, I decide I might as well relax. I close my eyes and try to think of what the first meeting will be like.

"How." I put up my right hand in a gesture of friendship and trust. I reach into my pocket and offer him beads.

But even in my mind he looks at me blank, his naked pink antennas waving in the breeze like a worm's underwear. Then I realize there isn't any breeze where we're going. So they stop waving and wilt.

I look around in my mind. We're alone, the two of us, in the middle of a vast plain, me in my business suit and him in his green skin. The scene looks familiar, like something I had experienced, or read about. . . . "We'll meet at Philippi," I think, and stab him with my sword.

Only then am I able to catch a few winks.

The month goes by. When I begin to think I'll never remember how to use a fork, the loudspeaker is turned on and I hear this very smooth, modulated voice, the tranquilized tones of a psychiatrist sucking glycerine, telling us it's just about over, and we should expect a slight jolt upon landing.

That slight jolt starts my life going by so fast I'm missing all the good parts. But finally the ship is still and all you can hear are the wheezes and sighs of the engines—the sounds remind me of Sadie when she's winding down from a good argument. I look around. Everybody is very white. Sadie's five fingers are around my upper arm like a tourniquet.

"We're here," I tell her. "Do I get a hacksaw or can you manage it yourself?"

"Oh, my goodness." She loosens her grip. She really looks a mess—completely pale, not blinking, not even nagging.

I take her by the arm and steer her into customs. All the time I feel that she's a big piece of unwilling luggage I'm smuggling in. There's no cooperation at all in her feet and her eyes are going every which way.

"Sadie, shape up!"

"If you had a little more curiosity about the world you'd be a better person," she says tolerantly.

While we're waiting to be processed by a creature in a suit like ours who surprises me by talking English, I sneak a quick look around.

It's funny. If I didn't know where we are I'd think we're in the back yard. The ground stretches out pure green, and it's only from the leaflet they give you in the ship to keep your mind off the panic that I know it's 100% Acrispan we're looking at, not grass. The air we're getting smells good, too, like fresh-cut flowers, but not too sweet.

By the time I've had a good look and a breathe, what's-its-name is handing us back our passports with a button that says to keep Mars beautiful don't litter.

I won't tell you about the troubles we had getting to the house, or the misunderstanding about the tip, because to be honest I wasn't paying attention. But we do manage to make it to the right door, and considering that the visit was a surprise, I didn't really expect they would meet us at the airport. My daughter must have been peeking, though, because she's in front of us even before we have a chance to knock.

"Mother!" she says, looking very round in the stomach. She hugs and kisses Sadie, who starts bawling. Five minutes later, when they're out of the clinch, Lorinda turns to me, a little nervous.

You can say a lot of things about me, but basically I'm a warm person, and we're about to be guests in this house, even if she is a stranger to me. I shake her hand.

"Is he home, or is he out in the back yard, growing new leaves?"

Her face (or what I can see of it through the climate adapter) crumples a little at the chin line, but she straightens it out and puts her hand on my shoulder.

"Mor had to go out, Daddy—something important came up—but he should be back in an hour or so. Come on, let's go inside."

Actually there's nothing too crazy about the house, or even interesting. It has walls, a floor and a roof, I'm glad to see, even a few relaxer chairs, and after the trip we just had, I sit down and relax. I notice my daughter is having a little trouble looking me straight in the face, which is only as it should be, and it isn't long before she and Sadie are discussing pregnancy, gravitational exercise, labor, hospitals, formulas and sleep-taught toilet training. When I'm starting to feel that I'm getting over-educated, I decide to go into the kitchen and make myself a bite to eat. I could have asked them for a little something but I don't want to interfere with their first conversation. Sadie has all engines going and is interrupting four times a sentence, which is exactly the kind of game they always had back home—my daughter's goal is to say one complete thought out loud. If Sadie doesn't spring back with a non sequitur, Lorinda wins that round. A full-fledged knockout with Sadie still champion is when my daughter can't get a sentence in for a week. Sometimes I can understand why she went to Mars.

Anyway, while they're at the height of their simultaneous monologues, I go quietly off to the kitchen to see what I can dig up. (Ripe parts of Mor, wrapped in plastic? Does he really regenerate, I wonder. Does Lorinda fully understand how he works, or one day will she make an asparagus omelet out of one of his appendages, only to learn that's the part that doesn't grow

181

back? "Oh, I'm so *sorry,*" she says. "Can you ever forgive me?")

The refrigerator, though obsolete on Earth, is well stocked—fruits of a sort, steaks, it seems, small chicken-type things that might be stunted pigeons. There's a bowl of a brownish, creamy mess—I can't even bring myself to smell it. Who's hungry, anyway, I think. The rumbling in my stomach is the symptom of a father's love turning sour.

I wander into the bedroom. There's a large portrait of Mor hanging on the wall—or maybe his ancestor. Is it true that instead of hearts, Martians have a large avocado pit? There's a rumor on Earth that when Martians get old they start to turn brown at the edges, like lettuce.

There's an object on the floor and I bend down and pick it up. A piece of material—at home I would have thought it was a man's handkerchief. Maybe it is a handkerchief. Maybe they have colds like us. They catch a germ, the sap rises to combat the infection, and they have to blow their stamens. I open up the drawer to put the piece of material in (I like to be neat), but when I close it, something gets stuck. Another thing I can't recognize. It's small, round and either concave or convex, depending on how you look at it. It's made of something black and shiny. A cloth bowl? What would a vegetable be doing with a cloth bowl? Some questions are too deep for me, but what I don't know I eventually find out—and not by asking, either.

I go back to the living room.

"Did you find anything to eat?" Lorinda asks. "Or would you like me to fix—"

"Don't even get up," Sadie says quickly. "I can find my way around any kitchen, I don't care whose."

"I'm not hungry. It was a terrible trip. I thought I'd never wake up from it in one piece. By the way, I heard a good riddle on the ship. What's round and black, either concave or convex, depending on how you look at it, and made out of a shiny material?"

Lorinda blushed. "A skullcap? But that's not funny."

"So who needs funny? Riddles have to be a laugh a minute all of a sudden? You think Oedipus giggled all the way home from seeing the Sphinx?"

"Look, Daddy, I think there's something I should tell you."

"I think there are all sorts of things you should tell me."

"No, I mean about Mor."

"Who do you think *I* mean, the grocery boy? You elope with a cucumber from outer space and you want I should be satisfied because he's human in all the important ways? What's important—that he sneezes and hiccups? If you tell me he snores, I should be ecstatic? Maybe he sneezes when he's

182

happy and hiccups when he's making love and snores because it helps him think better. Does that make him human?''

"Daddy, *please.*"

"Okay, not another word." Actually I'm starting to feel quite guilty. What if she has a miscarriage right on the spot? A man like me doesn't blithely torture a pregnant woman, even if she does happen to be his daughter. "What's so important it can't wait till later?"

"Nothing, I guess. Would you like some chopped liver? I just made some fresh.''

"What?''

"Chopped liver—you know, chopped liver."

Oh yes, the ugly mess in the refrigerator. "You made it, that stuff in the bowl?''

"Sure. Daddy, there's something I really have to tell you."

She never does get to tell me, though, because her husband walks in, bold as brass.

I won't even begin to tell you what he looks like. Let me just say he's a good dream cooked up by Mary Shelley. I won't go into it, but if it gives you a small idea, I'll say that his head is shaped like an acorn on top of a stalk of broccoli. Enormous blue eyes, green skin and no hair at all except for a small blue round area on top of his head. His ears are adorable. Remember Dumbo the Elephant? Only a little smaller—I never exaggerate, even for effect. And he looks boneless, like a filet.

My wife, God bless her, I don't have to worry about; she's a gem in a crisis. One look at her son-in-law and she faints dead away. If I didn't know her better, if I wasn't absolutely certain that her simple mind contained no guile, I would have sworn she did it on purpose, to give everybody something to fuss about. Before we know what's happening, we're all in a tight, frantic conversation about what's the best way to bring her around. But while my daughter and her husband are in the bathroom looking for some deadly chemical, Sadie opens both eyes at once and stares up at me from the floor.

"What did I miss?''

"You didn't miss anything—you were only unconscious for fifteen seconds. It was a cat nap, not a coma."

"Say hello, Hector. Say hello to him or so help me I'll close my eyes for good.''

"I'm very glad to meet you, Mr. Trumbnick," he says. I'm grateful that he's sparing me the humiliation of making the first gesture, but I pretend I don't see the stalk he's holding out.

"Smutual," I say.

"I beg your pardon?"

"Smutual. How are you? You look better than your pictures." He does, too. Even though his skin is green, it looks like the real thing up close. But his top lip sort of vibrates when he talks, and I can hardly bear to look at him except sideways.

"I hear you had some business this afternoon. My daughter never did tell me what your line is, uh, Morton."

"Daddy, his name is Mor. Why don't you call him Mor?"

"Because I prefer Morton. When we know each other better I'll call him something less formal. Don't rush me, Lorinda; I'm still getting adjusted to the chopped liver."

My son-in-law chuckles and his top lip really goes crazy. "Oh, were you surprised? Imported meats aren't a rarity here, you know. Just the other day one of my clients was telling me about an all-Earth meal he had at home."

"Your client?" Sadie asks. "You wouldn't happen to be a lawyer?" (My wife amazes me with her instant familiarity. She could live with a tyrannosaurus in perfect harmony. First she faints, and while she's out cold everything in her head that was strange becomes ordinary and she wakes up a new woman.)

"No, Mrs. Trumbnick. I'm a—"

"—rabbi, of course," she finishes. "I knew it. The minute Hector found that skullcap I knew it. Him and his riddles. A skullcap is a skullcap and nobody not Jewish would dare wear one—not even a Martian." She bites her lip but recovers like a pro. "I'll bet you were out on a Bar Mitzvah—right?"

"No, as a matter of fact—"

"—a Bris. I knew it."

She's rubbing her hands together and beaming at him. "A Bris, how *nice.* But why didn't you tell us, Lorinda? Why would you keep such a thing a secret?"

Lorinda comes over to me and kisses me on the cheek, and I wish she wouldn't because I'm feeling myself go soft and I don't want to show it.

"Mor isn't *just* a rabbi, Daddy. He converted because of me and then found there was a demand among the colonists. But he's never given up his own beliefs, and part of his job is to minister to the Kopchopees who camp outside the village. That's where he was earlier, conducting a Kopchopee menopausal rite."

"A what!"

"Look, to each his own," says my wife with the open mind. But me, I want facts, and this is getting more bizarre by the minute.

"Kopchopee. He's a Kopchopee priest to his own race and a rabbi to ours,

184

and that's how he makes his living? You don't feel there's a contradiction between the two, Morton?''

"That's right. They both pray to a strong silent god, in different ways of course. The way my race worships, for instance—''

"Listen, it takes all kinds," says Sadie.

"And the baby, whatever it turns out to be—will it be a Choptapi or a Jew?''

"Jew, shmoo," Sadie says with a wave of dismissal. "All of a sudden it's Hector the Pious—such a megilla out of a molehill." She turns away from me and addresses herself to the others, like I've just become invisible. "He hasn't seen the inside of a synagogue since we got married—what a rain that night—and now he can't take his shoes off in a house until he knows its race, color and creed." With a face full of fury, she brings me back into her sight. "Nudnick, what's got into you?''

I stand up straight to preserve my dignity. "If you'll excuse me, my things are getting wrinkled in the suitcase.''

Sitting on my bed (with my shoes on), I must admit I'm feeling a little different. Not that Sadie made me change my mind. Far from it; for many years now her voice is the white sound that lets me think my own thoughts. But what I'm realizing more and more is that in a situation like this a girl needs her father, and what kind of a man is it who can't sacrifice his personal feelings for his only daughter? When she was going out with Herbie the Hemopheliac and came home crying it had to end because she was afraid to touch him, he might bleed, didn't I say pack your things, we're going to Grossingers Venus for three weeks? When my twin brother Max went into kitchen sinks, who was it that helped him out at only four per cent? Always, I stood ready to help my family. And if Lorinda ever needed me, it's now when she's pregnant by some religious maniac. Okay—he makes me retch, so I'll talk to him with a tissue over my mouth. After all, in a world that's getting smaller all the time, it's people like me who have to be bigger to make up for it, no?

I go back to the living room and extend my hand to my son-in-law the cauliflower. (Feh.)

185

From Norman Spinrad, July 22, 1968:

Dear Damon:

Here are my nits to your kvetches on "The Big Flash":

... (P. 7) Yiddish transliterated into English is a matter of arbitrary spelling, since they have different alphabets. "Schwartzers" is a little bit closer to the pronunciation than "Schwartzes", which could be pronounced as the German plural for black, which would be wrong. (Only by super-goys, of course.) ...

(P. 8) The heartbeat thing. Let's fudge this and to hell with hard science. Boom-boom would throw the whole rhythm of the sequence off. Besides, it really goes: Boom-ba. Boom-ba.

To Spinrad, August 6, 1968:

Dear Norm,

I have done a probably fink thing—after reading the ending and your letter five or six times & wavering back & forth, just like you, I finally decided to stick with the inversion of 3 and 2 and the blank space under 0. No time to consult with you again, I just did it. The reason it now seems to me it has to be this way is that the story has to funnel down to a point; if we show both sets of guys pressing the firing buttons, that's two points, & the second is anticlimactic. The answer is to imply one of them, and that's what we get by the inversion. . . . Hope you will (a) agree, or (b) forgive me.

From Spinrad, August 26, 1968:

Dear Damon:

I did get your fink changes letter, but I am not sore. I tried to call you the day I got it, but I couldn't get you; you must've been on your way to Florida already. I agreed with the logic of your changes, but they left two consecutive sections, 3 and 4, from the Captain's viewpoint, and that I don't like.

So here are 2 new pages, pages 33 and 34. I've left the changes you've made alone, but I've reversed sections 4 and 5 (old numbering) on page 33. . . .

Phew! I think we've finally got the best version possible. I don't want to panic you, but the new Jefferson Airplane album has a cover consisting of the Airplane peeking out from a mushroom pillar cloud—title: "The Crown of Creation."

THE BIG FLASH

by *Norman Spinrad*

T minus 200 days . . . and counting . . .

They came on freaky for my taste—but that's the name of the game: freaky means a draw in the rock business. And if the Mandala was going to survive in LA, competing with a network-owned joint like The American Dream, I'd just have to hold my nose and out-freak the opposition. So after I had dug the Four Horsemen for about an hour, I took them into my office to talk turkey.

I sat down behind my Salvation Army desk (the Mandala is the world's most expensive shoestring operation) and the Horsemen sat down on the bridge chairs sequentially, establishing the group's pecking order.

First the head honcho, lead guitar and singer, Stony Clarke—blond shoulder-length hair, eyes like something in a morgue when he took off his steel-rimmed shades, a reputation as a heavy acid-head and the look of a speed-freak behind it. Then Hair, the drummer, dressed like a Hell's Angel, swastikas and all, a junkie, with fanatic eyes that were a little too close together, making me wonder whether he wore swastikas because he grooved behind the Angel thing or made like an Angel because it let him groove behind the swastika in public. Number three was a cat who called himself Super Spade and wasn't kidding—he wore earrings, natural hair, a Stokely Carmichael sweatshirt, and on a thong around his neck a shrunken head that had been whitened with liquid shoe polish. He was the utility infielder: sitar, bass, organ, flute, whatever. Number four, who called himself Mr. Jones, was about the creepiest cat I had ever seen in a rock group, and that is saying something. He was their visuals, synthesizer and electronics man. He was at least forty, wore Early Hippy clothes that looked like they had been made by Sy Devore, and was rumored to be some kind of Rand Corporation dropout. There's no business like show business.

187

"Okay, boys," I said, "you're strange, but you're my kind of strange. Where you worked before?"

"We ain't, baby," Clarke said. "We're the New Thing. I've been dealing crystal and acid in the Haight. Hair was drummer for some plastic group in New York. The Super Spade claims it's the reincarnation of Bird and it don't pay to argue. Mr. Jones, he don't talk too much. Maybe he's a Martian. We just started putting our thing together."

One thing about this business, the groups that don't have square managers, you can get cheap. They talk too much.

"Groovy," I said. "I'm happy to give you guys your start. Nobody knows you, but I think you got something going. So I'll take a chance and give you a week's booking. One A.M. to closing, which is two, Tuesday through Sunday, four hundred a week."

"Are you Jewish?" asked Hair.

"What?"

"Cool it," Clarke ordered. Hair cooled it. "What it means," Clarke told me, "is that four hundred sounds like pretty light bread."

"We don't sign if there's an option clause," Mr. Jones said.

"The Jones-thing has a good point," Charke said. "We do the first week for four hundred, but after that it's a whole new scene, dig?"

I didn't feature that. If they hit it big, I could end up not being able to afford them. But on the other hand $400 was light bread, and I needed a cheap closing act pretty bad.

"Okay," I said. "But a verbal agreement that I get first crack at you when you finish the gig."

"Word of honor," said Stony Clarke.

That's this business—the word of honor of an ex-dealer and speed-freak.

T minus 199 days . . . and counting . . .

Being unconcerned with ends, the military mind can be easily manipulated, easily controlled, and easily confused. Ends are defined as those goals set by civilian authority. Ends are the conceded province of civilians; means are the province of the military, whose duty it is to achieve the ends set for it by the most advantageous application of the means at its command.

Thus the confusion over the war in Asia among my uniformed clients at the Pentagon. The end has been duly set: eradication of the guerrillas. But the civilians have overstepped their bounds and meddled in means. The Generals regard this as unfair, a breach of contract, as it were. The Generals (or the faction among them most inclined to paranoia) are beginning to see the conduct of the war, the political limitation on means, as a ploy of the civilians for performing a putsch against their time-honored prerogatives.

This aspect of the situation would bode ill for the country, were it not for the fact that the growing paranoia among the Generals has enabled me to manipulate them into presenting both my scenarios to the President. The President has authorized implementation of the major scenario, provided that the minor scenario is successful in properly molding public opinion.

My major scenario is simple and direct. Knowing that the poor flying weather makes our conventional airpower, with its dependency on relative accuracy, ineffectual, the enemy has fallen into the pattern of grouping his forces into larger units and launching punishing annual offensives during the monsoon season. However, these larger units are highly vulnerable to tactical nuclear weapons, which do not depend upon accuracy for effect. Secure in the knowledge that domestic political considerations preclude the use of nuclear weapons, the enemy will once again form into division-sized units or larger during the next monsoon season. A parsimonious use of tactical nuclear weapons, even as few as twenty 100 kiloton bombs, employed simultaneously and in an advantageous pattern, will destroy a minimum of 200,000 enemy troops, or nearly two-thirds of his total force, in a twenty-four hour period. The blow will be crushing.

The minor scenario, upon whose success the implementation of the major scenario depends, is far more sophisticated, due to its subtler goal: public acceptance of, or, optimally, even public clamor for, the use of tactical nuclear weapons. The task is difficult, but my scenario is quite sound, if somewhat exotic, and with the full, if to-some-extent-clandestine support of the upper military hierarchy, certain civil government circles and the decision-makers in key aerospace corporations, the means now at my command would seem adequate. The risks, while statistically significant, do not exceed an acceptable level.

T minus 189 days . . . and counting . . .

The way I see it, the network deserved the shafting I gave them. They shafted me, didn't they? Four successful series I produce for those bastards, and two bomb out after thirteen weeks and they send me to the salt mines! A discotheque, can you imagine they make me producer at a lousy discotheque! A remittance man they make me, those schlockmeisters. Oh, those schnorrers made the American Dream sound like a kosher deal—20% of the net, they say. And you got access to all our sets and contract players, it'll make you a rich man, Herm. And like a yuk, I sign, being broke at the time, without reading the fine print. I should know they've set up the American Dream as a tax loss? I should know that I've *gotta* use their lousy sets and stiff contract players and have it written off against my gross? I should know their shtick is to run the American Dream at a loss and then do a network TV

189

show out of the joint from which I don't see a penny? So I end up running the place for them at a paper loss, living on salary, while the network rakes it in off the TV show that I end up paying for out of my end.

Don't bums like that deserve to be shafted? It isn't enough they use me as a tax loss patsy, they gotta tell me who to book! "Go sign the Four Horsemen, the group that's packing them in at the Mandala," they say. "We want them on *A Night With The American Dream.* They're hot."

"Yeah, they're hot," I say, "which means they'll cost a mint. I can't afford it."

They show me more fine print—next time I read the contract with a microscope. I *gotta* book whoever they tell me to and I gotta absorb the cost on my books! It's enough to make a Litvak turn anti-Semite.

So I had to go to the Mandala to sign up these hippies. I made sure I didn't get there till 12:30 so I wouldn't have to stay in that nuthouse any longer than necessary. Such a dive! What Bernstein did was take a bankrupt Hollywood-Hollywood club on the Strip, knock down all the interior walls and put up this monster tent inside the shell. Just thin white screening over two-by-fours. Real shlock. Outside the tent, he's got projectors, lights, speakers, all the electronic mumbo-jumbo, and inside is like being surrounded by movie screens. Just the tent and the bare floor, not even a real stage, just a platform on wheels they shlepp in and out of the tent when they change groups.

So you can imagine he doesn't draw exactly a class crowd. Not with the American Dream up the street being run as a network tax loss. What they get is the smelly hard-core hippies I don't let in the door and the kind of j.d. high-school kids that think it's smart to hang around putzes like that. A lot of dope-pushing goes on. The cops don't like the place and the rousts draw professional troublemakers.

A real den of iniquity—I felt like I was walking onto a Casbah set. The last group had gone off and the Horsemen hadn't come on yet, so what you had was this crazy tent filled with hippies, half of them on acid or pot or amphetamine or for all I know Ajax, high-school would-be hippies, also mostly stoned and getting ugly, and a few crazy schwartzers looking to fight cops. All of them standing around waiting for something to happen, and about ready to make it happen. I stood near the door, just in case. As they say, "the vibes were making me uptight."

All of a sudden the house lights go out and it's black as a network executive's heart. I hold my hand on my wallet—in this crowd, tell me there are no pickpockets. Just the pitch black and dead silence for what, ten beats, and then I start feeling something, I don't know, like something crawling along my bones, but I know it's some kind of subsonic effect and not my imagination, because all the hippies are standing still and you don't hear a sound.

Then from monster speakers so loud you feel it in your teeth, a heartbeat, but heavy, slow, half-time like maybe a whale's heart. The thing crawling along my bones seems to be synchronized with the heartbeat and I feel almost like I am that big dumb heart beating there in the darkness.

Then a dark red spot—so faint it's almost infrared—hits the stage which they have wheeled out. On the stage are four uglies in crazy black robes—you know, like the Grim Reaper wears—with that ugly red light all over them like blood. Creepy. Boom-ba-boom. Boom-ba-boom. The heartbeat still going, still that subsonic bone-crawl and the hippies are staring at the Four Horsemen like mesmerized chickens.

The bass player, a regular jungle-bunny, picks up the rhythm of the heartbeat. Dum-da-dum. Dum-da-dum. The drummer beats it out with earsplitting rim-shots. Then the electric guitar, tuned like a strangling cat, makes with horrible heavy chords. Whang-ka-whang. Whang-ka-whang.

It's just awful, I feel it in my guts, my bones; my eardrums are just like some great big throbbing vein. Everybody is swaying to it, I'm swaying to it. Boom-ba-boom. Boom-ba-boom.

Then the guitarist starts to chant in rhythm with the heartbeat, in a hoarse, shrill voice like somebody dying: *"The* big *flash . . . The* big *flash . . ."*

And the guy at the visuals console diddles around and rings of light start to climb the walls of the tent, blue at the bottom becoming green as they get higher, then yellow, orange and finally as they become a circle on the ceiling, eye-killing neon-red. Each circle takes exactly one heartbeat to climb the walls.

Boy, what an awful feeling! Like I was a tube of toothpaste being squeezed in rhythm till the top of my head felt like it was gonna squirt up with those circles of light through the ceiling.

And then they start to speed it up gradually. The same heartbeat, the same rim-shots, same chords, same circles of light, same *"The* big *flash . . . The* big *flash . . ."* same bass, same subsonic bone-crawl, but just a little faster. . . . Then faster! Faster!

Thought I would die! Knew I would die! Heart beating like a lunatic. Rim-shots like a machine gun. Circles of light sucking me up the walls, into the red neon hole.

Oy, incredible! Over and over faster faster till the voice was a scream and the heartbeat a boom and the rim-shots a whine and the guitar howled feedback and my bones were jumping out of my body—

Every spot in the place came on and I went blind from the sudden light—

An awful explosion-sound came over every speaker, so loud it rocked me on my feet—

I felt myself squirting out of the top of my head and loved it.

Then:

The explosion became a rumble—

The light seemed to run together into a circle on the ceiling, leaving everything else black.

And the circle became a fireball.

The fireball became a slow-motion film of an atomic bomb cloud as the rumbling died away. Then the picture faded into a moment of total darkness and the house lights came on.

What a number!

Gevalt, what an act!

So after the show, when I got them alone and found out they had no manager, not even an option to the Mandala, I thought faster than I ever had in my life.

To make a long story short and sweet, I gave the network the royal screw. I signed the Horsemen to a contract that made me their manager and gave me twenty percent of their take. Then I booked them into the American Dream at ten thousand a week, wrote a check as proprietor of the American Dream, handed the check to myself as manager of the Four Horsemen, then resigned as a network flunky, leaving them with a $10,000 bag and me with 20% of the hottest group since the Beatles.

What the hell, he who lives by the fine print shall perish by the fine print.

T minus 148 days . . . and counting . . .

"You haven't seen the tape yet, have you, B.D.?" Jake said. He was nervous as hell. When you reach my level in the network structure, you're used to making subordinates nervous, but Jake Pitkin was head of network continuity, not some office boy, and certainly should be used to dealing with executives at my level. Was the rumor really true?

We were alone in the screening room. It was doubtful that the projectionist could hear us.

"No, I haven't seen it yet," I said. "But I've heard some strange stories."

Jake looked positively deathly. "About the tape?" he said.

"About you, Jake," I said, deprecating the rumor with an easy smile. "That you don't want to air the show."

"It's true, B.D.," Jake said quietly.

"Do you realize what you're saying? Whatever our personal tastes—and I personally think there's something unhealthy about them—the Four

192

Horsemen are the hottest thing in the country right now and that dirty little thief Herm Gellman held us up for a quarter of a million for an hour show. It cost another two hundred thousand to make it. We've spent another hundred thousand on promotion. We're getting top dollar from the sponsors. There's over a million dollars one way or the other riding on that show. That's how much we blow if we don't air it.''

''I know that, B.D.,'' Jake said. ''I also know this could cost me my job. Think about that. Because knowing all that, I'm still against airing the tape. I'm going to run the closing segment for you. I'm sure enough that you'll agree with me to stake my job on it.''

I had a terrible feeling in my stomach. I have superiors too and The Word was that *A Trip With The Four Horsemen* would be aired, period. No matter what. Something funny was going on. The price we were getting for commercial time was a precedent and the sponsor was a big aerospace company which had never bought network time before. What really bothered me was that Jake Pitkin had no reputation for courage; yet here he was laying his job on the line. He must be pretty sure I would come around to his way of thinking or he wouldn't dare. And though I couldn't tell Jake, I had no choice in the matter whatsoever.

''Okay, roll it,'' Jake said into the intercom mike. ''What you're going to see,'' he said as the screening room lights went out, ''is the last number.''

On the screen:

A shot of empty blue sky, with soft, lazy electric guitar chords behind it. The camera pans across a few clouds to an extremely long shot on the sun. As the sun, no more than a tiny circle of light, moves into the center of the screen, a sitar-drone comes in behind the guitar.

Very slowly, the camera begins to zoom in on the sun. As the image of the sun expands, the sitar gets louder and the guitar begins to fade and a drum starts to give the sitar a beat. The sitar gets louder, the beat gets more pronounced and begins to speed up as the sun continues to expand. Finally, the whole screen is filled with unbearably bright light behind which the sitar and drum are in a frenzy.

Then over this, drowning out the sitar and drum, a voice like a sick thing in heat: *''Brighter . . . than a thousand suns . . .''*

The light dissolves into a closeup of a beautiful dark-haired girl with huge eyes and moist lips, and suddenly there is nothing on the sound track but soft guitar and voices crooning low: *''Brighter . . . Oh God, it's brighter . . . brighter . . . than a thousand suns . . .''*

The girl's face dissolves into a full shot of the Four Horsemen in their Grim Reaper robes and the same melody that had played behind the girl's face shifts into a minor key, picks up whining, reverberating electric guitar chords and a sitar-drone and becomes a dirge: *"Darker . . . the world grows darker . . ."*

And a series of cuts in time to the dirge:

A burning village in Asia strewn with bodies—

"Darker . . . the world grows darker . . ."

The corpse-heap at Auschwitz—

"Until it gets so dark . . ."

A gigantic auto graveyard with gaunt Negro children dwarfed in the foreground—

"I think I'll die . . ."

A Washington ghetto in flames with the Capitol misty in the background—

". . . before the daylight comes . . ."

A jump-cut to an extreme closeup on the lead singer of the Horsemen, his face twisted into a mask of desperation and ecstasy. And the sitar is playing double-time, the guitar is wailing and he is screaming at the top of his lungs: *"But before I die, let me make that trip before the nothing comes . . ."*

The girl's face again, but transparent, with a blinding yellow light shining through it. The sitar beat gets faster and faster with the guitar whining behind it and the voice is working itself up into a howling frenzy: *". . . the last big flash to light my sky . . ."*

Nothing but the blinding light now—

". . . and zap! the world is done . . ."

An utterly black screen for a beat that becomes black fading to blue at a horizon—

". . . but before we die let's dig that high that frees us from our binds . . . that blows all cool that ego-drool and burns us from our mind . . . the last big flash, mankind's last gas, the trip we can't take twice. . . ."

Suddenly, the music stops dead for half a beat. Then:

The screen is lit up by an enormous fireball—

A shattering rumble—

The fireball coalesces into a mushroom-pillar cloud as the roar goes on. As the roar begins to die out, fire is visible inside the monstrous nuclear cloud. And the girl's face is faintly visible superimposed over the cloud.

A soft voice, amplified over the roar, obscenely reverential now: *Brighter . . . great God, it's brighter . . . brighter than a thousand suns . . ."*

And the screen went blank and the lights came on.

I looked at Jake. Jake looked at me.

"That's sick," I said. "That's really sick."

"You don't want to run a thing like that, do you, B.D.?" Jake said softly.

I made some rapid mental calculations. The loathsome thing ran something under five minutes . . . it could be done. . . .

"You're right, Jake," I said. "We won't run a thing like that. We'll cut it out of the tape and squeeze in another commercial at each break. That should cover the time."

"You don't understand," Jake said. "The contract Herm rammed down our throats doesn't allow us to edit. The show's a package—all or nothing. Besides, the whole show's like that."

"All like that? What do you mean, all like that?"

Jake squirmed in his seat. "Those guys are . . . well, perverts, B.D.," he said.

"Perverts?"

"They're . . . well, they're in love with the atom bomb or something. Every number leads up to the same thing."

"You mean . . . they're *all* like that?"

"You got the picture, B.D.," Jake said. "We run an hour of *that* or we run nothing at all."

"Jesus."

I knew what I wanted to say. Burn the tape and write off the million dollars. But I also knew it would cost me my job. And I knew that five minutes after I was out the door, they would have someone in my job who would see things their way. Even my superiors seemed to be just handing down The Word from higher up. I had no choice. There was no choice.

"I'm sorry, Jake," I said. "We run it."

"I resign," said Jake Pitkin, who had no reputation for courage.

T minus 10 days . . . and counting . . .

"It's a clear violation of the Test-Ban Treaty," I said.

The Under Secretary looked as dazed as I felt. "We'll call it a peaceful use of atomic energy, and let the Russians scream," he said.

"It's insane."

"Perhaps," the Under Secretary said. "But you have your orders, General Carson, and I have mine. From higher up. At exactly eighty fifty-eight P.M. local time on July fourth, you will drop a fifty kiloton atomic bomb on the designated ground zero at Yucca Flats."

"But the people . . . the television crews . . ."

"Will be at least two miles outside the danger zone. Surely, SAC can manage that kind of accuracy under 'laboratory conditions.' "

I stiffened. "I do not question the competence of any bomber crew under my command to perform this mission," I said. "I question the reason for the mission. I question the sanity of the orders."

195

The Under Secretary shrugged, smiled wanly. "Welcome to the club."

"You mean you don't know what this is all about either?"

"All I know is what was transmitted to me by the Secretary of Defense, and I got the feeling he doesn't know everything, either. You know that the Pentagon has been screaming for the use of tactical nuclear weapons to end the war in Asia—you SAC boys have been screaming the loudest. Well, several months ago, the President conditionally approved a plan for the use of tactical nuclear weapons during the next monsoon season."

I whistled. The civilians were finally coming to their senses. Or were they?

"But what does that have to do with—?"

"Public opinion," the Under Secretary said. "It was conditional upon a drastic change in public opinion. At the time the plan was approved, the polls showed that seventy-eight point eight percent of the population opposed the use of tactical nuclear weapons, nine point eight percent favored their use and the rest were undecided or had no opinion. The President agreed to authorize the use of tactical nuclear weapons by a date, several months from now, which is still top secret, provided that by that date at least sixty-five percent of the population approved their use and no more than twenty percent actively opposed it."

"I see . . . Just a ploy to keep the Joint Chiefs quiet."

"General Carson," the Under Secretary said, "apparently you are out of touch with the national mood. After the first Four Horsemen show, the polls showed that twenty-five percent of the population approved the use of nuclear weapons. After the second show, the figure was forty-one percent. It is now forty-eight percent. Only thirty-two percent are now actively opposed."

"You're trying to tell me that a rock group—"

"A rock group and the cult around it, General. It's become a national hysteria. There are imitators. Haven't you seen those buttons?"

"The ones with a mushroom cloud on them that say 'Do it'?"

The Under Secretary nodded. "Your guess is as good as mine whether the National Security Council just decided that the Horsemen hysteria could be used to mold public opinion, or whether the Four Horsemen were their creatures to begin with. But the results are the same either way—the Horsemen and the cult around them have won over precisely that element of the population which was most adamantly opposed to nuclear weapons: hippies, students, dropouts, draft-age youth. Demonstrations against the war and against nuclear weapons have died down. We're pretty close to that sixty-five percent. Someone—perhaps the President himself—has decided that one more big Four Horsemen show will put us over the top."

"The President is behind this?"

"No one else can authorize the detonation of an atomic bomb, after all," the Under Secretary said. "We're letting them do the show live from Yucca Flats. It's being sponsored by an aerospace company heavily dependent on defense contracts. We're letting them truck in a live audience. Of course the government is behind it."

"And SAC drops an A-bomb as the show-stopper?"

"Exactly."

"I saw one of those shows," I said. "My kids were watching it. I got the strangest feeling . . . I almost wanted that red telephone to ring. . . ."

"I know what you mean," the Under Secretary said. "Sometimes I get the feeling that whoever's behind this has gotten caught up in the hysteria themselves . . . that the Horsemen are now using whoever was using them . . . a closed circle. But I've been tired lately. The war's making us all so tired. If only we could get it all over with . . ."

"We'd all like to get it over with one way or the other," I said.

T minus 60 minutes . . . and counting . . .

I had orders to muster *Backfish*'s crew for the live satellite relay of *The Four Horsemen's Fourth.* Superficially, it might seem strange to order the whole Polaris fleet to watch a television show, but the morale factor involved was quite significant.

Polaris subs are frustrating duty. Only top sailors are chosen and a good sailor craves action. Yet if we are ever called upon to act, our mission will have been a failure. We spend most of our time honing skills that must never be used. Deterrence is a sound strategy but a terrible drain on the men of the deterrent forces—a drain exacerbated in the past by the negative attitude of our countrymen toward our mission. Men who, in the service of their country, polish their skills to a razor edge and then must refrain from exercising them have a right to resent being treated as pariahs.

Therefore the positive change in the public attitude toward us that seems to be associated with the Four Horsemen has made them mascots of a kind to the Polaris fleet. In their strange way they seem to speak for us and to us.

I chose to watch the show in the missile control center, where a full crew must always be ready to launch the missiles on five-minute notice. I have always felt a sense of communion with the duty watch in the missile control center that I cannot share with the other men under my command. Here we are not Captain and crew but mind and hand. Should the order come, the will to fire the missiles will be mine and the act will be theirs. At such a moment, it will be good not to feel alone.

197

All eyes were on the television set mounted above the main console as the show came on and . . .

The screen was filled with a whirling spiral pattern, metallic yellow on metallic blue. There was a droning sound that seemed part sitar and part electronic and I had the feeling that the sound was somehow coming from inside my head and the spiral seemed etched directly on my retinas. It hurt mildly, yet nothing in the world could have made me turn away.

Then two voices, chanting against each other:

"Let it all come in. . . ."

"Let it all come out . . ."

"In . . . *out* . . . in . . . *out* . . . in . . . *out* . . ."

My head seemed to be pulsing— in-*out*, in-*out*, in-*out*—and the spiral pattern began to pulse color-changes with the words: yellow-on-blue (in) . . . green-on-red (*out*) . . . In-*out*-in-*out*-in-*out*-in-*out* . . .

In the screen . . . *out* my head . . . I seemed to be beating against some kind of invisible membrane between myself and the screen as if something were trying to embrace my mind and I were fighting it . . . But why was I fighting it?

The pulsing, the chanting, got faster and faster till *in* could not be told from *out* and negative spiral afterimages formed in my eyes faster than they could adjust to the changes, piled up on each other faster and faster till it seemed my head would explode—

The chanting and the droning broke and there were the Four Horsemen, in their robes, playing on some stage against a backdrop of clear blue sky. And a single voice, soothing now: "You are in . . ."

Then the view was directly above the Horsemen and I could see that they were on some kind of circular platform. The view moved slowly and smoothly up and away and I saw that the circular stage was atop a tall tower; around the tower and completely encircling it was a huge crowd seated on desert sands that stretched away to an empty infinity.

"And we are in and they are in . . ."

I was down among the crowd now; they seemed to melt and flow like plastic, pouring from the television screen to enfold me . . .

"And we are all in here together. . . ."

A strange and beautiful feeling . . . the music got faster and wilder, ecstatic . . . the hull of the *Backfish* seemed unreal . . . the crowd was swaying to it around me . . . the distance between myself and the crowd seemed to dissolve . . . I was there . . . they were here. . . . We were transfixed . . .

"Oh yeah, we are all in here together . . . together . . ."

Jeremy and I sat staring at the television screen, ignoring each other and everything around us. Even with the short watches and the short tours of duty, you can get to feeling pretty strange down here in a hole in the ground under tons of concrete, just you and the guy with the other key, with nothing to do but think dark thoughts and get on each other's nerves. We're all supposed to be as stable as men can be, or so they tell us, and they must be right because the world's still here. I mean, it wouldn't take much—just two guys on the same watch over the same three Minutemen flipping out at the same time, turning their keys in the dual lock, pressing the three buttons . . . Pow! World War III!

A bad thought, the kind we're not supposed to think or I'll start watching Jeremy and he'll start watching me and we'll get a paranoia feedback going. . . . But that can't happen; we're too stable, too responsible. As long as we remember that it's healthy to feel a little spooky down here, we'll be all right.

But the television set is a good idea. It keeps us in contact with the outside world, keeps it real. It'd be too easy to start thinking that the missile control center down here is the only real world and that nothing that happens up there really matters. . . . Bad thought!

The Four Horsemen . . . somehow these guys help you get it all out. I mean that feeling that it might be better to release all that tension, get it all over with. Watching The Four Horsemen, you're able to go with it without doing any harm, let it wash over you and then through you. I suppose they are crazy; they're all the human craziness in ourselves that we're got to keep very careful watch over down here. Letting it all come out watching the Horsemen makes it surer that none of it will come out down here. I guess that's why a lot of us have taken to wearing those "Do It" buttons off duty. The brass doesn't mind; they seem to understand that it's the kind of inside sick joke we need to keep us functioning.

Now that spiral thing they had started the show with—and the droning—came back on. Zap! I was right back in the screen again, as if the commercial hadn't happened.

"We are all in here together . . ."

And then a closeup of the lead singer, looking straight at me, as close as Jeremy and somehow more real. A mean-looking guy with something behind his eyes that told me he knew where everything lousy and rotten was at.

A bass began to thrum behind him and some kind of electronic hum that set my teeth on edge. He began playing his guitar, mean and low-down. And singing in that kind of drop-dead tone of voice that starts brawls in bars:

"I stabbed my mother and I mugged my paw . . ."

A riff of heavy guitar-chords echoed the words mockingly as a huge swastika (red-on-black, black-on-red) pulsed like a naked vein on the screen—

The face of the Horseman, leering—

"Nailed my sister to the toilet door . . ."

Guitar behind the pulsing swastika—

"Drowned a puppy in a ce-ment machine. . . . Burned a kitten just to hear it scream. . . ."

On the screen, just a big fire burning in slow-motion, and the voice became a slow, shrill, agonized wail:

"Oh God, I've got this red-hot fire burning in the marrow of my brain. . . .

"Oh yes, I got this fire burning . . . in the stinking marrow of my brain. . . .

"Gotta get me a blowtorch . . . and set some naked flesh on flame. . . ."

The fire dissolved into the face of a screaming Oriental woman, who ran through a burning village clawing at the napalm on her back.

"I got this message. . . . boiling in the bubbles of my blood . . . A man ain't nothing but a fire burning . . . in a dirty glob of mud. . . ."

A film-clip of a Nuremburg rally: a revolving swastika of marching men waving torches—

Then the leader of the Horsemen superimposed over the twisted flaming cross:

"Don't you hate me, baby, can't you feel somethin' screaming in your mind?

"Don't you hate me, baby, feel me drowning you in slime!"

Just the face of the Horseman howling hate—

"Oh yes, I'm a monster, mother. . . ."

A long view of the crowd around the platform, on their feet, waving arms, screaming soundlessly. Then a quick zoom in and a kaleidoscope of faces, eyes feverish, mouths open and howling—

"Just call me—"

The face of the Horseman superimposed over the crazed faces of the crowd—

"Mankind!"

I looked at Jeremy. He was toying with the key on the chain around his neck. He was sweating. I suddenly realized that I was sweating too and that my own key was throbbing in my hand alive. . . .

T minus 13 minutes . . . and counting . . .

A funny feeling, the Captain watching the Four Horsemen here in the *Backfish*'s missile control center with us. Sitting in front of my console watching the television set with the Captain kind of breathing down my neck . . . I got the feeling he knew what was going through me and I couldn't know what was going through him . . . and it gave the fire inside me a kind of greasy feel I didn't like. . . .

Then the commercial was over and that spiral-thing came on again and whoosh! it sucked me right back into the television set and I stopped worrying about the Captain or anything like that. . . .

Just the spiral going yellow-blue, red-green, and then starting to whirl and whirl, faster and faster, changing colors and whirling, whirling, whirling. . . . And the sound of a kind of Coney Island carousel tinkling behind it, faster and faster and faster, whirling and whirling and whirling, flashing red-green, yellow-blue, and whirling, whirling, whirling . . .

And this big hum filling my body and whirling, whirling, whirling . . . My muscles relaxing, going limp, whirling, whirling, whirling, all limp, whirling, whirling, whirling, oh so nice, just whirling, whirling . . .

And in the center of the flashing spiraling colors, a bright dot of colorless light, right at the center, not moving, not changing, while the whole world went whirling and whirling in colors around it, and the humming was coming from the dot the way the carousel-music was coming from the spinning colors and the dot was humming its song to me. . . .

The dot was a light way down at the end of a long, whirling, whirling tunnel. The humming started to get a little louder. The bright dot started to get a little bigger. I was drifting down the tunnel toward it, whirling, whirling, whirling . . .

T minus 11 minutes . . . and counting . . .

Whirling, whirling, whirling down a long, long tunnel of pulsing colors, whirling, whirling, toward the circle of light way down at the end of the tunnel . . . How nice it would be to finally get there and soak up the beautiful hum filling my body and then I could forget that I was down here in this hole in the ground with a hard brass key in my hand, just Duke and me, down here in a cave under the ground that was a spiral of flashing colors, whirling, whirling toward the friendly light at the end of the tunnel, whirling, whirling . . .

T minus 10 minutes . . . and counting . . .

The circle of light at the end of the whirling tunnel was getting bigger and bigger and the humming was getting louder and louder and I was feeling better and better and the *Backfish*'s missile control center was getting dimmer and dimmer as the awful weight of command got lighter and lighter, whirling, whirling, and I felt so good I wanted to cry, whirling, whirling . . .

T minus 9 minutes . . . and counting . . .

Whirling, whirling . . . I was whirling, Jeremy was whirling, the hole in the ground was whirling, and the circle of light at the end of the tunnel whirled closer and closer and—I was through! A place filled with yellow light. Pale metal-yellow light. Then pale metallic blue. Yellow. Blue. Yellow. Blue. Yellow-blue-yellow-blue-yellow-blue-yellow . . .

Pure light pulsing . . . and pure sound droning. And just the *feeling* of letters I couldn't read between the pulses—not-yellow and not-blue—too quick and too faint to be visible, but important, very important . . .

And then a voice that seemed to be singing from inside my head, almost as if it were my own:

"Oh, oh, oh . . . don't I really wanna know . . . Oh, oh, oh, . . . don't I really wanna know . . ."

The world pulsing, flashing around those words I couldn't read, couldn't quite read, had to read, could *almost* read . . .

"Oh, oh, oh, . . . great God I really wanna know. . . ."

Strange amorphous shapes clouding the blue-yellow-blue flickering universe, hiding the words I had to read . . . Dammit, why wouldn't they get out of the way so I could find out what I had to know!

"Tell me tell me tell me tell me tell me . . . Gotta know gotta know gotta know gotta know . . ."

T minus 7 minutes . . . and counting . . .

Couldn't read the words! Why wouldn't the Captain let me read the words?

And that voice inside me: *"Gotta know . . . gotta know . . . gotta know why it hurts me so. . . ."* Why wouldn't it shut up and let me read the words? Why wouldn't the words hold still? Or just slow down a little? If they'd slow down a little, I could read them and then I'd know what I had to do. . . .

T minus 6 minutes . . . and counting . . .

I felt the sweaty key in the palm of my hand . . . I saw Duke stroking his own key. Had to know! Now—through the pulsing blue-yellow-blue light and the unreadable words that were building up an awful pressure in the back of my brain—I could see the Four Horsemen. They were on their knees, crying, looking up at something and begging: *"Tell me tell me tell me tell me . . ."*

Then soft billows of rich red-and-orange fire filled the world and a huge voice was trying to speak. But it couldn't form the words. It stuttered and moaned—

The yellow-blue-yellow flashing around the words I couldn't read—the same words, I suddenly sensed, that the voice of the fire was trying so hard to form—and the Four Horsemen on their knees begging: *"Tell me tell me tell me . . ."*

The friendly warm fire trying so hard to speak—

"Tell me tell me tell me tell me. . . ."

T minus 4 minutes . . . and counting . . .

What were the words? What was the order? I could sense my men silently imploring me to tell them. After all, I was their Captain, it was my duty to tell them. It was my duty to find out!

"Tell me tell me tell me . . ." the robed figures on their knees implored through the flickering pulse in my brain and I could almost make out the words . . . almost . . .

"Tell me tell me tell me . . ." I whispered to the warm orange fire that was trying so hard but couldn't quite form the words. The men were whispering it too: "Tell me tell me . . ."

T minus 3 minutes . . . and counting . . .

The question burning blue and yellow in my brain: WHAT WAS THE FIRE TRYING TO TELL ME? WHAT WERE THE WORDS I COULDN'T READ?

Had to unlock the words! Had to find the key!

A key . . . *The* key? THE KEY! And there was the lock that imprisoned the words, right in front of me! Put the key in the lock . . . I looked at Jeremy. Wasn't there some reason, long ago and far away, why Jeremy might try to stop me from putting the key in the lock?

But Jeremy didn't move as I fitted the key into the lock. . . .

T minus 2 minutes . . . and counting . . .

Why wouldn't the Captain tell me what the order was? The fire knew, but it couldn't tell. My head ached from the pulsing, but I couldn't read the words.

"Tell me tell me tell me . . ." I begged.

Then I realized that the Captain was asking too.

T minus 90 seconds . . . and counting . . .

"Tell me tell me tell me . . ." the Horsemen begged. And the words I couldn't read were a fire in my brain.

Duke's key was in the lock in front of us. From very far away, he said: "We have to do it together."

Of course . . . our keys . . . our keys would unlock the words!

I put my key into the lock. One, two, three, we turned our keys together. A lid on the console popped open. Under the lid were three red buttons. Three signs on the console lit up in red letters: "ARMED."

T minus 60 seconds . . . and counting . . .

The men were waiting for me to give some order. I didn't know what the order was. A magnificent orange fire was trying to tell me but it couldn't get the words out. . . . Robed figures were praying to the fire. . . .

Then, through the yellow-blue flicker that hid the words I had to read, I saw a vast crowd encircling a tower. The crowd was on its feet begging silently—

The tower in the center of the crowd became the orange fire that was trying to tell me what the words were—

Became a great mushroom of billowing smoke and blinding orange-red glare. . . .

T minus 30 seconds . . . and counting . . .

The huge pillar of fire was trying to tell Jeremy and me what the words were, what we had to do. The crowd was screaming at the cloud of flame. The yellow-blue flicker was getting faster and faster behind the mushroom cloud. I could almost read the words! I could see that there were two of them!

T minus 20 seconds . . . and counting . . .

Why didn't the Captain tell us? I could almost see the words!

Then I heard the crowd around the beautiful mushroom cloud shouting: "DO IT! DO IT! DO IT! DO IT! DO IT!"

What did they want me to do? Did Duke know?

9

The men were waiting! What was the order? They hunched over the firing controls, waiting. . . . The firing controls . . . ?

"DO IT! DO IT! DO IT! DO IT! DO IT!"

8

"DO IT! DO IT! DO IT! DO IT! DO IT!": the crowd screaming.
"Jeremy!" I shouted. "I can read the words!"

7

My hands hovered over my bank of firing buttons . . . .
"DO IT! DO IT! DO IT! DO IT!" the words said.
Didn't the Captain understand?

6

"What do they want us to do, Jeremy?"

5

Why didn't the mushroom cloud give the order? My men were waiting! A good sailor craves action.
Then a great voice spoke from the pillar of fire: "DO IT . . . DO IT . . . DO IT. . . ."

4

"There's only one thing we can do down here, Duke."

3

"The order, men! Action! Fire!"

2

Yes, yes, yes! Jeremy—

1

I reached for my bank of firing buttons. All along the console, the men reached for their buttons. But I was too fast for them! I would be first!

0

THE BIG FLASH

From James Sallis, November 25, 1968:

Dear Damon, Kate—

Thank you for liking "Jim and Mary G," and for finding it appropriately dreadful. Comme il vos maison trouve ravi a juste titre. Comme fait tout le monde. Le Mouillage. La maison a s'ancrer. La maison de roi, du roi . . .

[On a separate sheet of orange paper]

Damon:

Quite frankly, I think (am certain) that "Jim and Mary G" is worth, deserving of, *much* more than a hundred dollars. But, as Jane points out, this house is worth vastly more than you are asking from us for it . . . So, with a sigh, and cursing equilibrium, I let my favorite story (and it shall remain my favorite story for some time) go; I let go and it plunges over the hundred-dollar brink, screaming. I cry a little. I will miss it . . .

JIM AND MARY G

by James Sallis

Getting his little coat down off the hook, then his arms into it, not easy because he's so excited and he always turns the wrong way anyhow. And all the time he's looking up at you with those blue eyes. We go park Papa, he says. We go see gulls. Straining for the door. The gulls are a favorite; he discovered them on the boat coming across and can't understand, he keeps looking for them in the park.

Wrap the muffler around his neck. Yellow, white. (Notice how white the skin is there, how the veins show through.) They call them scarves here don't they. Stockingcap—he pulls it down over his eyes, going Haha. He hasn't learned to laugh yet. Red mittens. Now move the zipper up and he's packed away. The coat's green corduroy, with black elastic at the neck and cuffs and a round hood that goes down over the cap. It's November. In

England. Thinking, the last time I'll do this. Is there still snow on the ground, I didn't look this morning.

Take his hand and go on out of the flat. Letting go at the door because it takes two hands to work the latch, Mary rattling dishes in the kitchen. (Good-bye, she says very softly as you shut the door.) He goes around you and beats you to the front door, waits there with his nose on the glass. The hall is full of white light. Go on down it to him. The milk's come, two bottles, with the *Guardian* leaning between them. Move the mat so we can open the door. We go park Papa, we seegulls. Frosty foggy air coming in. Back for galoshes, all the little brass-tongue buckles? No the snow's gone. Just some dirty slush. Careful. Down the steps.

Crunching down the sidewalk ahead of you, disappointed because there's no snow but looking back, Haha. We go park? The sky is flat and white as a sheet of paper. Way off, a flock of birds goes whirling across it, circling inside themselves—black dots, like iron filings with a magnet under the paper. The block opposite is lined with trees. What kind? The leaves are all rippling together. It looks like green foil. Down the walk.

Asking, Why is everything so still. Why aren't there any cars. Or a mailtruck. Or milkcart, gliding along with bottles jangling. Where is everyone. It's ten in the morning, where is everyone.

But there is a car just around the corner, stuck on ice at the side of the road where it parked last night with the wheels spinning Whrrrrrr. Smile, you understand a man's problems. And walk the other way. His mitten keeps coming off in your hand. Haha.

She had broken down only once, at breakfast.

The same as every morning, the child had waked them. Standing in his bed in the next room and bouncing up and down till the springs were banging against the frame. Then he climbed out and came to their door, peeking around the frame, finally doing his tiptoe shyly across the floor in his white wool nightshirt. Up to their bed, where they pretended to be still asleep. Brekpust, brekpust, he would say, poking at them and tugging the covers, at last climbing onto the bed to bounce up and down between them until they rolled over: Hello. Morninggg. He is proud of his *g*'s. Then, Mary almost broke down, remembering what today was, what they had decided the night before.

She turned her face toward the window (they hadn't been able to afford curtains yet) and he heard her breathe deeply several times. But a moment later she was up—out of bed in her quilted robe and heading for the kitchen, with the child behind her.

He reached and got a cigarette off the trunk they were using as a night

207

table. It had a small wood lamp, a bra, some single cigarettes and a jar-lid full of ashes and filters on it. Smoking, listening to water running, pans clatter, cupboards and drawers. Then the sounds stopped and he heard them together in the bathroom: the tap ran for a while, then the toilet flushed and he heard the child's pleased exclamations. They went back into the kitchen and the sounds resumed. Grease crackling, the child chattering about how good he had been. The fridge door opened and shut, opened again, Mary said something. He was trying to help.

He got out of bed and began dressing. How strange that she'd forgotten to take him to the bathroom first thing, she'd never done that before. Helpinggg, from the kitchen by way of explanation, as he walked to the bureau. It was square and ugly, with that shininess peculiar to cheap furniture, and it had been in the flat when they moved in, the only thing left behind. He opened a drawer and took out a shirt. All his shirts were white. Why, she had once asked him, years ago. He didn't know, then or now.

He went into the kitchen with the sweater over his head. "Mail?" Through the wool. Neither of them looked around, so he pulled it the rest of the way on, reaching down inside to tug the shirtcollar out. Then the sleeves.

"A letter from my parents. They're worried they haven't heard from us, they hope we're all right. Daddy's feeling better, why don't we write them."

The child was dragging his high-chair across the floor from the corner. Long ago they had decided he should take care of as many of his own needs as he could—a sense of responsibility, Mary had said—but this morning Jim helped him carry the chair to the table, slid the tray off, lifted him into it and pushed the chair up to the table. When he looked up, Mary turned quickly away, back to the stove.

Eggs, herring, toast and ham. "I thought it would be nice," Mary said. "To have a good breakfast." And that was the time she broke down.

The child had started scooping the food up in his fingers, so she got up again and went across the kitchen to get his spoon. It was heavy silver, with an ivory *K* set into the handle, and it had been her own. She turned and came back across the tile, holding the little spoon in front of her and staring at it. Moma cryinggg, the child said. Moma cryinggg. She ran out of the room. The child turned in his chair to watch her go, then turned back and went on eating with the spoon. The plastic padding squeaked as the child moved inside it. The chair was metal, the padding white with large blue asterisks all over it. They had bought it at a Woolworths. Twelve and six. Like the bureau, it somehow fit the flat.

A few minutes later Mary came back, poured coffee for both of them and sat down across from him.

208

"It's best this way," she said. "He won't have to suffer. It's the only answer."

He nodded, staring into the coffee. Then took off his glasses and cleaned them on his shirttail. The child was stirring the eggs and herring together in his bowl. Holding the spoon like a chisel in his hand and going round and round the edge of the bowl.

"Jim . . ."

He looked up. She seemed to him, then, very tired, very weak.

"We could take him to one of those places. Where they . . . take care of them . . . for you."

He shook his head, violently. "No, we've already discussed that, Mary. He wouldn't understand. It will be easier, my way. If I do it myself."

She went to the window and stood there watching it. It filled most of one wall. It was frosted over.

"How would you like to go for a walk after breakfast," he asked the child. He immediately shoved the bowl away and said, "Bafroom first?"

"You or me?" Mary said from the window.

Finally: "You."

He sat alone in the kitchen, thinking. Taps ran, the toilet flushed, he came out full of pride. "We go park," he said. "We go see gulls."

"Maybe." It was this, the lie, which came back to him later; this was what he remembered most vividly. He got up and walked into the hall with the child following him and put his coat on. "Where's his other muffler?"

"In the bureau drawer. The top one."

He got it, then began looking for the stockingcap and mittens. Walking through the rooms, opening drawers. There aren't any seagulls in London. When she brought the cap and mittens to him there was a hole in the top of the cap and he went off looking for the other one. Walking through rooms, again and again into the child's own.

"For God's sake go on," she finally said. "Please stop. O damn Jim, go on." And she turned and ran back into the kitchen.

Soon he heard her moving about. Clearing the table, running water, opening and shutting things. Silverware clicking.

"We go park?"

He began to dress the child. Getting his little coat down off the hook. Wrapping his neck in the muffler. There aren't any seagulls in London. Stockingcap, Haha.

Thinking. This is the last time I'll ever do this.

Now bump, bump, bump. Down the funny stairs.

209

When he returned, Mary was lying on the bed, still in the quilted robe, watching the ceiling. It seemed very dark, very cold in the room. He sat down beside her in his coat and put his hand on her arm. Cars moved past the window. The people upstairs had their radio on.

"Why did you move the bureau?" he asked after a while.

Without moving her head she looked down toward the foot of the bed. "After you left I was lying here and I noticed a traffic light or something like that out on the street was reflected in it. It was blinking on and off, I must have watched it for an hour. We've been here for weeks and I never saw that before. But once I did, I had to move it."

"You shouldn't be doing heavy work like that."

For a long while she was still, and when she finally moved, it was just to turn her head and look silently into his face.

He nodded, once, very slowly.

"It didn't . . ."

No.

She smiled, sadly, and he lay down beside her in the small bed. She seemed younger now, rested, herself again. There was warmth in her hand when she took his own and put them together on her stomach.

They lay quietly through the afternoon. Ice was reforming on the streets; outside, they could hear wheels spinning, engines racing. The hall door opened, there was a jangle of milkbottles, the door closed. Then everything was quiet. The trees across the street drooped under the weight of the ice.

There was a sound in the flat. Very low and steady, like a ticking. He listened for hours before he realized it was the drip of a faucet in the bathroom.

Outside, slowly, obscuring the trees, the night came. And with it, snow. They lay together in the darkness, looking out the frosted window. Occasionally, lights moved across it.

"We'll get rid of his things tomorrow," she said after a while.

From a reader, November 8, 1970:

Dear Mr. Knight:
   I have just finished reading *Orbit 7* and I have re-read "Jim and

210

Mary G" by James Sallis and can find absolutely *no* reason for the inclusion of this story in "an anthology of new science fiction." Did I miss something?

To the same, November 24, 1970:

> Dear Mrs. ——,
>   I think I understand your surprise at finding "Jim and Mary G" in a science fiction anthology, but look at it this way: the story is set in a parallel world in which children can be disposed of like pets. If that isn't science fiction, why not?

From another reader, January 15, 1971:

> Dear Sir:
>   You recently edited a book called *Orbit 7*—a science fiction anthology. I am a great fan of science fiction stories and purchase them frequently. This particular book I borrowed from the public library today and will return tomorrow. The second story I happened to read in it was entitled "Jim and Mary G" by James Sallis. I won't read another story in this book or in any of your other *Orbit* series for fear of coming across a similar work.
>   Possibly, I misread the plot but it was so abhorrent to me, I won't touch the book even to reassure myself that I am wrong. In my opinion, a cold, calculating murder of a baby can not by any stretch of the imagination be deemed good science fiction or even good writing. It is the work of a *sick mind*. My greatest bewilderment is how an editor of seven? successful? science fiction works can see fit to lower himself to acknowledge such a piece and how he can think that the public (however simple-minded) can accept and enjoy such absolute filth. I hope that I am completely wrong in my conclusions to this story but I sincerely doubt it.
>
>   Yours in DISGUST,

To the same, January 26, 1971:

> Dear Mrs. ——,
>   You were quite right to stop reading after "Jim and Mary G." If that mild little story offended you, heaven knows what you would have thought of the rest of the book.

211

From Thomas M. Disch, January 19, 1969:

Dear Damon and Kate,

Heaps of bad news and heaps of good and little time to write letters, but I'll try to squeeze it all in at the expense of narrative grace.

The house: one day last week the kitchen started flooding at a source in the bathroom. I was called, numb with novocaine, from the dentist in Matamoras to come back and turn off the water, which I did after much travail with the car (it had a flat tire exactly then), but the trouble seems to have been not with the plumbing but with the cesspool which was backing up the drains for as yet undiscovered causes. I was just into New York, and returned to discover this had happened twice again in my absence. Great difficulty, still, to get help from the locals, tho Jane has found one man willing to do the work. Snyder (I believe it was) never came by to do the work on the burnt doorframe, and the other man she found will do that and take care of the kitchen floor. The tiles are absolutely ruined (there was an earlier flooding when the radiator geysered in the John) and two layers of plywood must also be replaced (I'm told), and it is now under debate whether the insurance covers this. . . .

THE END

by Ursula K. Le Guin

On the shore of the sea he stood looking out over the long foam-lines far where vague the Islands lifted or were guessed. There, he said to the sea, there lies my kingdom. The sea said to him what the sea says to everybody. As evening moved from behind his back across the water the foam-lines paled and the wind fell, and very far in the west shone a star perhaps, perhaps a light, or his desire for a light.

He climbed the streets of his town again in late dusk. The shops and huts of his neighbors were looking empty now, cleared out, cleaned up, packed away in preparation for the end. Most of the people were up at the Weeping in Heights-Hall or down with the Ragers in the fields. But Lif had not been able to clear out and clean up; his wares and belongings were too heavy to throw away, too hard to break, too dull to burn. Only centuries could waste them. Wherever they were piled or dropped or thrown they formed what might have been, or seemed to be, or yet might be, a city. So he had not tried to get rid of his things. His yard was still stacked and piled with bricks, thousands and thousands of bricks of his own making. The kiln stood cold but ready, the barrels of clay and dry mortar and lime, the hods and barrows and trowels of his trade, everything was there. One of the fellows from Scriveners Lane had asked sneering, Going to build a brick wall and hide behind it when that old end comes, man?

—Another neighbor on his way up to the Heights-Hall gazed a while at those stacks and heaps and loads and mounds of well-shaped, well-baked bricks all a soft reddish gold in the gold of the afternoon sun, and sighed at last with the weight of them on his heart: Things, things! Free yourself of things, Lif, from the weight that drags you down! Come with us, above the ending world!

Lif had picked up a brick from the heap and put it in place on the stack and smiled in embarrassment. When they were all past he had gone neither up to the Hall nor out to help wreck the fields and kill the animals, but down to the beach, the end of the ending world, beyond which lay only water. Now back in his brickyard hut with the smell of salt in his clothes and his face hot with the seawind, he still felt neither the Ragers' laughing and wrecking despair nor the soaring and weeping despair of the communicants of the Heights; he felt empty; he felt hungry. He was a heavy little man and the seawind at the world's edge had blown at him all evening without moving him at all.

Hey, Lif! said the widow from Weavers Lane, which crossed his street a few houses down—I saw you coming up the street, and never another soul going by since sunset, and getting dark, and quieter than . . . She did not say what the town was quieter than, but went on, Have you had your supper? I was about to take my roast out of the oven, and the little one and I will never eat up all that meat before the end comes, no doubt, and I hate to see good meat go to waste.

Well thank you very much, says Lif, putting on his coat again; and they went down Masons Lane to Weavers Lane through the dark and the wind sweeping up steep streets from the sea. In the widow's lamplit house Lif played with her baby, the last born in the town, a little fat boy just learning how to stand up. Lif stood him up and he laughed and fell over, while the widow set out bread and hot meat on the table of heavy woven cane. They sat to eat, even the baby, who worked with four teeth at a hard hunch of bread.

—How is it you're not up on the Hill or in the fields? asked Lif, and the widow replied as if the answer sufficed to her mind, Oh, I have the baby.

Lif looked around the little house which her husband, who had been one of Lif's bricklayers, had built. —This is good, he said. I haven't tasted meat since last year sometime.

I know, I know! No houses being built any more.

Not a one, he said. Not a wall nor a henhouse, not even repairs. But your weaving, that's still wanted?

Yes; not the men, to be sure, but some of the women, they want new clothes right up to the end. This meat I bought from the Ragers that slaughtered all my lord's flocks, and I paid with the money I got for a piece of fine linen I wove for my lord's daughter's gown that she wants to wear at the end! —The widow gave a little derisive, sympathetic, feminine snort, and went on: But now there's no flax, and scarcely any wool. No more to spin, no more to weave. The fields burnt and the flocks dead.

Yes, said Lif, eating the good roast meat. Bad times, he said, the worst times.

And now, the widow went on, where's bread to come from, with the fields burnt? And water, now they're poisoning the wells? I sound like the Weepers up there, don't I. Help yourself, Lif. Spring lamb's the finest meat in the world, my man always said, till autumn came and then he'd say roast pork's the finest meat in the world. Come on now, give yourself a proper slice. . . .

That night in his hut in the brickyard Lif dreamed. Usually he slept as still as the bricks themselves, but this night he drifted and floated in dream all night to the Islands, and when he woke they were no longer a wish or a guess: like a star as daylight darkens they had become certain, he knew them. But what, in his dream, had borne him over the water? He had not flown, he had not walked, he had not gone underwater like the fish; yet he had come across the gray-green plains and wind-moved hillocks of the sea to the Islands, he had heard voices call, and seen the lights of towns.

He set his mind to think how a man could ride on water. He thought of how grass floats on streams, and saw how one might make a sort of mat of woven cane and lie on it pushing with one's hands: but the great canebrakes were still smoldering down by the stream, and the piles of withies at the basketmaker's had all been burnt. On the Islands in his dream he had seen canes or grasses half a hundred feet high, with brown stems thicker than his arms could reach around, and a world of green leaves spread sunward from the thousand outreaching twigs. On those stems a man might ride over the sea. But no such plants grew in his country nor ever had; though in the Heights-Hall was a knife-handle made of a dull brown stuff, said to come

214

from a plant that grew in some other land, and was called wood. But he could not ride across the bellowing sea on a knife-handle.

Greased hides might float; but the tanners had been idle now for weeks, there were no hides for sale. He might as well stop looking about for any help. He carried his barrow and his largest hod down to the beach that white windy morning and laid them in the still water of a lagoon. Indeed they floated, deep in the water, but when he leaned even the weight of one hand on them they tipped, filled, sank. They were too light, he thought.

He went back up the cliff and through the streets, loaded the barrow with useless well-made bricks, and wheeled a hard load down. As so few children had been born these last years there was no young curiosity about to ask him what he was doing, though a Rager or two, groggy from last night's wreckfest, glanced sidelong at him from a dark doorway through the brightness of the air. All that day he brought down bricks and the makings of mortar, and the next day, though he had not had the dream again, he began to lay his bricks there on the blustering beach of March with rain and sand handy in great quantities to set his cement. He built a little brick dome, oval with pointed ends like a fish, all of a single course of bricks laid spiral very cunningly. If a cupful or a barrowful of air would float, would not a brick domeful? And it would be strong. But when the mortar was set, and straining his broad back he overturned the dome and pushed it into the cream of the breakers, it dug deeper and deeper into the wet sand as if burrowing down like a clam or a sandflea. The waves filled it, and refilled it when he tipped it empty, and at last a green-shouldered breaker caught it with its white dragging backpull, rolled it over, smashed it back into its elemental bricks and sank them in the restless sodden sand. There stood Lif wet to the neck and wiping salt spray out of his eyes. Nothing lay westward on the sea but wavewrack and rainclouds. But they were there. He knew them, with their great grasses ten times a man's height, their wild golden fields raked by the sea-wind, their white towns, their white-crowned hills above the sea; and the voices of shepherds called on the hills.

I'm a builder, not a floater, said Lif after he had considered his stupidity from all sides. And he came doggedly out of the water and up the cliffside path and through the rainy streets to get another barrowload of bricks.

Free for the first time in a week of his fool dream of floating, he noticed now that Leather Street seemed deserted. The tannery was rubbishy and vacant. The craftsmen's shops lay like a row of little black gaping mouths, and the sleeping-room windows above them were blind. At the end of the lane an old cobbler was burning, with a terrible stench, a small heap of new shoes never worn. Beside him a donkey waited, saddled, flicking its ears at the stinking smoke.

Lif went on and loaded his barrow with bricks. This time as he wheeled it down, straining back against the tug of the barrow on the steep streets, swinging all the strength of his shoulders to balance its course on the winding cliff-path down to the beach, a couple of townsmen followed him. Two or three more from Scriveners Lane followed after them, and several more from the streets round the marketplace, so that by the time he straightened up, the seafoam fizzing on his bare black feet and the sweat cold on his face, there was a little crowd strung out along the deep single track of his barrow over the sand. They had the lounging listless air of Ragers. Lif paid them no heed, though he was aware that the widow of Weavers Lane was up on the cliffs watching with a scared face.

He ran the barrow out into the sea till the water was up to his chest, and tipped the bricks out, and came running in with a great breaker, his banging barrow full of foam.

Already some of the Ragers were drifting away down the beach. A tall fellow from the Scriveners Lane lot lounged by him and said with a little grin, Why don't you throw 'em from the top of the cliff, man?

They'd only hit the sand, said Lif.

And you want to drown 'em. Well, good. You know there was some of us thought you was building something down here! They was going to make cement out of you. Keep those bricks wet and cool, man.

Grinning, the Scrivener drifted off, and Lif started up the cliff for another load.

Come for supper, Lif, said the widow at the cliff's top with a worried voice, holding her baby close to keep it from the wind.

I will, he said. I'll bring a loaf of bread, I laid in a couple before the bakers left. —He smiled, but she did not. As they climbed the streets together she asked, Are you dumping your bricks in the sea, Lif?

He laughed wholeheartedly and answered yes.

She had a look then that might have been relief and might have been sadness; but at supper in her lamplit house she was quiet and easy as ever, and they ate their cheese and stale bread with good cheer.

Next day he went on carrying bricks down load after load, and if the Ragers watched him they thought him busy on their own kind of work. The slope of the beach out to deep water was gradual, so that he could keep building without ever working above water. He had started at low tide so that his work would never be laid bare. At high tide it was hard, dumping the bricks and trying to lay them in rough courses with the whole sea boiling in his face and thundering over his head, but he kept at it. Toward evening he brought down long iron rods and braced what he had built, for a crosscurrent tended to undermine his causeway about eight feet from its beginning. He

216

made sure that even the tips of the rods were underwater at low tide, so that no Rager might suspect an affirmation was being made. A couple of elderly men coming down from a Weeping in the Heights-Hall passed him clanging and battering his empty barrow up the stone streets in dusk, and gravely smiled upon him. It is well to be free of Things, said one softly, and the other nodded.

Next day, though still he had not dreamed of the Islands again, Lif went on building his causeway. The sand began to shelve off more steeply as he went farther. His method now was to stand on the last bit he had built and tip the carefully loaded barrow from there, and then tip himself off and work, floundering and gasping and coming up and pushing down, to get the bricks leveled and fitted between the preset rods; then up again, across the gray sand and up the cliff and bang-clatter through the quiet streets for another load.

Some time that week the widow said meeting him in his brickyard, Let me throw 'em over the cliff for you, it'll save you one leg of the trip.

It's heavy work loading the barrow, he said.

Oh well, said she.

All right, so long as you want to. But bricks are heavy bastards. Don't try to carry many. I'll give you the small barrow. And the little rat here can sit on the load and get a ride.

So she helped him on and off through days of silvery weather, fog in the morning, clear sea and sky all afternoon, and the weeds in crannies of the cliff flowering; there was nothing else left to flower. The causeway ran out many yards from shore now, and Lif had had to learn a skill which no one else had ever learned that he knew of, except the fish. He could float and move himself about on the water or under it, in the very sea, without touching foot or hand to solid earth.

He had never heard that a man could do this thing; but he did not think much about it, being so busy with his bricks, in and out of air and in and out of water all day long, with the foam, the bubbles of water-circled air or air-circled water, all about him, and the fog, and the April rain, a confusion of the elements. Sometimes he was happy down in the murky green unbreathable world, wrestling strangely willful and weightless bricks among the staring shoals, and only the need of air drove him gasping up into the spray-laden wind.

He built all day long, scrambling up on the sand to collect the bricks that his faithful helper dumped over the cliff's edge for him, load them in his barrow and run them out the causeway that went straight out a foot or two under sealevel at low tide and four or five feet under at high, then dump them at the end, dive in, and build; then back ashore for another load. He came up

217

into town only at evening, worn out, salt-bleared and salt-itching, hungry as a shark, to share what food turned up with the widow and her little boy. Lately, though spring was getting on with soft, long, warm evenings, the town seemed very dark and still.

One night when he was not too tired to notice this he spoke of it, and the widow said, Oh, they're all gone now, I think.

All? —A pause. —Where did they go?

She shrugged. She raised her dark eyes to his across the table and gazed through lamplit silence at him for a time. Where? she said. Where does your sea-road lead, Lif?

He stayed still awhile. To the Islands, he answered at last, and then laughed and met her look.

She did not laugh. She only said, Are they there? Is it true, then, there are Islands? —Then she looked over at her sleeping baby, and out the open doorway into the darkness of late spring that lay warm in the streets where no one walked and the rooms where no one lived. At last she looked back at Lif, and said to him, Lif, you know, there aren't many bricks left. A few hundred. You'll have to make some more. —Then she began to cry softly.

By God! said Lif, thinking of his underwater road across the sea that went for a hundred and twenty feet, and the sea that went on ten thousand miles from the end of it—I'll swim there! Now then, don't cry, dear heart. Would I leave you and the little rat here by yourselves? After all the bricks you've nearly hit my head with, and all the queer weeds and shellfish you've found us to eat lately, after your table and fireside and your bed and your laughter would I leave you when you cry? Now be still, don't cry. Let me think of a way we can get to the Islands, all of us together.

But he knew there was no way. Not for a brickmaker. He had done what he could do. What he could do went one hundred and twenty feet from shore.

Do you think, he asked after a long time, during which she had cleared the table and rinsed the plates in wellwater that was coming clear again now that the Ragers had been gone many days— Do you think that maybe . . . this . . . He found it hard to say but she stood quiet, waiting, and he had to say it: That this *is* the end?

Stillness. In the one lamplit room and all the dark rooms and streets and the burnt fields and wasted lands, stillness. In the black Hall above them on the hill's height, stillness. A silent air, a silent sky, silence in all places unbroken, unreplying. Except for the far sound of the sea, and very soft though nearer, the breathing of a sleeping child.

No, the woman said. She sat down across from him and put her hands upon the table, fine hands as dark as earth, the palms like ivory. No, she said, the end will be the end. This is still just the waiting for it.

Then why are we still here—just us?

Oh well, she said, you had your things—your bricks—and I had the baby. . . .

Tomorrow we must go, he said after a time. She nodded.

Before sunrise they were up. There was nothing at all left to eat, and so when she had put a few clothes for the baby in a bag and had on her warm leather mantle, and he had stuck his knife and trowel in his belt and put on a warm cloak that had been her husband's, they left the little house, going out into the cold wan light in the deserted streets.

They went downhill, he leading, she following with the sleepy child in a fold of her cloak. He turned neither to the road that led north up the coast nor to the southern road, but went on past the marketplace and out on the cliff and down the rocky path to the beach. All the way she followed and neither of them spoke. At the edge of the sea he turned.

I'll keep you up in the water as long as we can manage, he said.

She nodded, and said softly, Well, use the road you built, as far as it goes.

He took her free hand and led her into the water. It was cold. It was bitter cold, and the cold light from the east behind them shone on the foam-lines hissing on the sand. When they stepped on the beginning of the causeway the bricks were firm under their feet, and the child had gone back to sleep on her shoulder in a fold of her cloak.

As they went on, the buffeting of the waves got stronger. The tide was coming in. The outer breakers wet their clothes, chilled their flesh, drenched their hair and faces. They reached the end of his long work. There lay the beach a little way behind them, the sand dark silver under the cliff over which stood the silent, paling sky. Around them was wild water and foam. Ahead of them was the unresting water, the gulf, the great abyss, the gap.

A breaker hit them on its way in to shore and they staggered; the baby waked by the sea's hard slap cried, a little wail in the long, hissing mutter of the sea always saying the same thing.

Oh I can't! cried the mother, but the man took her hand more firmly and said aloud, Come on!

Lifting his head to take the last step from what he had done toward no shore, he saw the shape riding the western water, the leaping light, the white flicker like a swallow's breast catching the break of day. It seemed as if voices rang over the sea's voice. What is it? he said, but her head was bowed to her baby, trying to soothe the little wail that was all she heard in the vast babbling of the sea. He stood still and saw the whiteness of the sail, the little dancing light above the waves, dancing on toward them and toward the greater light that grew behind them.

Wait, the call came from the form that rode the gray waves and danced on the foam, Wait!— The voices rang very sweet, and as the sail leaned white above him he saw the faces and the reaching arms, and heard them say to him, Come, come on the ship, come with us to the Islands.

Hold on, he said softly to the woman, and took the last step.

From Harlan Ellison, January 22, 1969:

Dear Damon:

Gleefully, here is "Dogfight on 101," submitted to fulfill the obligation incurred by the $200 check advance from Dardis, which has not yet arrived, thereby taking you off the hook (if you like this as much as I do) for paying for a story before you have received it. As you can see, it runs 4,250, not 4,000, which makes a balance owing of $12.50 which I am magnanimously prepared to forget, in appreciation of the trust and favor extended by yourself in asking for advance payment.

On the other hand, if you are a shit and reject this story, I will demand the full payment of $212.50. . . .

Being that you don't drive, I know you won't enjoy the story, so I suggest you let Kate make the decision. After all, there are more of us who drive than throwbacks such as yourself.

To Ellison, January 27, 1969:

Dear Harlan,

This is a jazzy thing in some ways, but it is one of your jazzy stories & that is not what I want out of you for *Orbit*. What I want is the restrained, powerful, distant and mysterious Ellison, cf. "Goblin," so please write me a restrained, powerful &c. story, and don't rush it. I want it good, not quick.

Katie read your "Goblin" in her copy of 4 which just arrived (I haven't got mine yet) and was forced to admit that it is a work of

220

transcendent genius, etc. She was not sure before because had read it in ms. at dinner with author pacing up and down.

If I don't drive, who was it that almost ran you down in Milford a couple of years ago, Katie?

CONTINUED ON NEXT ROCK

by R. A. Lafferty

Up in the Big Lime country there is an upthrust, a chimney rock that is half fallen against a newer hill. It is formed of what is sometimes called Dawson Sandstone and is interlaced with tough shell. It was formed during the glacial and recent ages in the bottomlands of Crow Creek and Green River when these streams (at least five times) were mighty rivers.

The chimney rock is only a little older than mankind, only a little younger than grass. Its formation had been upthrust and then eroded away again, all but such harder parts as itself and other chimneys and blocks.

A party of five persons came to this place where the chimney rock had fallen against a newer hill. The people of the party did not care about the deep limestone below: they were not geologists. They *did* care about the newer hill (it was man-made) and they did care a little about the rock chimney; they were archeologists.

Here was time heaped up, bulging out in casing and accumulation, and not in line sequence. And here also was striated and banded time, grown tall, and then shattered and broken.

The five party members came to the site early in the afternoon, bringing the working trailer down a dry creek bed. They unloaded many things and made a camp there. It wasn't really necessary to make a camp on the ground. There was a good motel two miles away on the highway; there was a road along the ridge above. They could have lived in comfort and made the trip to the site in five minutes every morning. Terrence Burdock, however, believed that one could not get the feel of a digging unless he lived on the ground with it day and night.

The five persons were Terrence Burdock, his wife Ethyl, Robert Derby, and Howard Steinleser: four beautiful and balanced people. And Magdalen

221

Mobley who was neither beautiful nor balanced. But she was electric; she was special. They rouched around in the formations a little after they had made camp and while there was still light. All of them had seen the formations before and had guessed that there was promise in them.

"That peculiar fluting in the broken chimney is almost like a core sample," Terrence said, "and it differs from the rest of it. It's like a lightning bolt through the whole length. It's already exposed for us. I believe we will remove the chimney entirely. It covers the perfect access from the slash in the mound, and it is the mound in which we are really interested. But we'll study the chimney first. It is so available for study."

"Oh, I can tell you everything that's in the chimney," Magdalen said crossly. "I can tell you everything that's in the mound too."

"I wonder why we take the trouble to dig if you already know what we will find," Ethyl sounded archly.

"I wonder too," Magdalen grumbled. "But we will need the evidence and the artifacts to show. You can't get appropriations without evidence and artifacts. Robert, go kill that deer in the brush about forty yards northeast of the chimney. We may as well have deer meat if we're living primitive."

"This isn't deer season," Robert Derby objected. "And there isn't any deer there. Or, if there is, it's down in the draw where you couldn't see it. And if there's one there, it's probably a doe."

"No, Robert, it is a two-year-old buck and a very big one. Of course it's in the draw where I can't see it. Forty yards northeast of the chimney would have to be in the draw. If I could see it, the rest of you could see it too. Now go kill it! Are you a man or a *mus microtus*? Howard, cut poles and set up a tripod to string and dress the deer on."

"You had better try the thing, Robert," Ethyl Burdock said, "or we'll have no peace this evening."

Robert Derby took a carbine and went northeastward of the chimney, descending into the draw at forty yards. There was the high ping of the carbine shot. And after some moments, Robert returned with a curious grin.

"You didn't miss him, Robert, you killed him," Magdalen called loudly. "You got him with a good shot through the throat and up into the brain when he tossed his head high like they do. Why didn't you bring him? Go back and get him!"

"Get him? I couldn't even lift the thing. Terrence and Howard, come with me and we'll lash it to a pole and get it here somehow."

"Oh Robert, you're out of your beautiful mind," Magdalen chided. "It only weighs a hundred and ninety pounds. Oh, I'll get it."

Magdalen Mobley went and got the big buck. She brought it back, carrying it listlessly across her shoulders and getting herself bloodied, stopping sometimes to examine rocks and kick them with her foot, coming on easily with her load. It looked as if it might weigh two hundred and fifty pounds; but if Magdalen said it weighed a hundred and ninety, that is what it weighed.

Howard Steinleser had cut poles and made a tripod. He knew better than not to. They strung the buck up, skinned it off, ripped up its belly, drew it, and worked it over in an almost professional manner.

"Cook it, Ethyl," Magdalen said.

Later, as they sat on the ground around the fire and it had turned dark, Ethyl brought the buck's brains to Magdalen, messy and not half cooked, believing that she was playing an evil trick. And Magdalen ate them avidly. They were her due. She had discovered the buck.

If you wonder how Magdalen knew what invisible things were where, so did the other members of the party always wonder.

"It bedevils me sometimes why I am the only one to notice the analogy between historical geology and depth psychology," Terrence Burdock mused as they grew lightly profound around the campfire. "The isostatic principle applies to the mind and the upper-mind as well as it does to the surface and undersurface of the earth. The mind has its erosions and weatherings going on along with its deposits and accumulations. It also has its upthrusts and its stresses. It floats on a similar magma. In extreme cases it has its volcanic eruptions and its mountain building."

"And it has its glaciations," Ethyl Burdock said, and perhaps she was looking at her husband in the dark.

"The mind has its hard sandstone, sometimes transmuted to quartz, or half transmuted into flint, from the drifting and floating sand of daily events. It has its shale from the old mud of daily ineptitudes and inertias. It has limestone out of its more vivid experiences, for lime is the remnant of what was once animate: and this limestone may be true marble if it is the deposit of rich enough emotion, or even travertine if it has bubbled sufficiently through agonized and evocative rivers of the under-mind. The mind has its sulphur and its gemstones—" Terrence bubbled on sufficiently, and Magdalen cut him off.

"Say simply that we have rocks in our heads," she said. "But they're random rocks, I tell you, and the same ones keep coming back. It *isn't* the same with us as it is with the earth. The world gets new rocks all the time. But it's the same people who keep turning up, and the same minds. Damn, one of the samest of them just turned up again! I wish he'd leave me alone. The answer is still no."

Very often Magdalen said things that made no sense. Ethyl Burdock assured herself that neither her husband, nor Robert, nor Howard, had slipped over to Magdalen in the dark. Ethyl was jealous of the chunky and surly girl.

"I am hoping that this will be as rich as Spiro Mound," Howard Steinleser hoped. "It could be, you know, I'm told that there was never a less prepossessing site than that, or a trickier one. I wish we had someone who had dug at Spire."

"Oh, he dug at Spire," Magdalen said with contempt.

"He? Who?" Terrence Burdock asked. "No one of us was at Spiro. Magdalen, you weren't even born yet when that mound was opened. What could you know about it?"

"Yeah, I remember him at Spiro," Magdalen said, "always turning up his own things and pointing them out."

"*Were* you at Spiro?" Terrence suddenly asked a piece of the darkness. For some time, they had all been vaguely aware that there were six, and not five, persons around the fire.

"Yeah, I was at Spiro," the man said. "I dig there. I dig at a lot of the digs. I dig real well, and I always know when we come to something that will be important. You give me a job."

"Who are you?" Terrence asked him. The man was pretty visible now. The flame of the fire seemed to lean toward him as if he compelled it.

"Oh, I'm just a rich old poor man who keeps following and hoping and asking. There is *one* who is worth it all forever, so I solicit that one forever. And sometimes I am other things. Two hours ago I was the deer in the draw. It is an odd thing to munch one's own flesh." And the man was munching a joint of the deer, unasked.

"Him and his damn cheap poetry!" Magdalen cried angrily.

"What's your name?" Terrence asked him.

"Manypenny. Anteros Manypenny is my name forever."

"What are you?"

"Oh, just Indian. Shawnee. Choc, Creek, Anadarko, Caddo and pre-Caddo. Lots of things."

"How could anyone be pre-Caddo?"

"Like me. I am."

"Is Anteros a Creek name?"

"No. Greek. Man, I am a going Jessie, I am one digging man! I show you tomorrow."

Man, he was one digging man! He showed them tomorrow. With a short-handled rose hoe he began the gash in the bottom of the mound, working too swiftly to be believed.

224

"He will smash anything that is there. He will not know what he comes to," Ethyl Burdock complained.

"Woman, I will *not* smash whatever is there," Anteros said. "You can hide a wren's egg in one cubic meter of sand. I will move all the sand in one minute. I will uncover the egg wherever it is. And I will not crack the egg. I sense these things. I come now to a small pot of the proto-Plano period. It is broken, of course, but I do not break it. It is in six pieces and they will fit together perfectly. I tell you this beforehand. Now I reveal it."

And Anteros revealed it. There was something wrong about it even before he uncovered it. But it was surely a find, and perhaps it *was* of the proto-Plano period. The six shards came out. They were roughly cleaned and set. It was apparent that they would fit wonderfully.

"Why, it is perfect!" Ethyl exclaimed.

"It is too perfect," Howard Steinleser protested. "It was a turned pot, and who had turned pots in America without the potter's wheel? But the glyphs pressed into it do correspond to proto-Plano glyphs. It is fishy." Steinleser was in a twitchy humor today and his face was livid.

"Yes, it is the ripple and the spinosity, the fish-glyph," Anteros pointed out. "And the sun-sign is riding upon it. It is a fish-god."

"It's fishy in another way," Steinleser insisted. "Nobody finds a thing like that in the first sixty seconds of a dig. And there *could not be* such a pot. I wouldn't believe it was proto-Plano unless points were found in the exact site with it."

"Oh here," Anteros said. "One can smell the very shape of the flint points already. Two large points, one small one. Surely you get the whiff of them already? Four more hoe cuts and I come to them."

Four more hoe cuts, and Anteros *did* come to them. He uncovered two large points and one small one, spearheads and arrowhead. Lanceolate they were, with ribbon flaking. They were late Folsom, or they were proto-Plano; they were what you will.

"This cannot be," Steinleser groaned. "They're the missing chips, the transition pieces. They fill the missing place too well. I won't believe it. I'd hardly believe it if mastodon bones were found on the same level here."

"In a moment," said Anteros, beginning to use the hoe again. "Hey, those old beasts *did smell funny*! An elephant isn't in it with them. And a lot of it still clings to their bones. Will a sixth thoracic bone do? I'm pretty sure that's what it is. I don't know where the rest of the animal is. Probably somebody gnawed the thoracic here. Nine hoe cuts, and then very careful."

Nine hoe cuts—and then Anteros, using a mason's trowel, unearthed the old gnawed bone very carefully. Yes, Howard said almost angrily, it was a

225

sixth thoracic of a mastodon. Robert Derby said it was a fifth or a sixth; it is not easy to tell.

"Leave the digging for a while, Anteros," Steinleser said. "I want to record and photograph and take a few measurements here."

Terrence Burdock and Magdalen Mobley were working at the bottom of the chimney rock, at the bottom of the fluting that ran the whole height of it like a core sample.

"Get Anteros over here and see what he can uncover in sixty seconds," Terrence offered.

"Oh, him! He'll just uncover some of his own things."

"What do you mean, his own things? Nobody could have made an intrusion here. It's hard sandstone."

"And harder flint here," Magdalen said. "I might have known it. Pass the damned thing up. I know just about what it says anyhow."

"What it says? What do you mean? But it is marked! And it's large and dressed rough. Who'd carve in flint?"

"Somebody real stubborn, just like flint," Magdalen said. "All right then, let's have it out. Anteros! Get this out in one piece. And do it without shattering it or tumbling the whole thing down on us. He can do it, you know, Terrence. He can do things like that."

"What do you know about his doings, Magdalen? You never saw or heard about the poor man till last night."

"Oh well, I know that it'll turn out to be the same damned stuff."

Anteros did get it out without shattering it or bringing down the chimney column. A cleft with a digging bar, three sticks of the stuff and a cap, and he touched the leads to the battery when he was almost on top of the charge. The blast, it sounded as if the whole sky were falling down on them, and some of those sky-blocks were quite large stones. The ancients wondered why fallen pieces of the sky should always be dark rock-stuff and never sky-blue clear stuff. The answer is that it is only pieces of the night sky that ever fall, even though they may sometimes be most of the daytime in falling, such is the distance. And the blast that Anteros set off did bring down rocky hunks of the night sky even though it was broad daylight. They brought down darker rocks than any of which the chimney was composed.

Still, it was a small blast. The chimney tottered but did not collapse. It settled back uneasily on its base. And the flint block was out in the clear.

"A thousand spearheads and arrowheads could be shattered and chipped out of that hunk," Terrence marveled. "That flint block would have been a primitive fortune for a primitive man."

226

"I had several such fortunes," Anteros said dully, "and this one I preserved and dedicated."

They had all gathered around it.

"Oh the poor man!" Ethyl suddenly exclaimed. But she was not looking at any of the men. She was looking at the stone.

"I wish he'd get off that kick," Magdalen sputtered angrily. "I don't care *how* rich he is. I can pick up better stuff than him in the alleys."

"What are the women chirping about?" Terrence asked. "But those do look like true glyphs. Almost like Aztec, are they not, Steinleser?"

"Nahaut-Tanoan, cousins-german to the Aztec, or should I say cousins-yaqui?"

"Call it anything, but can you read it?"

"Probably. Give me eight or ten hours on it and I should come up with a contingent reading of many of the glyphs. We can hardly expect a rational rendering of the message, however. All Nahuat-Tanoan translations so far have been gibberish."

"And remember, Terrence, that Steinleser is a slow reader," Magdalen said spitefully. "And he isn't very good at interpreting *other* signs either."

Steinleser was sullen and silent. How had his face come to bear those deep livid claw-marks today?

They moved a lot of rock and rubble that morning, took quite a few pictures, wrote up bulky notes. There were constant finds as the divided party worked up the shag-slash in the mound and the core-flute of the chimney. There were no more really startling discoveries; no more turned pots of the proto-Plano period; how could there be? There were no more predicted and perfect points of the late Folsom, but there were broken and unpredictable points. No other mastodon thoracic was found, but bones were uncovered of *bison latifrons*, of dire wolf, of coyote, of man. There were some anomalies in the relationships of the things discovered, but it was not as fishy as it had been in the early morning, not as fishy as when Anteros had announced and then dug out the shards of the pot, the three points, the mastodon bone. The things now were as authentic as they were expected, and yet their very profusion had still the smell of a small fish.

And that Anteros was one digging man. He moved the sand, he moved the stone, he missed nothing. And at noon he disappeared.

An hour later he reappeared in a glossy station wagon, coming out of a thicketed ravine where no one would have expected a way. He had been to town. He brought a variety of cold cuts, cheeses, relishes, and pastries, a couple cases of cold beer, and some V.O.

227

"I thought you were a poor man, Anteros," Terrence chided.

"I told you that I was a rich old poor man. I have nine thousand acres of grassland, I have three thousand head of cattle, I have alfalfa land and clover land and corn land and hay-grazer land—"

"Oh, knock it off!" Magdalen snapped.

"I have other things," Anteros finished sullenly.

They ate, they rested, they worked in the afternoon. Magdalen worked as swiftly and solidly as did Anteros. She was young, she was stocky, she was light-burned-dark. She was not at all beautiful. (Ethyl was.) She could have any man there any time she wanted to. (Ethyl couldn't.) She was Magdalen, the often unpleasant, the mostly casual, the suddenly intense one. She was the tension of the party, the string of the bow.

"Anteros!" she called sharply just at sundown.

"The turtle?" he asked. "The turtle that is under the ledge out of the current where the backwater curls in reverse? But he is fat and happy and you do not want me to get that turtle."

"I do! There's eighteen pounds of him. He's fat. He'll be good. Only eighty yards, where the bank crumbles down to Green River, under the lower ledge that's shale that looks like slate, two feet deep—"

"I know where he is. I will go get the fat turtle," Anteros said. "I myself am the fat turtle. I am the Green River." He went to get it.

"Oh that damned poetry of his!" Magdalen spat when he was gone.

Anteros brought back the fat turtle. He looked as if he'd weigh twenty-five pounds; but if Magdalen said he weighed eighteen pounds, then it was eighteen.

"Start cooking, Ethyl," Magdalen said. Magdalen was a mere undergraduate girl permitted on the digging by sheer good fortune. The others of the party were all archeologists of moment. Magdalen had no right to give orders to anyone, except her born right.

"I don't know how to cook a turtle," Ethyl complained.

"Anteros will show you how."

"The late evening smell of newly exposed excavation!" Terrence Burdock burbled as they lounged around the campfire a little later, full of turtle and V.O. and feeling rakishly wise. "The exposed age can be guessed by the very timbre of the smell, I believe."

"Timbre of the smell! What is your nose wired up to?" from Magdalen.

And indeed, there was something time-evocative about the smell of the diggings: cool, at the same time musty and musky, ripe with old stratified water and compressed death. Stratified time.

"It helps if you already know what the exposed age is," said Howard

228

Steinleser. "Here there is an anomaly. The chimney sometimes acts as if it were younger than the mound. The chimney cannot be young enough to include written rock, but it is."

"Archeology is made up entirely of anomalies," said Terrence, "rearranged to make them fit in a fluky pattern. There'd be no system to it otherwise."

"Every science is made up entirely of anomalies rearranged to fit," said Robert Derby. "Have you unriddled the glyph-stone, Howard?"

"Yes, pretty well. Better than I expected. Charles August can verify it, of course, when we get it back to the university. It is a non-royal, non-tribal, non-warfare, non-hunt declaration. It does not come under any of the usual radical signs, any of the categories. It can only be categorized as un-categoried or personal. The translation will be rough."

"Rocky is the word," said Magdalen.

"On with it, Howard," Ethyl cried.

" 'You are the freedom of wild pigs in the sour-grass, and the nobility of badgers. You are the brightness of serpents and the soaring of vultures. You are passion on mesquite bushes on fire with lightning. You are serenity of toads.' "

"You've got to admit he's got a different line," said Ethyl. "Your own love notes were less acrid, Terrence."

"What kind of thing is it, Steinleser?" Terrence questioned. "It must have a category."

"I believe Ethyl is right. It's a love poem. 'You are the water in rock cisterns and the secret spiders in that water. You are the dead coyote lying half in the stream, and you are the old entrapped dreams of the coyote's brains oozing liquid through the broken eyesocket. You are the happy ravening flies about that broken socket.' "

"Oh, hold it, Steinleser," Robert Derby cried. "You can't have gotten all that from scratches on flint. What is 'entrapped dreams' in Nahaut-Tanoan glyph-writing?"

"The solid-person sign next to the hollow-person sign, both enclosed in the night sign—that has always been interpreted as the dream glyph. And here the dream glyph is enclosed in the glyph of the deadfall trap. Yes, I believe it means entrapped dreams. To continue: 'You are the cornworm in the dark heart of the corn, the naked small bird in the nest. You are the pustules on the sick rabbit, devouring life and flesh and turning it into your own serum. You are stars compressed into charcoal. But you cannot give, you cannot take. Once again you will be broken at the foot of the cliff, and the word will remain unsaid in your swollen and purpled tongue.' "

"A love poem, perhaps, but with a difference," said Robert Derby.

229

"I never was able to go his stuff, and I tried, I really tried," Magdalen moaned.

"Here is the change of person-subject shown by the canted-eye glyph linked with the self-glyph," Steinleser explained. "It is now a first-person talk. 'I own ten thousand back-loads of corn. I own gold and beans and nine buffalo horns full of watermelon seeds. I own the loincloth that the sun wore on his fourth journey across the sky. Only three loincloths in the world are older and more valued than this. I cry out to you in a big voice like the hammering of herons' (that sound-verb-particle is badly translated, the hammer being not a modern pounding hammer but a rock angling, chipping hammer) 'and the belching of buffalos. My love is sinewy as entwined snakes, it is steadfast as the sloth, it is like a feathered arrow shot into your abdomen—such is my love. Why is my love unrequited?' "

"I challenge you, Steinleser," Terrence Burdock cut in. "What is the glyph for 'unrequited'?"

"The glyph of the extended hand—with all the fingers bent backwards. It goes on, 'I roar to you. Do not throw yourself down. You believe you are on the hanging sky bridge, but you are on the terminal cliff. I grovel before you. I am no more than dog-droppings.' "

"You'll notice he said that and not me," Magdalen burst out. There was always a fundamental incoherence about Magdalen.

"Ah—continue, Steinleser," said Terrence. "The girl is daft, or she dreams out loud."

"That is all of the inscription, Terrence, except for a final glyph which I don't understand. Glyph writing takes a lot of room. That's all the stone would hold."

"What is the glyph that you don't understand, Howard?"

"It's the spear-thrower glyph entwined with the time glyph. It sometimes means 'flung forward or beyond.' But what does it mean here?"

"It means 'continued,' dummy, 'continued,' " Magdalen said. "Do not fear. There'll be more stones."

"I think it's beautiful," said Ethyl Burdock, "in its own context, of course."

"Then why don't you take him on, Ethyl, in his own context, of course?" Magdalen asked. "Myself, I don't care how many back-loads of corn he owns. I've had it."

"Take whom on, dear?" Ethyl asked. "Howard Steinleser can interpret the stones, but who can interpret our Magdalen?"

"Oh, I can read her like a rock," Terrence Burdock smiled. But he couldn't.

But it had fastened on them. It was all about them and through them: the brightness of serpents and the serenity of toads, the secret spiders in the water, the entrapped dreams oozing through the broken eyesocket, the pustules of the sick rabbit, the belching of buffalo, and the arrow shot into the abdomen. And around it all was the night smell of flint and turned earth and chuckling streams, the mustiness, and the special muskiness which bears the name Nobility of Badgers.

They talked archeology and myth talk. Then it was steep night, and the morning of the third day.

Oh, the sample digging went well. This was already a richer mound than Spiro, though the gash in it was but a small promise of things to come. And the curious twin of the mound, the broken chimney, confirmed and confounded and contradicted. There was time gone wrong in the chimney, or at least in the curious fluted core of it; the rest of it was normal enough, and sterile enough.

Anteros worked that day with a soft sullenness, and Magdalen brooded with a sort of lightning about her.

"Beads, glass beads!" Terrence Burdock exploded angrily. "All right! Who is the hoaxer in our midst? I will not tolerate this at all." Terrence had been angry of face all day. He was clawed deeply, as Steinleser had been the day before, and he was sour on the world.

"There have been glass-bead caches before, Terrence, hundreds of them," Robert Derby said softly.

"There have been hoaxers before, hundreds of them," Terrence howled. "These have 'Hong Kong Contemporary' written all over them, damned cheap glass beads sold by the pound. They have no business in a stratum of around the year seven hundred. All right, who is guilty?"

"I don't believe that any one of us is guilty, Terrence," Ethyl put in mildly. "They are found four feet in from the slant surface of the mound. Why, we've cut through three hundred years of vegetable loam to get to them, and certainly the surface was eroded beyond that."

"We are scientists," said Steinleser. "We find these. Others have found such. Let us consider the improbabilities of it."

It was noon, so they ate and rested and considered the improbabilities. Anteros had brought them a great joint of white pork, and they made sandwiches and drank beer and ate pickles.

"You know," said Robert Derby, "that beyond the rank impossibility of glass beads found so many times where they *could not be found*, there is a real mystery about *all* early Indian beads, whether of bone, stone, or antler. There are millions and millions of these fine beads with pierced holes finer

231

than any piercer ever found. There are residues, there are centers of every other Indian industry, and there is evolution of every other tool. Why have there been these millions of pierced beads, and never one piercer? There was no technique to make so fine a piercer. How were they done?''

Magdalen giggled. "Bead-spitter," she said.

"Bead-spitter! You're out of your fuzzy mind," Terrence erupted. "That's the silliest and least sophisticated of all Indian legends."

"But it *is* the legend," said Robert Derby, "the legend of more than thirty separate tribes. The Carib Indians of Cuba said that they got their beads from Bead-spitters. The Indians of Panama told Balboa the same thing. The Indians of the pueblos told the same story to Coronado. Every Indian community had an Indian who was its Bead-spitter. There are Creek and Alabama and Koasati stories of Bead-spitter; see Swanton's collections. And his stories were taken down within living memory.

"More than that, when European trade-beads were first introduced, there is one account of an Indian receiving some and saying, 'I will take some to Bead-spitter. If he sees them, he can spit them too.' And that Bead-spitter did then spit them by the bushel. There was never any other Indian account of the origin of their beads. *All* were spit by a Bead-spitter.''

"Really, this is very unreal," Ethyl said. Really it was.

"Hog hokey! A bead-spitter of around the year seven hundred could not spit future beads, he could not spit cheap Hong Kong glass beads of the present time!" Terrence was very angry.

"Pardon me, yes sir, he could," said Anteros. "A Bead-spitter can spit future beads, if he faces North when he spits. That has always been known.''

Terrence was angry, he fumed and poisoned the day for them, and the claw marks on his face stood out livid purple. He was angrier yet when he said that the curious dark capping rock on top of the chimney was dangerous, that it would fall and kill someone; and Anteros said that there was no such capping rock on the chimney, that Terrence's eyes were deceiving him, that Terrence should go sit in the shade and rest.

And Terrence became excessively angry when he discovered that Magdalen was trying to hide something that she had discovered in the fluted core of the chimney. It was a large and heavy shale-stone, too heavy even for Magdalen's puzzling strength. She had dragged it out of the chimney flute, tumbled it down to the bottom, and was trying to cover it with rocks and scarp.

"Robert, mark the extraction point!" Terrence called loudly. "It's quite plain yet. Magdalen, stop that! Whatever it is, it must be examined now.''

"Oh, it's just more of the damned same thing! I wish he'd let me alone.

232

With his kind of money he can get plenty girls. Besides, it's private, Terrence. You don't have any business reading it."

"You are hysterical, Magdalen, and you may have to leave the digging site."

"I wish I could leave. I can't. I wish I could love. I can't. Why isn't it enough that I die?"

"Howard, spend the afternoon on this," Terrence ordered. "It has writing of a sort on it. If it's what I think it is, it scares me. It's too recent to be in any eroded chimney rock formation, Howard, and it comes from far below the top. Read it."

"A few hours on it and I may come up with something. I never saw anything like it either. What did you think it was, Terrence?"

"What do you think I think it is? It's much later than the other, and that one was impossible. I'll not be the one to confess myself crazy first."

Howard Steinleser went to work on the incised stone; and two hours before sundown they brought him another one, a gray soapstone block from higher up. Whatever this was covered with, it was not at all the same thing that covered the shale-stone.

And elsewhere things went well, too well. The old fishiness was back on it. No series of finds could be so perfect, no petrification could be so well ordered.

"Robert," Magdalen called down to Robert Derby just at sunset, "in the high meadow above the shore, about four hundred yards down, just past the old fence line—"

"—there is a badger hole, Magdalen. Now you have me doing it, seeing invisible things at a distance. And if I take a carbine and stroll down there quietly, the badger will stick his head out just as I get there (I being strongly downwind of him), and I'll blam him between the eyes. He'll be a big one, fifty pounds."

"Thirty. Bring him, Robert. You're showing a little understanding at last."

"But, Magdalen, badger is rampant meat. It's seldom eaten."

"May not the condemned girl have what she wishes for her last meal? Go get it, Robert."

Robert went. The voice of the little carbine was barely heard at that distance. Soon, Robert brought back the dead badger.

"Cook it, Ethyl," Magdalen ordered.

"Yes, I know. And if I don't know how, Anteros will show me." But Anteros was gone. Robert found him on a sundown knoll with his shoulders hunched. The odd man was sobbing silently and his face seemed to be made out of dull pumice stone. But he came back to aid Ethyl in preparing the badger.

"If the first of today's stones scared you, the second should have lifted the hair right off your head, Terrence," Howard Steinleser said.

"It does, it does. All the stones are too recent to be in a chimney formation, but this last one is an insult. It isn't two hundred years old, but there's a thousand years of strata above it. What time is deposited there?"

They had eaten rampant badger meat and drunk inferior whisky (which Anteros, who had given it to them, didn't know was inferior), and the muskiness was both inside them and around them. The campfire sometimes spit angrily with small explosions, and its glare reached high when it did so. By one such leaping glare, Terrence Burdock saw that the curious dark capping rock was once more on the top of the chimney. He thought he had seen it there in the daytime; but it had not been there after he had sat in the shade and rested, and it had absolutely not been there when he climbed the chimney itself to be sure.

"Let's have the second chapter and then the third, Howard," Ethyl said. "It's neater that way."

"Yes. Well, the second chapter (the first and lowest and apparently the earliest rock we came on today) is written in a language that no one ever saw written before; and yet it's no great trouble to read it. Even Terrence guessed what it was and it scared him. It is Anadarko-Caddo hand-talk graven in stone. It is what is called the sign language of the Plains Indians copied down in formalized pictograms. And it *has* to be very recent, within the last three hundred years. Hand-talk was fragmentary at the first coming of the Spanish, and well developed at the first coming of the French. It was an explosive development, as such things go, worked out within a hundred years. This rock has to be younger than its *situs*, but it was absolutely found in place."

"Read it, Howard, read it," Robert Derby called. Robert was feeling fine and the rest of them were gloomy tonight.

" 'I own three hundred ponies,' Steinleser read the rock out of his memory. 'I own two days' ride north and east and south, and one day's ride west. I give you all. I blast out with a big voice like fire in tall trees, like the explosion of crowning pine trees. I cry like closing-in wolves, like the high voice of the lion, like the hoarse scream of torn calves. Do you not destroy yourself again! You are the dew on crazy-weed in the morning. You are the swift crooked wings of the night-hawk, the dainty feet of the skunk, you are the juice of the sour squash. Why can you not take or give? I am the humpbacked bull of the high plains, I am the river itself and the stagnant

234

pools left by the river, I am the raw earth and the rocks. Come to me, but do not come so violently as to destroy yourself.'

"Ah, that was the text of the first rock of the day, the Anadarko-Caddo hand-talk graven in stone. And final pictograms which I don't understand: a shot-arrow sign, and a boulder beyond."

" 'Continued on next rock,' of course," said Robert Derby. "Well, why *wasn't* hand-talk ever written down? The signs are simple and easily stylized and they were understood by many different tribes. It would have been natural to write it."

"Alphabetical writing was in the region *before* hand-talk was well developed," Terrence Burdock said. "In fact, it was the coming of the Spanish that gave the impetus to hand-talk. It was really developed for communication between Spanish and Indian, not between Indian and Indian. And yet, I believe, hand-talk *was* written down once; it was the beginning of the Chinese pictographs. And there also it had its beginning as communication between differing peoples. Depend on it, if all mankind had always been of a single language, there would never have been any written language developed at all. Writing always began as a bridge, and there had to be some chasm for it to bridge."

"We have one to bridge here," said Steinleser. "That whole chimney is full of rotten smoke. The highest part of it should be older than the lowest part of the mound, since the mound was built on a base eroded away from the chimney formation. But in many ways they seem to be contemporary. We must all be under a spell here. We've worked two days on this, parts of three days, and the total impossibility of the situation hasn't struck us yet.

"The old Nahuatlan glyphs for Time are the chimney glyphs. Present time is a lower part of a chimney and fire burning at the base. Past time is black smoke from a chimney, and future time is white smoke from a chimney. There was a signature glyph running through our yesterday's stone which I didn't and don't understand. It seemed to indicate something coming down out of the chimney rather than going up it."

"It really doesn't look much like a chimney," Magdalen said.

"And a maiden doesn't look much like dew on crazy-weed in the morning, Magdalen," Robert Derby said, "but we recognize these identities."

They talked a while about the impossibility of the whole business.

"There are scales on our eyes," Steinleser said. "The fluted core of the chimney is wrong. I'm not even sure the rest of the chimney is right."

"No, it isn't," said Robert Derby. "We can identify most of the strata of the chimney with known periods of the river and stream. I was above and below today. There is one stretch where the sandstone was not eroded at all,

235

where it stands three hundred yards back from the shifted river and is overlaid with a hundred years of loam and sod. There are other sections where the stone is cut away variously. We can tell when most of the chimney was laid down, we can find its correspondences up to a few hundred years ago. But when were the top ten feet of it laid down? There were no correspondences anywhere to that. The centuries represented by the strata of the top of the chimney, people, those centuries haven't happened yet.''

"And when was the dark capping rock on top of it all formed—?'' Terrence began. "Ah, I'm out of my mind. It isn't there. I'm demented.''

"No more than the rest of us,'' said Steinleser. "I saw it too, I thought, today. And then I didn't see it again.''

"The rock-writing, it's like an old novel that I only half remember,'' said Ethyl.

"Oh, that's what it is, yes,'' Magdalen murmured.

"But I don't remember what happened to the girl in it.''

"I remember what happened to her, Ethyl,'' Magdalen said:

"Give us the third chapter, Howard,'' Ethyl asked. "I want to see how it comes out.''

"First you should all have whisky for those colds,'' Anteros suggested humbly.

"But none of us have colds,'' Ethyl objected.

"You take your own medical advice, Ethyl, and I'll take mine,'' Terrence said. "I will have whisky. My cold is not rheum but fear-chill.''

They all had whisky. They talked a while, and some of them dozed.

"It's late, Howard,'' Ethyl said after a while. "Let's have the next chapter. Is it the last chapter? Then we'll sleep. We have honest digging to do tomorrow.''

"Our third stone, our second stone of the day just past, is another and even later form of writing, and it has never been seen in stone before. It is Kiowa picture writing. The Kiowas did their out-turning spiral writing on buffalo skins dressed almost as fine as vellum. In its more sophisticated form (and this is a copy of that) it is quite late. The Kiowa picture writing probably did not arrive at its excellence until influenced by white artists.''

"How late, Steinleser?'' Robert Derby asked.

"Not more than a hundred and fifty years old. But I have never seen it copied in stone before. It simply isn't stone-styled. There's a lot of things around here lately that I haven't seen before.

"Well then, to the text, or should I say the pictography? 'You fear the earth, you fear rough ground and rocks, you fear moister earth and rotting flesh, you fear the flesh itself, all flesh is rotting flesh. If you love not rotting flesh, you love not at all. You believe the bridge hanging in the sky, the bridge hung by tendrils and woody vines that diminish as they go up and up till they are no thicker than hairs. There is no sky-bridge, you cannot go upon it. Did you believe that the roots of love grow upside down? They come out of deep earth that is old flesh and brains and hearts and entrails, that is old buffalo bowels and snakes' pizzles, that is black blood and rot and moaning underground. This is old and worn-out and bloody time, and the roots of love grow out of its gore.' "

"You seem to give remarkable detailed translations of the simple spiral pictures, Steinleser, but I begin to get in the mood of it," Terrence said.

"Ah, perhaps I cheat a little," said Steinleser.

"You lie a lot," Magdalen challenged.

"No I do not. There is some basis for every phrase I've used. It goes on: 'I own twenty-two trade rifles. I own ponies. I own Mexico silver, eight-bit pieces. I am rich in all ways. I give all to you. I cry out with big voice like a bear full of mad-weed, like a bullfrog in love, like a stallion rearing against a puma. It is the earth that calls you. I am the earth, woollier than wolves and rougher than rocks. I am the bog earth that sucks you in. You cannot give, you cannot take, you cannot love, you think there is something else, you think there is a sky-bridge you may loiter on without crashing down. I am bristled-boar earth, there is no other. You will come to me in the morning. You will come to me easy and with grace. Or you will come to me reluctant and you be shattered in every bone and member of you. You be broken by our encounter. You be shattered as by a lightning bolt striking up from earth. I am the red calf which is in the writings. I am the rotting red earth. Live in the morning or die in the morning, but remember that love in death is better than no love at all.' "

"Oh brother! Nobody gets that stuff from such kid pictures, Steinleser," Robert Derby moaned.

"Ah well, that's the end of the spiral picture. And a Kiowa spiral pictograph ends with either an in-sweep or an out-sweep line. This ends with an out-sweep, which means—"

" 'Continued on next rock,' that's what it means," Terrence cried roughly.

"You won't find the next rocks," Magdalen said. "They're hidden, and most of the time they're not there yet, but they will go on and on. But for all that, you'll read it in the rocks tomorrow morning. I want it to be over with. Oh, I don't know what I want!"

"I believe I know what you want tonight, Magdalen," Robert Derby said. But he didn't.

The talk trailed off, the fire burned down, they went to their sleeping sacks.

Then it was long jagged night, and the morning of the fourth day. But wait! In Nahuat-Tanoan legend, the world ends on the fourth morning. All the lives we lived or thought we lived had been but dreams of third night. The loincloth that the sun wore on the fourth day's journey was not so valuable as one has made out. It was worn for no more than an hour or so.

And, in fact, there was something terminal about fourth morning. Anteros had disappeared. Magdalen had disappeared. The chimney rock looked greatly diminished in its bulk (something had gone out of it) and much crazier in its broken height. The sun had come up a garish gray-orange color through fog. The signature-glyph of the first stone dominated the ambient. It was as if something were coming down from the chimney, a horrifying smoke; but it was only noisome morning fog.

No it wasn't. There was something else coming down from the chimney, or from the hidden sky: pebbles, stones, indescribable bits of foul oozings, the less fastidious pieces of the sky; a light nightmare rain had begun to fall there; the chimney was apparently beginning to crumble.

"It's the damnedest thing I ever heard about," Robert Derby growled. "Do you think that Magdalen really went off with Anteros?" Derby was bitter and fumatory this morning and his face was badly clawed.

"Who is Magdalen? Who is Anteros?" Ethyl Burdock asked.

Terrence Burdock was hooting from high on the mound. "All come up," he called. "Here is a find that will make it all worthwhile. We'll have to photo and sketch and measure and record and witness. It's the finest basalt head I've ever seen, man-sized, and I suspect that there's a man-sized body attached to it. We'll soon clean it and clear it. Gah! What a weird fellow he was!"

But Howard Steinleser was studying a brightly colored something that he held in his two hands.

"What is it, Howard? What are you doing?" Derby demanded.

"Ah, I believe this is the next stone in sequence. The writing is alphabetical but deformed, there is an element missing. I believe it is in modern English, and I will solve the deformity and see it true in a minute. The text of it seems to be—"

Rocks and stones were coming down from the chimney, and fog, amnesic and wit-stealing fog.

"Steinleser, are you all right?" Robert Derby asked with compassion. "That isn't a stone that you hold in your hand."

"It isn't a stone. I thought it was. What is it then?"

"It is the fruit of the Osage orange tree, the American Meraceous. It isn't

238

a stone, Howard." And the thing was a tough, woody, wrinkled mock-orange, as big as a small melon.

"You have to admit that the wrinkles look a little bit like writing, Robert."

"Yes, they look a little like writing, Howard. Let us go up where Terrence is bawling for us. You've read too many stones. And it isn't safe here."

"Why go up, Howard? The other thing is coming down."

It was the bristled-boar earth reaching up with a rumble. It was a lightning bolt struck upward out of the earth, and it got its prey. There was explosion and roar. The dark capping rock was jerked from the top of the chimney and slammed with terrible force to the earth, shattering with a great shock. And something else that had been on that capping rock. And the whole chimney collapsed about them.

She was broken by the encounter. She was shattered in every bone and member of her. And she was dead.

"Who—who is she?" Howard Steinleser stuttered.

"Oh God! Magdalen, of course!" Robert Derby cried.

"I remember her a little bit. Didn't understand her. She put out like an evoking moth but she wouldn't be had. Near clawed the face off me the other night when I misunderstood the signals. She believed there was a sky-bridge. It's in a lot of the mythologies. But there isn't one, you know. Oh well."

"The girl is dead! Damnation! What are you doing grubbing in those stones?"

"Maybe she isn't dead in them yet, Robert. I'm going to read what's here before something happens to them. This capping rock that fell and broke, it's impossible, of course. It's a stratum that hasn't been laid down yet. I always did want to read the future and I may never get another chance."

"You fool! The girl's dead! Does nobody care? Terrence, stop bellowing about your find. Come down. The girl's dead."

"Come up, Robert and Howard," Terrence insisted. "Leave that broken stuff down there. It's worthless. But nobody ever saw anything like this."

"Do come up, men," Ethyl sang. "Oh, it's a wonderful piece! I never saw anything like it in my life."

"Ethyl, is the whole morning mad?" Robert Derby demanded as he came up to her. "She's dead. Don't you really remember her? Don't you remember Magdalen?"

"I'm not sure. Is she the girl down there? Isn't she the same girl who's been hanging around here a couple days? She shouldn't have been playing

239

on that high rock. I'm sorry she's dead. But just look what we're uncovering here!''

''Terrence. Don't *you* remember Magdalen?''

''The girl down there? She's a little bit like the girl that clawed the hell out of me the other night. Next time someone goes to town they might mention to the sheriff that there's a dead girl here. Robert, did you ever see a face like this one? And it digs away to reveal the shoulders. I believe there's a whole man-sized figure here. Wonderful, wonderful!''

''Terrence, you're off your head. Well, do you remember Anteros?''

''Certainly, the twin of Eros, but nobody ever made much of the symbol of unsuccessful love. Thunder! That's the name for him! It fits him perfectly. We'll call him Anteros.''

Well, it *was* Anteros, lifelike in basalt stone. His face was contorted. He was sobbing soundlessly and frozenly and his shoulders were hunched with emotion. The carving was fascinating in its miserable passion, his stony love unrequited. Perhaps he was more impressive now than he would be when he was cleaned. He was earth, he was earth itself. Whatever period the carving belonged to, it was outstanding in its power.

''The live Anteros, Terrence. Don't you remember our digging man, Anteros Manypenny?''

''Sure. He didn't show up for work this morning, did he? Tell him he's fired.''

''Magdalen is dead! She was one of us! Dammit, she was the main one of us!'' Robert Derby cried. Terrence and Ethyl Burdock were earless to his outburst. They were busy uncovering the rest of the carving.

And down below, Howard Steinleser was studying dark broken rocks before they would disappear, studying a stratum that hadn't been laid down yet, reading a foggy future.

To Thomas A. Dardis, January 29, 1969:

Dear Tom,

I can't tell much about any of the [copyeditor's] queries on *Orbit 6* without seeing the manuscript. The queries about ''The Second Inquisition'' sound like peculiarities of punctuation about

240

which I have decided it is good policy to humor Miss Russ. "Baygal" is the way Mr. Davidson likes to spell "bagel," and I like to humor *him*.

To Thomas A. Dardis, March 11, 1969:

Dear Tom,
Here is flap copy for *Orbit 5*.
As you know, we've had some complaints about the cover line, "The Best ALL NEW SF Stories of the Year." Algis Budrys, in his review of *Orbit 3*, kicked us for this. I think myself that it's an excessive & hucksterish claim, and that the phrase "best all new" is not English. How would you feel about substituting the following?

An Anthology of New SF Stories

It seems to me this would go nicely over the title, would define the book accurately, and would help build the image of quality I'm trying to establish. See what you think about this. I do hate to give a reviewer any stick to beat us with.

From Gene Wolfe, March 16, 1969:

Dear Damon,
I don't have to tell you, I hope, that I am very happy that you like "The Island of Doctor Death and Other Stories." I thought you would, but because I like it so much myself I was (by the twist of nature which I suppose is part of original sin) especially afraid you would not. I bled for that little boy; besides, it's a second person story and they're very rare, as you no doubt know. Edna Ferber (I think) is supposed to have done a novel in second person and there are a handful (supposedly) of short stories. I used it, of course, to contrast with the straightforward third person of the "Island of Doctor Death" story within a story. And the title is my all-time favorite among my own things.

THE ISLAND OF
DOCTOR DEATH AND
OTHER STORIES

by Gene Wolfe

Winter comes to water as well as land, though there are no leaves to fall. The waves that were a bright, hard blue yesterday under a fading sky today are green, opaque, and cold. If you are a boy not wanted in the house you walk the beach for hours, feeling the winter that has come in the night; sand blowing across your shoes, spray wetting the legs of your corduroys. You turn your back to the sea, and with the sharp end of a stick found half buried write in the wet sand *Tackman Babcock*.

Then you go home, knowing that behind you the Atlantic is destroying your work.

Home is the big house on Settlers Island, but Settlers Island, so called, is not really an island and for that reason is not named or accurately delineated on maps. Smash a barnacle with a stone and you will see inside the shape from which the beautiful barnacle goose takes its name. There is a thin and flaccid organ which is the goose's neck and the mollusk's siphon, and a shapeless body with tiny wings. Settlers Island is like that.

The goose neck is a strip of land down which a county road runs. By whim, the mapmakers usually exaggerate the width of this and give no information to indicate that it is scarcely above the high tide. Thus Settlers Island appears to be a mere protuberance on the coast, not requiring a name—and since the village of eight or ten houses has none, nothing shows on the map but the spider line of road terminating at the sea.

The village has no name, but home has two: a near and a far designation. On the island, and on the mainland nearby, it is called the Seaview place because in the earliest years of the century it was operated as a resort hotel. Mama calls it The House of 31 February; and that is on her stationery and is presumably used by her friends in New York and Philadelphia when they do not simply say, "Mrs. Babcock's." Home is four floors high in some places, less in others, and is completely surrounded by a veranda; it was once painted yellow, but the paint—outside—is mostly gone now and The House of 31 February is gray.

Jason comes out the front door with the little curly hairs on his chin trembling in the wind and his thumbs hooked in the waistband of his Levi's.

"Come on, you're going into town with me. Your mother wants to rest."

"Hey tough!" Into Jason's Jaguar, feeling the leather upholstery soft and smelly; you fall asleep.

Awake in town, bright lights flashing in the car windows. Jason is gone and the car is growing cold; you wait for what seems a long time, looking out at the shop windows, the big gun on the hip of the policeman who walks past, the lost dog who is afraid of everyone, even you when you tap the glass and call to him.

Then Jason is back with packages to put behind the seat. "Are we going home now?"

He nods without looking at you, arranging his bundles so they won't topple over, fastening his seatbelt.

"I want to get out of the car."

He looks at you.

"I want to go in a store. Come on, Jason."

Jason sighs. "All right, the drugstore over there, okay? Just for a minute."

The drugstore is as big as a supermarket, with long bright aisles of glassware and notions and paper goods. Jason buys fluid for his lighter at the cigarette counter, and you bring him a book from the revolving wire rack. "Please, Jason?"

He takes it from you and replaces it in the rack, then when you are in the car again takes it from under his jacket and gives it to you.

It is a wonderful book, thick and heavy, with the edges of the pages tinted yellow. The covers are glossy stiff cardboard, and on the front is a picture of a man in rags fighting a thing partly like an ape and partly like a man, but much worse than either. The picture is in color, and there is real blood on the ape-thing; the man is muscular and handsome, with tawny hair lighter than Jason's and no beard.

"You like that?"

You are out of town already, and without the street lights it's too dark in the car, almost, to see the picture. You nod.

Jason laughs. "That's camp. Did you know that?"

You shrug, riffling the pages under your thumb, thinking of reading alone, in your room tonight.

"You going to tell your mom how nice I was to you?"

"Uh-huh, sure. You want me to?"

"Tomorrow, not tonight. I think she'll be asleep when we get back. Don't wake her up." Jason's voice says he will be angry if you do.

"Okay."

"Don't come into her room."

243

"Okay."

The Jaguar says "*Hutntntaaa . . .*" down the road, and you can see the whitecaps in the moonlight now, and the driftwood pushed just off the asphalt.

"You got a nice, soft mommy, you know that? When I climb on her it's just like being on a big pillow."

You nod, remembering the times when, lonely and frightened by dreams, you have crawled into her bed and snuggled against her soft warmth—but at the same time angry, knowing Jason is somehow deriding you both.

Home is silent and dark, and you leave Jason as soon as you can, bounding off down the hall and up the stairs ahead of him, up a second, narrow, twisted flight to your own room in the turret.

I had this story from a man who was breaking his word in telling it. How much it has suffered in his hands—I should say in his mouth, rather—I cannot say. In essentials it is true, and I give it to you as it was given to me. This is the story he told.

Captain Philip Ransom had been adrift, alone, for nine days when he saw the island. It was already late evening when it appeared like a thin line of purple on the horizon, but Ransom did not sleep that night. There was no feeble questioning in his wakeful mind concerning the reality of what he had seen; he had been given that one glimpse and he knew. Instead his brain teemed with facts and speculations. He knew he must be somewhere near New Guinea, and he reviewed mentally what he knew of the currents in these waters and what he had learned in the past nine days of the behavior of his raft. The island when he reached it—he did not allow himself to say *if*—would in all probability be solid jungle a few feet back from the water's edge. There might or might not be natives, but he brought to mind all he could of the Bazaar Malay and Tagalog he had acquired in his years as a pilot, plantation manager, white hunter, and professional fighting man in the Pacific.

In the morning he saw that purple shadow on the horizon again, a little nearer this time and almost precisely where his mental calculations had told him to expect it. For nine days there had been no reason to employ the inadequate paddles provided with the raft, but now he had something to row for. Ransom drank the last of his water and began stroking with a steady and powerful beat which was not interrupted until the prow of his rubber craft ground into beach sand.

Morning. You are slowly awake. Your eyes feel gummy, and the light over your bed is still on. Downstairs there is no one, so you get a bowl and milk and puffed, sugary cereal out for yourself and light the oven with a kitchen match so that you can eat and read by its open door. When the cereal is gone you drink the sweet milk and crumbs in the bottom of the bowl and start a pot of coffee, knowing that will please Mother. Jason comes down, dressed but not wanting to talk; drinks coffee and makes one piece of cinnamon toast in the oven. You listen to him leave, the stretched buzzing of his car on the road, then go up to Mother's room.

She is awake, her eyes open looking at the ceiling, but you know she isn't ready to get up yet. Very politely, because that minimizes the chances of being shouted at, you say, "How are you feeling this morning, Mama?"

She rolls her head to look. "Strung out. What time is it, Tackie?"

You look at the little folding clock on her dresser. "Seventeen minutes after eight."

"Jason go?"

"Yes, just now, Mama."

She is looking at the ceiling again. "You go back downstairs now, Tackie. I'll get you something when I feel better."

Downstairs you put on your sheepskin coat and go out on the veranda to look at the sea. There are gulls riding the icy wind, and very far off something orange bobbing in the waves, always closer.

A life raft. You run to the beach, jump up and down and wave your cap. "Over here. Over here."

The man from the raft has no shirt but the cold doesn't seem to bother him. He holds out his hand and says, "Captain Ransom," and you take it and are suddenly taller and older; not as tall as he is or as old as he is, but taller and older than yourself. "Tackman Babcock, Captain."

"Pleased to meet you. You were a friend in need there a minute ago."

"I guess I didn't do anything but welcome you ashore."

"The sound of your voice gave me something to steer for while my eyes were too busy watching that surf. Now you can tell me where I've landed and who you are."

You are walking back up to the house now, and you explain to Ransom about you and Mother, and how she doesn't want to enroll you in the school here because she is trying to get you into the private school your father went to once. And after a time there is nothing more to say, and you show Ransom one of the empty rooms on the third floor where he can rest and do whatever he wants. Then you go back to your own room to read.

245

"Do you mean that you *made* these monsters?"

"*Made* them?" Dr. Death leaned forward, a cruel smile playing about his lips. "Did God *make* Eve, Captain, when he took her from Adam's rib? Or did Adam make the bone and God *alter* it to become what he wished? Look at it this way, Captain. I am God and Nature is Adam."

Ransom looked at the thing who grasped his right arm with hands that might have circled a utility pole as easily. "Do you mean that this thing is an animal?"

"Not an animal," the monster said, wrenching his arm cruelly. "Man."

Dr. Death's smile broadened. "Yes, Captain, man. The question is, what are you? When I'm finished with you we'll see. Dulling your mind will be less of a problem than upgrading these poor brutes; but what about increasing the efficacy of your sense of smell? Not to mention rendering it impossible for you to walk erect."

"*Not* to walk all-four-on-ground," the beast-man holding Ransom muttered, "*that* is the *law*."

Dr. Death turned and called to the shambling hunchback Ransom had seen earlier, "Golo, see to it that Captain Ransom is securely put away; then prepare the surgery."

A car. Not Jason's noisy Jaguar, but a quiet, large-sounding car. By heaving up the narrow, tight little window at the corner of the turret and sticking your head out into the cold wind you can see it: Dr. Black's big one, with the roof and hood all shiny with new wax.

Downstairs Dr. Black is hanging up an overcoat with a collar of fur, and you smell the old cigar smoke in his clothing before you see him; then Aunt May and Aunt Julie are there to keep you occupied so that he won't be reminded too vividly that marrying Mama means getting you as well. They talk to you: "How have you been, Tackie? What do you find to do out here all day?"

"Nothing."

"Nothing? Don't you ever go looking for shells on the beach?"

"I guess so."

"You're a handsome boy, do you know that?" Aunt May touches your nose with a scarlet-tipped finger and holds it there.

Aunt May is Mother's sister, but older and not as pretty. Aunt Julie is Papa's sister, a tall lady with a pulled-out, unhappy face, and makes you think of him even when you know she only wants Mama to get married again so that Papa won't have to send her any more money.

Mama herself is downstairs now in a clean new dress with long sleeves. She laughs at Dr. Black's jokes and holds onto his arm, and you think how nice her hair looks and that you will tell her so when you are alone. Dr. Black says, "How about it, Barbara, are you ready for the party?" and Mother, "Heavens no. You know what this place is like—yesterday I spent all day cleaning and today you can't even see what I did. But Julie and May will help me."

Dr. Black laughs. "After lunch."

You get into his big car with the others and go to a restaurant on the edge of a cliff, with a picture window to see the ocean. Dr. Black orders a sandwich for you that has turkey and bacon and three pieces of bread, but you are finished before the grown-ups have started, and when you try to talk to Mother, Aunt May sends you out to where there is a railing with wire to fill in the spaces like chicken wire only heavier, to look at the view.

It is really not much higher than the top window at home. Maybe a little higher. You put the toes of your shoes in the wire and bend out with your stomach against the rail to look down, but a grown-up pulls you down and tells you not to do it, then goes away. You do it again, and there are rocks at the bottom which the waves wash over in a neat way, covering them up and then pulling back. Someone touches your elbow, but you pay no attention for a minute, watching the water.

Then you get down, and the man standing beside you is Dr. Death.

He has a white scarf and black leather gloves and his hair is shiny black. His face is not tanned like Captain Ransom's but white, and handsome in a different way like the statue of a head that used to be in Papa's library when you and Mother used to live in town with him, and you think: Mama would say after he was gone how good looking he was. He smiles at you, but you are no older.

"Hi." What else can you say?

"Good afternoon, Mr. Babcock. I'm afraid I startled you."

You shrug. "A little bit. I didn't expect you to be here, I guess."

Dr. Death turns his back to the wind to light a cigarette he takes from a gold case. It is longer even than a 101 and has a red tip, and a gold dragon on the paper. "While you were looking down, I slipped from between the pages of the excellent novel you have in your coat pocket."

"I didn't know you could do that."

"Oh, yes. I'll be around from time to time."

"Captain Ransom is here already. He'll kill you."

Dr. Death smiles and shakes his head. "Hardly. You see, Tackman, Ransom and I are a bit like wrestlers; under various guises we put on our show again and again—but only under the spotlight." He flicks his cigarette over the rail and for a moment your eyes follow the bright spark out and down and see it vanish in the water. When you look back, Dr. Death is gone, and you are getting cold. You go back into the restaurant and get a free mint candy where the cash register is and then go to sit beside Aunt May again in time to have coconut cream pie and hot chocolate.

Aunt May drops out of the conversation long enough to ask, "Who was that man you were talking to, Tackie?"

"A man."

In the car Mama sits close to Dr. Black, with Aunt Julie on the other side of her so she will have to, and Aunt May sits way up on the edge of her seat with her head in between theirs so they can all talk. It is gray and cold outside; you think of how long it will be before you are home again, and take the book out.

Ransom heard them coming and flattened himself against the wall beside the door of his cell. There was no way out, he knew, save through that iron portal.

For the past four hours he had been testing every surface of the stone room for a possible exit, and there was none. Floor, walls, and ceiling were of cyclopean stone blocks; the windowless door of solid metal locked outside.

Nearer. He tensed every muscle and knotted his fists.

Nearer. The shambling steps halted. There was a rattle of keys and the door swung back. Like a thunderbolt of purpose he dove through the opening. A hideous face loomed above him and he sent his right fist crashing into it, knocking the lumbering beast-man to his knees. Two hairy arms pinioned him from behind, but he fought free and the monster reeled under his blows. The corridor stretched ahead of him with a dim glow of daylight at the end and he sprinted for it. Then—darkness!

When he recovered consciousness he found himself already erect, strapped to the wall of a brilliantly lit room which seemed to share the characters of a surgical theater and a chemical laboratory. Directly before his eyes stood a bulky object which he knew must be an operating table, and upon it, covered with a sheet, lay the unmistakable form of a human being.

He had hardly had time to comprehend the situation when Dr. Death entered, no longer in the elegant evening dress in which Ransom had beheld him last, but wearing white surgical clothing. Behind him limped the hideous Golo, carrying a tray of implements.

"Ah!" Seeing that his prisoner was conscious, Dr. Death

248

strolled across the room and raised a hand as though to strike him in the face, but, when Ransom did not flinch, dropped it, smiling. "My dear Captain! You are with us again, I see."

"I hoped for a minute there," Ransom said levelly, "that I was away from you. Mind telling me what got me?"

"A thrown club, or so my slaves report. My baboon-man is quite good at it. But aren't you going to ask about this charming little tableau I've staged for you?"

"I wouldn't give you the pleasure."

"But you are curious." Dr. Death smiled his crooked smile. "I shall not keep you in suspense. Your own time, Captain, has not come yet; and before it does I am going to demonstrate my technique to you. It is so seldom that I have a really appreciative audience." With a calculated gesture he whipped away the sheet which had covered the prone form on the operating table.

Ransom could scarcely believe his eyes. Before him lay the unconscious body of a girl, a girl with skin as white as silk and hair like the sun seen through mist.

"You are interested now, I see," Dr. Death remarked drily, "and you consider her beautiful. Believe me, when I have completed my work you will flee screaming if she so much as turns what will no longer be a face toward you. This woman has been my implacable enemy since I came to this island, and the time has come for me to"—he halted in mid-sentence and looked at Ransom with an expression of mingled slyness and gloating—"for me to illustrate something of your own fate, shall we say."

While Dr. Death had been talking his deformed assistant had prepared a hypodermic. Ransom watched as the needle plunged into the girl's almost translucent flesh, and the liquid in the syringe—a fluid which by its very color suggested the vile perversion of medical technique—entered her bloodstream. Though still unconscious the girl sighed, and it seemed to Ransom that a cloud passed over her sleeping face as though she had already begun an evil dream. Roughly the hideous Golo turned her on her back and fastened in place straps of the same kind as those that held Ransom himself pinned to the wall.

"What are you reading, Tackie?" Aunt May asked.
"Nothing." He shut the book.

249

"Well, you shouldn't read in the car. It's bad for your eyes."

Dr. Black looked back at them for a moment, then asked Mama, "Have you gotten a costume for the little fellow yet?"

"For Tackie?" Mama shook her head, making her beautiful hair shine even in the dim light of the car. "No, nothing. It will be past his bedtime."

"Well, you'll have to let him see the guests anyway, Barbara; no boy should miss that."

And then the car was racing along the road out to Settlers Island. And then you were home.

Ransom watched as the loathsome creature edged toward him. Though not as large as some of the others its great teeth looked formidable indeed, and in one hand it grasped a heavy jungle knife with a razor edge.

For a moment he thought it would molest the unconscious girl, but it circled around her to stand before Ransom himself, never meeting his eyes.

Then, with a gesture as unexpected as it was frightening, it bent suddenly to press its hideous face against his pinioned right hand, and a great, shuddering gasp ran through the creature's twisted body.

Ransom waited, tense.

Again that deep inhalation, seeming almost a sob. Then the beast-man straightened up, looking into Ransom's face but avoiding his gaze. A thin, strangely familiar whine came from the monster's throat.

"Cut me loose," Ransom ordered.

"Yes. This I came to. Yes, Master." The huge head, wider than it was high, bobbled up and down. Then the sharp blade of the machete bit into the straps holding Ransom. As soon as he was free he took the blade from the willing hand of the beast-man and freed the limbs of the girl on the operating table. She was light in his arms, and for an instant he stood looking down at her tranquil face.

"Come, Master." The beast-man pulled at his sleeve. "Bruno knows a way out. Follow Bruno."

A hidden flight of steps led to a long and narrow corridor, almost pitch dark. "No one use this way," the beast-man said in his harsh voice. "They not find us here."

"Why did you free me?" Ransom asked.

There was a pause, then almost with an air of shame the great,

250

twisted form replied, "You smell good. And Bruno does not like Dr. Death."

Ransom's conjectures were confirmed. Gently he asked, "You were a dog before Dr. Death worked on you, weren't you, Bruno?"

"Yes." The beast-man's voice held a sort of pride. "A St. Bernard. I have seen pictures."

"Dr. Death should have known better than to employ his foul skills on such a noble animal," Ransom reflected aloud. "Dogs are too shrewd in judging character; but then the evil are always foolish in the final analysis."

Unexpectedly the dog-man halted in front of him, forcing Ransom to stop too. For a moment the massive head bent over the unconscious girl. Then there was a barely audible growl. "You say, Master, that I can judge. Then I tell you Bruno does not like this female Dr. Death calls Talar of the Long Eyes."

You put the open book face-down on the pillow and jump up, hugging yourself and skipping bare heels around the room. Marvelous! Wonderful!

But no more reading tonight. Save it, save it. Turn the light off, and in the delicious dark put the book reverently away under the bed, pushing aside pieces of the Tinker Toy set and the box with the filling station game cards. Tomorrow there will be more, and you can hardly wait for tomorrow. You lie on your back, hands under head, covers up to chin and when you close your eyes, you can see it all: the island, with jungle trees swaying in the sea wind; Dr. Death's castle lifting its big, cold grayness against the hot sky.

The whole house is still, only the wind and the Atlantic are out, the familiar sounds. Downstairs Mother is talking to Aunt May and Aunt Julie and you fall asleep.

You are awake! Listen! Late, it's very late, a strange time you have almost forgotten. Listen!

So quiet it hurts. Something. Something. Listen!

On the steps.

You get out of bed and find your flashlight. Not because you are brave, but because you cannot wait there in the dark.

There is nothing in the narrow, cold little stairwell outside your door. Nothing in the big hallway of the second floor. You shine your light quickly from end to end. Aunt Julie is breathing through her nose, but there is nothing frightening about that sound, you know what it is: only Aunt Julie, asleep, breathing loud through her nose.

Nothing on the stairs coming up.

251

You go back to your room, turn off your flashlight, and get into bed. When you are almost sleeping there is the scrabbling sound of hard claws on the floorboards and a rough tongue touching your fingertips. "Don't be afraid, Master, it is only Bruno." And you feel him, warm with his own warm and smelling of his own smell, lying beside your bed.

Then it is morning. The bedroom is cold, and there is no one in it but yourself. You go into the bathroom where there is a thing like a fan but with hot electric wires to dress.

Downstairs Mother is up already with a cloth thing tied over her hair, and so are Aunt May and Aunt Julie, sitting at the table with coffee and milk and big slices of fried ham. Aunt Julie says, "Hello, Tackie," and Mother smiles at you. There is a plate out for you already and you have ham and toast.

All day the three women are cleaning and putting up decorations—red and gold paper masks Aunt Julie made to hang on the wall, and funny lights that change color and go around—and you try to stay out of the way, and bring in wood for a fire in the big fireplace that almost never gets used. Jason comes, and Aunt May and Aunt Julie don't like him, but he helps some and goes into town in his car for things he forgot to buy before. He won't take you, this time. The wind comes in around the window, but they let you alone in your room and it's even quiet up there because they're all downstairs.

Ransom looked at the enigmatic girl incredulously.

"You do not believe me," she said. It was a simple statement of fact, without anger or accusation.

"You'll have to admit it's pretty hard to believe," he temporized. "A city older than civilization, buried in the jungle here on this little island."

Talar said tonelessly, "When you were as he"—she pointed at the dog-man—"is now, Lemuria was queen of this sea. All that is gone, except my city. Is not that enough to satisfy even Time?"

Bruno plucked at Ransom's sleeve. "Do not go, Master! Beast-men go sometimes, beast-men Dr. Death does not want, few come back. They are very evil at that place."

"You see?" A slight smile played about Talar's ripe lips. "Even your slave testifies for me. My city exists."

"How far?" Ransom asked curtly.

"Perhaps half a day's travel through the jungle." The girl paused, as though afraid to say more.

"What is it?" Ransom asked.

252

"You will lead us against Dr. Death? We wish to cleanse this island which is our home."

"Sure. I don't like him any more than your people do. Maybe less."

"Even if you do not like my people you will lead them?"

"If they'll have me. But you're hiding something. What is it?"

"You see me, and I might be a woman of your own people. Is that not so?" They were moving through the jungle again now, the dog-man reluctantly acting as rear guard.

"Very few girls of my people are as beautiful as you are, but otherwise yes."

"And for that reason I am high priestess to my people, for in me the ancient blood runs pure and sweet. But it is not so with all." Her voice sunk to a whisper. "When a tree is very old, and yet still lives, sometimes the limbs are strangely twisted. Do you understand?"

"Tackie? Tackie are you in there?"

"Uh-huh." You put the book inside your sweater.

"Well, come and open this door. Little boys ought not to lock their doors. Don't you want to see the company?" You open, and Aunt May's a gypsy with long hair that isn't hers around her face and a mask that is only at her eyes.

Downstairs cars are stopping in front of the house and Mother is standing at the door dressed in Day-Glo robes that open way down the front but cover her arms almost to the ends of her fingers. She is talking to everyone as they come in, and you see her eyes are bright and strange the way they are sometimes when she dances by herself and talks when no one is listening.

A woman with a fish for a head and a shiny, silver dress is Aunt Julie. A doctor with a doctor's coat and listening things and a shiny thing on his head to look through is Dr. Black, and a soldier in a black uniform with a pirate thing on his hat and a whip is Jason. The big table has a punchbowl and cakes and little sandwiches and hot bean dip. You pull away when the gypsy is talking to someone and take some cakes and sit under the table watching legs.

There is music and some of the legs dance, and you stay under there a long time.

Then a man's and a girl's legs dance close to the table and there is suddenly a laughing face in front of you—Captain Ransom's. "What are you doing under there, Tack? Come out and join the party." And you crawl

253

out, feeling very small instead of older, but older when you stand up. Captain Ransom is dressed like a castaway in a ragged shirt and pants torn off at the knees, but all clean and starched. His love beads are seeds and sea shells, and he has his arm around a girl with no clothes at all, just jewelry.

"Tack, this is Talar of the Long Eyes."

You smile and bow and kiss her hand, and are nearly as tall as she. All around people are dancing or talking, and no one seems to notice you. With Captain Ransom on one side of Talar and you on the other you thread your way through the room, avoiding the dancers and the little groups of people with drinks. In the room you and Mother use as a living room when there's no company, two men and two girls are making love with the television on, and in the little room past that a girl is sitting on the floor with her back to the wall, and men are standing in the corners. "Hello," the girl says. "Hello to you all." She is the first one to have noticed you, and you stop.

"Hello."

"I'm going to pretend you're real. Do you mind?"

"No." You look around for Ransom and Talar, but they are gone and you think that they are probably in the living room, kissing with the others.

"This is my third trip. Not a good trip, but not a bad trip. But I should have had a monitor—you know, someone to stay with me. Who are those men?"

The men in the corners stir, and you can hear the clinking of their armor and see light glinting on it and you look away. "I think they're from the City. They probably came to watch out for Talar," and somehow you know that this is the truth.

"Make them come out where I can see them."

Before you can answer Dr. Death says, "I don't really think you would want to," and you turn and find him standing just behind you wearing full evening dress and a cloak. He takes your arm. "Come on, Tackie, there's something I think you should see." You follow him to the back stairs and then up, and along the hall to the door of Mother's room.

Mother is inside on the bed, and Dr. Black is standing over her filling a hypodermic. As you watch, he pushes up her sleeve so that all the other injection marks show ugly and red on her arm, and all you can think of is Dr. Death bending over Talar on the operating table. You run downstairs looking for Ransom, but he is gone and there is nobody at the party at all except the real people and, in the cold shadows of the back stoop, Dr. Death's assistant Golo, who will not speak, but only stares at you in the moonlight with pale eyes.

The next house down the beach belongs to a woman you have seen sometimes cutting down the dry fall remnant of her asparagus or hilling up her roses while you played. You pound at her door and try to explain, and after a while she calls the police.

    . . . across the sky. The flames were licking at the roof timbers now. Ransom made a megaphone of his hands and shouted. "Give up! You'll all be burned to death if you stay in there!" but the only reply was a shot and he was not certain they had heard him. The Lemurian bowmen discharged another flight of arrows at the windows.
    Talar grasped his arm: "Come back before they kill you."
    Numbly he retreated with her, stepping across the massive body of the bull-man, which lay pierced by twenty or more shafts.

You fold back the corner of a page and put the book down. The waiting room is cold and bare, and although sometimes the people hurrying through smile at you, you feel lonely. After a long time a big man with gray hair and a woman in a blue uniform want to talk to you.

The woman's voice is friendly, but only the way teachers' voices are sometimes. "I'll bet you're sleepy, Tackman. Can you talk to us a little still before you go to bed?"

"Yes."

The gray-haired man says, "Do you know who gave your mother drugs?"

"I don't know. Dr. Black was going to do something to her."

He waves that aside. "Not that. You know, medicine. Your mother took a lot of medicine. Who gave it to her? Jason?"

"I don't know."

The woman says, "Your mother is going to be well, Tackman, but it will be a while—do you understand? For now you're going to have to live for a while in a big house with some other boys."

"All right."

The man: "Amphetamines. Does that mean anything to you? Did you ever hear that word?"

You shake your head.

The woman: "Dr. Black was only trying to help your mother, Tackman. I know you don't understand, but she used several medicines at once, mixed them, and that can be very bad."

They go away and you pick up the book and riffle the pages, but you do not read. At your elbow Dr. Death says, "What's the matter, Tackie?" He
255

smells of scorched cloth and there is a streak of blood across his forehead, but he smiles and lights one of his cigarettes.

You hold up the book. "I don't want it to end. You'll be killed at the end."

"And you don't want to lose me? That's touching."

"You will, won't you? You'll burn up in the fire and Captain Ransom will go away and leave Talar."

Dr. Death smiles. "But if you start the book again we'll all be back. Even Golo and the bull-man."

"Honest?"

"Certainly." He stands up and tousles your hair. "It's the same with you, Tackie. You're too young to realize it yet, but it's the same with you."

To Edward Bryant, April 25, 1969:

Dear Ed,

Well, you will hate this, but I have already bought two stories about the upcoming civil disturbances, both pretty good, but don't want to turn *Orbit* into Gripping Black Power Stories. I do think you are coming up closer to present time, so please persevere.

I think I have spotted something else that's holding you back; noticed it in the last one you sent me and again in this. Each story is a series of vignettes, and you get a feeling that any one of them could be cut out without doing the story any particular damage. This is bad news. Scenes & incidents should build, and every one should be* essential to the story. If they don't & aren't, something is wrong.

*or, anyhow, seem to be. If an incident doesn't seem necessary, it may be that the trouble is not that the incident itself is intrusive or unnecessary, but that something else necessary has been left out. In the present case, I think that's it, & that what you need is a thread to string your pearls on. . . .

256

To Stanley Schmidt, May 21, 1969:

Dear Mr. Schmidt,
 Glad to get a look at this one, & it's ingeniously worked out, but it's the kind of story that could only exist in the context of the s.f. magazines, where a lot of things can be skipped because the readers have seen them all before and take them for granted. I'm trying to get away from this kind of thing because I think it leads to boredom inside the field and incomprehension outside it. Am trying to publish only stories that can stand on their own, something I think a good story ought to be able to do anyhow. If you can't do that with the 1,941st interstellar spaceflight story, because it would be tedious to repeat what has already been done in the other 1,940, that only suggests to me that the topic is exhausted and that we ought to try something else.

To an author whose name I suppress, June 18, 1969:

Dear ——,
 This is a good story completely covered with gingerbread. Every damn sentence is tortured out of its natural shape and encrusted with useless modifiers. Here is one horrible example, from p. 1: "He crouched in goosefleshed, arthritic pain to gaze at its near-comprehensible incomprehensibility, at once pristine and futuristic." This is what happens when you try to write like a goddam thesaurus; you lose the ability to say what you mean. Pain can be arthritic, but it can't be goosefleshed. You can't gaze at incomprehensibility, only at an incomprehensible thing. The prize is this sentence, however, is the last phrase, which is just glued on because it looks so pretty. Somebody has got to rap you on the knuckles for this kind of thing, or you will go right on doing it.

From Gardner R. Dozois, undated, 1968:

Dear Damon,
 It was nice to hear from you again; thanks for replying so quickly. Also thank you for the SFWA address. It's spring over here: green and golden and beautiful, with the smell of manure laced through wet air and snow busily melting and frothing into white-running rivers. My work goes slowly and limpingly as
257

usual, but I have managed to get a few things finished, although at this rate starving to death is beginning to seem like a distinct possibility. Still wrestling with shadows: my thoughts and emotions are curiously intertwined and knotted, solid things fade, ghosts become substantial, myths become reality . . .

From Dozois, February 19, 1969:

Dear Damon,

. . . I am presently living in a cramped garret apartment on the top floor of a pre-WWII house in a suburb of Nurnburg, swimming through seas of unwashed dishes and empty tin cans, and alternately wrestling with shadows, staring grimly at my incredible shrinking bankbook, staring grimly out the window at the ancient graveyard below and staring grimly at my typewriter. . . . my parents have glumly predicted for years that I would end up starving in a garret if I didn't watch it. And so here I am. Interesting.

From Dozois, undated, 1969:

Dear Damon,

Dozois *is* French, believe it or not; at least that's what my grandfather always claimed, and he was a naturalized citizen who wandered into New Hampshire from out of the Canadian woods. Very probably it's a corruption of some other common French name, because I've never heard of another Dozois, other than relatives. I usually pronounce it as a flat Doze-wa, although some of my more flamboyant relations like to do it up grand as Doze-*wah* in the traditional French fashion, and you're likely to get an eyeful of spit. . . .

I can't really think of anything better than "Horse of Air" offhand—I'm lousy at titles. If you have any suggestions, let me know. . . . I find myself doing some very strange things lately, including a couple of pieces I laughingly call "poems" . . . one about half as long as *The Rime of the Ancient Mariner*, which is perhaps a bit pretentious now that I think of it. Somewhere Dylan Thomas is spinning in his grave like the sea.

To Dozois, August 27, 1969:

Dear Gardner,

Thanx for your two letters. About titles, I like "A Kingdom by the Sea," but have a feeling you would really prefer "Horse of Air" in spite of my explaining why it is inappropriate, so what the hell, it is your story, & I will run your title on it.

"A Fine and Private Place" is a jazzy title, but has been used by Peter S. Beagle, who won a National Book Award with it a year or so ago.

Can't help relocate you, I'm afraid—have never lived anywhere but here, & all I know is what Harry Harrison tells me. If you were coming back to the States I would get to meet you, which would be cool, but if you are going to write about this country maybe you should stay out of it awhile. Come here if you are going to write about Germany. That's about all I know.

Still have an uneasy feeling that you don't know exactly how that mesh is attached to the wall. I talked to a carpenter and heard a lot about concrete nails and screws, also holes drilled in stone, plugged with wood or lead, & screws put in. But I did not explain to him all about your story; he would have thought I was a nut.

. . .

HORSE OF AIR

by Gardner R. Dozois

Sometimes when the weather is good I sit and look out over the city, fingers hooked through the mesh.

—The mesh is weather-stained, beginning to rust. As his fingers scrabble at it, chips of rust flake off, staining his hands the color of crusted blood. The heavy wire is hot and smooth under his fingers, turning rougher and drier at a rust spot. If he presses his tongue against the wire, it tastes slightly of lemons. He doesn't do that very often—

The city is quieter now. You seldom see motion, mostly birds if you do. As I watch, two pigeons strut along the roof ledge of the low building several stories below my balcony, stopping every now and then to pick at each other's feathers. They look fatter than ever. I wonder what they eat these days? Probably it is better not to know. They have learned to keep away from me anyway, although the mesh that encloses my small balcony floor to ceiling makes it difficult to get at them if they do land nearby. I'm not really hungry, of course, but they are noisy and leave droppings. I don't really bear any malice toward them. It's not a personal thing; I do it for the upkeep of the place.

(I hate birds. I will kill any of them I can reach. I do it with my belt buckle, snapping it between the hoops of wire.)

—He hates birds because they have freedom of movement, because they can fly, because they can shift their viewpoint from spot to spot in linear space, while he can do so only in time and memory, and that imperfectly. They can fly here and look at him and then fly away, while he has no volition: if he wants to look at them, he must wait until they decide to come to him. He flicks a piece of plaster at them, between the hoops—

Startled by something, the pigeons explode upward with a whir of feathers. I watch them fly away: skimming along the side of a building, dipping with an air current. They are soon lost in the maze of low roofs that thrust up below at all angles and heights, staggering toward the Apartment Towers in the middle distance. The Towers stand untouched by the sea of brownstones that break around their flanks, like aloof monoliths wading in a surf of scummy brown brick. Other Towers march off in curving lines toward the horizon, becoming progressively smaller until they vanish at the place where a misty sky merges with a line of low hills. If I press myself against the mesh at the far right side of the balcony, I can see the nearest Tower to my own, perhaps six hundred yards away, all of steel and concrete with a vertical line of windows running down the middle and rows of identical balconies on either side.

Nearest to me on the left is a building that rises about a quarter of the way up my Tower's flank: patterns of dark brown and light red bricks, interlaced with fingers of mortar; weathered gray roof shingles, a few missing here and there in a manner reminiscent of broken teeth; a web of black chimney and sewage pipes crawling up and across the walls like metallic creepers. All covered with the pale splotches of bird droppings. The Towers are much cleaner; not so many horizontal surfaces. Windows are broken in the disintegrating buildings down there; the dying sunlight glints from fangs of shattered glass. Curtains hang in limp shreds that snap and drum when a wind comes up. If you squint, you can see that the wind has scattered broken twigs and rubbish all over the floors inside. No, I am much happier in one of the Towers.

(I hate the Towers. I would rather live anywhere than here.)

—He hates the Towers. As the sun starts to dip below the horizon, settling down into the concrete labyrinth like a hog into a wallow, he shakes his head blindly and makes a low noise at the back of his throat. The shadows of buildings are longer now, stretching in toward him from the horizon like accusing fingers. A deep grey gloom is gathering in the corners and angles of walls, shot with crimson sparks from the foundering sun, now dragged under and wrapped in chill masonry. His hands go up and out, curling again around the hoops of the mesh. He shakes the mesh violently, throwing his weight against it. The mesh groans in metallic agony but remains solid. A few chips of concrete pull from the places where the ends of the mesh are anchored to the walls. He continues to tear at the mesh until his hands bleed, half-healed scabs torn open again. Tiny blood droplets spatter the heavy wire. The blood holds the deeper color of rust—

If you have enough maturity to keep emotionalism out of it, the view from here can even be fascinating. The sky is clear now, an electric, saturated blue, and the air is as sharp as a jeweler's glass. Not like the old days. Without factories and cars to keep it fed, even the eternal smog has dissipated. The sky reminds me now of an expensive aquarium filled with crystal tropical water, me at the bottom: I almost expect to see huge eyes peering in from the horizon, maybe a monstrous nose pressed against the glass. On a sunny day you can see for miles.

But it is even more beautiful when it rains. The rain invests the still landscape with an element of motion: long fingers of it brushing across the rooftops or marching down in zigzag sheets, the droplets stirring and rippling the puddles that form in depressions, drumming against the flat concrete surfaces, running down along the edges of the shingles, foaming and sputtering from downspouts. The Towers stand like lords, swirling rain mists around them as a fine gentleman swirls his jeweled cloak. Pregnant grey clouds scurry by behind the Towers, lashed by wind. The constant stream of horizontals past the fixed vertical fingers of the Towers creates contrast, gives the eye something to follow, increases the relief of motion. Motion is heresy when the world has become a still-life. But it soothes, the old-time religion. There are no atheists in foxholes, nor abstainers when the world begins to flow. But does that prove the desirability of God or the weakness of men? I drink when the world flows, but unwillingly, because I know the price. I have to drink, but I also have to pay. I will pay later when the motion stops and the world returns to lethargy, the doldrums made more unbearable by the contrast known a moment before. That is another cross that I am forced to bear.

But it is beautiful, and fresh-washed after. And sometimes there is a

261

rainbow. Rain is the only esthetic pleasure I have left, and I savor it with the unhurried leisure of the aristocracy.

—When the rain comes, he flattens himself against the mesh, arms spread wide as if crucified there, letting the rain hammer against his face. The rain rolls in runnels down his skin, mixing with sweat, counterfeiting tears. Eyes closed, he bruises his open mouth against the mesh, trying to drink the rain. His tongue dabs at the drops that trickle by his mouth, licks out for the moisture oozing down along the links of wire. After the storm, he sometimes drinks the small puddles that gather on the balcony ledge, lapping them noisily and greedily, although the tap in the kitchen works, and he is never thirsty—

Always something to look at from here. Directly below are a number of weed-overgrown yards, chopped up unequally by low brick walls, nestled in a hollow square formed by the surrounding brownstones. There is even a tree in one corner, though it is dead and its limbs are gnarled and splintered. The yards were never neatly kept by the rabble that lived there, even in the old days: they are scattered with trash and rubbish, middens of worn-out household items and broken plastic toys, though the weeds have covered much. There was a neat, bright flower bed in one of the further yards, tended by a bent and leather-skinned foreign crone of impossible age, but the weeds have overgrown that as well, drowning the rarer blossoms. This season there were more weeds, fewer flowers—they seem to survive better, though God knows they have little else to recommend them, being coarse and ill-smelling.

In the closest yard an old and ornate wicker-back chair is still standing upright; if I remember correctly, a pensioner bought it at a rummage sale and used it to take the sun, being a parasite good for nothing else. Weeds are twining up around the chair; it is half-hidden already. Beyond is a small concrete court where hordes of ragged children used to play ball. Its geometrical white lines are nearly obliterated now by rain and wind-drifted gravel. If you look sharp at this clearing, sometimes you can see the sudden flurry of a small darting body through the weeds: a rat or a cat, hard to tell at this distance.

Once, months ago, I saw a man and a woman there, my first clear indication that there are still people alive and about. They entered the court like thieves, crawling through a low window, the man lowering the girl and then jumping down after. They were dressed in rags, and the man carried a rifle and a bandolier. After reconnoitering, the man forced one of the rickety doors into a brownstone, disappearing inside. After a while he came out dragging a mattress—filthy, springs jutting through fabric—and carried it into the ball court. They had intercourse there for the better part of the

262

afternoon, stopping occasionally while the man prowled about with the rifle. I remember thinking that it was too bad the gift of motion had been wasted on such as these. They left at dusk. I had not tried to signal them, leaving them undisturbed to their rut, although I was somewhat sickened by the coarse brutality of the act. There *is* such a thing as *noblesse oblige*.

(I hate them. If I had a gun I would kill them. At first I watch greedily as they make love, excited, afraid of scaring them away if they should become aware of me watching. But as the afternoon wears on, I grow drained, and then angry, and begin to shout at them, telling them to get out, get the hell out. They ignore me. Their tanned skin is vivid against asphalt as they strain together. Sweat makes their locked limbs glisten in the thick sunlight. The rhythmic rise and fall of their bodies describes parabolic lines through the crusted air. I scream at them and tear at the mesh, voice thin and impotent. Later they make love again, rolling from the mattress in their urgency, sprawling among the lush weeds, coupling like leopards. I try to throw plaster at them, but the angle is wrong. As they leave the square, the man gives me the finger.)

Thinking of those two makes me think of the other animals that howl through the world, masquerading as men. On the far left, hidden by the nearest brownstones but winding into sight further on, is a highway. Once it was a major artery of the city, choked with a chrome flood of traffic. Now it is empty. Once or twice at the beginning I would see an ambulance or a fire engine, once a tank. A few weeks ago I saw a jeep go by, driving square in the middle of the highway, ridden by armed men. Occasionally I have seen men and women trudge past, dragging their possessions behind them on a sledge. Perhaps the wheel is on the way out.

Against one curb is the overturned, burned-out hulk of a bus: small animals use it for a cave now, and weeds are beginning to lace through it. I saw it burning, a week after the Building Committee came. I sat on the balcony and watched its flames eat up at the sky, although it was too dark to make out what was happening around it; the street lights had been the first things to go. There were other blazes in the distance, glowing like campfires, like blurred stars. I remember wondering that night what was happening, what the devil was going on. But I've figured it out now.

It was the niggers. I hate to say it. I've been a liberal man all my life. But you can't deny the truth. They are responsible for the destruction, for the present degeneration of the world. It makes me sad to have to say this. I had always been on their side in spirit, I was more than willing to stretch out a helping hand to those less fortunate than myself. I always said so; I always said that. I had high hopes for them all. But they got greedy, and brought us to this. We should have known better, we should have listened to the

263

so-called racists, we should have realized that idealism is a wasting disease, a cancer. We should have remembered that blood will tell. A hard truth: it was the niggers. I have no prejudice; I speak of cold facts. I had always wished them well.

(I hate niggers. They are animals. Touching one would make me vomit.)

—He hates niggers. He has seen them on the street corners with their women, he has seen them in their jukeboxed caves with their feet in sawdust, he has heard them speaking in a private language half devised of finger snaps and motions of liquid hips, he has felt the inquiry of their eyes, he has seen them dance. He envies them for having a culture separate from the bland familiarity of his own, he envies their tang of the exotic. He envies their easy sexuality. He fears their potency. He fears that in climbing up they will shake him down. He fears generations of stored-up hate. He hates them because their very existence makes him uncomfortable. He hates them because sometimes they have seemed to be happy on their tenement street corners, while he rides by in an air-conditioned car and is not. He hates them because they are not part of the mechanism and yet still have the audacity to exist. He hates them because they have escaped—

Dusk has come, hiding a world returned to shame and barbarism. It occurs to me that I may be one of the few members of the upper class left. The rabble were always quick to blame their betters for their own inherent inferiority and quick to vent their resentment in violence when the opportunity arose. The other Apartment Towers are still occupied, I think; I can see the lights at night, as they can see mine, if there is anyone left there to see. So perhaps there are still a few of us left. Perhaps there is still some hope for the world after all.

Although what avail to society is their survival if they are as helpless as I? We may be the last hope of restoring order to a land raped by Chaos, and we are being wasted. We are born to govern, to regulate, prepared for it by station, tradition and long experience: leadership comes as naturally to us as drinking and fornication come to the masses of the Great Unwashed. We are being wasted, our experience and foresight pissed away by fools who will not listen.

And we dwindle. I speak of us as a class, as a corporate "we." But there are fewer lights in the other Towers every month. Last night I counted less than half the number I could see a year ago. On evenings when the wind grows bitter with autumn cold, I fear that I will soon be the only one left with the courage to hold out. It would be so easy to give in to despair; the quietus of hopelessness is tempting. But it is a siren goddess, made of tin. Can't the others see that? To give up is to betray their blood. But still the lights dwindle. At times I have the dreadful fancy that I will sit here one night and

264

watch the last light flicker out in the last Tower, leaving me alone in darkness, the only survivor of a noble breed. Will some improbable alien archaeologist come and hang a sign on my cage: the last of the aristocracy?

Deep darkness now. The lights begin to come on across the gulfs of shadow, but I am afraid to count them. Thinking of these things has chilled me, and I shudder. The wind is cold, filled with dampness. There will be a storm later. Distant lightning flickers behind the Towers, each flash sending jagged shadows leaping toward me, striking blue highlights from every reflecting surface. Each lightning stroke seems to momentarily reverse the order of things, etching the Towers in black relief against the blue-white dazzle of the sky, then the brilliance draining, leaving the Towers as before: islands of light against an inky background of black. The cycle is repeated, shadows lunging in at me, in at me, thrusting swords of nigger-blackness. It was on a hellish night like this that the Building Committee came.

It was a mistake to give them so much power. I admit it. I'm not too proud to own up to my own mistakes. But we were tired of struggling with an uncooperative and unappreciative society. We were beaten into weariness by a horde of supercilious bastards, petty and envious little men hanging on our coattails and trying to chivy us down. We were sick of people with no respect, no traditions, no heritage, no proper ambitions. We were disgusted by a world degenerating at every seam, in every aspect. We had finally realized the futility of issuing warnings no one would listen to. Even then the brakes could have been applied to our skidding society if someone had bothered to listen, if anyone had had the guts and foresight to take the necessary measures. But we were tired, and we were no longer young.

So we traded our power for security. We built the Towers; we formed a company, turned our affairs over to them, and retired from the world into our own tight-knit society. Let the company have the responsibility and the problems, let them deal with the pressures and the decisions, let them handle whatever comes; we will be safe and comfortable regardless. They are the bright, ambitious technicians; let them cope. They are the expendable soldiers; let them fight and be expended as they are paid for doing; we shall be safe behind the lines. Let them have the mime show of power; we are civilized enough to enjoy the best things of life without it. We renounce the painted dreams; they are hollow.

It was a mistake.

It was a mistake to give them the voting proxies; Anderson was a fool, senile before his time. It was all a horrible mistake. I admit it. But we were no longer young.

And the world worsened, and one day the Building Committee came.

It was crisis, they said, and Fear was walking in the land. And the charter

265

specified that we were to be protected, that we must not be disturbed. So they came with the work crews and meshed over my balcony. And welded a slab of steel over my door as they left. They would not listen to my protest, wrapped in legalities, unvulnerable in armor of technical gobbledygook. Protection was a specific of the Charter, they said, and with the crisis this was the only way they could ensure our protection should the outer defenses go down; it was a temporary measure.

And the work crews went about their business with slap-dash efficiency, and the balding, spectacled foreman told me he only worked here. So I stood quietly and watched them seal me in, although I was trembling with rage. I am no longer young. And I would not lose control before these vermin. Every one of them was waiting for it, hoping for it in their petty, resentful souls, and I would let myself be flayed alive before I would give them the satisfaction. It is a small comfort to me that I showed them the style with which a gentleman can take misfortune.

(When I finally realize what they are doing, I rage and bluster. The foreman pushes me away. "It's for your own good," he says, mouthing the cliché halfheartedly, not really interested. I beat at him with ineffectual fists. Annoyed, he shrugs me off and ducks through the door. I try to run after him. One of the guards hits me in the face with his rifle butt. Pain and shock and a brief darkness. And then I realize that I am lying on the floor. There is blood on my forehead and on my mouth. They have almost finished maneuvering the steel slab into place, only a man-sized crack left open. The guard is the only one left in the room, a goggled technician just squeezing out through the crack. The guard turns toward the door. I hump myself across the room on my knees, crawling after him, crying and begging. He plants his boot on my shoulder and pushes me disgustedly away. The room tumbles, I roll over twice, stop, come up on my elbows and start to crawl after him again. He says, "Fuck off, Dad," and slaps his rifle, jangling the magazine cartridge in the breech. I stop moving. He glares at me, then leaves the room. They push the slab all the way closed. It makes a grinding, rumbling sound, like a subway train. Still on my knees, I throw myself against it, but it is solid. Outside there are welding noises. I scream.)

There is a distant rumbling now. Thunder: the storm is getting nearer. The lightning flashes are more intense, and closer together. They are too bright, too fast, blending into one another, changing the dimensions of the world too rapidly. With the alternating of glare and thrusting shadow there is too much motion, nothing ever still for a second, nothing you can let your eye rest on. Watching it strains your vision. My eyes ache with the motion.

I close them, but there are squiggly white afterimages imprinted on the insides of my eyelids. A man of breeding should know how to control his emotions. I do; in the old circles, the ones that mattered, I was known for my self-discipline and refinement. But this is an unseasonable night, and I am suddenly afraid. It feels like the bones are being rattled in the body of the earth, it feels like maybe It will come now.

But that is an illusion. It is not the Time; It will not come yet. Only I know when the Time is, only I can say when It will come. And It will not come until I call for It, that is part of the bargain. I studied military science at Annapolis. I shall recognize the most strategic moment, I shall know when the Time is at hand for vengeance and retribution. I shall know. And the Time is not now. It will not come tonight. This is only an autumn storm.

I open my eyes. And find my stare returned. Windows ring me on all sides like walls of accusing, lidless eyes. Lightning oozes across the horizon: miniature reflections of the electric arc etched in cold echoes across a thousand panes of glass, a thousand matches struck simultaneously in a thousand dusty rooms.

A sequence of flares. The sky alternates too quickly to follow. Blue-white, black. Blue-white. Black again. The roofs flicker with invested motion, brick dancing in a jerky, silent-movie fashion.

Oh God, the chimneys, humped against dazzle, looming in shadow. Marching rows of smoky brick gargoyles, ash-cold now with not an ember left alive. The rows sway closer with every flash. I can hear the rutch of mortar-footed brick against tile, see the waddling, relentless rolling of their gait. They are people actually, the poor bastard refugees of the rabble frozen into brick, struck dumb with mortar. I saw it happen on the night of the Building Committee, thousands of people swarming like rats over the roofs to escape the burning world, caught by a clear voice of crystal that metamorphosed them with a single word, fixing them solid to the roofs, their hands growing into their knees, their heels into their buttocks, their heads thrown back with mouths gaped in a scream, flesh swapped for brick, blood for mortar. They hump toward me on their blunt knees in ponderously bobbing lines. With a sound like fusing steel, nigger-black shadows humping *in* on me. Christ hands sealing my eyes with clay stuffing down my mouth my throat filling Oh God oh christ christ *christ*

It is raining now. I will surely catch a chill standing here; there are vapors in the night air. Perhaps it would be advisable to go inside. Yes, I do think that would be best. Sometimes it is better to forget external things.

—He crawls away from the mesh on his hands and knees, although he is healthy and perfectly able to stand. He often crawls from place to place in the apartment; he thinks it gives him a better perspective. Rain patters on the balcony behind, drums against the glass of the French windows that open into the apartment. He claws at the framework of the windows, drags himself to his feet. He stands there for a moment, face pressed flat against the glass, trembling violently. His cheeks are wet. Perhaps he has been crying. Or perhaps it was the rain—

I turn on the light and go inside, closing the French windows firmly behind me. It is the very devil of a night outside. In here it is safe, even comfortable. This place is only a quarter of my actual apartment of course. The Building Committee sealed me in here, cut me off from the rest of my old place, which occupied most of this floor. Easier to defend me this way, the bastards said. So this apartment is smaller than what I'm used to living in, God knows. But in a strange way the smallness makes the place more cozy somehow, especially on a piggish night like this when fiends claw the windowpane.

I cross to the kitchen cubicle, rummage through the jars and cans; there's some coffee left from this week's shipment, I think. Yes, a little coffee left in one of the jars: instant; coarse, murky stuff. I had been used to better; once we drank nothing but fine-ground Colombian, and I would have spat in the face of any waiter who dared to serve me unpercolated coffee. This is one of the innumerable little ways in which we pay for our folly. A thousand little things, but together they add up into an almost unbearable burden, a leering Old Man of the Sea wrapped leech-fashion around my shoulders and growing heavier by the day. But this is defeatist talk. I am more tired than I would allow myself to admit. Here the coffee will help; even this bitter liquid retains that basic virtue in kind with the more palatable stuff. I heat some water, slosh it over the obscene granules into a cup. The cup is cracked, no replacement for it: another little thing. A gust of wind rattles the glass in the French windows. I will not listen to it.

Weary, I carry the steaming cup into the living room, sit down in the easy chair with my back to the balcony. I try to balance the cup on my knee, but the damn thing is too hot; I finally rest it on the chair arm, leaving a moist ring on the fabric, but that hardly matters now. Can my will be weakening? Once I would have considered it sacrilege to sully fine furniture and would have gone to any length to avoid doing so. Now I am too wrapped in lassitude to get up and go into the kitchen for a coaster. Coffee seeps slowly into fabric, a widening brownish stain, like blood. I am almost too tired to lift the cup to my lips.

Degeneration starts very slowly, so deviously, so patiently that it almost seems to be a living thing; embodied it would be a weasellike animal armed with sly cunning and gnawing needle teeth. It never goes for your throat like a decent monster, so that you might have a chance of beating it down: it lurks in darkness, it gnaws furtively at the base of your spine, it burrows into your liver while you sleep. Like the succubi I try to guard against at night, it saps your strength, it sucks your breath in slumber, it etches away the marrow of your bones.

There is enough water in the tank for one more bath this week; I should wash, but I fear I'm too tired to manage it. Another example? It takes such a lot of *effort* to remain civilized. How tempting to say, "It no longer matters." It does matter. I say it does. I will make it matter. I cannot afford the seductive surrender of my unfortunate brethren; I have a responsibility they don't have. Perhaps I am luckier to have it in a way. It is an awesome responsibility, but carrying it summons up a corresponding strength, it gives me a reason for living, a goal outside myself. Perhaps my responsibility is what enables me to hang on, the knowledge of what is to come just enough to balance out the other pressures. The game has not yet been played to an end. Not while I still hold my special card.

Thinking of the secret, I look at the television set, but the atmospherics are wrong tonight for messages, and it's probably too late for the haphazard programming they put out now. Some nights I leave the test pattern on, enjoying the flickering highlights it sends across the walls and ceilings, but tonight I think it will be more comfortable with just the pool of yellow glow cast by the lamp next to my chair, a barrier against the tangible darkness.

Looking at the television always reawakens my curiosity about the outside world. What is the state of society? The city I can see from my balcony seems to have degenerated into savagery, civilization seems to have been destroyed, but there are contradictions, there are ambiguities. Obviously the Building Committee must still be in existence somewhere. The electric lights and the plumbing still work in the Towers, a shipment of food supplies rattles up the pneumatic dumbwaiter into the kitchen cubicle twice a week, there are old movies and cartoons on television, running continuously with no commercials or live programming, never a hint of news. Who else could it be for but us? Who else could be responsible for it but the Building Committee? I've seen the city; it is dark, broken, inhabited by no one but a few human jackals who eke out a brute existence and hunt each other through the ruins. These facilities are certainly not operated for them—the other Towers are the only lighted buildings visible in the entire wide section of city visible from here.

No, it is the Building Committee. It must be. They are the only ones with the proper resources to hold a circle of order against a widening chaos. Those resources were vast. I know: we built them, we worked to make them flexible, we sweated to make them inexhaustible. We let their control pass out of our hands. One never finishes paying for past sins.

What a tremendous amount of trouble they've gone to, continuing to operate the Towers, even running a small television station somewhere to force-feed us the "entertainment" specified in the Charter. And never a word, never a glimpse of them, even for a second. Why? Why do they bother to keep up the pretense, the mocking hypocrisy of obeying the Charter? The real power is theirs now, why do they bother to continue the sham and lip service? Why don't they just shut down the Towers and leave us to starve in our plush cells? Is it the product of some monstrous, sadistic sense of humor? Or is it the result of a methodical, fussily prim sense of order that refuses to deny a legal technicality even when the laws themselves have died? Do they laugh their young men's laughter when they think of the once-formidable old beasts they have caged?

I feel a surge of anger. I put the half-emptied cup down on the rug. My hand is trembling. The Time is coming. It will be soon now. Soon they will heap some further indignity on me and force my hand. I will not have them laughing at me, those little men with maggots for eyes. Not when I still have it in my power to change it all. Not while I still am who I am. But not just yet. Let them have their victory, their smug laughter. An old tiger's fangs may be blunt and yellowing, but they can still bite. And even an old beast can still rise for one more kill.

I force myself to my feet. I have the inner strength, the discipline. They have nothing, they are the rabble, they are children trying out as men and parading in adult clothing. It was we who taught them the game, and we still know how to play it best. I force myself to wash, to fold the bed out from the wall, to lie still, fighting for calm. I run my eyes around the familiar dimensions of the apartment, cataloguing: pale blue walls, red draw curtains for the French windows, bookshelves next to the curtains, a black cushioned stool, the rug in patterns of orange and green against brown, a red shaggy chair and matching couch, the archways to the kitchen and bath cubicles. Nothing alien. Nothing hostile. I begin to relax. Thank God for familiarity. There is a certain pleasure in looking at well-known, well-loved things, a certain unshakable sense of reality. I often fall asleep counting my things.

(I hate this apartment. I hate everything in this apartment. I cannot stand to live here any longer. Someday I will chop everything to unrecognizable fragments and pile it in the middle of the floor and burn it, and I will laugh while it burns.)

—He is wakened by a shaft of sunlight that falls through the uncurtained French windows. He groans, stirs, draws one foot up, heel against buttock, knee toward the ceiling. His hand clenches in the bedclothes. The sound of birds reaches him through the insulating glass. For a moment, waking, he thinks that he is elsewhere, another place, another time. He mutters a woman's name and his hand goes out to grope across the untouched, empty space beside him in the double bed. His hand encounters only the cool of

270

sheets, no answering warmth of flesh. He grimaces, his bent leg snaps out to full length again, his suddenly desperate hand rips the sheet free of the mattress, finding nothing. He wrenches to his feet, neck corded, staggering. By the time his eyes slide open he has begun to scream—

I will not allow it. Do you hear me, bastards? *I will not allow it.* I will not stand for it. You've gone too far, I warn you, too far, I'll kill you. D'you hear? Niggers and thieves. The past is all I have. I will not have you touching it, I will not have you sliming and defiling it with your shitty hands. You leave her out of it, you leave her alone. What kind of men are you using her against me? *What kind of men are you?* Rabble not worth breath. Defiling everything you touch, everything better than you finer than you. I will not allow it.

It is time. It is *Time.*

The decision brings a measure of calm. I am committed now. They have finally driven me too far. It is time for me to play the final card. I will not let them remain unpunished for this another second, another breath. I will call for It, and It will come. I must keep control, there must be no mistakes. This is retribution. This is the moment I have waited for all these agonizing months. I must keep control, there must be no mistakes. It must be executed with dispatch, with precision. I breathe deeply to calm myself. There will be no mistakes, no hesitations.

Three steps take me to the television. I flick it on, waiting for it to warm. Impatience drums within me, tightly reined as a rearing Arabian stallion. So long, so long.

A picture appears on the screen: another imbecilic movie. I think of the Building Committee, unaware, living in the illusion of victory. Expertly, I remove the back of the television, my skilled fingers probing deep into the maze of wires and tubes. I work with the familiarity of long practice. How many hours did I crouch like this, experimenting, before I found the proper frequency of the Others by trial and error? Patience was never a trait of the rabble; it is a talent reserved for the aristocracy. They didn't count on my patience. Mayflies themselves, they cannot understand dedication of purpose. They didn't count on my scientific knowledge, on my technical training at Annapolis. They didn't count on the resources and ingenuity of a superior man.

I tap two wires together, creating sparks, sending messages into ether. I am sending on the frequency of the Others, a prearranged signal in code: the Time is now. Let It come. Sweat in my eyes, fingers cramping, but I continue to broadcast. The Time is now. Let It come. At last a response, the Others acknowledging that they've received my order.

It is over.

Now It will come.

Now they will pay for their sins.

I sit back on my heels, drained. I have done my part. I have launched It on Its way, given birth to retribution, sowed the world with dragon's teeth. And they laughed. Now It is irreversible. Nothing can stop It. An end to all thieves and niggers, to all little men, to all the rabble that grow over the framework like weeds and ruin the order of the world. I stagger to the French windows, throw them open. Glass shatters in one frame, bright fragments against the weave of the rug. Onto the balcony where buildings press in at me unaware of Ragnarok. I collapse against the mesh, fingers spread, letting it take my weight. No motion in the world, but soon there will be enough. Far north, away from the sight of the city, the spaceships of the Others are busy according to plan, planting the thermal charges that will melt the icecap, shattering the earth-old ice, liberating the ancient waters, forming a Wave to thunder south and drown the world. I think of the Building Committee, of the vermin in the ruins of the city, even of my fellows in the other Towers. I am not sorry for them. I am no longer young, but I will take them with me into darkness. There will be no other eyes to watch a sun I can no longer see. I have no regrets. I've always hated them. I hate them all.

(I hate them all.)

—He hates them all—

A moaning in the earth, a trembling, a drumming as of a billion billion hooves. The Tower sways queasily. A swelling, ragged shriek of sound.

The Wave comes.

Over the horizon, climbing, growing larger, stretching higher, filling up the sky, cutting off the sunlight, water in a green wall like glass hundreds of feet high, topped with fangs of foam, the Wave beginning to topple in like the closing fist of God. Its shadow over everything, night at noon as it sweeps in, closes down. The Towers etched like thin lines against its bulk. It is curling overhead is the sky now there is no sky now but the underbelly of the Wave coming down. I have time to see the Towers snapped like matchsticks broken stumps of fangs before it hits with the scream of grating steel and blackness clogs my throat to

(I have destroyed the world.)

—The shadow of the mesh on his face—

Sometimes you can see other people in the other Tower apartments, looking out from their own balconies. I wonder how they destroy the world?

—He turns away, dimly remembering a business appointment. Outside the lazy hooting of rush-hour traffic. There is a cartoon carnival on Channel Five—

Damon:

Here is the final revised version of the story. As you will see, I ran it through the machine again, and integrated all but two of your suggestions. The two were in the areas of what you called "self-indulgence," and as I said in my last note, to remove those (even to the admitted betterment of the total story) would be to negate some of the reason for my having written the story in the first place. I can't quibble with you on literary grounds. All I can say is that writing, for me, is a combination of release, panacea and therapy. To negate those elements of the story that provided these three, would be merely to become a commercial writer. I can't do that. So . . . you're right, 100% right . . . but I don't care.

To Harlan Ellison, August 16, 1969:

Dear Harlan,

I found "One Life," and send it herewith one more time, with copyediting marks on. Most of these are just punctuation & things like that, but there are a few you might want to change back. A good story now, & I don't even mind the goddamn Red-Red lipstick; maybe I am used to it.

ONE LIFE, FURNISHED IN EARLY POVERTY
by *Harlan Ellison*

And so it was—strangely, strangely—that I found myself standing in the backyard of the house I had lived in when I was seven years old. At thirteen minutes till midnight on no special magical winter's night, in a town that had held me only till I was physically able to run away. In Ohio, in winter, near midnight—certain I could go back.

Not truly knowing *why* I even wanted to go back. But certain that I could.

Without magic, without science, without alchemy, without supernatural assistance; just *go back*. Because I had to, I needed to . . . go back.

Back; thirty-five years and more. To find myself at the age of seven, before any of it had begun; before any of the directions had been taken; to find out what turning point in my life it had been that had wrenched me from the course all little boys took to adulthood and set me on the road of loneliness and success that ended here, back where I'd begun, in a backyard at now-twelve minutes to midnight.

At forty-two I had come to the point in my life I had struggled toward since I was a child: a place of security, importance, recognition. The only one from this town who had made it. The ones who had had the most promise in school were now milkmen, used-car salesmen, married to fat, stupid *dead* women who had themselves been girls of exceeding promise in high school. *They* had been trapped in this little Ohio town, never to break free. To die there, unknown. I had broken free, had done all the wonderful things I'd said I would do.

Why should it all depress me now?

Perhaps it was because Christmas was nearing and I was alone, with bad marriages and lost friendships behind me.

I walked out of the studio, away from the wet-ink-new fifty-thousand-dollar contract, got in my car and drove to International Airport. It was a straight line made up of inflight meals and jet airliners and rental cars and hastily purchased winter clothing. A straight line to a backyard I had not seen in over thirty years.

I had to find the dragoon to go back.

Crossing the rime-frosted grass that crackled like cellophane, I walked under the shadow of the lightning-blasted pear tree. I had climbed in that tree endlessly when I was seven years old. In summer, its branches hung far over and scraped the roof of the garage. I could shinny out across the limb and drop onto the garage roof. I had once pushed Johnny Mummy off that garage roof . . . not out of meanness, but simply because I had jumped from it many times and I could not understand anyone's not finding it a wonderful thing to do. He had sprained his ankle, and his father, a fireman, had come looking for me. I'd hidden on the garage roof.

I walked around the side of the garage, and there was the barely visible path. To one side of the path I had always buried my toy soldiers. For no other reason than to bury them, know I had a secret place, and later dig them up again, as if finding treasure.

(It came to me that even now, as an adult, I did the same thing. Dining in a Japanese restaurant, I would hide small pieces of *pakkai* or pineapple or *teriyaki* in my rice bowl and pretend to be delighted when, later in the meal, my chopsticks encountered the tiny treasures down in among the rice grains.)

I knew the spot, of course. I got down on my hands and knees and began digging with the silver penknife on my watch chain. It had been my father's penknife—almost the only thing he had left when he died.

The ground was hard, but I dug with enthusiasm, and the moon gave me more than enough light. Down and down I dug, knowing eventually I would come to the dragoon.

He was there. The bright paint rusted off his body, the saber corroded and reduced to a stub. Lying there in the grave I had dug for him thirty-five years before. I scooped the little metal soldier out of the ground and cleaned him off as best I could with my paisley dress handkerchief. He was faceless now, and as sad as I felt.

I hunkered there, under the moon, and waited for midnight, only a minute away, knowing it was all going to come right for me. After so terribly long.

The house behind me was silent and dark. I had no idea who lived there now. It would have been unpleasant if the strangers who now lived here had been unable to sleep and, rising to get a glass of water, had idly looked into the backyard. *Their* backyard. I had played here and built a world for myself here, from dreams and loneliness. Using talismans of comic books and radio programs and matinee movies and potent charms like the sad little dragoon in my hand.

My wristwatch said midnight, one hand laid straight on the other.

The moon faded. Slowly, it went gray and shadowy, till the glow was gone, and then even the gray afterimage was gone.

The wind rose. Slowly, it came from somewhere far away, and built around me. I stood up, pulling the collar of my topcoat around my neck. The wind was neither warm nor cold, yet it rushed, without even ruffling my hair. I was not afraid.

The ground was settling. Slowly, it lowered me the tiniest fractions of inches. But steadily, as though the layers of tomorrows that had been built up were vanishing.

My thoughts were of myself: *I'm coming to save you. I'm coming, Gus. You won't hurt anymore . . . you'll never have hurt.*

The moon came back. It had been full; now it was new. The wind died. It had carried me where I'd needed to go. The ground settled. The years had been peeled off.

I was alone in the backyard of the house at 89 Harmon Drive. The snow was deeper. It was a different house, though it was the same. It was not recently painted. The Depression had not been long ago; money was still tight. It wasn't weather-beaten, but in a year or two my father would have it painted. Light yellow.

There was a sumac tree growing below the window of the dinette. It was nourished by lima beans and soup and cabbage.

"You'll just sit there until you finish every drop of your dinner. We're not wasting food. There are children starving in Russia."

I put the dragoon in my topcoat pocket. He had worked more than hard enough. I walked around the side of the house. I smiled as I saw again the wooden milk box by the side door. In the morning, very early, the milkman would put three quarts of milk there, but before anyone could bring them in, this very cold winter morning in December, the cream would push its way up and the little cardboard caps would be an inch above the mouths of the bottles.

The gravel talked beneath my feet. The street was quiet and cold. I stood in the front yard, beside the big oak tree, and looked up and down.

It was the same. It was as though I'd never been away. I started to cry. Hello.

Gus was on one of the swings in the playground. I stood outside the fence of Lathrop Grade School, and watched him standing on the seat, gripping the ropes, pumping his little legs. He was smaller than I'd remembered him. He wasn't smiling as he tried to swing higher. It was serious to him.

Standing outside the hurricane fence, watching Gus, I was happy. I scratched at a rash on my right wrist, and smoked a cigarette, and was happy.

I didn't see them until they were out of the shadows of the bushes, almost on him.

One of them rushed up and grabbed Gus's leg, and tried to pull him off the seat, just as he reached the bottom of his swing. Gus managed to hold on, but the chain ropes twisted crazily and when the seat went back up, it hit the metal leg of the framework.

Gus fell, rolled face down in the dust of the playground, and tried to sit up. The boys pushed through between the swings, avoiding the berserk one that clanged back and forth.

Gus managed to get up, and the boys formed a circle around him. Then Jack Wheeldon stepped out and faced him. I remembered Jack Wheeldon.

He was taller than Gus. They were *all* taller than Gus, but Wheeldon was beefier. I could see shadows surrounding him. Shadows of a boy who would grow into a man with a beer stomach and thick arms. But the eyes would always remain the same.

276

He shoved Gus in the face. Gus went back, dug in and charged him. Gus came at him low, head tucked under, fists tight, arms braced close to the body. He hit him in the stomach and wrestled him around. They struggled together like inept club fighters, raising dust.

One of the boys in the circle took a step forward and hit Gus hard in the back of the head. Gus turned his face out of Wheeldon's stomach, and Wheeldon punched him in the mouth. Gus started to cry.

I'd been frozen, watching it happen, but he was crying—

I looked both ways down the fence and found the break far to my right. I threw the cigarette away as I dashed down the fence, trying to look behind me. Then through the break and I was running toward them the long distance from far right field of the baseball diamond, toward the swings and seesaws. They had Gus down now, and they were kicking him.

When they saw me coming, they started to run away. Jack Wheeldon paused to kick Gus once more in the side; then he, too, ran.

Gus was lying there, on his back, the dust smeared into mud on his face. I bent down and picked him up. He wasn't moving, but he wasn't really hurt. I held him very close and carried him toward the bushes that rose on a small incline at the side of the playground. The bushes were cool overhead and they canopied us, hid us; I laid him down and used my handkerchief to clean away the dirt. His eyes were very blue. I smoothed the straight brown hair off his forehead. He wore braces; one of the rubber bands hooked onto the pins of the braces, used to keep them tension-tight, had broken. I pulled it free.

He opened his eyes and started crying again.

Something hurt in my chest.

He started snuffling, unable to catch his breath. He tried to speak, but the words were only mangled sounds, huffed out with too much air and pain.

Then he forced himself to sit up and rubbed the back of his hand across his runny nose.

He stared at me. It was panic and fear and confusion and shame at being seen this way. "Th-they hit me from in back," he said, snuffling.

"I know. I saw."

"D'jou scare'm off?"

"Yes."

He didn't say thank you. It wasn't necessary. The backs of my thighs hurt from squatting. I sat down.

"My name is Gus," he said, trying to be polite. I didn't know what name to give him. I was going to tell him the first name to come into my head, but heard myself say, "My name is Mr. Rosenthal."

He looked startled. "That's *my* name, too. Gus Rosenthal!"

"Isn't that peculiar," I said. We grinned at each other, and he wiped his nose again.

I didn't want to see my mother or father. I had those memories. They were sufficient. It was little Gus I wanted to be with. But one night I crossed into the backyard at 89 Harmon Drive from the empty lots that would later be a housing development.

And I stood in the dark, watching them eat dinner. There was my father. I hadn't remembered him being so handsome. My mother was saying something to him, and he nodded as he ate. They were in the dinette. Gus was playing with his food. *Don't mush your food around like that, Gus. Eat, or you can't stay up to hear* Lux Presents Hollywood.

But they're doing "Dawn Patrol."

Then don't mush your food.

"Momma," I murmured, standing in the cold, "Momma, there are children starving in Russia." And I added, thirty-five years late, "Name two, Momma."

I met Gus downtown at the newsstand.

"Hi."

"Oh. Hullo."

"Buying some comics?"

"Uh-huh."

"You ever read *Doll Man* and *Kid Eternity*?"

"Yeah, they're great. But I got them."

"Not the new issues."

"Sure do."

"Bet you've got *last* month's. He's just checking in the new comics right now."

So we waited while the newsstand owner used the heavy wire snips on the bundles, and checked off the magazines against the distributor's long white mimeographed sheet. And I bought Gus *Airboy* and *Jingle Jangle Comics* and *Blue Beetle* and *Whiz Comics* and *Doll Man* and *Kid Eternity*.

Then I took him to Isaly's for a hot fudge sundae. They served it in a tall tulip glass with the hot fudge in a little pitcher. When the waitress had gone to get the sundaes, little Gus looked at me. "Hey, how'd you know I only liked crushed nuts, an' not whipped cream or a cherry?"

I leaned back in the high-walled booth and smiled at him.

"What do you want to be when you grow up, Gus?"

He shrugged. "I don't know."

278

Somebody put a nickel in the Wurlitzer in his booth, and Glenn Miller swung into "String of Pearls."

"Well, did you ever think about it?"

"No, huh-uh. I like cartooning, maybe I could draw comic books."

"That's pretty smart thinking, Gus. There's a lot of money to be made in art." I stared around the dairy store, at the Coca-Cola posters of pretty girls with pageboy hairdos, drawn by an artist named Harold W. McCauley whose style would be known throughout the world, whose name would never be known.

He stared at me. "It's fun, too, isn't it?"

I was embarrassed. I'd thought first of money, he'd thought first of happiness. I'd reached him before he'd chosen his path. There was still time to make him a man who would think first of joy, all through his life.

"Mr. Rosenthal?"

I looked down and across, just as the waitress brought the sundaes. She set them down and I paid her. When she'd gone, Gus asked me, "Why did they call me a dirty Jewish elephant?"

"Who called you that, Gus?"

"The guys."

"The ones you were fighting that day?"

He nodded. "Why'd they say elephant?"

I spooned up some vanilla ice cream, thinking. My back ached, and the rash had spread up my right wrist onto my forearm. "Well, Jewish people are supposed to have big noses, Gus." I poured the hot fudge out of the little pitcher. It bulged with surface tension for a second, then spilled through its own dark-brown film, covering the three scoops of ice cream. "I mean, that's what some people *believe*. So I suppose they thought it was smart to call you an elephant, because an elephant has a big nose . . . a trunk. Do you understand?"

"That's dumb. I don't have a big nose . . . do I?"

"I wouldn't say so, Gus. They most likely said it just to make you mad. Sometimes people do that."

"That's dumb."

We sat there for a while and talked. I went far down inside the tulip glass with the long-handled spoon, and finished the deep dark, almost black bittersweet hot fudge. They hadn't made hot fudge like that in many years. Gus got ice cream up the spoon handle, on his fingers, on his chin, and on his T-shirt. We talked about a great many things.

We talked about how difficult arithmetic was. (How I would still have to use my fingers sometimes even as an adult.) How the guys never gave a short kid his "raps" when the sandlot ball games were in progress. (How I

279

overcompensated with women from doubts about stature.) How different kinds of food were pretty bad-tasting. (How I still used ketchup on well-done steak.) How it was pretty lonely in the neighborhood with nobody for friends. (How I had erected a façade of charisma and glamor so no one could reach me deeply enough to hurt me.) How Leon always invited all the kids over to his house, but when Gus got there, they slammed the door and stood behind the screen laughing and jeering. (How even now a slammed door raised the hair on my neck and a phone receiver slammed down, cutting me off, sent me into a senseless rage.) How comic books were great. (How my scripts sold so easily because I had never learned how to rein in my imagination.)

We talked about a great many things.

"I'd better get you home now," I said.

"Okay." We got up. "Hey, Mr. Rosenthal?"

"You'd better wipe the chocolate off your face."

He wiped. "Mr. Rosenthal . . . how'd you know I like crushed nuts, an' not whipped cream or a cherry?"

We spent a great deal of time together. I bought him a copy of a pulp magazine called *Startling Stories* and read him a story about a space pirate who captures a man and his wife and offers the man the choice of opening one of two large boxes—in one is the man's wife, with twelve hours of air to breathe, in the other is a terrible alien fungus that will eat him alive. Little Gus sat on the edge of the big hole he'd dug, out in the empty lots, dangling his feet, and listening. His forehead was furrowed as he listened to the marvels of Jack Williamson's "Twelve Hours to Live," there on the edge of the fort he'd built.

We discussed the radio programs Gus heard every day: *Tennessee Jed, Captain Midnight, Jack Armstrong, Superman, Don Winslow of the Navy.* And the nighttime programs: *I Love a Mystery, Suspense, The Adventures of Sam Spade.* And the Sunday programs: *The Shadow, Quiet, Please, The Mollé Mystery Theater.*

We became good friends. He had told his mother and father about "Mr. Rosenthal," who was his friend, but they'd spanked him for the *Startling Stories,* because they thought he'd stolen it. So he stopped telling them about me. That was all right; it made the bond between us stronger.

One afternoon we went down behind the Colony Lumber Company, through the woods and the weeds to the old condemned pond. Gus told me he used to go swimming there, and fishing sometimes, for a black oily fish with whiskers. I told him it was a catfish. He liked that. Liked to know the names

280

of things. I told him *that* was called nomenclature, and he laughed to know there was a name for knowing names.

We sat on the piled logs rotting beside the black mirror water, and Gus asked me to tell him what it was like where I lived, and where I'd been, and what I'd done, and everything.

"I ran away from home when I was thirteen, Gus."

"Wasn't you happy there?"

"Well, yes and no. They loved me, my mother and father. They really did. They just didn't understand what I was all about."

There was a pain on my neck. I touched a fingertip to the place. It was a boil beginning to grow. I hadn't had a boil in years, many years, not since I was a . . .

"What's the matter, Mr. Rosenthal?"

"Nothing, Gus. Well, anyhow, I ran away, and joined the carny."

"Huh?"

"A carnival. The Tri-State Shows. We moved through Illinois, Ohio, Pennsylvania, Missouri, even Kansas . . ."

"Boy! A carnival! Just like in *Toby Tyler or Ten Weeks with the Circus?* I really cried when Toby Tyler's monkey got killed, that was the worst part of it, did you do stuff like that when you were with the circus?"

"Carnival."

"Yeah. Uh-huh. Didja?"

"Something like that. I carried water for the animals sometimes, although we only had a few of those, and mostly in the freak show. But usually what I did was clean up and carry food to the performers in their tops—"

"What's that?"

"That's where they sleep, in rigged tarpaulins. You know, tarps."

"Oh. Yeah, I know. Go on, huh."

The rash was all the way up to my shoulder now. It itched like hell, and when I'd gone to the drugstore to get an aerosol spray to relieve it, so it wouldn't spread, I had only to see those round wooden display tables with their glass centers, under which were bottles of Teel tooth liquid, Tangee Red-Red lipstick and nylons with a seam down the back, to know the druggist wouldn't even know what I meant by Bactine or Liquid Band-Aid.

"Well, along about K.C. the carny got busted because there were too many moll dips and cannons and paperhangers in the tip . . ." I waited, his eyes growing huge.

"What's all *thaaat* mean, Mr. Rosenthal?"

"Ah-ha! Fine carny stiff *you'd* make. You don't even know the lingo."

281

"Please, Mr. Rosenthal, please tell me!"

"Well, K.C. is Kansas City, Missouri . . . when it isn't Kansas City, Kansas. Except, really, on the other side of the river is Weston. And busted means thrown in jail, and . . ."

"You were in *jail*?"

"Sure was, little Gus. But let me tell you now. Cannons are pickpockets and moll dips are lady pickpockets, and paperhangers are fellows who write bad checks. And a tip is a group."

"So what happened, what happened?"

"One of these bad guys, one of these cannons, you see, picked the pocket of an assistant district attorney, and we all got thrown in jail. And after a while everyone was released on bail, except me and the Geek. Me, because I wouldn't tell them who I was, because I didn't want to go home, and the Geek, because a carny can find a wetbrain in *any* town to play Geek."

"What's a Geek, huh?"

The Geek was a sixty-year-old alcoholic. So sunk in his own endless drunkenness that he was almost a zombie . . . a wetbrain. He was billed as The Thing, and he lived in a portable pit they carried around, and he bit the heads off snakes and ate live chickens and slept in his own dung. And all for a bottle of gin every day. They locked me in the drunk tank with him. The smell. The smell of sour liquor, oozing with sweat out of his pores, it made me sick, it was a smell I could never forget. And the third day, he went crazy. They wouldn't fix him with gin, and he went crazy. He climbed the bars of the big freestanding drunk tank in the middle of the lockup, and he banged his head against the bars and ceiling where they met, till he fell back and lay there, breathing raggedly, stinking of that terrible smell, his face like a pound of raw meat.

The pain in my stomach was worse now. I took Gus back to Harmon Drive and let him go home.

My weight had dropped to just over a hundred and ten. My clothes didn't fit. The acne and boils were worse. I smelled of witch hazel. Gus was getting more antisocial.

I realized what was happening.

I was alien to my own past. If I stayed much longer, God only knew what would happen to little Gus . . . but certainly I would waste away. Perhaps just vanish. Then . . . would Gus's future cease to exist, too? I had no way of knowing; but my choice was obvious. I had to return.

And couldn't! I was happier here than I'd ever been before. The bigotry and violence Gus had known before I came to him had ceased. They knew he was being watched over. But Gus was becoming more erratic. He was shoplifting toy soldiers and comic books from the Kresge's and constantly defying his parents. It was turning bad. I had to go back.

I told him on a Saturday. We had gone to see a Lash La Rue Western and Val Lewton's *The Cat People* at the Lake Theater. When we came back I parked the car on Mentor Avenue, and we went walking in the big, cool, dark woods that fronted Mentor where it met Harmon Drive.

"Mr. Rosenthal," Gus said. He looked upset.

"Yes, Gus?"

"I gotta problem, sir."

"What's that, Gus?" My head ached. It was a steady needle of pressure above the right eye.

"My mother's gonna send me to a military school."

I remembered. *Oh, God,* I thought. It had been terrible. Precisely the thing *not* to do to a child like Gus.

"They said it was 'cause I was rambunctious. They said they were gonna send me there for a *year* or two. Mr. Rosenthal . . . don't let'm send me there. I didn't mean to be bad. I just wanted to be around you."

My heart slammed inside me. Again. Then again. "Gus, I have to go away."

He stared at me. I heard a soft whimper.

"Take me with you, Mr. Rosenthal. Please. I want to see Galveston. We can drive a dynamite truck in North Carolina. We can go to Matawatchan, Ontario, Canada, and work topping trees, we can sail on boats, Mr. Rosenthal!"

"Gus . . ."

"We can work the carny, Mr. Rosenthal. We can pick peanuts and oranges all across the country. We can hitchhike to San Francisco and ride the cable cars. We can ride the boxcars, Mr. Rosenthal . . . I promise I'll keep my legs inside an' not dangle 'em. I remember what you said about the doors slamming when they hook'm up. I'll keep my legs inside, honest I will. . . ."

He was crying. My head ached hideously. But he was *crying!*

"I'll *have* to go, Gus!"

"You don't care!" He was shouting. "You don't care about me, you don't care what happens to me! You don't care if I die . . . you don't—"

He didn't have to say it: *you don't love me.*

"I do, Gus. I swear to God, I do!"

I looked up at him; he was supposed to be my friend. But he wasn't. He was going to let them send me off to that military school.

283

"I hope you die!"

Oh, dear God, Gus, I am! I turned and ran out of the woods as I watched him run out of the woods.

I drove away. The green Plymouth with the running boards and the heavy body; it was hard steering. The world swam around me. My eyesight blurred. I could feel myself withering away.

I thought I'd left myself behind, but little Gus had followed me out of the woods. Having done it, I now remembered: why had I remembered none of it before? As I drove off down Mentor Avenue, I came out of the woods and saw the big green car starting up, and I ran wildly forward, crouching low, wanting only to go with him, my friend, me. I threw in the clutch and dropped the stick into first and pulled away from the curb as I reached the car and climbed onto the rear fender, pulling my legs up, hanging onto the trunk latch. I drove weaving, my eyes watering and things going first blue then green, hanging on for dear life to the cold latch handle. Cars whipped around, honking madly, trying to tell me that I was on the rear of the car, but I didn't know what they were honking about, and scared their honking would tell me I was back there, hiding.

After I'd gone almost a mile, a car pulled up alongside, and a woman sitting next to the driver looked down at me crouching there, and I made a *please don't tell* sign with my finger to my freezing lips, but the car pulled ahead and the woman rolled down her window and motioned to me. I rolled down my window and the woman yelled across through the rushing wind that I was back there on the rear fender. I pulled over and fear gripped me as the car stopped and I saw me getting out of the door, and I crawled off the car and started running away. But my legs were cramped and cold from having hung on back there, and I ran awkwardly; then coming out of the dark was a road sign, and I hit it, and it hit me in the side of the face, and I fell down, and I ran toward myself, lying there, crying, and I got to him just as I got up and ran off into the gravel yard surrounding the Colony Lumber Company.

Little Gus was bleeding from the forehead where he'd struck the metal sign. He ran into the darkness, and I knew where he was running . . . I had to catch him, to tell him, to make him understand why I had to go away.

I came to the hurricane fence and ran and ran till I found the place where I'd dug out under it, and I slipped down and pulled myself under and got my clothes all dirty, but I got up and ran back behind the Colony Lumber Company, into the sumac and the weeds, till I came to the condemned pond back there. Then I sat down and looked out over the black water. I was crying.

I followed the trail down to the pond. It took me longer to climb over the fence than it had taken him to crawl under it. When I came down to the pond, he was sitting there with a long blade of saw grass in his mouth, crying softly.

I heard him coming, but I didn't turn around.

I came down to him, and crouched behind him. "Hey," I said quietly. "Hey, little Gus."

I wouldn't turn around. I wouldn't.

I spoke his name again, and touched him on the shoulder, and in an instant he was turned to me, hugging me around the chest, crying into my jacket, mumbling over and over, "Don't go, please don't go, please take me with you, please don't leave me here alone . . ."

And I was crying, too. I hugged little Gus, and touched his hair, and felt him holding onto me with all his might, stronger than a seven-year-old should be able to hold on, and I tried to tell him how it was, how it would be: "Gus . . . hey, hey, little Gus, listen to me . . . I *want* to stay, you *know* I want to stay . . . but I can't."

I looked up at him; he was crying, too. It seemed so strange for a grown-up to be crying like that, and I said, "If you leave me *I'll* die. I will!"

I knew it wouldn't do any good to try explaining. He was too young. He wouldn't be able to understand.

He pulled my arms from around him, and he folded my hands in my lap, and he stood up, and I looked at him. He was gonna leave me. I knew he was. I stopped crying. I wouldn't let him see me cry.

I looked down at him. The moonlight held his face in a pale photograph. I wasn't fooling myself. He'd understand. He'd know. I turned and started back up the path. Little Gus didn't follow. He sat there looking back at me. I only turned once to look at him. He was still sitting there like that.

He was watching me. Staring up at me from the pond side. And I knew what instant it had been that had formed me. It wasn't all the people who'd called me a wild kid, or a strange kid, or any of it. It wasn't being poor or being lonely.

I watched him go away. He was my friend. But he didn't have no guts. He didn't. But I'd show him! I'd really show him! I was gonna get out of here, go away, be a big person and do a lot of things, and some day I'd run into him someplace and see him and he'd come up and shake my hand and I'd spit on him. Then I'd beat him up.

He walked up the path and went away. I sat there for a long time, by the pond. Till it got real cold.

I got back in the car, and went to find the way back to the future, where I belonged. It wasn't much, but it was all I had. I would find it . . . I still had the dragoon . . . and there were many stops I'd made on the way to becoming me. Perhaps Kansas City; perhaps Matawatchan, Ontario, Canada; perhaps Galveston; perhaps Shelby, North Carolina.

And crying, I drove. Not for myself, but for myself, for little Gus, for what I'd done to him, forced him to become. Gus . . . Gus!

But . . . oh, God . . . what if I came back again . . . and again? Suddenly, the road did not look familiar.

To Edward Bryant, August 28, 1969:

Dear Ed,
This has a feeling that I recognize from my own work—a bricks-without-straw kind of feeling. When I had a little bitty idea for a story & went ahead and wrote it, because what the hell, why not?, I would get something a lot like this, and sometimes I would sell it and sometimes not. A story like this has just the one thing going for it, just the idea, so it's like a one-legged tripod. If you like to put signs up on your wall, try this one: A TRIPOD HAS THREE LEGS.

To Harlan Ellison, August 29, 1969:

Dear Harlan,
You nit, the only relevant part of this whole mess is paragraph 10 which you wrote into the contract for "Story Without a Title," and that's the part you did not send, so who knows what you wrote? Whatever it was, however, it could not be any use to God or man, because (a) the story has not been published yet and therefore there isn't any copyright to assign, and (b) how the hell is the Register of Copyrights supposed to know that "Story Without a Title" is "One Life, Furnished in Early Poverty?"

From W. Macfarlane, September 3, 1969:

Dear Damon,

. . . While you have been having a good time moving, I have been writing the Apple Day booklet. On the assumption that you are a desultory reader of cereal boxes & the like, I'll put you on the mailing list. Apple Day is the 4th & 5th of October this year so do not hold your breath. Besides, I done the deed in 18 derriere-weary hours.

. . . The reason I had to write the Apple Day booklet was because the woman who wanted to, did a foul job. And do you know what? She signed a covering note to me: Be Sweet.

To Gardner R. Dozois, September 16, 1969:

Dear Gardner,

"Traveler" is way out of reach for *Orbit*, alas, but I like it a lot. Am not going to be much use about marketing because I know damn-all about "mainstream" or the literary markets: the latter, my guess, more likely than former, but chancy to try to sell anything this length to either. Aside from market considerations, I think the ms. would benefit from cutting—parts of it to my eye much better than other parts. Where it works for me is where you have struck some sharp detail: where it doesn't work is where you are wrestling with generalities. . . . Some of these passages look to me like tentative sketches for much longer sections, in which case maybe what you have here is the first cut at a novel. If this has not already occurred to you, please think about.

Please come and stay with us for a week or ten days if you can manage it; no jobs here worth mentioning, but you could rest and recover forces, and make phone calls, write letters &c.

To Barry N. Malzberg, Sept. 15, 1969:

Dear Barry,

I like this one, but what I get is a mild little plip on the dial instead of a great big pizzazz. This indicates to me that 1) all I'm supposed to get is a mild little plip, or 2) my dial is defective, or else 3) the story was supposed to emit a pizzazz but fails to do so. You would tell me that I should be able to decide between 2) and 3) at least, but I maintain that in my present state of evolution I can't.

287

RITE OF SPRING

by *Avram Davidson*

"The winter meat is about all *gone*," said Mrs. Robinson.

"So's the winter, for that matter," her husband said. "Al*most* . . ."

". . . *and* the potatoes . . ."

Mr. Robinson got up rather quickly and looked in the bin. "Guess there's enough, though. I can do without greens with my meat. If I have to. But I sure hate to do without potatoes."

"Yes," she said, drily. "I've noticed."

He looked at her, as though for a moment mildly surprised or puzzled. Then, with a faint smile, he put his arm around her. For a moment she stood there, her head bent and touching his. With a little sound of content, next, she moved away. She gestured toward one of the cabinets. "There'll be all *that* to do."

He nodded. "Not time *yet*, though . . . Alice . . ."

"Yes?"

Mr. Robinson coughed. "Boy was trying to get in the girl's room again last night."

She whirled around, quicker than you might have thought. A look of alarm or concern faded from her face. "He didn't, though . . ."

Mr. Robinson shook his head. "Scuttled off quick enough, he heard me coming." And did quick brief mimicry of himself, bleary-eyed, clutching an imaginary bathrobe, coughing a rheumy, old-man's-nighttime cough, and shuffling along noisily. Abruptly he stopped and straightened up, ceased to be an ill and probably querulous old man, was once again stalwart, thickset, and vigorous, for all his gray hairs. He and his wife chuckled.

"Well," he said, "it's natural enough. Healthy young boy. Pretty young girl."

"*That*," she said, "is beside the point— You speak to him, now, Henry. I'll speak to her."

"Done and done and Bradstreet," said Mr. Robinson. He looked out the tightly closed windows. "Getting to be about that time of the season. Fact, it *is* that time of the season. Oh, I shouldn't be surprised . . . any day now . . . Boy out to the shed?"

His wife nodded. As he started getting into his sweater and jacket, she said, "Button up warm now."

Mr. Robinson stepped out the back door and started across the yard. The remnants of last year's vegetable garden lay stark and dead beneath his feet. Looking down, he said, "Well, old friend, we'll put new life into you very

288

soon now." He pushed open the door of a weathered and sturdy old outbuilding. Its smell was cold and faint. Hanging from a beam was a block and tackle and rope and chain. Mr. Robinson pulled, tested, made adjustments, grunted his approval, and went out.

The sound of sawing and chopping ceased as he appeared in the door of the shed. "You doing pretty good, Roger," he said. "Yes, sir, you doing pretty good, Mr. Ames."

Roger picked up an armful of wood and carried it over and stacked it. He wiped his face. He had on it a few freckles and a few pimples and a few hairs. Mr. Robinson put a hand on the boy's biceps and doubled up the boy's arm. "That's good, too," he said. "Better than lifting dumbbells."

A sudden look of cunning came over Roger's stolid face. He swiftly seized the older man in a wrestling hold, heaved. They swayed together for a moment. Then, suddenly, Roger lay on the sawdusty floor and Mr. Robinson was pinning his shoulders to it. "Can't do it yet, can you?" he asked.

"Hey," said Roger. The grip relaxed, the boy started to get up, Mr. Robinson flopped him down again. "Pretty good for an old man with one foot in the grave and another on a banana peel . . . *Now* . . . I got something to tell you, young Roger Ames, and you are going to listen to it, too. You were trying to sneak into Betty's room last night. Weren't you. Yes you were." Roger's face, only faintly flushed, still, from the wrestling, now flooded as red as his shirt. "Now you listen. I am not some old prune who doesn't know that females are built different from men. I know all about that. You ever learn as much about that as me, you be doing pretty well. *I* know what's fun and natural between the sects. *But*. And here's the point, you see, boy. There is a *time*. You been *told* that. And when the time comes, why fine. That's what makes the world go round. That's what makes the grasses grow. The flowers bloom. But that time has not yet come for you. You just *wait*, now, till it does. *I* waited. It won't kill you." He got up.

Roger scrambled up as well. He looked embarrassed and, at the same time, respectful. And, for the present moment, just a bit uncertain. Mr. Robinson said, "Well, now. You've cut wood. You've wrestled. So now let's see you practice catching for a while." And for a while there, in the winter-stale garden between the old house and the out-buildings, he watched and instructed Roger as Roger practiced catching. Somewhere in the house a little bell rang.

Mrs. Robinson was putting things on a tray with attention and dispatch at the same time as she was speaking with Betty. "Toast, butter, jam, honey, cocoa," she counted. "Bless me, *how* that woman does eat. It's a pleasure to behold . . . cookies . . . is there any piece of crisp bacon, cold, from breakfast? She is *very* fond of that . . . What was I saying . . . Oh, there's always so much to think about and to *do* at this time of the year . . ."

"About Roger and, *you* know," Betty said: a slim young girl, rather blossomy about the bosom, with a pale-and-pink and shiny face. "Well, I never encouraged him. I don't even . . . well . . . oh . . . I guess I do *like* him okay, but, oh, sort of like a brother, if you know what I mean, Grandma Robinson." The little bell rang and rang.

Grandma Robinson said that she did know what Betty meant. A little smile crinkled the corners of her mouth and eyes. "As for 'a brother,' well, my, many a girl says that, until a certain time comes, and *then* her mind gets changed quick enough." She deftly laid a neatly ironed napkin over the tray and picked it up. Betty went ahead and opened doors. "Oh, I've no reason to complain of you, dear," said the older woman. "You've been as nice as any girl who's ever lived with us. And I'm sure your mother will be pleased, too. Because it's just as she *said*, child, it's just as she *said*. It's hard raising children right, in the city, teaching them the right ways, the old ways, the things to *know* . . . to *do* . . . and, for *that* matter, *not* to do . . ."

Betty said, "And all those things, you know, in the woods, too . . ."

Mrs. Robinson turned her face, slightly creased with the effort of carrying the tray, and nodded over her shoulder. Betty knocked on the last door. There was a noise from inside, and she opened the door, standing aside for the other to go in.

"Well, Mrs. Machick," said Grandma Robinson, cheerfully, "and here we are, with your half-past ten snack." The room was clean, but it did not smell so.

"Half-past *ten*? You mean more like half-past *twelve*," the woman sitting on the bed said. She was fat. She was very, very fat. Betty deftly pulled up a little table. Mrs. Robinson set the tray down. "No, dear, it's only half-past ten," she said.

"*Sure* it is," said Mrs. Machick, in a low, tight voice. "Oh, sure." She had a small, tight, tiny-tiny mouth, set into the middle of a vast, loose face. Her eyes darted quickly between the lady of the house and the girl, but she didn't meet their own eyes, and then she had eyes only for the tray and what was on it.

"Now. Is that all right?" Mrs. Robinson cocked her head.

"Could you spare it?" the woman on the bed asked. Her brows made quirky little motions. She sighed. She shrugged. All down the front of her nightgown were food stains.

"Now, if there's anything else you'd like, just ring your little bell for it," Mrs. Robinson said, without the slightest trace of annoyance. "If we have it, we'll be glad to bring it to you."

290

"*Sure* you would," Mrs. Machick said. "*Oh*, yeah." She fluttered her nostrils with the breath of the long-suffering, gave her frowzy head a little shake, and began to feed.

Betty and Grandma closed the door and exchanged faint sighs. They were halfway across the front room when a low whistle was heard from outside. They looked at each other, wide-eyed and open-mouthed, then turned and tiptoed swiftly to the windows, not touching the lace curtains. A bird was on the ground in front of the house, investigating the sere remains of last year's grass. Out from behind an evergreen came Roger. It was a marvel how, body crouched, on the tips of his toes, hands out just so, how swiftly and how silently he sped; for all his size and all.

It was over in a matter of seconds.

Everybody cried out, but not very loudly. Roger, followed by Mr. Robinson, turned toward the house. Grandma and Betty bustled about, taking things from drawers and closets. The men came in, Roger with a wide and surprised-silly grin on his face. "Welcome, welcome, first harbinger of spring," said Mrs. Robinson; and, "Sir, we bid you welcome," her husband said, with a slight bow. She poured wine into a silver goblet. The bird's head peeped out between the boy's fingers. He held them over the goblet, as though he were offering the bird a drink. Mr. Robinson took its head between the thumb and forefinger of his left hand and with his right hand he took the shears Betty gave him and cut off its head. The bright blood made little swirls in the pale wine, till Mrs. Robinson, with a silver spoon on the handle of which were quaint and curious engravings much more than half-obscured, stirred the goblet. Then the liquid turned pink. She gave everybody a spoonful of it.

For a moment the house was utterly still.

Then Betty gave her lips an absentminded smack. Then she went absolutely pale. Her eyes flew to Roger. From her now white lips came a sound like the rim of a glass being squeaked. His mouth fell open. His eyes bulged. She fled the room in an instant. The door to the hall slammed behind her. Then another door slammed—the back one. But in between the two times, Roger, uttering a noise between a growl and a howl, had begun his pursuit. There was a crash. ("Didn't even *try* to open *that* one," Mr. Robinson said.) There was a cry, first shrill, then full-throated. There were two noises, quick together, as it might be thud-*thump* or thump-*thud*.

"Well, now," said Mr. Robinson, gently. "He did wait. And it didn't kill him." There were some more noises. A lot more. "Isn't killing *her*, either, presumably," he added.

"It always pays to do things right," his wife said. "You'll get some good greens and potatoes and garden truck *this* year, I shouldn't wonder."

He gave a slow, reflective nod. "You decided what kind of annuals you want out front?" he asked. She started to reply; then, with a tongue click of self-reproof, flung open the front door and emptied the goblet in a wide-scattered toss. Her lips moved. "*There,*" she said, after a moment, closing up. The two older people looked at each other in quiet contentment. They sighed. Nodded briskly.

"Plenty to do," he said. "Even before *those* two are ready to help us. Got to get all those knives and cleavers out of the cabinet and sharpen— Oh. *Oh*, yes. Before I forget." He fetched a pad and an envelope, ink bottle and pen, sat. "To the Editor, Dear Sir," he wrote, in his neat, slow hand. "This morning at"—he pursed his lips, consulted his pocket watch, considered—"at about a quarter-to eleven we sighted the first robin of spring in our front yard. Wonder if this is any kind of a record for recent years? Would be glad to hear from any devoted 'robin-watchers' and followers of other good old ways and customs, who may write me directly if they care to."

In her room across the other side of the house, fat Mrs. Machick rang her little bell.

To W. Macfarlane, September 17, 1969:

Dear Wally,
  This is a pretty good specimen of its kind, but being a well-intentioned person full of illusions about mankind you probably would not believe how many times this story has already been written and published. Dumb aliens keep running into morons and going away. Or children. Blind men. Mules. Camels. Science fiction editors. I am not making up any of these except the last, and I believe if hard pressed I could produce a specimen of that.
  Forgive, and try something next time without any spaceships in it. It is my theory that the stultification of modern s.f. is largely due to spaceships.

292

To Liz Hufford, September 29, 1969:

Dear Liz,
    There are one or two slightly wonky things on the first page of the story; after that it goes beautifully. Could you do something about the pink tongue that appears at the corner of Lorena's mouth? I get all hung up on whose it is, how much is hanging out, etc.

From Virginia Kidd, October 17, 1969:

    . . . Have just worked all night, when a really lovely dawn kind of interrupted me for a quarter hour, and while mulling over what I had accomplished remembered that I had not transmitted a message.

Letter from Lafferty says:

      Re yours of 7 October, or 8, first, sure, Damon can punctuate or arrange the last lines of "All Pieces of a River Shore" any way that seems best. I've said it before that he's probably the best last-line man in the business. And I'm likely the worst. I'm tempted sometimes to put "Uh—ah—that's all" at the end of one of my pieces.

    Of course, he concludes his letter, a page later, with
    Uh—ah—that's all. Love, Raphael A. Lafferty.

To Don Bensen, November 6, 1969:

    . . . The stories in *Orbit* are written by established professionals, as a rule, and it is not up to us to instruct them in matters of style. This extends even to punctuation, where the author's use of commas may be idiosyncratic, not because he doesn't know any better but because that's the way he wants them. It goes even farther than this in some instances. Lafferty's use of substitutes for "said," which I would condemn in anybody else, is part of his personal style and I leave it alone. Grammatical errors, in many cases, are deliberate; this applies most obviously to dialog and first-person narrative, but even in straight narration it

293

is not safe to assume that the author did not know what he was doing.

Orbit's policy for some time has been to make none but the most trivial and obvious editorial changes without the consent of the author. The manuscripts as I submit them have been through this process, and should be regarded as having already been copyedited for style, consistency, &c. Some errors do get by me, and I would be grateful to anybody who would catch these, but they should be unequivocal errors—misspelled words and the like. Anything that is possibly debatable should be allowed to stand.

From Gardner R. Dozois, undated, 1969·

Dear Damon and Kate,
  Well, I made it to New York more or less in one piece. Right at the moment I'm crashing at my friend Doug's place in the East Village. It's a really crummy hole, but at least it's someplace to live. New York so far has been interesting. I got robbed Tuesday night. I was just entering the building when a young Negro came up behind me and pressed a knife against my throat. He forced me up the stairs to the landing just before the roof and went through my pockets, telling me that he was "sick" (a junkie) and that he was going to go to the hospital Saturday but he needed money now or he'd die and not to make any noise or he'd cut my throat. The woman on the landing below almost caught us, and he was so jumpy I'm sure he would have stabbed me if we'd been surprised by anyone. The woman must have heard something, because she came out onto the landing directly below us and looked *down* the stairwell; she didn't look up, or she'd have seen us. All the while, we were crouched on the landing above her, and he was pricking the knife into my throat. Hairy. But she didn't look up, and went away after a minute or so. He finished going through my pockets (he only got $10; fortunately that was all I had on me), told me to be quiet, backed down to the next landing while menacing me with the knife, and then turned and ran. I didn't even bother to tell the cops; the residents tell me this happens constantly here, and in the even "heavier" areas just to the east, they usually beat up or slash or even kill their victims, just for the hell of it. Fun City. I guess New York really is a Summer Festival.

294

To Thom Lee Wharton, December 4, 1969:

Dear Thom,

As I told you over the phone, it was a lucky coincidence that you got in touch when you did. Would have sent "The Bystander" back months ago if I had known where to find you, because the series I wanted it for, "Soundings," aroused zero enthusiasm and I gave it up. Was not then courageous enough to buy the story for *Orbit*. Not sure why I am now, but anyhow, have slipped "The Bystander" into *Orbit 8* between stories by Avram Davidson and R. A. Lafferty, and it looks perfectly natural there, and I am delighted to have it.

THE BYSTANDER

by *Thom Lee Wharton*

Harry Van Outten was sitting on the tall stool behind the bar at Decline And Fall when the chunky man with the straw snap-brim and the attaché case came in. He stood blinking as his eyes got used to the dark, and Harry got a good long look at him and decided who he was. The man ambled over to the bar and Harry took the usual deep breath and waited. The case was put down gently between the man and Harry, and of course the man did not sit down.

"If it's about the fire policy, you'll have to go see Pardie in the Maritime and Commercial Building. Suite H, tell him I sent you."

"Mr. Van Outten?"

"Doctor. DDS. No matter. Listen, I'd like to help you, but the lawyer said I wasn't to mess around with this insurance mess."

"Dr. Harry Van Outten, Orthodontic Surgeon, NLP, 22053 Oceanic Avenue, Bournemouth, N.J." (He said it "EnJay.") "This address."

"NLP?"

"No Longer Practicing."

"How'd you know that? Would you like a drink?"

"My name is Roseboom," said the chunky man, and pulled out a little

295

vinyl card case with his picture and thumbprint set into it. The card had "Federal Bureau of Investigation" printed across the top.

"*Oh*, yeah," said Harry, leaning forward on the stool. "What can I do for you, Mr. Rosenbloom?"

"That's Rose-boom." The man looked at Harry's hand and took it and shook it.

"Sorry," said Harry. "Drink?" He clinked the rocks in his gin-gin.

"Maybe later." He looked closely at Harry for a moment. "You know, Doctor . . . Mister. . . ."

"Call me Harry," said Harry.

"You know, Doctor, you don't look very much like your description."

"I've been sick. What description?"

"Bureau files description."

"Why would the FBI have a description of me?"

"Oh, you'd be surprised," said Roseboom vaguely. "Could I talk to you? For a while?"

"How long? What about?"

"A while. Some of your . . . associates."

"Which?"

"Your business associates."

"You mean Joe the Nuts?"

"I hoped you'd come to the point."

"We'll come to the point of an icepick in here," said Harry in a raspy whisper, "this place is bugged to the ears. We'll go for a ride."

Roseboom led the way out the door by several yards, and Harry gimped across the parking lot after him. "Slow down," he called, "this hot blacktop is murder."

"You could've gotten your shoes. I'd wait."

"Never wear 'em. Here." Harry jumped up on the running board of an absolutely mint 1934 Packard Twin Six Phaeton, in buff aluminum with red piping and gray watered-silk upholstery. He twitched his scorched toes for a few seconds and scraped his feet on the running board, then deftly swung the door open and fell behind the towering wheel. "Come on."

Roseboom walked cautiously around the beast and climbed up and in the passenger's side. Harry piloted the big silver car out of the parking lot and turned north on Oceanic Avenue. Roseboom craned his neck to look behind, then slowly turned again to the front.

"That second windshield keeps the wind off your neck if you're riding in front and is vital if you're in back." Roseboom looked over the dash, which was real ebony, taking in the expanse of dials and instruments. "This hickey here is a stopwatch for testing your speedometer, this is a brake fluid gauge, this is a . . . now what the hell is this? Might be a manifold pressure gauge, but then again. . . ."

"What would a car like this cost?"

"Invaluable. Priceless. There *aren't* any more, you see."

Roseboom looked straight ahead through the tall windshield. "You are a successful orthodontist," he said. "Yet most of your income comes from that gin mill we just left. You command a very great deal of money. But I think a toy like this might be beyond even you." He looked over at Harry.

"The car was a gift," said Harry.

"From whom, may I ask?"

"Why?"

"I'm wondering—this is for the record—if any taxes were paid on this gift."

"I honestly wouldn't know," said Harry, glancing back at Roseboom for an instant. The agent narrowed his eyes but saw no guile in Harry's face. "My lawyer takes care of the money."

"Which brings us back to the source of the gift."

"Oh, Joe saw the thing at the opera one night—parked outside the opera house, that is—in Hollywood, I think it was. Said it reminded him of *The Untouchables*." Harry gave one soundless snicker.

"And he bought it then."

"I've got a bill of sale, title, everything's in order."

"I know," said Roseboom after a time. He sat quietly, watching the honky-tonks on Oceanic Avenue fly past. Shortly, Harry noticed that the agent was inspecting him again.

"Something the matter?"

"This nags at me. There are only two elements of the description we have of you that jibe with your actual appearance. The height. The glasses. Now, it says here"—and he was not looking at any paper—"six feet, two thirty-five,,brown hair, gray eyes—"

"Gray is right," said Harry.

"If you like. And you are about six feet. The stoop fools you. *White* hair now, and you weigh"—a pause and a sidewise glance—"about one sixty, one fifty-five."

"I told you I was sick."

"Also, the beard. And mustache."

"I quit shaving when I sold my practice. Only psychiatrists get away with beards. Who brings their kids to a dentist with a beard? You know, that poopsheet you have on me sounds like about four, five years ago."

"At date of compilation, subject forty-two years of age."

"I'm forty-six. This birthday." He thumped the wheel with the heel of his hand. "You must've gotten that stuff from my driver's license or something."

"Mmmm," said Roseboom, nodding vaguely, "I concede that you were sick."

"*Oh*, yeah," said Harry.

"What with?"

"Gastroenteritis," said Harry, after a pause. "Recurrent. Gets worse as you get older, I guess."

"I knew dysentery was recurrent. I never heard that about gastrowhoozis. When contracted?"

"You sound like a doctor."

"Small talk. I don't care—professionally—what you've got. What *illness*."

"I picked it up in the Caribbean about four years ago," said Harry, softly. "Somebody forgot to wash their hands Before Leaving This Rest Room and went and put together our hors d'oeuvres."

" 'Our'?"

"My wife and boy. They died of it. The boy on the island, my wife in Miami. After she heard. Never eat raw fish."

"I'm sorry."

"Thanks. I mean it," he added quickly.

"To get back to Joe the Nuts," said Roseboom.

"Just a minute," said Harry. There was a pause of ten or fifteen seconds, then Harry braked the car to a near stop and turned sharply to the right, up a dirt road that was really only two ruts through a vacant lot overgrown with brown marsh grass. They breasted a low hill—really a sand dune, Roseboom realized—and saw the ocean. Harry let the car roll ahead a little into softening sand and then stopped it and turned off the motor. "Come on," said Harry. They got out of the car. Roseboom sank to his ankles in soft, hot sand. "Leave your shoes and socks." Roseboom sat on the wide running board and pulled them off. He knocked the shoes together, sending a cloud of sand downwind. "Don't get it on the car," called Harry.

Roseboom caught up with him, and they trudged together through the sand and grass tufts toward a tall oblong structure half on the beach and half in the low surf. There was a rusty metal ladder set in its landward side. Harry shouldered ahead, heaved himself up, and continued to climb without a word. Roseboom saw him disappear into a low doorway about twenty feet from the ground and then followed him. Roseboom heaved himself into a low-ceilinged room about thirty feet square and saw Harry on the seaward side, looking out a narrow horizontal window. The walls, Roseboom saw, must have been a foot thick. There were pocks and cracks in them, and bits of rusty reinforcing skeleton were visible here and there. He guessed that the thing must have been fifty feet high altogether. "What's upstairs?"

"Another room like this. Roof. We could go up there now, but it's like a frying pan this time of day." He intercepted Roseboom's look. "Watchtower left from War Two. There were a lot of tankers getting sunk off this coast. There'd be six or eight guys in here, Coast Guard, all weathers, looking for submarines, smoke, like that."

Roseboom looked at him with a grin. "Not bugged?"

"Someday the thing'll fall into the water. Anyway, I don't think anybody knows the way I come here. At least nobody ever followed me or was here, except some kids who come to roast marshmallows and screw and like that."

"You come here often."

"*Oh*, yeah. I like to watch the sea," he said simply, looking out the view slit again.

"How did you know your own place was bugged?"

"Well, I did it myself. Early in the game, that was. Then somebody, I don' know, maybe Christmas Angel, some of the boys, added some little hickeys of their own. You can hear 'em on the phones. Lights dim out every once in a while. You'd be surprised—no, I guess you wouldn't—at what goes on in those back rooms some nights." Roseboom nodded and continued to look straight at Harry, who wiped his rust-stained palms on his spotless white bell-bottomed slacks, looked once around the room, then back out at the ocean.

"You bought into Decline And Fall in nineteen sixty-six," prompted Roseboom.

"*Oh*, yeah. I came back here, tried to pick up my practice. You know. I had this big-ass house down the coast, in Lochmere, on the Bay. Hundred'n a quarter thousand. Pool. Heated pool. Vacuum cleaners in the baseboards. Boat dock. Big playroom. You know how I felt when I saw that playroom. Jesus Christ.

"Well, I tried to stick it out there. The place wasn't quite paid off, I had a good practice, lots of consulting work, my own lab, four bright young kid associates, going to all be partners someday. Whole floor in a new building. Eight chairs, little operating theater, even. Mostly just for show.

"And. I never had much time to indulge myself, really, just in that upper-middle suburbs kind of way. The lawn. The parties. The concerts. Running the pie throw at the church fair. You know. I really didn't know how to go about it any other way.

"I tried. I had the people from Dunhill's come down and survey the place, turn the next-to-biggest bathroom into a room-size humidor. Bought three thousand Royal Jamaica Churchills. Ever smoke a Churchill?'' Roseboom shook his head. ''Here. Buck twenty-five a crack.''

Roseboom did not smoke. He took the big cigar anyway.

''Then I called Frederick Wildman. I don't mean Frederick Wildman's goddamn secretary, I mean Frederick. Wildman. He came down. Him. We put together a wine and cordial celler. He also sold me a couple of barrels of scotch. Glenlivet Waters, it's called. Apparently they don't bottle it at all. That's how Decline And Fall got such a reputation for wines and brandies, by the way. That's *my* cellar down in the cellar. If you follow me.

''Then I had a few more alterations made. A sauna. A seven-foot-deep bathtub. That just about killed my wife's insurance. Turned the Buick in on a Cad with a few refinements. Mostly a bar.

''I got myself a maid after the first couple of big dinner parties I gave to dispel the . . . what? It wasn't *gloom*, exactly. . . . A maid, after a decent period of mourning. Lives-in-gives-out, as the saying goes. *That* was a little girl. Between her and that fountain of booze, I wouldn't have lasted long. It was that empty, empty house. And I hadn't even gotten *started* on drugs yet.'' He was talking quietly, conversationally, but Roseboom saw that he was wringing his hands very slowly and very hard.

''Then one night. I think it was New Year's, sixty-six, I was driving along Oceanic Avenue, blitzed out of my mind, as usual, when all of a sudden, this fire engine comes blasting by me on the *right*. Of course I was probably driving on the left anyway. Well, this aroused some atavistic drunk-ass response in me, so I took off chasing it. Now that was a wild ride. I should mention that there were a bunch of others behind me. I kept those red lights in sight up ahead and drove. Spray was coming over the seawall and freezing in the air, and that road was just like glass. Anyway, I stayed alive until I came up on the place that was burning. I spun out turning into the lot—hit the big marble seal by the exit sign—and crumpled the Cad up a little.

''Anyway, I was out there looking over the damage, freezing to death and staggering and falling on my face, half from ice and half from booze, up comes this little guy with tears running down his face, yelling, 'No insurance! No insurance! No insurance even for fires! You might's well go away, no money for you here!'

''Well, I told him I wasn't going to sue, it was my fault, I was drunk, and so on for about a minute. After the third time I said 'drunk,' his face lit up, and he grabbed me and hugged me and said 'Me, too!' And be damned if he didn't have half a Pinch bottle under his apron.

''So then, we got in the Cad and watched the fire and butchered the Pinch.

What he'd left. The place didn't burn badly, just a lot of decor and the kitchen wiped out. And there were some fur coats and so on that they were going to be liable for. Just for the record, his name was Tibor Telredy, and the place was called Ungaria, Goulash Our Specialty. Telredy was a Hungarian Freedom Fighter who'd gone into his family pretty deep to set up the place; his mother did the cooking, his father played violin and so on, besides their life savings on the line. He just hadn't had anything left over for insurance.

"I don't know if it was booze, boredom, or genius, but I started to talk the deal right then and there. Him being drunk didn't hurt any. Anyhow, we worked it out, sitting there in that bunged-up Cadillac with the heater running fit to roast your ass off, guzzling raw booze right from that bulky bottle. My collar was wilted next morning from what ran down my chin that night. Anyhow, we worked it out. I'd cover all his liabilities, pay for incidentals like legal fees and so on, and buy him out for . . ." Harry looked appraisingly at the FBI man for a second. "If you want to know, I guess you could find out. Ninety thou. Go on, you say it if you want. Others have accused me of setting bombs in orphanages.

"I had to sell the house to cover it all, which wasn't a bad idea. Didn't take much of a loss. It cost me about forty to cover liabilities—there were a few cars on fire behind the place that he neglected to point out at the time—and about another sixty to get the place fixed up the way I wanted. The way it is now. With my penthouse on the third floor, the pool tables, the stage and all. You know, I looked up the original title on that land and house. Decline And Fall is a restaurant, bar, cocktail lounge, grill, and cabaret with occasional dinner-theater, which can seat four hundred people on two floors and in the Wine Cellar Room. It was built in nineteen ten as a *summer* house for *one* family! We've lost something somewhere."

"What happened to the former owner?"

"I got a postcard from him about a year ago. He's teaching Slavic history at Southern California. Asked if I wanted to join the Minutemen."

"Did you?"

"Why should I? When I've got the Mafia?"

They looked each other in the eye for a little while, and then Harry looked back out to sea.

"Well, Decline And Fall opened, all right. I handed over the practice to the boys—taught them how to incorporate, first—and arranged for them to pay me a percentage for ninety-nine years or until my death, whichever happens first. Then I moved in on the third floor and tended bar and washed glasses. Didn't even get help, at first. But this resort-area trade just keeps coming and coming. I got tired out at last. But it took time to build up a

301

clientele, especially without a working kitchen—I didn't know much about the business then—and I had some problems."

"Such as what?"

"I'll skip over the little ones, because you want to hear about Joe and his Family. Anyway, that summer, there was a motorcycle gang hit town. Remember?"

"No."

"Well, they hit it. First it was just messing around a lot in the streets. Then the cops got on 'em and they had to go to ground someplace." Harry looked over his shoulder at the FBI man. "Usually it's a bar they pick."

"And it was yours."

"You bet it was. My regular customers—gone! The furniture was crumbling. The bastards never drank anything but draft beer and they'd get on a jag where they'd break glasses after each round. Then they dragged some woman in off the street and just about gangbanged her on the pool table before I got back from upstairs with the shotgun. I kept it under the bar after that."

"Got a permit?"

"You be damned. Anyhow, that cooled them down a little. Things were halfway back to normal. Things looked good, I was meeting expenses and beating trade out of the other locals. Then. Then one night the Big Sprocket or whatever they call him got paroled and crushed into town from California. The whole bunch came in and set up a long course of getting pie-eyed for themselves. They chased off the other customers in about five minutes.

"Except for a bunch of guys sitting in the back. In the big booth. These were guys I'd never seen before, off a charter boat. They were the usual fishing types—baseball caps, polo shirts, three-day beards—you know. They weren't paying any attention to what was going on up front, and the Big Sprocket saw that they weren't. He hitched up his jeans and walked back there and told them to buy a round for the house or get the hell out. One says, 'Can we drink up before we leave?' but Big Sprocket had wandered away.

"I guess somebody must've gone to the phone. I don't know who or when. Anyway, a half hour later, Big Sprock remembered them, and he went back with a mug of beer in each hand and said, 'Are you mutherfuckers still here?' And the first guy he'd talked to stood up, very soft-spoken and almost fatherly, and said, 'We better take this discussion outside,' and Big Sprocket says, 'You bet your ass we better,' and he led the way out, with his whole mob following him. And those fishing types.

"By this time, *I* was on the phone, but somebody'd popped the wires out. So I had a gin-gin and I got the shotgun and filled my pockets with shells and started for the porch. By then, there were sounds of a real, earnest difference

302

of opinion to be heard issuing from the front parking lot.'' Harry grinned and smacked his lips at the memory.

"I opened those swinging doors and walked out like Long John Silver onto that quarterdeck,'' said Harry, "and there was quite a rumble out there. But it was just about over. Down at the end of each driveway, somebody had parked a dump truck. In the middle of the lot there was a big pile of motorcycle parts. There were four or five guys down there, taking their time about tossing these little bits of motorcycles onto the one truck, the one parked in the 'enter' driveway. Then there were four or five guys with sledgehammers and spud bars tearing what must've been the last few motorcycles apart and throwing the bits and pieces onto the pile. And right in front of the big front steps were forty or fifty guys with baseball bats, brass knucks, sandbags, blackjacks, loaded canes, and what-all, just beating the living hell out of Big Sprocket and his mob.

"I just sort of stood there. Frozen, you know, at the sight. I thought I was really going to have to shoot somebody, and I was so relieved that I didn't have to, at least right away, that I just fell into one of those big rattan chairs. You saw 'em, the ones on the front porch for the neckers and honeymooners, moon over the vasty sea, and all that. Then, somebody put a hand on my shoulder. I practically had a stroke. Then I looked over beside me. There were those fishermen, sitting in these chairs, taking their lordly ease, sipping fresh boozes—and I don't know where they came from, I didn't serve 'em—watching the show just like they'd watch the Wednesday night fights.

" 'Here, old buddy,' says one of them, the one closest to me, who'd put his hand on my shoulder. 'Have a drink. These are almost as good as yours.' And I took it. What it was, I couldn't tell you. I made it go in three seconds, and he grinned at me, and squeezed my shoulder really buddy-buddy and handed me another one.

"Well, to keep from boring you, those guys in the lot and in the driveway finished beating those motorbikers to a bloody pulp and disposing of their mounts at the same time. Some of them took a whack or two at some of the bodies, then started to throw the remains onto the other truck, the one parked in the exit.

" 'Hey, Frank!' the guy beside me calls out. One of the batmen turned and came a few paces toward us. 'Dump 'em in the quarry. My quarry, not yours. Show 'em the Hand.' And the guy nodded and laughed and went about his business. Then the guy next to me turned and said, 'And now a gentleman can drink in peace,' and he drained his drink. Then he said, 'You've got one of the best places I ever saw. Come on back in and build us some more.' Then he said, 'You like Italian food?' ''

303

Harry looked at Roseboom. "I guess that was the first hint I ever had." Roseboom nodded.

"We got back into the bar," said Harry, "and I was setting them up for the house—the fishermen and about five others—when he introduced himself. 'I'm Joe Nucci,' he said, and I told him who I was. He nodded and said, 'Uh-huh. Glad to meet you.' Then he told me who the other guys were." Harry looked at Roseboom again. "All out-of-towners, except Christmas Angel."

"Yeah," said Roseboom.

"Well, we all socked 'em down with both hands for about two hours, and a couple of guys all covered with dust, T-shirts, work pants, you know, came in, and they looked at Joe and he lifted his eyebrows and they just nodded and sat down at the other end of the bar. I just served them two triples and they said 'Thank you,' and 'Thank you.'

"I guess it was that 'Italian food' business that got Joe and I talking about . . . business. 'Goddamn it, Harry old buddy,' he kept saying, 'a guy who runs such a hell of a bar has got to have a kitchen, too! And what could it be with a name like that but a *guinea* kitchen?' And I explained how I was going to get the kitchen running early next year, with help and all, and hire a pianist, and have a free lunch in the bar, and he kept pounding on the bar and hissing. 'Yeah! Right! Great!' Hell, I told it to him just like it is now—you saw it. And he nodded, and grinned, and kept punching me in the shoulder, and I never had a chance to think about closing time, so they stayed till four thirty. But somebody thought to shut off the sign." Harry stared off at the sea, remembering. "We were telling each other our life stories all night. Then he waved from the front porch, wiggled his fingers, he still had a drink in each hand, and he yelled, 'Don't forget what I said, Harry, boy!' and he said, 'Don't worry any more about that dentist shit! You're a *community service* now!' " Harry turned around. "And you know, I'm as good a restaurateur as I ever was an orthodontist?"

"What then?" asked Roseboom.

"Well, I started to get phone calls. This designer. That manufacturer. Beautiful terms. If I sounded reluctant, why, they'd come down a few thousand! I couldn't afford *not* to get that goddamn kitchen all outfitted and working! Then, when the stuff was all installed, and painted, and the drawers full of knives and like that, and we had lots of flour and all around, this fat guy comes walking in one day. 'I am Ercole Barone,' he says. 'Where is my kitchen?' " Harry paused. "You don't know who Ercole Barone is."

"No," said Roseboom. "Should I?"

Harry sighed. "Vulgarian," he said. "I shouldn't say that, because I

304

didn't know myself. All I knew was that this huge guy who looked like Oliver Hardy, if Oliver Hardy had been born in Rome, had come in and started to turn out these unbelievable meals. There was one sent to me on the third floor, every day, nine a.m., three thirty, and nine p.m., unless I sent word to hold it. My God,'' said Harry, remembering.

He recovered himself. "Ercole Barone is the master chef of a well-known restaurant in New York whose name I dare not divulge. He plans the menus for a shipping line and four airlines on the side. He works in town nine months out of the year." Harry looked at Roseboom, saw he was not impressed, and scowled. "The other three, he works for me. The Italian legation and the Italian Mission to the UN drives here once a week, summers, in DPL-licensed cars, to eat Barone's cooking. I have seen a silver-haired diplomat weeping into a plate of *scampi Fra Diavolo*, and there is hardly a man among them who is not in tears when he has to leave.

"Then there is the little old lady who comes in every day to make the pasta dough and pizza crusts. She does not speak a word of English. She arrives in a rented limousine. She turns out more starch than the farms of Idaho, finishes at four p.m., walks to the back door, and Barone gives her two twenty-dollar bills I have given him for this purpose. I ask why only forty bucks? Why two twenties? And I always get the same reply: 'Twenty for pay, twenty for carfare.' She comes in by private plane from *somewhere*, is met by a limousine, driven to my doorstep, and then every day at four, driven back to meet her plane at the local airport.

"Then there's the clientele. And the entertainment. The old days of serving gin and tonics to the beach bums are long gone. Sure, we let the suntanned, windblown crowd in afternoons, but at night, it's different. If we ever had a fire like poor Telredy's, the bill for the furs in the checkroom would be bigger than the cost of the whole building, burned flat. We don't just get the gold-plate trade from the trotting track, and the wanderers from the city! There were plates from nineteen states in that parking lot one night!"

Harry caught himself and lowered his voice. "The entertainment. Yeah. We don't *have* any. It's taxed. But what do we do when a truck rolls up one afternoon, delivers us a very special concert piano, and at nine that night, a certain blind jazz pianist shows up for dinner and then kids on the keys for a few hours afterward? Or when a British rock group comes for *fettucine Alfredo* and gigs until five the next morning? Now, this is not every day. The everyday stuff is Joe the Nuts singing Verdi, or his buddies singing . . . what they sing. What *he* sings."

Roseboom started to speak, and Harry put up his hand wearily. "I'm not naming any names." He scratched his chest reflectively. "One night he even had his *daughter* with him. Nobody even thought to turn out the sign that night.

"And then there's Joe. He's really pretty good. And he puts his heart into it, it's as much fun to watch as to listen. You know how he worked as a singing waiter when he was a kid. Do you know one thing that preys on Joe's mind? That he's never been able to get Franco Corelli to come in for a few days. Corelli is his idol."

"A *capo don* of the Mafia," said Roseboom, "working as a singing waiter. Dear God, no!"

"We don't say 'Mafia,' " said Harry. " 'Mafia' is a bad word. Old hat. It's usually 'the Family,' or 'the Honored Society,' or—this is Joe talking—'We the People.' "

Roseboom gave him a hard look. "When were the firm financial arrangements made?"

"Weren't," said Harry.

"You keep no records? I think, just speaking off the top of my head, that you people are all in trouble."

"Records? My taxes are in order. I'm not a vital industry, subject to audits by state or federal governments. As somebody or other once said, as long as the law can't require me to be literate, it can't make me keep records. They tell me I've got a pretty good tax lawyer."

"Don't you know for sure?"

"I'm in pretty good shape," said Harry, quietly. "I'm rich, and I'm not in jail. I'm enjoying life for the first time . . . in a long time."

Roseboom was silent for a while. Then he said, "I was going to ask you—I *do* ask you to testify at some future date, to a grand jury soon to be constituted, against your Mafia connections."

"Why?" said Harry.

"Why?" yelled Roseboom. "They've taken over your business, they've put you under their thumb—"

"How's that? *I* run my business. And I do a good job. What they're doing is throwing business my way and helping me keep on top. And, mister, it's pure cream." He paused reflectively. "Now, it is true that Joe put a safe in my office that only he and Christmas Angel know the combination to, and that the Angel handles the receipts. But the Angel is Joe's employee, and Joe is my friend. My own take has gone up every year, and I can't see anything significant being drained off."

" 'Thou shalt not muzzle the ox, when that he treadeth out the grain,' " said Roseboom, through his teeth. "What do you mean by 'significant'?"

"I mean that two places have changed hands on that strip this year.
306

Nothing to do with the Family. They just couldn't hack it. If I was being milked the way you seem to think I am, I'd be in the street myself. As it is, I was asked to bid on one of them. By the owner's lawyer, not by the Family. And as far as being under any thumbs," Harry continued, "I went to Martinique last spring to visit my son's grave. To Miami to visit my wife's. I visited my uncle in Chicago, he's a surgeon. I went to St. Petersburg to look into some real estate stuff I got into in the fifties. I could've run out any time, if I wanted to. Your point eludes me."

"Listen to me," said Roseboom. "Joe the Nuts, born Giuseppe Nucci, known as Joseph Nucci, is a *capo don*. He is a big, big gangster, if I may use an old-hat word." He sneering just the slightest bit. "He has operated all over the country as a special representative of the Mafia, gouging small businessmen into signing over their livelihoods to his . . . organization."

"Did you ever hear of the Supreme Protective Agency in New York?" asked Harry. "They go around hitting shopkeepers for ten bucks a month, for 'protection.' Now, that is *really* old hat. And all they do for that ten is to string tape around the edges of the shopwindows, you know, like a burglar alarm, but without alarm wires in it."

"Well?" said Roseboom.

"But it *works*," said Harry. "That green tape is like a danger signal. Joe described it to me once in very memorable terms. He said, 'Those storefronts are *Territory*.'" He paused. "Maybe what you're saying is that I'm Territory, too."

"Yes," said Roseboom, between his teeth, "I guess you are."

"And there's another thing," said Harry. "Joe Nucci is my friend. Now, I've had friends who were drunks. Queers. *Cruel* people, both men and women, and that's the worst of all. Joe is just a nice little guy who loves singing and booze and screwing and who takes pleasure keeping his house in order. That could be *me*, except I can't sing. When I compare him to some of the other friends I've had, he comes out pretty good.

"And now you come in here and tell me that I've got to chuck away my livelihood, my friend, and put myself in criminal suspicion, just because somebody sent you a report or a memo or what the hell to that effect. 'Casino owner'—these places like mine are always 'casinos' in your language—'with Mafia connections,' that's what I'll be for the rest of my life."

"Wait a minute," said Roseboom.

"No. Let me finish with the most cogent argument I've got, again, so as not to stretch this interview out unduly. Now, suppose I *am* a Mafia patsy. What happens? I'm caught between them and you, remember. They come to me and they threaten to cut off my balls, pull out my tongue, kill me, sink me in a block of cement into the bottom of New York Harbor. Kill a few of my friends, burn my house—and my business, they're in the same building—poison my cats, sink my boat . . . and so on.

"Now, what do you threaten? You threaten to put me in *jail*." Harry looked at Roseboom for a long time. Roseboom was looking at the floor. "I'm afraid, Mr. Roseboom, that the Mafia is leading in the bidding for my ass."

"Don't you know we can protect you?" asked Roseboom, but Harry could see that he was tired, and he himself knew that he spoke without conviction.

"Thirty years?" asked Harry. "I might live thirty years. But the chances are against it if I listen to you."

Roseboom stood up and automatically brushed a cloud of cement dust off the seat of his pants. He moved toward the doorway, turned and faced Harry, then stepped gingerly down onto the ladder.

Harry took one last look at the sea, sighed deeply, and followed him down.

* * *

Sleet and snow were racketing at the front windows of Decline And Fall, and Harry looked up, and then curled closer to the blaze in the new fireplace in the empty cocktail lounge. He guessed that he had another hour before the first of the wintertime regulars pulled in—if they came out at all on a night like this. The floodlit pillar Joe the Nuts had sent from Leptis Magna was sheathed in ice. Harry looked out at it and grinned to himself. "Good for the image," Joe had said. God knew it was phallic and classic and Roman enough for anybody. Harry had his sixth gin-gin of the evening at hand and was feeling no pain, literally. The small of his back had begun to bother him late in the fall. He pulled out the letter that had arrived with the pillar and read it again.

Dear Harry:
　　Thanks for the news about Uncle Freddie once again. Everybody needs a vacation. But you know them bastards wouldnt even let me in to SICILY? Then when I left Palermo I couldn't get into Rome. Anyway I got the pillar for you then, don't ask me how, you keep your nose clean like always. Beirut was nice but I like Spain much better. This is just a little fishing village Harry the name of which I will divulge when you call at Wagon-Lits In-

internationales, Barcelona. There are lots of Swede college girls
here, made me think of my man the DUTCHMAN. Im making out
OK with the wife of the local boss of guardia civil, thats state cops.
Harry the wine here is as good as real Vino Rosso and is thirtyfive
cents a quart. Oops thats a leter here in the old country. I never was
as happy travel ng for the family as I am here. To tell you the truth
Harry I think them bastards are just as happy if I stay over here
indefinitely. I didn't mention I get to sing in the local bar, what
they call a bodega! And for money! Its the greatest moment of my
life, more fun than when I was a kid. You know I love to sing. All I
realy need to die happy is to get paid to sing in your place Harry
with Corelli beside me. But its real good here too. When are you
coming over Harry? It isn't going to be too cool for you now that
theres been all that noise around there. Frankie Buttons was pulled
in to a special grand jury that convened just for him. You
remember Frank. Come over here Harry, well have a ball. Between the two of us theres nothing we cant do.

Joe (The Nuts)

Harry refolded the letter and put it back in his breast pocket. He was glad
Joe had gotten out. Of course, he thought, it would be easy anywhere for
Joe. He was like a cat, always landed on his feet. Now, he, Harry . . . But
that was water under the bridge. Harry drained the gin-gin. He got up—it
took him a distressingly long time—and walked to the bar. The barman came
to him, but he continued around behind it. "Never mind," he said. "I'll
build my own."

He sat on the high stool—his high stool—as he worked. He could not feel
the rung of the stool under his feet, and knew that his ankles and feet must be
swelling again. Sitting there reminded him of the previous summer, when
Inspector Roseboom had finally appeared, as Harry had known he, or some
other, would.

Roseboom had been blown to tatters by the bomb under the floorboards of
his car two days after the interview with Harry. Then an anonymous call had
sent FBI men from the local office after one Angelo Christofori, known as
Christmas Angel, who was suspected of killing an agent. The Angel might
have gotten clear if he hadn't locked his car. As he stood there, panting,
trying to work the lock on his Lincoln Continental, two agents had come up
on him and shot him eleven times, as he attempted to escape and/or resist
arrest. The coroner noted that no single one of these bullets lodged in a vital
spot.

After that, it had gone back and forth, for five months or more. An agent here, two or three torpedoes there, killed, bombed, wounded, taken into custody. A file of documents confiscated. An informer made to disappear. A little war, up and down the Jersey coast from the storm center at Decline And Fall. Harry thought that what he had done was better than what Roseboom had wanted him to do. First Harry had warned the Family, through Joe, that the FBI was interested in Decline And Fall. Joe had escaped, Roseboom was murdered, and Harry had blown the whistle on Christmas Angel. By then both sides were at each other, and Harry saw in each day's papers how the battle raged around him. Each morning's edition was delivered by special courier to Decline And Fall at eleven fifteen the previous night. Harry liked a head start on the news.

He had known for fourteen months that he was dying. The back pains had been cancer of both kidneys. It was a while before he could handle his gin-gins altogether comfortably. But Harry persevered. He had been a dentist, and a good one, all his life, except for a few timid and colorless childhood years. His student days were a blank to him once they had passed. He had never been able to get close to any woman but his dead wife. The passing of the boy who had been partly his wife and partly himself had burned something out of him. He reflected that he had not lied completely to Roseboom when he laid his sickness to a plate of pickled fish on a hot night in Martinique. Then he had bought Decline And Fall; he had discovered that his only pleasure was in making, rather than merely doing. He had made Decline And Fall well, and it would be his monument. With Joe's help, he had made it good beyond his dreams. Then came the thing that would unmake him and his creation, and he had done a bit of unmaking himself. Except for Joe, they were all expendable; and he would live—he would—to see the outcome of the battle that he had posed between his enemies as it raged around his house.

He finished the mixing and laid the long spoon down carefully, took up the fresh gin-gin and walked slowly back to his chair by the fire. The paper boy was on his way out but came back for his tip. Harry sat down gently and opened the paper, flipping it so that the pages stood by themselves, the headline boldly exposed. He could hardly wait to see what he had done tonight.

From Gene Wolfe, December 3, 1969:

Dear Damon,

So I'm not wild enough, aren't I? I know what you mean, but actually you've got it backward. Subversion, vice, and riotous living are civilized, and in the worst sense of the word *tame* things. We truly wild creatures are concerned about getting enough to eat and taking care of our cubs. The truth is that you wish me wild enough for painted women, but I am in fact far more wild than that—wild enough for painted dolls and red toy trains.

I am about as wild as mechanical engineers ever get.

And—though I pale to admit it—I have my vice. It is writing, and in everyday circles that is viewed a good deal more seriously than, say, pot probably is in yours. In short, your business is my besetting weakness; your business letters are my pornography, your shop talk my dissipation.

Which gives me a story idea. A nobleman, a pillar of the Jockey Club, who (on alternate Thursdays) creeps away from the Faubourg St. Germain to become (heh, heh!) a Montmartre used-lace merchant. Can't you just see him gloating fierce gloats as he speculates on Society's reaction to the news that he is secretly a *petit commercant*? That's me except that I reverse it—I steal away to become a nobleman.

And you know what the petite bourgeoisie think of that.

(Notice how I'm sneaking in all the French, which I looked up?)

Anyway, I don't know French. *I* got Mouton Saint-Menehould out of a cookbook, a Xerox of which is attached. What I wanted was not to hammer home the "leg" idea again—"leg" occurs (Wessleman's) in the sentence before but one, and "legacy" in the same sentence as the *mouton Saint-Menehould* (which I just realized I misspelled in the story, influenced I suppose by Santa). What I wanted (I think) was "dead as mutton" combined with the gourmet TV dinner idea. *Gigot de mouton* would be okay.

But the food in Crane Wessleman's freezer would be *bad* and *expensive*. Not leg of lamb. (That is, not by that name.)

Anyhow (just for the sake of argument) my little Collins French-English English-French Dictionary says: mouton (moo-*tohn*) nm. sheep, mutton, sheepskin; pl. whitehorses (waves). And my Dictionary Library (an incredible book bound in cheesecloth and printed in blackletter on rejected newspaper stock):

mouton n.m. 1 sheep, 2 (viande) mutton. moutonner vi. (mer) to foam.

The big New Cassell's French Dictionary has: mouton (mu'tō), n.m. Sheep, wether; (Cook) mutton; sheepskin (leather); ram; beetle, monkey (rammer); timber support for bell; balls (of fluff); (fig.) lamb (person), ninny;—

And so on and so on. I think the balls (of fluff) are what my father used to call goofer feathers. His theory was that the goofers played baseball (baisbal?) under my bed at night and lost the feathers sliding into third. He never said who won.

Anyway, darn it Damon, it has to be *mutton*. All American animals after the Norman conquest turned into French meats when they died. Deer to venison, the humble peasants' cows to beef, and so on.

But you'll get back at me. "The Fifth Head of Cerberus" has some French in it, and after all this it's bound to be wrong.

Yes I *would* believe Doubleday has lost eleven stories; in fact I'd believe eleven hundred. Fortunately the carbon of "Horars" looks quite good, so I'm taking you up and sending it. Also the SFWA Bulletin says Harry Harrison's *Nova 1* will be out in February, and if that's not too late we could tear it out of there. Meanwhile carbon enclosed.

I doubt if I could talk much about the encounter group without boring both of us. I went because it was voluntary. In my company you can get out of a direct order pretty often if you've got a good excuse, but when something's strictly voluntary you'd damn well better do it. The idea was to teach you that everyone should participate in decision making and you should thrash things out on a non win-lose basis. (They talked like that.) It's not going to work much. The attractions of me chief, you indian are too great. I had always thought (this is one thing I learned) that the reason for bossy bosses was that nice feeling we all got as kids when we pushed a smaller kid off the sidewalk; but after butting up against it in Grid a few times I find (big discovery—I mean really) that it's not mostly that at all. These people are *scared* of letting go "the reins of power," or even loosening up a little. If you let the indian argue with you eyeball to eyeball you might lose the argument, and what a humiliation! They're really afraid their tender psyches might not stand it.

Does it do some good? Yeah, a little bit.

To Gene Wolfe, December 6, 1969:

Dear Gene,

Aha, now I understand all! (Ah, maintenant je comprends tout!) *Mouton Sainte-Menehould* is a *dish* (un mets), not a cut of meat. For Chrissake. (Zut alors.) So all I have to do is say that Sonya found a *package of* Mouton, etc. If I am wrong about this please advise me, otherwise will go ahead and do it. Whew.

Am saving your letter for some future use. Too good to waste on just me. (I like Chesterton, too.)

THE ENCOUNTER
by Kate Wilhelm

The bus slid to an uneasy stop, two hours late. Snow was eight inches deep, and the white sky met the white ground in a strange world where up and down had become meaningless, where the snow fell horizontally. Crane, supported by the wind and the snow, could have entered the station by walking up the wall, or across the ceiling. His mind seemed adrift, out of touch with the reality of his body. He stamped, scattering snow, bringing some feeling back to his legs, making himself feel the floor beneath his feet. He tried to feel his cheek, to see if he was feverish, but his hands were too numb, his cheek too numb. The heating system of the bus had failed over an hour ago.

The trouble was that he had not dressed for such weather. An overcoat, but no boots, no fur-lined gloves, no woolen scarf to wind and wind about his throat. He stamped and clapped his hands. Others were doing the same.

There had been only nine or ten people on the bus, and some of them were being greeted by others or were slipping out into the storm, home finally or near enough now. The bus driver was talking to an old man who had been in the bus station when they arrived, the ticket agent, probably. He was wearing two sweaters, one heavy, hip-length green that looked home-knit; under it, a turtle-neck gray wool with too-long sleeves that hung from

313

beneath the green sleeves. He had on furry boots that came to his knees, with his sagging pants tucked tightly into them. Beyond him, tossed over one of the wooden benches, was a greatcoat, fleece-lined, long enough to hang to his boot tops. Fleecy gloves bulged from one of the pockets.

"Folks," he said, turning away from the bus driver, "there won't be another bus until sometime in the morning, when they get the roads plowed out some. There's an all-night diner down the road, three-four blocks. Not much else in town's open this time of night."

"Is there a hotel?" A woman, fur coat, shiny patent boots, kid gloves. She had got on at the same station that Crane had; he remembered the whiff of expensive perfume as she had passed him.

"There's the Laughton Inn, ma'am, but it's two miles outsida town and there's no way to get there."

"Oh, for God's sake! You mean this crummy burg doesn't even have a hotel of its own?"

"Four of them, in fact, but they're closed, open again in April. Don't get many people to stay overnight in the wintertimes."

"Okay, okay. Which way's the diner?" She swept a disapproving glance over the bleak station and went to the door, carrying an overnight bag with her.

"Come on, honey. I'm going there, too," the driver said. He pulled on gloves and turned up his collar. He took her arm firmly, transferred the bag to his other hand, then turned to look at the other three or four people in the station. "Anyone else?"

Diner. Glaring lights, jukebox noise without end, the smell of hamburgers and onions, rank coffee and doughnuts saturated with grease. Everyone smoking. Someone would have cards probably, someone a bottle. The woman would sing or cry, or get a fight going. She was a nasty one, he could tell. She'd be bored within an hour. She'd have the guys groping her under the table, in the end booth. The man half-turned, his back shielding her from view, his hand slipping between her buttons, under the blouse, under the slip, the slippery smooth nylon, the tightness of the bra, unfastening it with his other hand. Her low laugh, busy hands. The hard nipple between his fingers now, his own responsive hardness. She had turned to look at the stranded passengers when the driver spoke, and she caught Crane's glance.

"It's a long wait for a Scranton bus, honey," she said.

"I'd just get soaked going to the diner," Crane said, and turned his back on her. His hand hurt, and he opened his clenched fingers and rubbed his hands together hard.

"I sure as hell don't want to wait all night in this rathole," someone else said. "Do you have lockers? I can't carry all this gear."

314

"Lock them up in the office for you," the ticket agent said. He pulled out a bunch of keys and opened a door at the end of the room. A heavyset man followed him, carrying three suitcases. They returned; the door squeaked. The agent locked it again.

"Now, you boys will hold me up, won't you? I don't want to fall down in all that snow."

"Doll, if you fall on your pretty little ass, I'll dry you off personally," the driver said.

"Oh, you will, will you?"

Crane tightened his jaw, trying not to hear them. The outside door opened and a blast of frigid air shook the room. A curtain of snow swept across the floor before the door banged again, and the laughing voices were gone.

"You sure you want to wait here?" the ticket agent asked. "Not very warm in here. And I'm going home in a minute, you know."

"I'm not dressed to walk across the street in this weather, much less four blocks," Crane said.

The agent still hesitated, one hand on his coat. He looked around, as if checking on loose valuables. There was a woman on one of the benches. She was sitting with her head lowered, hands in her lap, legs crossed at the ankles. She wore a dark cloth coat, and her shoes were skimpier than Crane's, three crossing strips of leather attached to paper-thin soles. Black cloth gloves hid her hands. She didn't look up, in the silence that followed, while the two men scrutinized her. It was impossible to guess her age in that pose, with only the dark clothes to go by.

"Ma'am, are you all right?" the agent asked finally.

"Yes, of course. Like the gentleman, I didn't care to wade through the snow. I can wait here."

She raised her head and with a touch of disappointment Crane saw that she was as nondescript as her clothing. When he stopped looking at her, he couldn't remember what she looked like. A woman. Thirty. Thirty-five. Forty. He didn't know. And yet. There was something vaguely familiar about her, as if he should remember her, as if he might have seen her or met her at one time or another. He had a very good memory for faces and names, an invaluable asset for a salesman, and he searched his memory for this woman and came up with nothing.

"Don't you have nothing with you that you could change into?" the agent asked peevishly. "You'd be more comfortable down at the diner."

"I don't have anything but some work with me," she said. Her voice was very patient. "I thought I'd be in the city before the storm came. Late bus, early storm. I'll be fine here."

Again his eyes swept through the dingy room, searching for something to

315

say, not finding anything. He began to pull on his coat, and he seemed to gain forty pounds. "Telephone under the counter, back there," he said finally. "Pay phone's outside under a drift, I reckon."

"Thank you," she said.

The agent continued to dawdle. He pulled on his gloves, checked the rest room to make sure the doors were not locked, that the lights worked. He peered at a thermostat, muttering that you couldn't believe what it said anyways. At the door he stopped once more. He looked like a walking heap of outdoor garments, a clothes pile that had swallowed a man. "Mr.—uh—"

"Crane. Randolph Crane. Manhattan."

"—Uh, yes. Mr. Crane, I'll tell the troopers that you two are up here. And the road boys. Plow'll be out soon's it lets up some. They'll keep an eye open for you, if you need anything. Maybe drop in with some coffee later on."

"Great," Crane said. "That'd be great."

"Okay, then. I wouldn't wander out if I was you. See you in the morning, then. Night."

The icy blast and the inrushing snow made Crane start to shake again. He looked over at the woman who was huddling down, trying to wrap herself up in the skimpy coat.

His shivering eased and he sat down and opened his briefcase and pulled out one of the policies he had taken along to study. This was the first time he had touched it. He hoped the woman would fall asleep and stay asleep until the bus came in the morning. He knew that he wouldn't be able to stretch out on the short benches, not that it would matter anyway. He wasn't the type to relax enough to fall asleep anywhere but in bed.

He stared at the policy, a twenty-year endowment, two years to go to maturity, on the life of William Sanders, age twenty-two. He held it higher, trying to catch the light, but the print was a blur; all he could make out were the headings of the clauses, and these he already knew by heart. He turned the policy over; it was the same on the back, the old familiar print, and the rest a blur. He started to refold the paper to return it to the briefcase. She would think he was crazy, taking it out, looking at it a moment, turning it this way and that, and then putting it back. He pursed his lips and pretended to read.

Sanders, Sanders. What did he want? Four policies, the endowment, a health and accident, a straight life, and a mortgage policy. Covered, protected. Insurance-poor, Sanders had said, throwing the bulky envelope onto Crane's desk. "Consolidate these things somehow. I want cash if I can get it, and out from under the rest."

"But what about your wife, the kids?"

"Ex-wife. If I go, she'll manage. Let her carry insurance on me."

Crane had been as persuasive as he knew how to be, and in the end he had had to promise to assess the policies, to have figures to show cash values, and so on. Disapprovingly, of course.

"You know, dear, you really are getting more stuffy every day," Mary Louise said.

"And if he dies, and his children are left destitute, then will I be so stuffy?"

"I'd rather have the seven hundred dollars myself than see it go to your company year after year."

"That's pretty shortsighted."

"Are you really going to wear that suit to Maggie's party?"

"Changing the subject?"

"Why not? You know what you think and I know what I think and they aren't even within hailing distance of each other."

Mary Louise wore a red velvet gown that was slit to her navel, molded just beneath her breasts by a silver chain, and almost completely bare in the back, down to the curve of her buttocks. The silver chain cut into her tanned back slightly. Crane stared at it.

"New?"

"Yes. I picked it up last week. Pretty?"

"Indecent. I didn't know it was a formal thing tonight."

"Not really. Optional anyway. Some of us decided to dress, that's all." She looked at him in the mirror and said, "I really don't care if you want to wear that suit."

Wordlessly he turned and went back to the closet to find his dinner jacket and black trousers. How easy it would be, a flick of a chain latch, and she'd be stripped to her hips. Was she counting on someone's noticing that? Evers maybe? Or Olivetti! Olivetti? What had he said? Something about women who wore red in public. Like passing out a dance card and pencil, the promise implicit in the gesture?

"Slut!" he said, through teeth so tightly pressed together that his jaws ached.

"What? I'm sorry."

He looked up. The woman in the bus station was watching him across the aisle. She still looked quite cold.

"I am sorry," she said softly. "I thought you spoke."

"No." He stuffed the policy back in his case and fastened it. "Are you warm enough?"

"Not really. The ticket agent wasn't kidding when he said the thermostat lies. According to it, it's seventy-four in here."

317

Crane got up and looked at the thermostat. The adjustment control was gone. The station was abysmally cold. He walked back and forth for a few moments, then paused at the window. The white world, ebbing and growling, changing, changeless. "If I had a cup or something, I could bring in some snow and chill the thermostat. That might make the heat kick on."

"Maybe in the rest room. . . ." He heard her move across the floor, but he didn't turn to look. There was a pink glow now in the whiteness, like a fire in the distance, all but obscured by the intervening clouds of snow. He watched as it grew brighter, darker, almost red; then it went out. The woman returned and stood at his side.

"No cups, but I folded paper towels to make a funnel thing. Will it do?"

He took the funnel. It was sturdy enough, three thicknesses of brown, unabsobent toweling. "Probably better than a cup," he said. "Best stand behind the door. Every time it opens, that blizzard comes right on in."

She nodded and moved away. When he opened the door the wind hit him hard, almost knocking him back into the room, wrenching the door from his hand. It swung wide open and hit the woman. Distantly he heard her gasp of surprise and pain. He reached out and scooped up the funnel full of snow and then pushed the door closed again. He was covered with snow. Breathless, he leaned against the wall. "Are you all right?" he asked after a few moments.

She was holding her left shoulder. "Yes. It caught me by surprise. No harm done. Did you get enough snow?"

He held up the funnel for her to see and then pushed himself away from the wall. Again he had the impression that there was no right side up in the small station. He held the back of one of the benches and moved along it. "The wind took my breath away," he said.

"Or the intense cold. I think I read that breathing in the cold causes as many heart attacks as overexertion."

"Well, it's cold enough out there. About zero by now, I guess." He scooped out some of the snow and held it against the thermostat. "The furnace must be behind this wall, or under this area. Feel how warm it is."

She put her hand on the wall and nodded. "Maybe we can fasten the cup of snow up next to the thermostat." She looked around and then went to the bulletin board. She removed several of the notices and schedules there and brought him the thumbtacks. Crane spilled a little snow getting the tacks into the paper towel and then into the wall. In a few minutes there was a rumble as the furnace came on and almost immediately the station began to feel slightly warmer. Presently the woman took off her coat.

"Success," she said, smiling.

318

"I was beginning to think it had been a mistake after all, not going to the diner."

"So was I."

"I think they are trying to get the snowplows going. I saw a red light a couple of minutes ago. It went out again, but at least someone's trying."

She didn't reply, and after a moment he said, "I'm glad you don't smoke. I gave it up a few months ago, and it would drive me mad to have to smell it through a night like this. Probably I'd go back to them."

"I have some," she said. "I even smoke once in a while. If you decide that you do want them . . ."

"No. No. I wasn't hinting."

"I just wish the lights were better in here. I could get in a whole night's work. I often work at night."

"So do I, but you'd put your eyes out. What—"

"That's all right. What kind of work do I do? An illustrator for Slocum House Catalogue Company. Not very exciting, I'm afraid."

"Oh, you're an artist."

"No. Illustrator. I wanted to become an artist, but . . . things didn't work out that way."

"I'd call you an artist. Maybe because I'm in awe of anyone who can draw, or paint, or do things like that. You're all artists to me."

She shrugged. "And you're an insurance salesman." He stiffened and she got up, saying, "I saw the policy you were looking over, and the briefcase stuffed full of policies and company pamphlets and such. I knew an insurance salesman once."

He realized that he had been about to ask where she was going, and he clamped his jaw again and turned so that he wouldn't watch her go into the ladies' room.

He went to the window. The wind was still at gale force, but so silent. With the door closed, the station seemed far removed from the storm, and looking at it was like watching something wholly unreal, manufactured to amuse him perhaps. There were storm windows, and the building was very sturdy and probably very well insulated. Now, with the furnace working, it was snug and secure. He cupped his hands about his eyes, trying to see past the reflections in the window, but there was nothing. Snow, a drift up to the sill now, and the wind driven snow that was like a sheer curtain being waved from above, touching the windows, fluttering back, touching again, hiding everything behind it.

She was taking a long time. He should have gone when she left. Now he had the awkward moment to face, of excusing himself or not, of timing it so

319

that she wouldn't think he was leaving deliberately in order to dodge something that one or the other said or hinted. She had done it so easily and naturally. He envied people like her. Always so sure of themselves.

"Which face are you wearing tonight, Randy?" Mary Louise reached across the table and touched his cheek, then shook her head. "I can't always tell. When you're the successful salesman, you are so assured, so poised, charming, voluble even."

"And the other times? What am I these times?"

"Afraid."

Drawing back from her hand, tight and self-contained again, watchful, he said, "Isn't it lucky that I can keep the two separated then? How successful a salesman would I be if I put on the wrong face when I went to work?"

"I wonder if mixing it up a little might not be good for you. So you wouldn't sell a million dollars' worth of insurance a year, but you'd be a little happier when you're not working."

"Like you?"

"Not like me, God forbid. But at least I haven't given up looking for something. And you have."

"Yeah. You're looking. In a bottle. In someone else's bed. In buying sprees."

"*C'est la vie.* You can always buzz off, you know."

"And add alimony to my other headaches? No thanks."

Smiling at him, sipping an old-fashioned, infinitely wise and infinitely evil. Were wise women always evil? "My poor Randy. My poor darling. You thought I was everything you were not, and instead you find that I am stamped from the same mold. Number XLM 119543872—afraid of life, only not quite afraid of death. Someone let up on the pressure there. Hardly an indentation even. So I can lose myself and you can't. A pity, my darling Randy. If we could lose ourselves together, what might we be able to find? We are so good together, you know. Sex with you is still the best of all. I try harder and harder to make you let go all the way. I read manuals and take personalized lessons, all for your sake, darling. All for you. And it does no good. You are my only challenge, you see."

"Stop it! Are you crazy?"

"Ah. Now I know who you are tonight. There you are. Tight mouth, frowning forehead full of lines, narrowed eyes. You are not so handsome with this face on, you know. Why don't you look at me, Randy?" Her hands across the table again, touching his cheeks, a finger trailing across his lips, a caress or mockery. "You never look at me, you know. You never look at me at all."

He leaned his forehead against the window, and the chill roused him.

320

Where was the woman? He looked at his watch and realized that she had been gone only a few minutes, not the half hour or longer that he had thought. Was the whole night going to be like that? Minutes dragging by like hours? Time distorted until a lifetime could be spent in waiting for one dawn?

He went to the men's room. When he returned, she was sitting in her own place once more, her coat thrown over her shoulders, a sketch pad in her lap.

"Are you cold again?" He felt almost frozen. There was no heat in the men's room.

"Not really. Moving about chilled me. There's a puddle under the funnel, and the snow is gone, but heat is still coming from the radiator."

"I'll have to refill it every half hour or so, I guess."

"The driver said it's supposed to go to ten or fifteen below tonight."

Crane shrugged. "After it gets this low, I don't care how much farther it drops. As long as I don't have to be out in it."

She turned her attention to her pad and began to make strong lines. He couldn't tell what she was drawing, only that she didn't hesitate, but drew surely, confidently. He opened his briefcase and got out his schedule book. It was no use, he couldn't read the small print in the poor lighting of the station. He rummaged for something that he would be able to concentrate on. He was grateful when she spoke again:

"It was so stupid to start out tonight. I could have waited until tomorrow. I'm not bound by a time clock or anything."

"That's just what I was thinking. I was afraid of being snowed in for several days. We were at Sky Mount Ski Lodge, and everyone else was cheering the storm's approach. Do you ski?"

"Some, not very well. The cold takes my breath away, hitting me in the face like that."

He stared at her for a moment, opened his mouth to agree, then closed it again. It was as if she was anticipating what he was going to say.

"Don't be so silly, Randy. All you have to do is wear the muffler around your mouth and nose. And the goggles on your eyes. Nothing is exposed then. You're just too lazy to ski."

"Okay, lazy. I know this, I'm bored to death here. I haven't been warm since we left the apartment, and my legs ache. That was a nasty fall I had this morning. I'm sore. I have a headache from the glare of the snow, and I think it's asinine to freeze for two hours in order to slide down a mountain a couple of times. I'm going back to the city."

"But our reservation is through Saturday night. Paid in advance."

"Stay. Be my guest. Have yourself a ball. You and McCone make a good pair, and his wife seems content to sit on the sidelines and watch you. Did

321

you really think that anemic blonde would appeal to me? Did you think we'd be too busy together to notice what you were up to?''

"Tracy? To tell the truth I hadn't given her a thought. I didn't know she didn't ski until this afternoon. I don't know why Mac brought her here. Any more than I know why you came along."

"Come on home with me. Let's pack up and leave before the storm begins. We can stop at that nice old antique inn on the way home, where they always have pheasant pie. Remember?''

"Darling, I came to ski. You will leave the car here, won't you? I'll need it to get the skis back home, and our gear. Isn't there a bus or something?''

"Mary Louise, this morning on the slope, didn't you really see me? You know, when your ski pole got away from you.''

"What in the world are you talking about? You were behind me. How could I have seen you? I didn't even know you had started down.''

"Okay. Forget it. I'll give you a call when I get to the apartment.''

"Yes, do. You can leave a message at the desk if I don't answer.''

The woman held up her sketch and narrowed her eyes. She ripped out the page and crumpled it, tossed it into the wastecan.

"I think I'm too tired after all.''

"It's getting cold in here again. Your hands are probably too cold.'' He got up and took the funnel from the wall. "I'll get more snow and see if we can't get the furnace going again.''

"You should put something over your face, so the cold air won't be such a shock. Don't you have a muffler?''

He stopped. He had crushed the funnel, he realized, and he tried to smooth it again without letting her see what he had done. He decided that it would do, and opened the door. A drift had formed, and a foot of snow fell into the station. The wind was colder, sharper, almost deliberately cutting. He was blinded by the wind and the snow that was driven into his face. He filled the funnel and tried to close the door again, but the drift was in the way. He pushed, trying to use the door as a snowplow. More snow was being blown in, and finally he had to use his hands, push the snow out of the way, not outside, but to one side of the door. At last he had it clear enough and he slammed the door, more winded this time than before. His throat felt raw, and he felt a constriction about his chest.

"It's getting worse all the time. I couldn't even see the bus, nothing but a mountain of snow.''

"Ground blizzard, I suspect. When it blows like this you can't tell how much of it is new snow and how much is just fallen snow being blown about. The drifts will be tremendous tomorrow.'' She smiled. "I remember how we loved it when this happened when we were kids. The drifts are exciting, so pure, so high. Sometimes they glaze over and you can play Glass Mountain. I used to be the princess.''

Crane was shivering again. He forced his hands to be steady as he pushed the thumbtacks into the funnel to hold it in place next to the thermostat. He had to clear his throat before he could speak. "Did the prince ever reach you?''

''No. Eventually I just slid back down and went home.''

''Where? Where did you live?''

''Outside Chicago, near the lake.''

He spun around. ''Who are you?'' He grabbed the back of a bench and clutched it hard. She stared at him. He had screamed at her, and he didn't know why. ''I'm sorry,'' he said. ''You keep saying things that I'm thinking. I was thinking of that game, of how I never could make it to the top.''

''Near Lake Michigan?''

''On the shores almost.''

She nodded.

''I guess all kids play games like that in the snow,'' he said. ''Strange that we should have come from the same general area. Did your milk freeze on the back steps, stick up out of the bottle, with the cap at an angle?''

''Yes. And those awful cloakrooms at school, where you had to strip off snowsuits and boots, and step in icy water before you could get your indoors shoes on.''

''And sloshing through the thaws, wet every damn day. I was wet more than I was dry all through grade school.''

''We all were,'' she said, smiling faintly, looking past him.

He almost laughed in his relief. He went to the radiator and put his hands out over it, his back to her. Similar backgrounds, that's all, he said to himself, framing the words carefully. Nothing strange. Nothing eerie. She was just a plain woman who came from the same state, probably the same county that he came from. They might have gone to the same schools, and he would not have noticed her. She was too common, too nondescript to have noticed at the time. And he had been a quiet boy, not particularly noteworthy himself. No sports besides the required ones. No clubs. A few friends, but even there, below average, because they had lived in an area too far removed from most of the kids who went to his school.

''It's only two. Seems like it ought to be morning already, doesn't it.'' She was moving about and he turned to see what she was doing. She had gone behind the counter, where the ticket agent had said there was a telephone. ''A foam cushion,'' she said, holding it up. ''I feel like one of the Swiss Family Robinson, salvaging what might be useful.''

"Too bad there isn't some coffee under there."

"Wish you were in the diner?"

"No. That bitch probably has them all at each other's throats by now, as it is."

"That girl? The one who was so afraid?"

He laughed harshly and sat down. "Girl!"

"No more than twenty, if that much."

He laughed again and shook his head.

"Describe her to me," the woman said. She left the counter and sat down on the bench opposite him, still carrying the foam cushion. It had a black plastic cover, gray foam bulged from a crack. It was disgusting.

Crane said. "The broad was in her late twenties, or possibly thirties—"

"Eighteen to twenty."

"She had a pound of makeup on, nails like a cat."

"Fake nails, chapped hands, calluses. Ten-cent store makeup."

"She had expensive perfume, and a beaver coat. I think beaver."

She laughed gently. "Drugstore spray cologne. Macy's Basement fake fur, about fifty-nine to sixty-five dollars, unless she hit a sale."

"And the kid gloves, and the high patent-leather boots?"

"Vinyl, both of them." She looked at him for an uncomfortable minute, then examined the pillow she had found. "On second thought, I'm not sure that I would want to rest my head on this. It's a little bit disgusting, isn't it?"

"Why did you want me to describe that woman? You have your opinion of what she is; I have mine. There's no way to prove either of our cases without having her before us."

"I don't need to prove anything. I don't care if you think you're right and I'm wrong. I felt very sorry for the girl. I noticed her."

"I noticed her, too."

"What color was her hair, her eyes? How about her mouth, big, small, full? And her nose? Straight, snub, broad?"

He regarded her bitterly for a moment, then shrugged and turned toward the window. He didn't speak.

"You can't describe what she really was like because you didn't see her. You saw the package and made up your mind about the contents. Believe me, she was terrified of the storm, of those men, everything. She needed the security of the driver and people. What about me? Can you describe me?"

He looked, but she was holding the pillow between them and he could see only her hands, long, pale, slender fingers, no rings.

"This is ridiculous," he said after a second. "I have one of those

324

reputations for names and faces. You know, never forget a name, always know the names of the kids, the wife, occupation, and so on."

"Not this side of you. This side refuses to see anyone at all. I wonder why."

"What face are you wearing tonight, Randy?" Mary Louise touching him. "Do you see me? Why don't you look at me?"

Wind whistling past his ears, not really cold yet, not when he was standing still anyway, with the sun warm on him. But racing down the slope, trees to his right, the precipice to his left, the wind was icy. Mary Louise a red streak ahead of him, and somewhere behind him the navy and white blur that was McCone. Holding his own between them. The curve of the trail ahead, the thrill of the downward plummet, and suddenly the openmouthed face of his wife, silent scream, and in the same instant, the ski pole against his legs, tripping him up, the more exciting plunge downward, face in the snow, blinded, over and over, skis gone now, trying to grasp the snow, trying to stop the tumbling, over and over in the snow.

Had his wife tried to kill him?

"Are you all right, Mr. Crane?"

"Yes, of course. Let me describe the last man I sold insurance to, a week ago. Twenty-four, six feet one inch, a tiny, almost invisible scar over his right eyebrow, crinkle lines about his eyes, because he's an outdoor type, very tanned and muscular. He's a professional baseball player, incidentally. His left hand has larger knuckles than the right . . ."

The woman was not listening. She had crossed the station and was standing at the window, trying to see out. "Computer talk," she said. "A meaningless rundown of facts. So he bought a policy for one hundred thousand dollars, straight life, and from now on you won't have to deal with him, be concerned with him at all."

"Why did you say one hundred thousand dollars?"

"No reason. I don't know, obviously."

He chewed his lip and watched her. "Any change out there?"

"Worse, if anything. I don't think you'll be able to use this door at all now. You'd never get it closed. It's half covered with a drift."

"There must be a window or another door that isn't drifted over."

"Storm windows. Maybe there's a back door, but I bet it opens to the office, and the ticket agent locked that."

Crane looked at the windows and found that she was right. The storm windows couldn't be opened from inside. And there wasn't another outside door. The men's room was like a freezer now. He tried to run the water, thinking that possibly cold water would work on the thermostat as well as snow, but nothing came out. The pipes must have frozen. As he started to close the door, he saw a small block-printed sign: "Don't close door all the way, no heat in there, water will freeze up." The toweling wouldn't hold water anyway.

He left the door open a crack and rejoined the woman near the window. "It's got to be this door," he said. "I guess I could open it an inch or two, let that much of the drift fall inside and use it."

"Maybe. But you'll have to be careful."

"Right out of Jack London," he said. "It's seventy-two on the thermometer. How do you feel?"

"Coolish, not bad."

"Okay, we'll wait awhile. Maybe the wind will let up."

He stared at the puddle under the thermostat, and at the other larger one across the room near the door, where the snowdrift had entered the room the last time. The drift had been only a foot high then, and now it was three or four feet. Could he move that much snow without anything to work with, if it came inside?

He shouldn't have started back to town. She had goaded him into it, of course. Had she suspected that he would get stranded somewhere, maybe freeze to death?

"Why don't you come right out and say what you're thinking?" Red pants, red ski jacket, cheeks almost as red.

"I'm not thinking anything. It was an accident."

"You're a liar, Randy! You think I guessed you were there, that I let go hoping to make you fall. Isn't that what you think? Isn't it?"

He shook his head hard. She hadn't said any of that. He hadn't thought of it then. Only now, here, stranded with this half-mad woman. Half-mad? He looked at her and quickly averted his gaze. Why had that thought come to him? She was odd, certainly, probably very lonely, shy. But half-mad?

Why did she watch him so? As if aware of his thoughts, she turned her back and walked to the ladies' room. He had to go too, but he remembered the frozen pipes in the men's room. Maybe she'd fall asleep eventually and he'd be able to slip into her rest room. If not, then he'd wait until morning. Maybe this night had come about in order to give him time to think about him and Mary Louise, to really think it through all the way and come to a decision.

He had met her when he was stationed in Washington, after the Korean War. He had been a captain, assigned to Army Intelligence. She had worked as a private secretary to Senator Robertson of New York. So he had done all right without her up to then. She had introduced him to the president of the company that he worked for now. Knowing that he wanted to become a writer, she had almost forced him into insurance. Fine. It was the right choice. He had told her so a thousand times. But how he had succeeded was still a puzzle to him. He never had tested well on salesmanship on aptitude tests. Too introverted and shy.

"You make other people feel stupid, frankly," she had said once. "You are so tight and so sure of yourself that you don't allow anyone else to have an opinion at all. It's not empathy, like it is with so many good salesmen. It's a kind of sadistic force that you apply."

"Oh, stop it. You're talking nonsense."

"You treat each client like an extension of the policy that you intend to sell to him. Not like a person, but the human counterpart of the slick paper with the clauses and small print. You show the same respect and liking for them as for the policies. They go together. You believe it and make them believe it. Numbers, that's what they are to you. Policy numbers."

"Why do you hang around if you find me so cold and calculating?"

"Oh, it's a game that I play. I know there's a room somewhere where you've locked up part of yourself, and I keep searching for it. Someday I'll find it and open it just a crack, and then I'll run. Because if it ever opens, even a little, everything will come tumbling out and you won't be able to stop any of it. How you'll bleed then, bleed and bleed, and cry and moan. I couldn't stand that. And I can't stand for it not to be so."

Crane put his head down in his hands and rubbed his eyes hard. Without affect, that was the term that she used. Modern man without affect. Schizoid personality. But he also had a nearly split personality. The doctor had told him so. In the six sessions that he had gone to he had learned much of the jargon, and then he had broken it off. Split personality. Schizoid tendencies. Without affect. All to keep himself safe. It seemed to him to be real madness to take away any of the safeties he had painstakingly built, and he had quit the sessions.

And now this strange woman that he was locked up with was warning him not to open the door a crack. He rubbed his eyes harder until there was solid pain there. He had to touch her. The ticket agent had seen her, too, though. He had been concerned about leaving her alone with a strange man all night. So transparently worried about her, worried about Crane. Fishing for his name. He could have told the fool anything. He couldn't remember his face at all, only his clothes.

All right, the woman was real, but strange. She had an uncanny way of anticipating what he was thinking, what he was going to say, what he feared. Maybe these were her fears too.

She came back into the waiting room. She was wearing her black coat buttoned to her neck, her hands in the pockets. She didn't mention the cold.

327

Soon he would have to get more snow, trick the fool thermostat into turning on the furnace. Soon. A maniac must have put it on that wall, the only warm wall in the building. A penny-pinching maniac.

"If you decide to try to get more snow, maybe I should hold the door while you scoop it up," she said, after a long silence. The cold had made her face look pinched, and Crane was shivering under his overcoat.

"Can you hold it?" he asked. "There's a lot of pressure behind that door."

She nodded.

"Okay. I'll take the wastecan and get as much as I can. It'll keep in the men's room. There's no heat in there."

She held the doorknob until he was ready, and when he nodded, she turned it and, bracing the door with her shoulder, let it open several inches. The wind pushed, and the snow spilled through. It was over their heads now, and it came in the entire height of the door. She gave ground and the door was open five or six inches. Crane pulled the snow inside, using both hands, clawing at it. The Augean stable, he thought bitterly, and then joined her behind the door, trying to push it closed again. At least no blast of air had come inside this time. The door was packing the snow, and the inner surface of it was thawing slightly, only to refreeze under the pressure and the cold from the other side. Push, Crane thought at her. Push, you devil. You witch.

Slowly it began to move, scrunching snow. They weren't going to get it closed all the way. They stopped pushing to rest. He was panting hard, and she put her head against the door. After a moment he said, "Do you think you could move one of the benches over here?"

She nodded. He braced himself against the door and was surprised at the increase in the pressure when she left. He heard her wrestling with the bench, but he couldn't turn to see. The snow was gaining again. His feet were slipping on the floor, wet now where some of the snow had melted and was running across the room. He saw the bench from the corner of his eye, and he turned to watch her progress with it. She was pushing it toward him, the back to the wall; the back was too high. It would have to be tilted to go under the doorknob. It was a heavy oak bench. If they could maneuver it in place, it would hold.

For fifteen minutes they worked, grunting, saying nothing, trying to hold the door closed and get the bench under the knob without losing any more ground. Finally it was done. The door was open six inches, white packed snow the entire height of it.

Crane fell onto a bench and stared at the open door, not able to say anything. The woman seemed equally exhausted. At the top of the door, the snow suddenly fell forward, into the station, sifting at first, then falling in a stream. Icy wind followed the snow into the room, and now that the top of the column of snow had been lost, the wind continued to pour into the station, whistling shrilly.

"Well, we know now that the drift isn't really to the top of the building," the woman said wearily. She was staring at the opening.

"My words, almost exactly," Crane said. She always said what he planned to say. He waited.

"We'll have to close it at the top somehow."

He nodded. "In a minute. In a minute."

The cold increased and he knew that he should get busy and try to close the opening, but he felt too numb to cope with it. The furnace couldn't keep up with the draft of below-zero air. His hands were aching with cold, and his toes hurt with a stabbing intensity. Only his mind felt pleasantly numb and he didn't want to think about the problem of closing up the hole.

"You're not falling asleep, are you?"

"For God's sake!" He jerked straight up on the bench and gave her a mean look, a guilty look. "Just shut up and let me try to think, will you?"

"Sorry." She got up and began to pace briskly, hugging her hands to her body. "I'll look around, see if I can find anything that would fit. I simply can't sit still, I'm so cold."

He stared at the hole. There had to be something that would fit over it, stay in place, keep out the wind. He narrowed his eyes, staring, and he saw the wind-driven snow as a liquid running into the station from above, swirling about, only fractionally heavier than the medium that it met on the inside. One continuum, starting in the farthest blackest vacuum of space, taking on form as it reached the highest atmospheric molecules, becoming denser as it neared Earth, almost solid here, but not yet. Not yet. The hole extended to that unimaginable distance where it all began, and the chill spilled down, down, searching for him, wafting about here, searching for him, wanting only to find him, willing then to stop the ceaseless whirl. Coat him, claim him. The woman belonged to the coldness that came from the black of space. He remembered her now.

Korea. The woman. The village. Waiting for the signal. Colder than the station even, snow, flintlike ground, striking sparks from nails in boots, sparks without warmth. If they could fire the village, they would get warm, have food, sleep that night. Harrison, wounded, frozen where he fell. Lorenz, frostbitten; Jakobs, snow-blind. Crane, too tired to think, too hungry to think, too cold to think. "Fire the village." The woman, out of nowhere, urging him back, back up the mountain to the bunkers that were half filled with ice, mines laid now between the bunkers and the valley. Ordering the woman into the village at gunpoint. Spark from his muzzle.

Blessed fire and warmth. But a touch of ice behind the eyes, ice that didn't let him weep when Lorenz died, or when Jakobs, blinded, wandered out and twitched and jerked and pitched over a cliff under a fusillade of bullets. The snow queen, he thought. She's the snow queen, and she touched my eyes with ice.

"Mr. Crane, please wake up. Please!"

He jumped to his feet reaching for his carbine, and only when his hands closed on air did he remember where he was.

"Mr. Crane, I think I know what we can use to close up the hole. Let me show you."

She pulled at his arm and he followed her. She led him into the ladies' room. At the door he tried to pull back, but she tugged. "Look, stacks of paper towels, all folded together. They would be about the right size, wouldn't they? If we wet them, a block of them, and if we can get them up to the hole, they would freeze in place, and the drift could pile up against them and stop blowing into the station. Wouldn't it work?"

She was separating the opened package into thirds, her hands busy, her eyes downcast, not seeing him at all. Crane, slightly to one side of her, a step behind, stared at the double image in the mirror. He continued to watch the mirror as his hands reached out for her and closed about her throat. There was no struggle. She simply closed her eyes and became very limp, and he let her fall. Then he took the wad of towels and held it under the water for a few moments and returned to the waiting room with it. He had to clear snow from the approach to the door, and then he had to move the bench that was holding the door, carefully, not letting it become dislodged. He dragged a second bench to the door and climbed on it and pushed the wet wad of towels into the opening. He held it several minutes, until he could feel the freezing paper start to stiffen beneath his fingers. He climbed down.

"That should do it," the woman said.

"But you're dead."

Mary Louise threw the sugar bowl at him, trailing a line of sugar across the room.

He smiled. "Wishful thinking," he/she said.

"You're dead inside. You're shriveled up and dried up and rotting inside. When did you last feel anything? My God! You can't create anything, you are afraid of creating anything, even our child!"

"I don't believe it was our child."

"You don't dare believe it. Or admit that you know it was."

He slapped her. The only time that he ever hit her. And her so pale from the operation, so weak from the loss of blood. The slap meant nothing to him, his hand meeting her cheek, leaving a red print there.

330

"Murderer!"

"You crazy bitch! You're the one who had the abortion! You wanted it!"

"I didn't. I didn't know what I wanted. I was terrified. You made the arrangements, got the doctor, took me, arranged everything, waited in the other room writing policies. Murderer."

"Murderer," the woman said.

He shook his head. "You'd better go back to the ladies' room and stay there. I don't want to hurt you."

"Murderer."

He took a step toward her. He swung around abruptly and almost ran to the far side of the station, pressing his forehead hard on the window.

"We can't stop it now," the woman said, following him. "You can't close the door again now. I'm here. You finally saw me. Really saw me. I'm real now. I won't be banished again. I'm stronger than you are. You've killed off bits and pieces of yourself until there's nothing left to fight with. You can't send me away again."

Crane pushed himself away from the glass and made a halfhearted attempt to hit her with his fist. He missed and fell against the bench holding the door. He heard the woman's low laugh. All for nothing. All for nothing. The bench slid out from under his hand, and the drift pushed into the room like an avalanche. He pulled himself free and tried to brush the snow off his clothes.

"We'll both freeze now," he said, not caring any longer.

The woman came to his side and touched his cheek with her fingers; they were strangely warm. "Relax now, Crane. Just relax."

She led him to a bench where he sat down resignedly. "Will you at least tell me who you are?" he said.

"You know. You've always known."

He shook his head. One last attempt, he thought. He had to make that one last effort to get rid of her, the woman whose face was so like his own. "You don't even exist," he said harshly, not opening his eyes. "I imagined you here because I was afraid of being alone all night. I created you. *I created you.*"

He stood up. "You hear that, Mary Louise! Did you hear that! I created something. Something so real that it wants to kill me."

"Look at me, Crane. Look at me. Turn your head and look. Look with me, Crane. Let me show you. Let me show you what I see. . . ."

He was shaking again, chilled through, shaking so hard that his muscles were sore. Slowly, inevitably he turned his head and saw the man half-standing, half-crouching, holding the bench with both hands. The man had gray skin, and his eyes were mad with terror.

"Let go, Crane. Look at him and let go. He doesn't deserve anything from

331

us ever again." Crane watched the man clutch his chest, heard him moaning for Mary Louise to come help him, watched him fall to the floor.

She heard the men working at the drift, and she opened the office door to wait for them. They finally got through and the ticket agent squirmed through the opening they had made.

"Miss! Miss? Are you all right?"

"Yes. I broke into the office, though."

"My God, I thought . . . When we saw that the door had given under the drift, and you in here . . . alo—" The ticket agent blinked rapidly several times.

"I was perfectly all right. When I saw that the door wasn't going to hold, I broke open the inner office and came in here with my sketch book and pencils. I've had a very productive night, really. But I could use some coffee now."

They took her to the diner in a police car, and while she waited for her breakfast order, she went to the rest room and washed her face and combed her hair. She stared at herself in the mirror appraisingly. "Happy birthday," she said softly then.

"Your birthday?" asked the girl who had chosen to wait the night out in the diner. "You were awfully brave to stay alone in the station. I couldn't have done that. You really an artist?"

"Yes, really. And last night I had a lot of work to get done. A lot of work and not much time."

From Gardner R. Dozois, undated, 1969:

Dear Damon and Kate,
   Just a quick note. . . .
   Saturday afternoon found myself giving Starving Lessons to several of the generation authors, mostly Clarion kids. Let them in on neat tricks like buying a package of six frozen veal cutlets for 99 cents and living on that for a week, one a day, have onion sandwiches or something on the seventh, rest and all like that. These kids were thinking they'd be poorhouse bait if they didn't

make more than $2,000 a year; babes in the woods, told 'em I'd made $600 since January. Went on to tell 'em how you can cut baby food with a little water and milk and make soup out of it. Circle of paling faces, jaws dropping a little, mouths pursing into Ecckkkkss. . . .

David Gerrold drove me back to New York. He was going to crash for the night at my place, but took a look around, eyed the hardcases drifting in and out, turned pale, excused himself and took off for Brooklyn instead, trying to find the Carrs. These West Coast boys just can't stand the gaff.

To Virginia Kidd, December 6, 1969:

Dear Virginia,

I return you herewith a story which represents an excursion of twenty yards from a base camp established forty years ago—like —— ——, handsomely equipped in Norwegian pullover, snow goggles and hiking boots, tramping around and around what was once an exploration site, now the parking lot of a Howard Johnson's.

To Virginia Kidd, December 13, 1969:

Dear Virginia,

I return two with regrets. The Russ is very nice indeed but too Christmasy for *Orbit*. In the first paragraph of "Touching Venus" I thought —— had finally got hold of something, but then it all pissed away as usual. I suspect writing is therapeutic for him because it helps him define and then evade the things that are bothering him.

GLEEPSITE

by *Joanna Russ*

I try to make my sales at night during the night shift in office buildings; it works better that way. Resistance is gone at night. The lobbies are deserted, the air filters on half power; here and there a woman stays up late amid piles of paper; things blow down the halls just out of the range of vision of the watch-ladies who turn their keys in the doors of unused rooms, who insert the keys hanging from chains around their necks in the apertures of empty clocks, or polish with their polishing rags the surfaces of desks, the bare tops of tables. You make some astonishing sales that way.

I came up my thirty floors and found on the thirty-first Kira and Lira, the only night staff: two fiftyish identical twins in the same gray cardigan sweaters, the same pink dresses, the same blue rinse on their gray sausage-curls. But Kira wore on her blouse (over the name tag) the emblem of the senior secretary, the Tree of Life pin with the cultured pearl, while Lira went without, so I addressed myself to the (minutes-) younger sister.

"We're closed," they said.

Nevertheless, knowing that they worked at night, knowing that they worked for a travel agency whose hints of imaginary faraway places (Honolulu, Hawaii—they don't exist) must eventually exacerbate the longings of even the most passive sister, I addressed myself to them again, standing in front of the semicircular partition over which they peered (alarmed but bland), keeping my gaze on the sans-serif script over the desk—or is it roses!—and avoiding very carefully any glance at the polarized vitryl panels beyond which rages hell's own stew of hot winds and sulfuric acid, it gets worse and worse. I don't like false marble floors, so I changed it.

Ladies.

"We're closed!" cried Miss Lira.

Here I usually make some little illusion so they will know who I am; I stopped Miss Kira from pressing the safety button, which always hangs on the wall, and made appear beyond the nearest vitryl panel a bat's face as big as a man's: protruding muzzle, pointed fangs, cocked ears, and rats' shiny eyes, here and gone. I snapped my fingers and the wind tore it off.

No, no, no, no! cried the sisters.

May I call you Flora and Dora? I said. *Flora and Dora in memory of that glorious time centuries past when ladies like yourselves danced on tables to the applause of admiring gentlemen, when ladies wore, like yourselves, scarlet petticoats, ruby stomachers, chokers and bibs of red velvet, pearls*

334

and maroon high-heeled boots, though they did not always keep their petticoats decorously about their ankles.

What you have just seen, ladies, is a small demonstration of the power of electrical brain stimulation—mine, in this case—and the field which transmitted it to you was generated by the booster I wear about my neck, metallic in this case, though they come in other colors, and tuned to the frequency of the apparatus which I wear in this ring. You will notice that it is inconspicuous and well designed. I am allowed to wear the booster only at work. In the year blank blank, when the great neurosurgical genius, Blank, working with Blank and Blank, discovered in the human forebrain what has been so poetically termed the Circle of Illusion, it occurred to another great innovator, Blank, whom you know, to combine these two great discoveries, resulting in a Device that has proved to be of inestimable benefit to the human race. (We just call it the Device.) Why not, thought Blank, employ the common, everyday power of electricity for the stimulation, the energization, the concretization of the Center of Illusion or (to put it bluntly) an aide-mémoire, crutch, companion and record-keeping book for that universal human talent, daydreaming? Do you daydream, ladies? Then you know that daydreaming is harmless. Daydreaming is voluntary. Daydreaming is not night dreaming. Daydreaming is normal. It is not hallucination or delusion or deception but creation. It is an accepted form of mild escape. No more than in a daydream or reverie is it possible to confuse the real and the ideal; try it and see. The Device simply supplements the power of your own human brain. If Miss Kira—

"No, no!" cried Miss Lira, but Miss Kira had already taken my sample ring, the setting scrambled to erase the last customer's residual charge.

You have the choice of ten scenes. No two persons will see the same thing, of course, but the parameters remain fairly constant. Further choices on request. Sound, smell, taste, touch, and kinesthesia optional. We are strictly prohibited from employing illegal settings or the use of variable condensers with fluctuating parameters. Tampering with the machinery is punishable by law.

"But it's so hard!" said Miss Kira in surprise. "And it's not real at all!" That always reassures them. At first.

It takes considerable effort to operate the Circle of Illusion even with mechanical aid. Voltage beyond that required for threshold stimulation is banned by law; even when employed, it does not diminish the necessity for effort, but in fact increases it proportionately. No more than in life, ladies, can you get something for nothing.

Practice makes perfect.

335

Miss Kira, as I knew she would, had chosen a flowery meadow with a suggestion of honeymoon; Miss Lira chose a waterfall in a glade. Neither had put in a Man, although an idealized figure of a Man is standard equipment for our pastoral choices (misty, idealized, in the distance, some even see him with wings) and I don't imagine either sister would ever get much closer.

Miss Lira said they actually had a niece who was actually married to a man.

Miss Kira said a half-niece.

Miss Lira said they had a cousin who worked in the children's nursery with real children and they had holidays coming *and if I use a variable condenser, what's it to you?*

Behind me, though I cannot imagine why, is a full-length mirror, and in this piece of inconstancy I see myself as I was when I left home tonight, or perhaps not, I don't remember: beautiful, chocolate-colored, naked, gold braided into my white hair. Behind me, bats' wings.

A mirror, ladies, produces a virtual image, and so does the Device.

Bats' faces.

Hermaphroditic.

It is no more addicting than thought.

Little snakes waving up from the counter, a forest of them. Unable to stand the sisters' eyes swimming behind their glasses, myopic Flora and Dora, I changed the office for them, gave them a rug, hung behind them on the wall original Rembrandts, made them younger, erased them, let the whole room slide, and provided for Dora a bedroom beyond the travel office, a bordello in white and gold baroque, embroidered canopy, goldfish pool, chihuahuas on the marble and bats in the belfry.

I have two heads.

Flora's quite a whore.

The younger sister, not quite willing to touch the ring again, said they'd think about it and Kira, in a quarrel that must have gone back years, began in a low, vapid whisper—

Why, they're not bats at all, I said, over at the nearest vitryl panel; *I was mistaken,* and Lira, Don't open that! We'll suffocate!

No one who is sane, of course, opens anything any more into that hell outside, but this old, old, old place had real locks on the vitryl and real seams between, and a narrow balcony where someone had gone out perhaps fifty years ago (in a diving suit) to admire the updrafts between the dead canyons where papers danced on the driving murk and shapes fluttered between the raw lights; one could see several streets over to other spires, other shafts, the hurricane tearing through the poisoned air. Nighttime makes a kind of inferno out of this and every once in a while someone decides on a gaudy exit: the lungs eaten away, the room reeking of hydrosulfurous acid, torn paper settling on the discolored rug.

When you have traveled in the tubes as much as I have, when you have seen the playground in Antarctica time after time, when your features have melted enough between black and brown and white, man and woman, as plastic as the lazy twist of a thought, you get notions. You get ideas. I saw once in a much more elegant office building a piece of polished wood, so large, so lovely, a curve fully six feet long and so beautiful that if you could have made out of that wood an idea and out of that idea a bed, you could have slept on that bed. When you put your hand on the vitryl panels at night, the heat makes your hand sweat onto the surface; my hand's melted through many times, like oil on water. I stood before the window, twisting shapes for fun, seeing myself stand on the narrow balcony, bored with Kira and Lira, poor Kira, poor Lira, poor as-I-once-was, discussing whether they can afford it.

". . . an outlet for creativity . . ."

". . . she *said* it's only . . ."

What effort it takes, and what an athlete of illusion you become! able to descend to the bottom of the sea (where we might as well be, come to think of it), to the manless moon, to the Southern Hemisphere where the men stay, dreaming about us; but no, they did away with themselves years ago, they were inefficient, and did themselves in (I mean all the men except themselves) in blank-blank. Only three percent of the population male, my word!

". . . legal . . ."

". . . never . . ."

"Don't!" cried Miss Kira.

They know what I'm going to do. Ever since I found out those weren't bats' faces. As Miss Kira and Miss Lira sign the contract (thumbsy-up, thumbsy-down) I wrench the lock off the vitryl and squeeze through, what a foul, screaming wind! shoving desperately at the panels, and stumble off the narrow, railless balcony, feeling as I go my legs contract, my fingers grow, my sternum arch like the prow of a boat, little bat-man-woman with sketchy turned-out legs and grasping toes, and hollow bones and fingers down to my ankles, a thumb-and-forefinger grasper at the end of each wing, and that massive wraparound of the huge, hollow chest, all covered with blonde fur; in the middle of it all, sunk between the shoulders, is the human face. Miss Kira would faint. I would come up to Miss Lira's waist. Falling down the nasty night air until I shrug up hard, hard, hard, into a steep upward glide and ride down the currents of hell past the man-made cliff where Kira and Lira, weeping with pain, push the vitryl panel back into place. The walls inside are blackening, the fake marble floor is singed. It is comfy-cold, it is comfy-nice, I'm going to mate in midair, I'm going to give shuddering birth on the ledge of a cliff, I'm going to scream at the windows when I like. They found no corpse, no body.

Kira and Lira, mouths like O's, stare out as I climb past. They do a little dance.

> She was a Floradora baby
> With a chance to meet the best,
> But she had to go and marry Abie,
> The drummer with the fancy vest!

Tampering with the machinery is punishable by law, says Kira.
Oh my dear, we'll tinker a bit. says Lira.
And so they will.

From James Sallis, December 22, 1969 (written after I showed him a letter from an unpublished author):

Dear Mr. Knight:
I am enclosing two stories. Please give them serious considera-tion before rejecting them. Or if you haven't that much time to hand, at least read them. I think they are exactly as I want them. I think they are very very good. I would be very very grateful if you could tell me why they are not good, why they are not well written, why you don't want them, why they are not sci-fi, or anything else like that.

I am a struggling, sniveling young faggot writer and I am trying very hard to get my work published. My friends like it, and so does my girl friend, so I can't understand why my work isn't "snapped up." I am hoping you can help me or at least give me some good advice. My favorite writers are Poul Anderson, Dr. McNelly, Robert Moore Williams, Bob Silverberg (I met Bob once), and

338

Anne McCaffrey. *And you!* I mean, of course, in science fiction, because I read a lot of mainstream literature of course.

I will be waiting to hear from you. If you don't like these stories I have a lot more that I can send!

BINARIES

by *James Sallis*

CRITICAL MASS

It's happened again, I'm in bed with a stranger. Don't know her name. If I want to remember the curve of the bottom of her breasts, the way they rest on her ribs or rise to her shoulder, I'll have to reach out and touch them. Do I know her? She has a name, an address (which she refuses to give me), three telephone numbers at which I might reach her. Along with the last she has given me a chart showing the time of day I'm most likely to find her at each number. She has long hair. She is wearing a tight violet dress. Her eyes are violet. She is overweight but that's something you always forget until you look at her again.

Also: I am being pursued. I saw the frost of his breath on the glass just a moment ago. Her lover, husband, father, a mutual friend? How am I to know? even that there is a connection? Each time I try and confront him, he flees. Last week in the press of crowds at 14th Street he took the only way open to him and was crushed to death in the doors of one of the uptown trains. His last words were I kept my promise, Tell them. My suit is still stained with his blood. And for a moment I envied the dead man: he kept his promise, I have to live up to mine. The next morning there was a certain wariness to his movements.

She has small breasts. When she lies down they hardly exist. Her hips are wide and solid, her thighs large, full, the whole lower half of her body out of proportion to the upper—the breasts, the slender torso, the fragile arms. Her legs are short. Her feet small, delicate. She is nude in the photograph, I can't remember what clothes she wore.

339

Someone has written a collection of short stories and published them under my name; they have even put my photograph on the back cover. I received a copy in the morning post. Anonymous, no return address, postmarked Grnd Cntrl Stn. The stories reveal my deepest secrets. The most intense and intimate movements, relations of my life. Only one person could have written them. Or had reason to. My attorney is investigating the possibility of a lawsuit against the publisher but, as the work was copyrighted in my own name, there seems little we can do. The publisher expressed to my attorney his desire to meet the author, his admiration for the book. He relayed an invitation to a party at his home last night. Which is how I met this girl.

He follows me everywhere. Perhaps I am looking for associations where there are none. Perhaps he is nothing more than a hired assassin. Plotting my rotation around the events of the day. The occasions of the moment. Then, certain, he will strike. Perhaps he has nothing to do with what I am doing.

She was standing in a group and she said You're here, You finally came, and took my arm. She was in the park by the fountain and we watched the pigeons dive for pennies then silently, without words, walked away together. We were afraid of words. It was a clear blue day. The water was silver. It would never rain again. She was in the library. We had requested the same book and sat side by side at one of the long tables in the Special Collections room reading it. She was working at a restaurant, to show me the way to the table where I never arrived. I ate, instead, on the bed in my single room. With her beside me. In the Village. She was sitting beside me on the plane from London and we never got off. She was sitting on the fire escape, crying softly, and I opened the window.

They are moving the city again and I am occasionally lost somewhere between her house and mine. It was at one of these times, coming up out of the subway into what I thought to be midtown Manhattan, and finding myself in the open space of Queens, that I first approached my pursuer. He turned and threw himself onto the back of a truck which was just then pulling away, carrying off the skating rink from Rockefeller Plaza.

Her face is fine and precise as an etching. No part of it could ever be changed. It was drawn with a crow-quill pen and always grins. Her eyes are astonished. Her hair is a different length and colour each time I see her. Her neck is a perfect curve, the wing of a sparrow. Her shoulders are narrow. Her hands are soft. And strong. Her eyes are astonished. They move slowly, as though sliding through oil. When they touch you, you smile.

Ice is crashing off the roof and onto the ground outside. There are pigeons frozen alive inside it. She is gone. He has taken away the photograph. He has gone away himself. And I am sitting here saying ——, ——, ——. Her name. And it all makes sense.

It does, it does.

MOMENTUM

I am waiting for a train. To take me a little farther away. Here at Paddington Station. Out of the taxi with my single bag. Ducking. Halfcrown tip, smile, Ta. Now I'm larger. On the pavement walking away from the cab. Before that was a coach from Brighton, whatever I was doing in Brighton and an 82 bus. Now I'm smaller. Inside the station. Waiting for a train etc. I'd like a ticket please. Certainly your destination sir. Anywhere. Ailleurs. Just a little farther away. I see and would that be return fare. No. God no never. I see sir that there is a departure from Gate D at eight o five that would be a halfhour from now sir the train arrives I forget where he said at ten twelve if that would be satisfactory sir. Yes. That would be two pounds eight sir. Stamp rubber ink. Thank you have a pleasant journey sir I hope you enjoy wherever he said. Politeness, that much politeness. A weapon. Now down through Gate D and onto a coach and tea and to look out at the backs of all these houses. And to take me a little farther away. To wonder how much further can I go. To check do I have my passport. To realize the train is going to Paris. To be more careful what I say from now on.

I am French. I was born in a large house off the rue de Tournon, in the 6th arrondissement. Of a Polish mother who died before she saw what I was. Of a father born in Paris, 32 and he'd spent a total of three of them there. Of a father who belonged too much to France to stay there. He read to me, peering over the slats of my petit berceau, Cendrars' Prose du transsibérien et de la petite Jeanne de France and Les Pâques à New York, and when I was 6 it was to New York that, bundled up, with my French abécédaires and my grammaires anglaises, I was sent pour faire de l'education. To that place that could never exist. That was something created in Cendrars' poems. That about to acquire a History possessed already its ruins. From which I would never return. Or wish to.

Are you still sitting on the beach with your book and the tiny glass of green tea. You'll never finish the book you know. With the old people all around you. The people from Hove who come to stare at the sea and wait to die. That strange beach without sand. Rocks. Where I told you one day Your ears are like shells and you turned back to me in the sun and your copper sweater and you smiled. And looked in the water. And it took your face away, to Greece and Istanbul. Where we watched a weary father lift an arm and point to the water and say to his two little girls France is just over there. Both of us

341

smiling at that, we could no more believe him than could the children. To an American France can never be just over there. France is thousands of miles away. A hundred years away. Ten hours by plane. We find it hard enough to believe France exists at all. Do you still believe, you said it once, that I'm "always returning." And each morning do you still set a place for me and make the tea very strong because I might come. With my eyes blurred, I've worked all night. With my hands trembling. Do you still keep cigarettes in the flat for me. And do you go down to the London trains each weekend, still. Because. I might come.

None of you could ever understand, perhaps even believe, my impotence while writing. You always . . . go away. You said. I didn't want to hurt you. But you always had to come too close. And incredible, the unerring instinct by which you'd know whenever I set to work. Get randy and turn up at my flat. Compete, demand attention, you probably wanted to tear up the pages. Crawl under the desk and fondle me as I wrote. And to say again and again I have only so much energy. Not enough for it all. Not enough—even as it drained into you on the studio bed and stained the coverings. And that little shout of yours to tell me I was empty again.

I am English. Turning over my passport. At the Embassy. Impossible to say is this an American or Briton smiling at me now, I trust you've given this matter serious consideration young man it is of grave import, I cannot stress strongly enough the profound significance and implications of your action I can only hope that you are yourself fully aware of it. And. And of what you are doing. Yes sir I'm quite aware thank you. And you wish to carry on. Most assuredly. I see. Well I should think yes everything seems to be in order. The girl is. French. O yes of course French. And both. Yes both of us. Quite, well then as I say everything is in order. You should be receiving the new passport within the fortnight. Through the other Embassy of course. They should I suppose be requiring new photographs. Yes sir I'm off to that now the little shop just up the way on Oxford. That would be the one across from Heals. Yes. Splendid. Best of luck young man. And to go down the steps now. Cold.

He won't be coming round anymore. You can take your Joan Baez records out of the cupboard and put them back on the shelf with the others. You can stop putting new paper in the typewriter every day. You can put away the notebooks for your novel. You can get rid of the French books on Fourth Avenue or in Soho and you don't have to dust off Heidegger any longer, you can just let it sit there on the table till it turns to dust. And. And you can tear down those wretched Cézanne reproductions. He hated them too.

I am in hospital. In Poland. Dying. They have scraped out the inside of my chest like a curetage till there's nothing more they can scrape out but moi-même. Which for some reason they're reluctant to do. I have donated the organs of my body to others. Whatever they can salvage. Three times a day doctors gather at the foot of my bed and talk quietly among themselves, glancing up towards me from time to time. I lie here smoking and reading Bergson. Duration. I have the general impression that they are bargaining for the various pumps vehicles containers of my body. Wypuść mu flaki. I am 24. Led to slaughter. I almost survived. That when it comes, not much longer now, I will hear far away in the corridors, the corridors where they would all be waiting, friends, attorneys, publishers, a few young writers, perhaps even a family, the quiet firm sound of applause.

Bump bump bump. Down the stairs. Bag slapping on your bare leg. Snow on the bottom now, I mean it this time. You always mean it. And a cab waiting. Black. And the snow. And two cups of tea on the table inside.

I'm an American. It's a complex fate, to be an American, Henry James. And it doesn't matter. Any train, plane, coach, cab, that's where I'll always arrive. This is New York say hello. To New York. Again. No. No I don't remember whose picture that is on the passport with me. It should say, page 9 I think. America say hello to one of your own. You'll never lose him and he can't get rid of you. America knows how to welcome a failure. It should. Les statues meurent aussi. And the French lady is crying into the sea. Si lourde. Sourde. Rain in the City. Noise. Smoke. Wheels. The low sob of a million machines and machinations. A thousand new plots. I am as far away as I can get now, from you. From everything. And it's not even snowing. And there's no beach.

Here.

CENTRE

The car died again today.

Each morning the grocer leaves a pound of coffee and a carton of cigarettes outside the door for me. Mail is delivered with the morning papers. Today none were there.

There is nothing on the radio. Even static.

Or maybe last night. In the dark and cold. Dying in snow. In the bright sun I gently pried open its hood, cleaned the plugs and checked they were firmly in place. Dried out the carburetor and blew into the fuel pump, opened the feed a bit wider. Scraped the battery terminals and choked it manually. It wouldn't come around.

I can get nothing on the phone but recordings. I've listened to Let It Bleed four times now.

K came. As always, punctually, at ten. With breakfast in a paper bag. She is 45, close to that, old enough to be my mother but when I think of her it's only her body I remember, her legs in tight jeans, the perfect curve of her bottom like an inverted heart, her short colourless hair and the smallness of her. Her smile and the eyes too light and soft to be blue. So much energy, so calm I think she's never been unhappy before this. She leaves herself behind in rooms from Kensington to Mayfair. The sense of her presence so strong you hardly realize she's gone. When she is. But she's stopped all that. Now, she comes only to this room. Only here. And sits on the grey unmade bed. And smiles whenever I look up at her. Why. Why do you keep coming here. I ask her. A whale's penis even in repose is taller than I am.

Next week I am being sent to another country, to learn the language. After which I am to return and teach others. I have no idea why. Nor do I seem to have much choice.

I have moved away from the window. K is painting them black and she's turned on the radio, to listen as she works. Black. Like a bat, penis libre, tail. Jumper stretching tight to show the bra, strap and buckle, the pinch of her waist and an inch of bare skin. I think we once had a discussion of something or another.

A call from D/K. Quite upset. They were unable to pay the bill. Hospital policy, no discharge of patients until such time as the bill is met. D standing at the desk. On the white floor. In his corduroy jacket. And a bargain struck. The hospital allowed K to leave but insists upon keeping the baby. They are permitted to visit it. From 2 to 4 in the afternoon. From 6 to 8 at night. K spoke to me. I could hear D crying softly in the background.

They have taken the car. Dragging it away across the fields of broken cornstalks and through the snow. It left a thin trail of oil behind.

One of her breasts is set lower on her chest than the other. Lower and slightly off to the side, towards her arm. The nipple of that one is inverted, the other 3/4 of an inch long. The obvious facts, of her jumper. Both breasts are small. And solid under your hand. Her husband would have strong fingers.

I am burning the book. It is snowing into the sea. The radio is on. I drop the last match and look up at her. Why do you keep coming back here. They are talking about the weather again.

ROTATION

The pills. A white one, a green one, a red one. They are lined up as always on the bedside table. Each night beside me. And the light. In the room, si légère.

She is wearing grey slacks tonight. When she comes. Of a thick material that follows the taper of her legs down, to fit close about the ankle. Where there are white socks. The tops turned down, and loafers. Brown. Her legs are crossed at the knee. Feet at rest sur le coussin. A band of skin on the left one showing which reminds him what he once said to her, cuisine à cuisse à toi. She is always smoking. Her breasts move in the light cashmere as she inhales. Rise, then sink. With his eyes. You smoke too much.

Some instants a man knows, even as they occur, at the very moment of occurrence, he will never forget. He will carry this with him through the rest of his life. It will always be beside him. A second shadow. And the life will seem longer, or shorter, because of it. He will never be able to make it go away. Or himself from it. And he knew, now, even before the words, when he looked up and saw her there. This was one of those times.

Cher,   Je lutte avec les anges de ta lettre,   Jacob.

Kind of you to notice. No, Hell, I meant that. Who really cares how much someone smokes, who gives a damn, really. You do. I meant it.

Living together off and on. For twenty years now, and she hasn't changed. Nothing about her has changed. She looks the same as that first time, twenty years ago. At the party they left together. And three days later thought to ask one another's name. While his own age rattles inside him. Like a turtle's blunt head. Butting dumbly, again and again, the glass slabs. That contain him.

Tu,   Bientôt une réponse. Tant bien que mal. Et dès maintenant, jamais, garderais l'oiseau.

Other times she would dress in black and move about the house, moving the furniture around inside the rooms, and he couldn't see her. Just the sound of her breath in the dark. The rasp of legs that don't want to be changed. And once. Late, lying in bed, her plan to have a peacock tail tattooed on her bottom, in full colour. When she felt he was losing interest in her. Or she would turn up some day, maybe she'd been gone for months, with her pubic hair shaved down till just two initials remained. And maybe they would be his and maybe they wouldn't. But he was pretending sleep. Just the sound of her breath in the dark.

Réponse.   Judas was a moral man. He did what he had to do.   A vous.

I don't like, no, the States. We all know now it's a failure and we're ashamed. That's what the French, the Polish, reading, that's what it all means. I feel I'm spiritually European. Or want to be. Then why do you stay here. Why did you come back. Because I belong here.

Artaud. Giving his reading. In Paris, he'd been locked away in mental asylums for nine years, all the Paris élite came. And every few minutes he'd stop and look out at the audience, out at Gide and Breton and Jean Paulhan and Camus and Pichette and his friend Adamov and all the others. In despair.

And he would try to explain, When you come round you simply cannot find yourself again. Life itself has been permanently debased, and a portion of original goodness and joy lost forever. He would say, I have agreed once and for all to give in to my own inferiority. He would stop and look around at all the faces and surrender. Give up in the middle of a poem, Putting myself in your place I can see how completely uninteresting everything that I am saying must seem. What can I do to be completely sincere? And then to go back and read L'Inconditionné. She is sitting up in bed. As he tells her this, again. Naked. Her breasts are larger than you think, perhaps in contrast to the smallness of her body in the tall window now. The motel sign red on the glass. Or the weight she's lost. She has seen a story of his in a magazine. Though he has been careful never to show them to her. And asks about the title. That Buddhism sees the Self, Etre, Being as a bubble. Nothing inside. Nothing at the centre. And Sartre's Cartesian phenomenology too but go ahead and call it existentialism if you want to. Sartre doesn't care. And I don't. And so there are just gestures, that's all we have. And the bubbles are all the time going higher and higher, getting larger. Like lies. Which essentially they are of course. And soon to burst. She hated it when he talked like that.

Do I. Belong here. Yes. Quel sens. Then to ask another name. To watch her. To turn her face away.

She would come back with her body bruised and torn. No explanation, I am doing what I have to do. And nothing else would have changed. Or had the power to change. Effects. And that pale residue of sadness inside. Somewhere.

A quote for you. Like many young men in the South, he became overly subtle and had trouble ruling out the possible.   C'est moi.

Living now in this house in Pennsylvania. And she comes round. All the questions unanswered. Or unasked. Peirce's old house down the road with a little plaque out front to tell everyone who he was. And Peirce who once wrote, Actuality is something brute. There is no reason for it. I instance putting your shoulder against a door and trying to force it open against an unseen, silent, and unknown resistance.

So let me tell you how it will be. The end. One night you will be lying alone in bed. You will hear sounds downstairs. You will hear feet coming slowly up the stairs. You will hear them pause at the door. You will hear the doorknob turning. You will hear the door open. You will hear the footsteps again. On the rug now. You will be lying alone in bed. You will never see his face. You will never know his name.

To Virginia Kidd, February 16, 1970:

> . . . If by magic wand I could make writers forget all the *Thrilling Wonders* they ever read, I would do it. Nine out of ten writers in this field are still writing for Sam Merwin, & it is sad.

From Gene Wolfe, April 27, 1970:

> Dear Damon,
> If Gene Wolfe stories you don't like are refreshing I can make you feel like you're twelve years old and have just stepped from under a Benzedrine shower. Of course I don't really have a hypnotic ray that will reach from the banks of the Great Miami to Milford and turn your bones to Jell-O.* (Just my "thing," which is a black box containing only a *drawing* of a hypnotic ray which will reach etc. It works better when it's not turned on.)
>
>   * Lemon-lime, but who cares?

To Miriam Allen deFord, April 30, 1970:

> Dear Miriam,
> Can't believe you're serious about brain transplants, although it is not hard to think of some people who could use them.

To Virginia Kidd, May 12, 1970:

> Dear Virginia,
> I return with regrets Joanna's piece with the Latin subtitle which I will not try to reproduce. I think this falls under the heading of literary criticism; effective as such, though somewhat like shooting fish in a barrel, but not a story. I sometimes think *Orbit* should use critical material, but anyhow it never has, & this is not the one I am going to break precedent for. Tell her to put the whole thing in Latin, why not.

To James Tiptree, Jr., July 7, 1970:

> Dear Tip,
> Yes, I know what you mean, & that's funny, all right, category "It only hurts when I laugh." Sorry to have put the story down for

what seemed like the wrong reason, but you are a good guy and will recover, and besides I will convince you someday that it was the right reason. All that alien-planet apparatus that we have clung to so long . . . not to mention the robots, laser guns, girls in tinfoil brassieres, etc. . . . Honest to God, what is it for and who needs it?

Another piece of my ancient typewriter has just broken. It is surprising how many you can get along without.

To Wanda Carol Pugner, July 11, 1970:

Dear Miss Pugner,

. . . People in fiction frequently devote their lives to revenge, but in real life they generally find something else to do.

To Joe W. Haldeman, July 19, 1970:

Dear Joe,

I like the careful background in the early pages of this one, & had great hopes for it, but then along about p. 3 we started to get the men's-magazine clichés, gee whiz, followed eventually by the revelation that all this is a therapeutic simulation—another cliché, alas. This is the third story I have bounced this month for the same reasons. What makes it embarrassing is that I wrote one like this myself a couple of years ago and sold it to Harry Harrison. But if I spit on the sidewalk, it's still spitting on the sidewalk.

From Edward Bryant, July 20, 1970:

Dear Damon,

Remember the evening at Milford when we all discussed the horrible present/future, breakdown of lawandorder, and everyone told their horror stories of being mugged, raped, beaten, murdered, etc.? Well. Let me add my name. Last night I finally arrived in Fun City. First thing, got out of the taxi at 149 Avenue A, my host met me at the door. Then a herd of black teens rampaged over from Tompkins Square Park (across the street), grabbed me there in the foyer, stuck knives in my back (not too deep, luckily), and relieved me of cash, cards, ID's, travelers' checks, etc. What a welcome to the big city. Ah well, they didn't

348

get my typewriter, which I would have defended with my life. They *did* take my ACLU card, which was a bitter blow.

To Pamela Sargent, July 22, 1970:

Dear Pam,

This is pretty good grim stuff but I think the first person screws it up. People who tell you how easy first person is average out about 99% amateurs. It is easy to do, all right, but if you want to do it well, it is very hard. . . . Please watch out for this tendency to populate the world with yoyos. People do dumb things, but there are always reasons for it.

To Neil Shapiro, September 1, 1970:

Dear Neil,

Please bear in mind that I have been reading science fiction since 1933; I read *Amazing Stories* and *Thrilling Wonder* and *Future* and *Astonishing*, and I got to the point about fifteen years ago where I just could not make my eyes track over stuff like this any more. So I am not a judge of whether it is a good thing of its kind or not. I will say, though, that your punctuation is still peculiar. Every time you begin a sentence with "but" or "and," along comes that comma, & it is wrong every time.

I bet I know why that judge asked you to come in; he wants to measure your skull. How many days overdue would that inspection sticker have to be before you would think it was okay for them to bust you? Robin [Wilson] was one day over & they got him, and he will never see thirty again unless he uses a time machine.

AL

by Carol Emshwiller

Sort of a plane crash in an uncharted region of the park.

> *We were flying fairly low over the mountains. We had come to the last ridge when there, before us, appeared this incredible valley . . .*
>
> *Suddenly the plane sputtered. (We knew we were low on gas but we had thought to make it over the mountains.)*
>
> *"I think I can bring her in." (John's last words.)*
>
> *I was the only survivor.*

A plane crash in a field of alfalfa, across the road from it the Annual Fall Festival of the Arts. An oasis on the edge of the parking area. One survivor. He alone, Al, who has spent considerable time in France, Algeria and Mexico, his paintings without social relevance (or so the critics say) and best in the darker colors, not a musician at all yet seems to be one of us. He, a stranger, wandering in a land he doesn't remember and not one penny of our kind of money, creeping from behind our poster, across from it the once-a-year art experience for music lovers. Knowing him as I do now, he must have been wary then, view from our poster: ENTRANCE sign, vast parking lot, our red and white tent, our EXIT on the far side, maybe the sound of a song, a frightening situation under the circumstance, all the others dead and Al having been unconscious for who knows how long? (the scar from that time is still on his cheek) stumbling across the road then and into our ticket booth.

"Hi."

I won't say he wasn't welcome. Even then we were wondering were we facing stultification? Already some of our rules had become rituals. Were we, we wondered, doomed to a partial relevance in our efforts to make music meaningful in our time? And now Al, dropped to us from the skies (no taller than Tom Disch, no wider and not quite so graceful). Later he was to say: "Maybe the artful gesture is lost forever."

We had a girl with us then as secretary, a long-haired changeling child, actually the daughter of a prince (there still are princes) left out in the picnic area of a western state forest to be found and brought up by some old couple in the upper middle class (she still hasn't found this out for sure, but has always suspected something of the sort) so when *I* asked Al to *my* (extra) bedroom it was too late. (By that time he had already pounded his head

350

against the wall some so he seemed calm and happy and rather well adjusted to life in our valley.) The man from the Daily asked him how did he happen to become interested in art? He said he came from a land of cultural giants east of our outermost islands where the policemen were all poets. That's significant in two ways.

About the artful gesture being lost, so many lost arts and soft, gray birds, etc., etc., etc. (The makers of toe shoes will have to go when the last toe dancer dies.)

However, right then, there was Al, mumbling to us in French, German and Spanish. We gave him two tickets to our early evening concert even though he couldn't pay except in what looked like pesos. Second row, left side. (Right from the beginning there was something in him I couldn't resist.) We saw him craning his neck there, somehow already with our long-haired girl beside him. She's five hundred years old though she doesn't look a day over sixteen and plays the virginal like an angel. Did her undergraduate work at the University of Utah (around 1776 I would say). If she crossed the Alleghenies *now* she'd crumble into her real age and die, so later on I tried to get them to take a trip to the Ann Arbor Film Festival together, but naturally she had something else to do. Miss Haertzler.

> *As our plane came sputtering down I saw the tents below, a village of nomads, God knows how far from the nearest outpost of civilization. They had, no doubt, lived like this for thousands of years.*
>
> *These thoughts went rapidly through my mind in the moments before we crashed and then I lost consciousness.*

"COME, COME YE SONS OF ART." That's what our poster across the street says—quotes, that is. Really very nice in dayglo colors. "COME, COME AWAY . . ." etc., on to "TO CELEBRATE, TO CELEBRATE THIS TRIUMPHANT DAY," which meant to me, in some symbolic way even at that time, the day Al came out from behind it and stumbled across the road to our booth, as they say: "A leading force, even then, among the new objectivists and continues to play a major role among them up to the present time" (which was a few years ago). Obtained his bachelor's degree in design at the University of Michigan with further study at the Atelier Chaumière in Paris. He always says, "Form speaks." I can say I knew him pretty well at that time. I know he welcomes criticism but not too early in the morning. Ralph had said (he was on the staff of the Annual Fall Festival), "Maybe artistic standards are no longer relevant." (We were wondering at the time how to get the immediacy of the war into our concerts more meaningfully

351

than the *1812 Overture*. Also something of the changing race relations.) Al answered, but just then a jet came by or some big oil truck and I missed the key word. That leaves me still not understanding what he meant. The next morning the same thing happened and it may have been more or less the answer to everything.

By then we had absorbed the major San Francisco influences. These have remained with us in some form or other up to the present time.

I would like you, Tom Disch, to write a poem about this plane crash in an uncharted region, but really, you know, kind of alfalfa field thing. I'd like the Annual Fall Festival of the Arts (and literature, too, if you must) in it and SONS OF ART. I know you can do it, can do anything which is a very nice way to be and being twenty-eight too and having your kind of future which isn't everyone's, not Al's either in spite of some similarities. Al is, after all, more my age, so even Al might be wishing to be Tom Disch though he wouldn't give up his long hooked nose and very black hair even for a tattooed eagle on his chest. Tom is kind of baroque and jolly. Al is more somber. Both having had quite an influence on all of us already. Jolly, somber. Somber, jolly. To be shy or not to be or less so than Al? He changed the art exhibit we had in the vestibule to his kind of art as soon as Miss Haertzler went to bed with him. We had a complete new selection of paintings by Friday afternoon, all hung in time for the early performance (Ralph hung them) and by then, or at least by Saturday night, I knew I was, at last, really in love for the first time in my life.

> *When I came to I found we had crashed in a cultivated field planted with some sort of weedlike bush entirely unfamiliar to me. I quickly ascertained that my three companions were beyond my help, then extricated myself from the wreckage and walked to the edge of the field. I found myself standing beneath a giant stele where strange symbols swirled in brilliant, jewellike colors. Weak and dazed though I was, I felt a surge of delight. Surely, I thought, the people who made this cannot be entirely uncivilized.*

Miss Haertzler took her turn onstage like the rest of us. She was the sort who would have cut off her right breast the better to bow the violin, but, happily, she played the harpsichord. Perhaps Al wouldn't have minded anyway. Strange man. From some entirely different land and I could never quite figure out where. Certainly he wouldn't have minded. She played only the very old and the very new, whereas *I* had suddenly discovered Beethoven (over again) and talked about Romanticism during our staff

352

meetings. Al said, "In some ways a return to Romanticism is like a return to the human figure." I believe he approved of the idea.

He spent the first night, Tuesday night that was, the twenty-second, in our red and white tent under the bleachers at the back. A touch of hay fever woke him early.

By Wednesday Ralph and I had already spent two afternoons calculating our losses owing to the rain, and I longed for a new experience of some sort that would lift me out of the endless problems of the Annual Fall Festival of the Arts. I returned dutifully, however, to the area early the next day to continue my calculations in the quiet of the morning and found him there.

"Me, Al. You?" Pointing finger.

"Ha, ha," (I *must* get rid of my nervous laugh!)

I wanted to redefine my purposes not only for his sake, but for my own.

I wanted to find out just what role the audience should play.

I wanted to figure out, as I mentioned before, how we could best incorporate aspects of the war and the changing race relations into our concerts.

I wondered how to present musical experiences in order to enrich the lives of others in a meaningful way, how to engage, in other words, their total beings.

I wanted to expand their musical horizons.

"I've thought about these things all year," I said, "ever since I knew I would be a director of the Annual Fall Festival. I also want to mention the fact," I said, "that there's a group from the college who would like to disrupt the unity of our performances (having other aims and interests), but," I told him, "the audience has risen to the occasion, at least by last night, when we had, not only good weather, but money and an enthusiastic reception."

"I have recognized," he replied, "here in this valley, a fully realized civilization with a past history, a rich present, and a future all its own, and I have understood, even in my short time here, the vast immigration to urban areas that must have taken place and that must be continuing into the present time."

How could I help falling in love with him? He may have spent the second night in Miss Haertzler's bed (if my conjectures are correct) but, I must say, it was with me he had all his discussions.

I awoke the next morning extremely hungry, with a bad headache and with sniffles and no handkerchief yet, somehow, in spite of this, in fairly good spirits though I did long for a good hot cup of almost anything. Little did I realize then, or I might not have felt so energetic, the hardships I was to encounter here in this strange, elusive, never-never land. Even just getting something to eat was to prove difficult.

Somewhat later that day I asked him out to lunch and I wish I could describe his expression eating his first grilled cheese and bacon, sipping his first clam chowder . . .

Ralph, I tell you, this really happened and just as if we haven't *all* crash-landed here in some sort of unknown alfalfa field. As if we weren't *all* penniless or about to be, waiting for you to ask us out to lunch. Three of our friends are dead and already there are several misunderstandings. You may even be in love with me for all I know, though that may have been before I had gotten to be your boss in the Annual Fall Festival.

That afternoon I gave Al a job, Ralph, cleaning up candy wrappers and crumpled programs with a nail on a stick and I invited him to our after-performance party for the audience. Paid him five dollars in advance. That's how much in love I was, so there's no sense in you coming over anymore. Besides, I'm tired of people who play instruments by blowing.

I found the natives to be a grave race, sometimes inattentive, but friendly and smiling, even though more or less continuously concerned about the war. The younger ones frequently live communally with a charming innocence, by threes or fours or even up to sixes or eights in quite comfortable apartments, sometimes forming their own family groups from a few chosen friends, and, in their art, having a strange return to the very old or the primitive along with their logical and very right interest in the new, though some liked Beethoven.

We had invited the audience to our party after the performance. The audience was surprised and pleased. It felt privileged. It watched us now with an entirely different point of view and it wondered at its own transformation while I wondered I hadn't thought of doing this before and said so to Al as the audience gasped, grinned, clapped, fidgeted and tried to see into the wings.

We had, during that same performance, asked the audience to come forward, even to dance if it was so inclined. We had discussed this thoroughly beforehand in our staff meetings. It wasn't as though it were not a completely planned thing, and we had thought some Vivaldi would be a good way to start them off. Al had said, "Certainly something new must happen every day." Afterward I said to the audience, "Let me introduce Al, who has just arrived by an unfortunate plane crash from a far-off land, a leading force among the new objectivists, but penniless at the moment, sleeping out under our bleachers . . ." However, that very night I heard that Miss Haertzler and Al went for a walk after our party up to the gazebo on the hill or either they went rowing on the lake, and Tom Disch said, though not necessarily referring to them, "Those are two, thin, young people in the woods and they're quite conscious that they don't have clothes on and that they're very free spirits." And he said, "She has a rather interesting brassiere," though that was at a different time, and also, "I wonder if he's a faggot because of the two fingers coming down so elegantly."

I found it hard to adjust to some of the customs of this hardy and lively people. This beautiful, slim young girl invited me to her guest room on my second night there and then entered as I lay in bed, dropping her simple, brightly colored shift at her feet. Underneath she wore only the tiniest bit of pink lace, and while I was wondering was she, perhaps, the king's daughter or the chief's mistress? what dangers would I be opening myself up to? and thinking besides that this was my first night in a really comfortable bed after a very enervating two days, also my first night with a full stomach and would I be able to? then she moved, not toward me, but to the harpsichord . . .

I had much to learn.

Mornings, sometimes as early as nine thirty, Al could be found painting in purples, browns, grays and blacks in the vestibule area of the front of our tent. The afternoons many of us, Al included, frequently spent lounging on the grass outside the tent (on those days it didn't rain), candidly confessing the ages of, and the natures of our very first sexual experiences and discussing other indiscretions, with the sounds of the various rehearsals as our background music. (Miss Haertzler's first sexual experience, from what I've been told, may have actually taken place fairly recently and in our own little red ticket booth.) During the evening concerts I can still see Al, as though it were yesterday, in his little corner backstage scribbling on his manifesto of the new art:

"Why should painting remain shackled by outmoded laws? Let us proclaim, here and at once, a new world for art where each work is judged by its own internal structures, by the manifestations of its own being, by its self-established decrees, by its self-generated commands.

"Let us proclaim the universal properties of the thing itself without the intermediary of fashion.

"Let us proclaim the fragment, the syllable, the single note (or sound) as the supreme elements out of which everything else flows . . ."

And so forth.

(Let us also proclaim what Tom Disch has said: "I don't understand people who have a feeling of comfortableness about art. There's a kind of art that they feel comfortable seeing and will go and see that kind of thing again and again. I get very bored with known sensations. . . .")

But, even as he worked, seemingly so contented, and even as he welcomed color TV, the discovery of DNA and the synthesizing of an enzyme, Al had his doubts and fears just like anyone else.

Those mountains that caught the rays of the setting sun and burned so red in the evenings! That breath-taking view! How many hours have I spent gazing at them when I should have been writing on my manifesto, aching with their beauty and yet wondering whether I would ever succeed in crossing them? How many times did my conversation at that time contain hidden references to bearers and guides? Once I learned of a trail that I might follow by myself if I could get someone to furnish me with a map. It was said only to be negotiable through the summer to the middle of October and to be too steep for mule or motorcycle. Later on I became acquainted with a middle-aged, homosexual flute player named Ralph A. who was willing to answer all my questions quite candidly. We became good friends and, as I got to know him better, I was astounded at the sophistication of his views on the nature of the universe. He was a gentle, harmless person, tall and tanned from a sun lamp. Perhaps I should mention that he never made any sexual advances to me, that I was aware of at any rate.

"After the meeting between Ralph A. and Al W.," the critics write, "Ralph A.'s work underwent an astonishing change. Obviously he was impressed by the similarities between art and music and he attempted to interpret in musical terms those portions of Al W.'s manifesto that would lend themselves to this transposition. His 'Three Short Pieces for Flute, Oboe and Prepared Piano' is, perhaps, the finest example of his work of this period."

By then Al had lent his name to our town's most prestigious art gallery. We had quoted him often in our programs. I had discussed with him the use of public or private funds for art. I had also discussed, needless to say, the problem of legalized abortion and whether the state should give aid to parochial schools. Also the new high-yield rice. I mentioned our peace groups including our Women's March for Peace. I also tried to tell him Miss Haertzler's real age and I said that, in spite of her looks, it would be very unlikely that she could ever have any children, whereas I, though not particularly young anymore, could at least do that, I'm (fairly) sure.

And then, all too soon, came the day of the dismantling of the Annual Fall Festival tent and the painting over of our billboard, which Al did (in grays, browns, purples and blacks), making it into an ad for the most prestigious art gallery, and I, I was no longer a director of anything at all. The audience, which had grown fat and satiated on our sounds, now walked in town as separate entities . . . factions . . . fragments . . . will-o'-the-wisps . . . meaningless individuals with their separate reactions. Al walked with them, wearing his same old oddly cut clothes as unself-consciously as ever, and, as ever, with them, but not of them. He had worked for us until the very last moment, but now I had no more jobs to give. Tom Disch had had a job as a copywriter for a while and made quite a bit of money, but he gave it all up for the sake of literature and I expected Al to give up these little jobs for the sake of his art as soon as he had some money. The trouble was, he couldn't find another little job to tide him over and while the critics and many others, too, liked his paintings, no one wanted to buy them. They were fairly expensive and the colors were too somber. I helped him look into getting a grant, but in the end it went to a younger man (which I should have anticipated). I gave him, at about that time, all my cans of corned-beef hash even though I knew he still spent some time in Miss Haertzler's guest room, though, by then, a commune (consisting of six young people of both sexes in a three-room apartment) had accepted him as one of them. (I wonder sometimes that he never asked Miss Haertzler to marry him, but he may have been unfamiliar with marriage as we know it. We never discussed it that I remember and not too many people in his circle of friends were actually married to each other.)

Ralph had established himself as the local college musical figure, musician in residence, really, and began to walk with a stoop and a slight limp and to have a funny way of clearing his throat every third or fourth word. I asked him to look into a similar job for Al, but they already had an artist in residence, a man in his sixties said to have a fairly original eye and to be profoundly concerned with the disaffection of the young, so they couldn't do a thing for Al for at least a year, they said, aside from having him give a lecture or two, but even that wouldn't be possible until the second semester.

Those days I frequently saw Al riding around on a borrowed motor scooter (sometimes not even waving), Miss Haertzler on the back with her skirts pulled up. He still painted. The critics have referred to this time in his life as one of hardship and self-denial while trying to get established.

Meanwhile it grew colder.

Miss Haertzler bought him a shearling lamb jacket. Also one for herself. I should have suspected something then, but I knew it was the wrong time of year for a climb. There was already a little bit of snow on the top of the highest of our mountains and the weatherman had forecast a storm front on the way that was or was not to be there by that night or the next afternoon. We all thought it was too early for a blizzard.

> *I was to find Miss (Vivienne) Haertzler an excellent traveling companion. Actually a better climber than I was myself in many ways and yet, for all that vigor, preserving an essential femininity. Like many others of her race, she had small hands and feet and a fair-skinned look of transparency and yet an endurance that matched my own. But I did notice about her that day an extraordinary anxiety that wasn't in keeping with her nature at all (nor of the natives in general). I didn't give a second thought, however, to any of the unlikely rumors I had heard, but I assumed it was due to the impending storm that we hoped would hide all traces of our ascent.*

A half a day later a good-sized group of our more creative people were going after one of the most exciting minds in the arts with bloodhounds. A good thing for Miss Haertzler, too, since the two of them never even got halfway. I saw them back in town a few days afterward still looking frostbitten and it wasn't long after that that I had a very pleasant discussion with Al. I had asked him out to our town's finest Continental restaurant. We talked, among other things, about alienation in our society, population control, impending atomic doom. In passing I mentioned a psychologist I had once gone to for certain anxieties of my own of a more private nature. Soon after that I heard that Al was in therapy himself and had nearly conquered his perennial urge to cross the mountains and, as the psychologist put it, leave our happy valley in his efforts to escape from something in himself. It would be a significant moment in both modern painting and modern music (and perhaps in literature, too, Tom Disch might say) when Al would finally be content to remain in his new-found artistic milieu. I can't help but feel that the real beginning of Al's participation (sponsored) within our culture as a whole was right here on my couch in front of the fireplace with a cup of hot coffee and a promise of financial assistance from two of our better-known art patrons. It was right here that he began living out some sort of universal human drama of life and death in keeping with his special talents.

From Carol and Terry Carr, August 22, 1970:

> Dear Damon,
> We are safe so far. Igor like sausage—make Igor sweat. Proficiency in language increases. This morning I ordered ein hamburger, ein beer & ein coke. Sweet little university town, looks like Ashland, Oregon with turrets. Convention is weird, but so far we are safe. Igor Coleman sends love also.

To a writer whose name I suppress, September 3, 1970:

> Dear Mr. ——,
> . . . There is a standard form for manuscript preparation which you should learn to use. Don't use a colored ribbon and don't furnish the blurb—the editor will do that. The first page should have your name and address, single-spaced, in the upper left-hand corner, and an approximate word-count (to the nearest 100 words) in the upper right. Then space down almost to the middle of the page and put the title, centered, with the by-line under it; skip a couple of spaces and begin the text. Following pages should have your last name in the upper left corner and the page number—just the number, not the word "page"—in the upper right. Leave about an inch margin at the top.
> And good luck.

To George Alec Effinger, April 25, 1968:

> Dear Piglet,
> I used to write things just like this and show them to people, and

359

they would say, "Nice try, but it isn't a story." I don't recall that this did me any good, because I couldn't see why it wasn't a story, even if it wasn't exactly like other people's stories.

When I was 16 or some such age, my father took me along to the U. of Oregon where he was taking a summer course and I enrolled for a couple of art classes. Life class was okay, but I was a washout in the painting class. The instructor sent me out to make sketches, and I wandered around looking at the conventional pretty views, river with weeping willows, cottages, etc., but could not see any point in producing one more example of calendar art, and doubted my ability to handle all those tough things like trees, water, etc., anyhow; thought I ought to begin with something simpler. So I wound up in the cemetery sketching simple designs of gravestones—nice rectangular shapes, arranged in different patterns. Instructor turned these down after one glance, sent me out again to do something more complex. Still rebelling against calendar views, I found a vacant lot full of junk and sketched that. It was complicated enough to suit anybody, but it was a shock to me when the instructor looked at it with approval, pointing out various dynamic relationships which I had not put into the drawing—had just drawn the damn junk the way it lay. Well, anyhow, he gave me a sheet of butcher paper and told me to paint it, and I did, and of course it was an unholy mess—you can't paint in oils on butcher paper—and that was the end of my painting for a while. I still think he would have done better to give me a piece of canvas and let me paint those gravestones.

I could tell you all the rules you have broken in this story and discourage the piss out of you, but I don't see what good that would do. I have a feeling that beginning writers have to work through a few simple things, finger exercises; at any rate I did. You have to build a few henhouses, I guess, before you can do a garage. Maybe I mean birdhouses, which is as far as I got in carpentry; don't think I could build anything as complicated as a henhouse. But this metaphor is not going to get us anywhere unless I can explain why I think your story is a birdhouse.

This is the kind of a story an editor who did not know you would send back with a rejection slip, and if he bothered to write anything on it, he would probably write, "So what?", the two most offensive words in the English language. But what he would mean by this is that the story is trivial—a birdhouse—that there's

360

nothing in it that's important to the reader or the people in the story.

This is what I could not grasp when people tried to explain it to me, because God damn it I was not ready to do "important" things like trees and cottages; I wanted to do simple things like gravestones, and could not see why that was not all right. As a writer I never did learn to do trees and cottages until long after I started selling stories, and then it did not matter, because I had found out how to do trivial things and get away with it. (For "trees and cottages" read "underground movements against the tyrannical government of 2000 AD, battles between fleets of spaceships, etc.") What turned me off when people talked to me about rules, I now realize, is that there is no rule in writing that you can't break if you know how. This story is trivial because if your guy never found out about the garbage, what would it matter? But having a baby is not trivial, so this could be a real story, you could make it important, but you would have to write it like a bastard. It would be a difference of emphasis—you'd have to make your two people come alive and seem real, even in the context of this light story. I don't recommend that you try it with this one, because there are other things wrong with it. The idea of angels running around turning garbage into living things is a little too cornball-sentimental, like Jack Frost painting all the leaves in autumn, and at the same time, when you bring in the baby, it turns definitely unpleasant. So you've got something that is saccharine and nasty at the same time, and you can't beat that for a sure loser. But next time, even if you've got an idea that you sense somebody else might call trivial, go ahead and write it, but bear down on making your people as real as you can. I will mention a rule here, and you can make your own decision about whether to try to break it or not: Don't write in the first person, and especially don't write about yourself and Diana. Pick other people, because you can see them from the outside; you're too close to yourself & D. And use third person because although 1st person seems natural and therefore easy, it is technically much harder to do well. In third person you can tell and show what the character is like, how he looks, how he moves, &c.; in first, you have to do it all by indirection, and since nobody can see himself objectively, you have to convey things that the character does not know about himself. It can be done, but oh boy, it is not easy. One more rule, with the same escape clause.

Don't try to embellish your style for the sake of embellishment. Tools are for use, not for display. Use the words that say what you mean directly and economically—e.g., if you mean garbage truck, say "garbage truck."

I don't know if this is any damn use; I sometimes suspect that the world would get along better if nobody ever wrote anything about other people's stories. Anyhow, it is well meant. If you have survived it, send me another and I'll do it again.

From Effinger, August 18, 1970:

Dear Damon:
Here is the German story. I finished it a lot sooner than I expected. It turned into a different story than I expected, too. I picked up the serious strain and used it to unify the three voices somewhat. The thing turned allegorical (as all my things are wont to do), and I ended up saying Meaningful Things about vengeance, race hatred, war in general, Indochina, and man's inhumanity to man.

Buy it. We need the money more than Berkley does.

To Effinger, October 1, 1970:

Dear Piglet,
Because of space problems I suddenly have to drop "Things" from *Orbit 10* and put "Berchtesgaden" in instead, and no time to send you the copyedited ms. But will tell you what I did, & if you object to any of it will change it back when the ms. comes back from Putnam's. Also. P. 2, I changed *krona* to *kronor*, which my dictionary says is the plural—hard to believe—and I also changed, p. 3, *Strassendirne* to *Strassendirnen*, although it occurred to me you might have meant this for a collective singular. I changed spectre to specter, p. 4. I moved some of your commas and periods inside quotation marks. . . . That is about all, and it is a jazzy story. Had not planned to run this one first, but I kind of like the idea of introducing Weinraub from a distance.

LIVE, FROM BERCHTESGADEN

by George Alec Effinger

"In Düsseldorf, as in certain other Rhinish *Hauptstädten*, there is a large, yellow-brick building very close to the railroad terminal. I am told that a great many good German *Bürger* make their periodic, Kaabic journey to this yellow institution; inside one is confronted by a bewildering array of charming and less charming photos, blurrily enticing Kodachromes of *Mädchen* that may be rung up in the manner to which one has become accustomed.

"It is sometimes difficult for the uninitiated to know how to react to this. Europe, by its very nature, is like this, in all ways and throughout its continental extent. This pure geographic propinquity of nations lulls the tourist's sense of culture. How easy it is to cross a border and find oneself immediately in an entirely different milieu of mores and folkways. It is necessary to change your ethics at the booth while you change your pounds sterling or kronor.

"Do you have inhibitions? Lose them, or be unhappy, for sooner or later you will have one or another offended. No matter how grotesque the practice, how bestial the behavior, if you live Continental long enough you will find the neighborhood where it is merely *comme il faut*. For some, it is not the superficiality of 'When in Rome . . .' but a matter of survival."

"*Mein Herr Doktor*, how is it that she speaks so? What language is it?"

"It is English she speaks, Frau Kämmer. She is delirious; oftentimes they will babble so in another language. But it is strange that she is so coherent. It is almost as if she recites."

"*Aber*, Herr Freischütz, my Gretchen knows no English. It cannot be English that she speaks."

"Far away now, beyond the political and other walls that we have built, beneath the impossible burden of years, look: Unter den Linden. Berlin! The mention of that brightest and most sophisticated of capitals did not always carry with it the indelible tinge of guilt, the subtlest pricks of fear. Unter den Linden: no other avenue in metropolitan Europe quite held the imagination of the literate world to such a degree; no other city's showplace was ever so rich with the modish, the absolute *dernier cri*. The broad, shaded way runs from the former Royal Palace down to the Vopos at Checkpoint Charlie. As in any large city, the Unter den Linden of old was frequented by the

363

ubiquitous *Strassendirnen*; but, whether or not it was merely the effect of the reflection of old Berlin's loveliness, these easier matches did not offend the grace and charm of the street. It was only after the war that Berlin learned shame.

"This shame was not previously totally unknown. It was, however, unnecessary. Beginning with Carolus Magnus, or Charlemagne, the Germans began their expansion eastward—the notorious *Drang nach Osten*—late in the eighth century. To this day the land to the west of the River Elbe is known as the 'old Germany,' and the land east, the 'new Germany.' Thus, historical precedent has given way to shame; the shame is shared by those who know the old Germany, for these are immersed in the most ancient of traditions. The new Germany is comparatively younger, but no one, not the oldest *Weisskopf*, is able to remember the initial annexation. Whatever shame is felt, therefore, is hereditary in nature. It is false shame."

    "Guten Nachmittag, Herr Doktor."
    "Ja, und auch Ihnen."
    "Wie geht es Ihnen?"
    "Sehr gut, danke. Ihre Tochter hat gut geschlafen. Wie geht's Ihnen?"
    "Ach, comme çi, comme ça. Pas mal."

"Where *is* Germany? Do you find Germany in the thousands of Volkswagens on the American highways? Is Germany to be found by searching amongst the sausages and waltzes and *Buddenbrooks* of the world? Where is Germany? What, now, is Germany?

"Germany has traded *Weltschmerz* for *ethischer Fortschritt*. The sensuousness of the Italians, the chauvinism of the French, the snobbery of the British, the unbridled passions of the Danish and the Swedes, the inscrutability of the Finnish, all these are as nothing compared to the sincerity of the German concern for morality. 'May God punish the sinful French' is a slogan for the masses; it is also, perhaps, an indication of the direction the German *Weltanschauung* has taken. It is no longer permissible to allow the nationalities of our continent to squander their precious energies in lustful abandon. It is time for a cleansing.

"But does this mean, I hear you ask, does this mean that a new wave of Puritanism must o'ersweep us, one and all? No, I reply, for extremism does not fit in with our own and exquisitely German idea of *Weltpolitik*.

"We cannot yet look for Germany in those isolated and expensive places in the sun. The specter of doom rises, and falls, and rises again: such is the natural course of events. It must rise once more like the *Unterseeboot*, to an economic and social periscope depth. There must be some effectual Curt Jurgens at the helm, and the tubes must be kept cleared for action. 'Bearing zero five four, two thousand yards . . . Mark!' This must be the watchword. *'Torpedos . . . Los!'* must be the countersign.''

''What is she saying? Does she still go on in English?''
''Yes, Nurse. But she becomes less coherent. What is this inflammatory rhetoric? Such pseudo-poetry! Ah, such a strange coma.''
''*Herr Doktor*, can nothing be done? She rambles on so; the other patients complain of the constant disturbance.''
''*Naja*, then. Give her *ein Glas Schnaps*.''

''There is no hiding this shame. It hides *im Bahnhof*, it lurks *im Postamt*, there is no peeling it from your shaking shoulders. *'Ich bekenne mich die Anklage, ''nicht schuldig.''* ' How many of us stop our laughter when we buy soap, when we touch the lampshade? When the SS and the SA march away, whose minds do they take with them, even now? *'Wenn wir fahren gegen England!'*

'' 'Isn't the Jew a human being too? Of course he is; none of us ever doubted it,' wrote Joseph Goebbels. 'All we doubt is that he is a *decent* human being.'
''*Ich bekenne mich die Anklage, 'nicht schuldig.'*
'' 'But in all, we can say that we fulfilled this heaviest of tasks in love to our people. And we suffered no harm in our essence, in our soul, in our character. . . .' Heinrich Himmler wrote that.
'' 'Paragraph 1: Jews may receive only those first names which are listed in the directives of the Ministry of the Interior concerning the use of first names.
'' 'Paragraph 2: If Jews should bear first names other than those permitted to Jews according to Par. 1, they must, as of January 1, 1939, adopt an additional name. For males, that name shall be Israel, for females Sara.'
'' 'On May 11, another transport of Jews (1,000 pieces) arrived in Minsk from Vienna, and was taken from the station directly to the above-mentioned ditch . . .'

''*Ich bekenne mich . . .*
''I plead 'not guilty.' ''

''Ah, Frau Kämmer, so good of you to come. I must speak to you about your daughter. Gretchen is a tragic case. Her coma is now nearly a year. She takes little food, she is wasting away; she is but a human skeleton. But, you know, she never ceases to talk. Her voice is anguished, Frau Kämmer, so that it pains one to listen. But what she says? Still delirium.

"But now, our country is at war. We march against the czar. Our Wilhelm takes us against the Russians, and today we are at war also with the French. There has been a general call for doctors, and I must now tell you that the sanatorium is closing. Your Gretchen may be taken home; I had been already considering that recommendation. It may do her more good than this close but impersonal attention . . ."

"Why am I here? I can't remember my husband here.

"As I recall, we were driving to Mainz. Our little brown VW. We pronounced it *fow*-vay in Germany. Driving along the Autobahn. I remember this Mercedes. We had the temerity to pass this black Mercedes. In our little VW.

"This feeling, I'm twisting . . .

"Here . . .

"Ich . . ."

"How is she today?"

"Better, poor thing. She's just wasted away from being in that awful hospital. She sounds as if she's just out of her head, pure and simple."

"And now, what with the war . . ."

"It is interesting to leaf through the documents that were discovered following the surrender. For instance, this communication: 'We started with three and a half million Jews here. Of that number, only a few work companies remain. Everybody else has—let us say—emigrated.'

"Where are all those soldiers now? Sousaphone players in the Bratwurst Festival?

"How can I say that I am not guilty?

"I cannot listen anymore. I cannot listen to the charges.

"Please, stop."

"Mama, does Gretchen know the news?"

"No, *Liebchen*, she cannot understand."

"Will you tell her about the *Lusitania*?"

"Nein, sie wurde es nicht verstehen."

"We must keep to ourselves. Everyone—the Russians, the French, the English, especially the Americans—they all watch. They hope to catch us, like little boys stealing the pfennigs from Mama's purse.

"We are here. We know what we have done; it is only left to atone for our deeds, or to justify them.

"We cannot know which course is the more horrible."

"Ernst. My husband's name is Ernst. He was born near Gelnhausen. We met in New York, during the Depression. But I can't remember . . ."

"Have you heard enough? Then consider the *Sonderkommando*.

"Little wooden and concrete block outhouses. Signs indicated that they were baths. How thoughtful of the German High Command. The inmates were gathered together; those who could play musical instruments were commandeered to play cheerful tunes from *The Merry Widow*. Everyone watched as the band played; soon everyone would have their turn for the delousing.

"They got a couple of thousand in one of those buildings. They got their money's worth out of the hydrogen cyanide.

"Twenty minutes later, after the spasms had stopped, they called in the *Sonderkommando*. They were male Jews who were promised immunity from execution for their services. They went into the gas chambers and pulled the tangled corpses apart with hooks. They hosed down the walls, cleaning off the blood and fouler material. They extracted the gold teeth of their kinsmen. A week later, they were gassed, too.

"You've heard it before, don't kid yourself.

"It is said that God appeared to Paul Joseph Goebbels dressed in a leather corset, tightly laced high-heeled hip boots, and brandishing a riding crop. To this day the breezes, according to the neighborhood fools around Bayreuth, to this day you may hear gentle whisperings, wind whistles of the *Horst Wessel*, and you know that it's just a matter of time before *die Fahne* is again *hoch*.

"After reading about Argentine political murders, can you spare some outrage for the merry pranks of thirty years past?

"Picture: It is night. The darkness is made more complete by the storm clouds which obscure the moon and stars. There is nothing to be seen but the light of a small lantern shining through the window of a farmhouse, about a hundred yards away. It is early December near Metz; it is very cold. There is ice on the Moselle, whose banks curve away about three kilometers beyond the farm. The German patrol halts on the rutted dirt road. Two of the six soldiers are sent up to the farmhouse. They knock loudly on the door. There is a long pause before the door is opened; then the light spills out through the narrow crack. Someone inside the house gasps, someone cries, another curses softly. The Germans force their way into the house. Sometimes in this situation there are shots, sounds of breaking glass, objects falling to the floor. At last one *vert-de-gris* comes to the door. He calls the other four, who still stand in the road, slapping their gloved hands and stamping their jackbooted feet.

"The six Germans are named Gerd, Thomas, Heinrich, Karl, Sigmund, and Gottlob. Their job is to stay in the farmhouse and guard it against the Allies. All over Europe there are similar pockets of Deutschland; this is how the war was fought, from farmhouses. Sometimes they are attacked by Burt Lancaster. Generally Heinrich, stranded hundreds of kilometers from the collaborating *dévoreuses* of Paris, goes mad and shoots a couple of his mates, or dies of lockjaw. In the end the Allies arrive in force, and the Boche are made to abandon the house, throwing their Lugers on a pile and crying '*Kamerad!*'

"And so, these days, as you take your Polaroid Swinger shots of the *Kölner Dom*, you will meet a man. He is selling green and yellow balloons, ice cream and peanuts, plastic novelties. You speak to him in your halting German, '*Bitte, können Sie mir sagen, wie komme ich zur Bedürfnis-anstalt?*' He smiles at you and answers in flawless English. 'The public lavatory that you seek is located there, built into the side of the Victory Monument. My name is Sigmund. You must be Americans. How charming; I was a Stormtrooper, myself.'

"This never happens. If you ask a German student about the *Nazizeit*, he says, 'Terrible. Simply terrible. It is frightening to believe that an entire nation could be so deluded. It was all like a monstrous dream.' A dream.

" 'Yes,' you say, 'but what did *your* father do during the war?'

"His eyes shift nervously, his tongue licks his full, Aryan lips, and he coughs. 'My father? Oh, during the war he was taking care of some mining interests in South America. We lived in São Paulo then; we never had any actual contact with the Reich.'

"So much for atrocities.

"You must be the conscience for your family: your daughter is busy with ecology, and your husband leads the commuters' fight with the Long Island Railroad. You must keep those memories alive, before you are seduced away by the plight of the American Indian."

* * *

"We have shown the way. It is always Germany that develops, *nicht wahr*, it is always Germany that knows its resources, that knows what to do with its people."

"Ach, what is it now, Herr Müller? In what new and resourceful way are we now superior?"

"You have right, Frau Kämmer, in calling us resourceful. For, indeed, we are the practical nation. How did they fight wars? How did the human race battle previously? Why, by loosing various missiles at the enemy, and hoping that the paths of the projectiles and the opposing soldiery might intersect. Ah, look at the probability. Very low, *n'est-ce pas?* What we have done, what the German Command has done, April 22, 1915, at Ypres, is to harness the potential of the very air as a weapon! The atmosphere has become our ally, spreading our new and tiny globules of death. We use gas. The new aircraft dispense thick yellow clouds, and the French are overcome, they are disabled, or they die."

"Perhaps we could drop from those same aircraft a sort of jellied petroleum product. It could be ignited, and those same foes would then have something to contend with, eh?"

"You do not know what you ask, Frau Kämmer. There are still conventions. We do have several sorts of gas, thanks to the Krupps of Essen and to the Interessen Gemeinschaft with their famous German professors. We have such variety; 'poison gas' is then a misnomer. We should refer, rather, to 'chemical warfare.' That is better, it is more *gemütlich*. We have the gas chemicals, and also the liquid chemicals which act in much the same way. Of our asphyxiating substances we have had success with simple chlorine, phosgene, chloropicrin, and others. We have produced lachrymators, vesicant or blistering compounds, sternutatory or sneezing compounds, and toxic compounds such as prussic acid. We have been disappointed so far with the arsenic compounds. Major V. Lefebure documents all this in his jocularly titled volume *The Riddle of the Rhine*. He discusses the new developments in mustard gas and states that 'these inherent possibilities of organic chemistry, flexibility in research and production, make chemical warfare the most important war problem in the future reconstruction of the world.' "

"I couldn't agree more. Though we win, I would still see those canisters thrown into the sea."

"Yes, and how goes your daughter, Frau Kämmer?"

"My daughter? Gutrune? Why, she begins to go to school soon. It is very kind of you to ask after her."

"I am sorry. I meant to inquire about your other."

"My other? Perhaps you mean Gretchen? Ah, she sleeps. We have little to do with her these days. She needs such little attention. She is so thin, she looks like a skeleton. And her eyes! Sometimes they open, and stare . . . We do not go into her room often these days."

"I don't have any idea how I came here. I mean, I don't even know where I am. No one talks to me. They treat me as if I'm not here at all. I'm paralyzed in this bed; I must have been in an accident, the way they shake their heads when they think I won't notice. Am I disfigured, startingly mangled now?

"I don't know how I got here. Christ, I don't even remember who I am! Oh, my god. *Who am I?* What a dumb-ass question. ·

"Okay, don't panic. I'm Gretchen Weinraub.

"I'm on vacation. I'm in Europe. Our first trip back to Europe! We're in Germany, visiting Munich, just finished in Heidelberg and Stuttgart. Going on to Nuremberg next. Ernst and our grandson, Stevie. Where are they? I haven't seen them at all.

"How long have I been here?

"This isn't a hospital. I remember a doctor looking at me a few times, but he seemed old and worried, dressed in a funny-smelling old dark suit. The ceiling above me is pointed, as if I were stuck up under the eaves. The mattress I'm lying on is very soft and comfortable. The bed is piled up with lovely hand-sewn quilts: it must be winter.

"It was July in Munich.

"Where am I? What in hell's happened?

"Where's Ernst?"

"Weh, how she tosses and turns tonight. She is troubled."

"Mama, do you think she has dreams all this time? Her long sleep, is it like we have every night?"

"A full year. I pray the good Lord that it has been peaceful for her."

"Oh, Mama! A full year of nightmare! Oh, how horrible it would be! To be chased, or lost, or falling for a year—"

"*Schweigst du*, little one. God in Heaven watches her."

"Does God understand what she says?"

"Yes, *Liebchen*, God understands what everyone says. Our Gretchen mutters still in English, but she says yet those German words."

"You can understand then, Mama?"

"Yes, but such silly words they are! '*Geheime Staatspolizei* . . .' What good are *secret* police, police that you can't even find when you need them? A 'Gestapo'?"

"Are we winning, Mama?"

"Yes, of course we are. God knows who's been good and who's been bad."

"Has Daddy been good?"

370

"Yes, dear. He was wounded in the chest just last week. He will win the Iron Cross, Second Class, he thinks. I hope that he does. That will show that landlord of ours in München."

"Does Gretchen know?"

"No, *Liebchen*. Poor, poor Gretchen knows nothing of our great struggle."

"Will you be here when *I* die too, Mama?"

"Hush, now, *Liebchen*. sit down. Watch the war."

* * *

"I could have taken any of several tacks in doing this. Should I instead have stayed only with the contrite and apologetic? Would it have been better, or even believable, to try to persuade that things weren't really all that bad? Can you believe the canard that seventy-five million Germans were only carrying out their instructions and today can't even recall that they did? No. The question is too big. There are too many angles, and the extenuating circumstances are too difficult to explain.

"The apology must suffice. A necessary prologue, perhaps, for one in my position; but enough. *Also, denn. 'Hier stehe ich.'*

"I borrow those words, of course, from Martin Luther. He knew how it felt to have the responsibility of putting the abstract feelings of a nation, a world, into coherent form. It is for me, having attempted the apology with all the conscience that I can muster, to say, 'Here we are.' I am supposed to point into the shadows, into our nation's superstitious submind, beckoning, saying to my fellows, 'Come out! It is over. *Abierunt ad plures.* They are dead, they are dead.' *They* are the memories, the guilt-demons that take on almost hallucinatory presence.

"And they should be dead. Why are we guilty no longer? Walk among us now. *O felix culpa!* Have the vanquished ever found such prosperity in defeat? To despair of forgiveness from God is the gravest of sins: why then should we bear the enmity of nations beyond the reasonable limit? The Führer was a captain who saw himself sinking and, in his perverse logic, thought it necessary to take his ship with him. Of course, the *Heimatland* suffered, but it was cleansed in its own Iron and Blood.

"No more brownshirts, blackshirts put away, too, with the photos of polished Mussolini, farewell *Ade Polenland, ade weisse Hand; fest ist der Tritt, fest ist der Tritt* up the steps into the attic, packed away in the trunks with the Hitler Youth badges, *die Jugend marschiert*, thirty, count 'em, thirty extermination camps, hundreds of thousands of cheering people.

371

"Speak of this amazing recovery of the divided German republic. It is remarkable; it would not have been possible, ironically, without Hitler's terrible and unifying nationalistic zeal. The extremities which are his epitaph are the product of his absolute power. But today, and all that counts *is* today, our country is in a far stronger economic position than before the war. You may go into the *Sowjet* zone, if you wish, and cluck your tongue at the difference.

"The continued animosity of our former enemies grows a bit silly. Certainly, we erred; we have learned from our mistakes. Not, I might add, like more than one of our accusers, to whom the term 'genocide' seems, to them, inapplicable because they lack the publicity that attended *our* Treblinkas and Buchenwalds. I fall into the *tu quoque* fallacy: you without sin, you be the first to cast the stone.

"We have a land. It is our *Vaterland*; that term cannot be discredited. If you insist on pulling open your older wounds, we insist on reacting with natural pride in our homes, ourselves, and our accomplishments.

"We still live."

"Gretchen? We once had a daughter named Gretchen, but last spring we lost her."

"Oh, I'm terribly sorry. Did she ever regain consciousness?"

"Oh, no. You misunderstand. We have no idea if she is still alive. You see, as time passed we saw less and less of her. She did not produce in us such a great amount of interest. We dusted her features often, and changed the flowers in the vase monthly, but otherwise we rarely thought of her. Then, one day, she was gone."

"But after so long a confinement to her bed, and in her starved condition, surely she couldn't have gone off by herself?"

"We think so, too. Perhaps we merely mislaid her. I remember one time, when we had taken her outside for the fresher air, we couldn't for the life of us recall where we had put her. We have recently written to the *Gastwirt* at the inn at St. Blasien, to see if we inadvertently left her in our rooms. But, personally, I don't think we even took her along."

"I can't remember who I am.

"Sometimes, like last night, I think I'm Gretchen Kämmer. Sometimes I'm Gretchen Weinraub. Right now, I don't have any name at all.

"I can't remember where I'm from, or where I am now.

"I remember getting here, or there, in a brown Volkswagen. It was the car we rented in Hamburg. I don't remember who the others who make up the 'we' are.

372

"For some reason I feel absolutely no desire to know, I feel no horror at being totally lost. It's rather warm and soft, like anesthesia. The only reasonable thing now, I guess, is to start again somewhere. I don't know which way to head, and I suppose I'll make mistakes I've made before. I forget . . .

"And I cannot yet forgive, but I forget."